MOUNTAIN MAN

by

Sean Edge

Anfield Publications
20 Fairfields
Saint Martin Field
East Looe
Cornwall PL13 1HD

Published by Anfield Publishing 1993

ISBN 0 9521647 0 1

Printed and bound in England by
Anfield Publishing

Set in Times Roman

Cover Design: Omnibus Graphics
Limited, London SE27

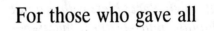

For those who gave all

Be not afraid, oh mountain man
Truth's not confined to the heart,
Look beyond the peaks, above the eagle
And the earth crumbling at thy feet.

Aloft, high places bless with solitude,
Ignobling man's feeble franchise:
Freedom's offered by a superior hand
That moves the clouds and frees the earth.

Come, my brave, reflect all ways,
Spill thy mind in desolate places;
On Calvary, you'll respect thy neighbours
All equal in their Maker's eyes.

And when you've learnt, oh mountain man
The simple beauty of truth,
Forget not the lessons of the wild
Or that this is not thy home.

Author.

PROLOGUE

One of the severest winters in North American history exploded in a cataclysm of spring madness: rushing water, melting snow and tumbling ice blocks thundered down the Colorado Rockies rearranging the high country; crushed the lowland beyond recognition.

Boulders, torn from the warming earth had crashed into trees and vegetation, revising river courses and blocking creeks. Acres of pine forest were uprooted; slopes and flat land, now littered with broken trunks, lay glistening like open wounds in the March sunshine.

The insanity had ended swiftly as nature blew away her winter temper; the warm chinook winds now breathed merciful life back into the devastation.

Stunned, the mountain animals began moving through the ruins like humans after a bombing raid; mooched ill tempered among the debris searching for food and showing their displeasure. Only the beavers took advantage of the fallen timber for their underwater lodges – and the grizzly he-bear who lived on Devil Mountain.

Named for its twin horned peaks, Devil Mountain was a fourteen *thousand feet colossus. It dominated the untamed wilderness with its incomparable magnificence.*

Situated on the eastern fringe of the Roan Plateau skirting the Arapahoe National Forest, Devil Mountain dwarfed its surroundings. Billions of tons of impregnable landmass thrown together before the Ice Age and gouged fom the earth's core, had merged into a vast tangle of rock sweeping savegely up to the sky. The mammoth devil-horned peaks thrust out from the morass and soared for ever upwards beyond the clouds.

The mountain, a terrifying presence plagued by the cruellest elements, was shrouded with superstition of missing men who had ventured too high; feared for the he-bear who prowled its wretched spaces.

Like his mountain home, the grizzly was majestic. A splendid eight hundred pound Titan, he was the supreme power among the animals. Eight feet tall on his powerful hind legs, his call would fill the high country and rich forests and meadows below, forever warning his dominance and perpetual anger.

Nor did the grizzly like man, or the male lion from the nearby box canyon, constantly urged by its greedy mate for more territory. There had been ongoing friction between the he-bear and the large cats ever since he had claimed the mountain as his own twelve summers ago.

Dismissing his enemies, he hurried along the windline, the heady pleasure of his old female's smell, strong in his large nostrils. She would be with the cubs.

High on the wing, a female eagle planed over the valley, surveying winter's legacy and the land creatures hiding from the he-bear.

Cresting a rise, the grizzly moved quickly into the pine forest tottering on the steep approaches to his mountain. Totally, his mountain! *He had been born there, lived, loved and hunted through the seasons there. One day, he would lie down and rest there. Forever.*

But today, he was exultant. Spring fever had arisen from winter's violence; thawed ice and snow promised an abundance of fish and beaver and the tiny roots that he craved – and the return of the she-bear with his cubs.

Catching trout from a newly formed creek, the late breakfast fired his jubilance. The thought of his old mate and the two cubs electrified him. He knew they would be playing in the valley on the wet carpet of scrub below the big timber and his mountain.

A stiff wind flung their scent and he growled approvingly. Excited, he galloped, his great bulk hurdling nimbly over the fallen pine. He stopped abruptly at the far edge of the forest where the ground fell sharply into a narrow defile bordering the scrub.

Once more, he tested the air; stiffened as a familiar odour triggered a warning signal: Man was closing in on his family. Man with his noise of death.

He panicked, for his woman and children were upwind; unable to detect the hunters' smell.

Climbing a tree, he saw her romping below in the open ground. His warning cry was reduced to a moan, for, unaware of the danger, his family also failed to hear his high pitched scream. Dropping to the ground, he stood on his hind legs. Frustrated, he beat the air with his paws; massive body shuddering with fear and anger.

His roar echoed defiantly across the valley at the strengthening smell of man.

With enormous strides, he charged down the slope, leapt over the defile and bounded across country towards the scrub. Making the lower ground, he saw the hunters off to his right squatting behind a boulder. To the left, his female grunted and tossed happily with the cubs.

Experienced hunters from Buffalo Creek, the two men had remained upwind, stalking the bears from the safety of high ground. Now, they watched mother and young through powerful anti-glare binoculars as the animals larked and called to one another in play.

Silently, the men prepared for the kill.

A big female, she rolled over and over, droplets of dew shooting from her fur into the sunlight. Copying ungainly, the cubs bounced off timber and rock, their cries ignored by the exultant female as she wrestled with them in human fashion far out into the open scrub.

Time stood still for the she-bear as she frolicked with her young.

With the rising sun at their backs, the two hunters had an uninterrupted line of fire. Both carried high-powered rifles.

'Like takin' candy off a baby, huh, Jake,' whispered one man tugging at a wild beard. 'Your Wilma's gonna love this birthday coat,' centring the cross-hairs on the female's chest. 'Gen-u-ine fur, huh! About a hundred an' fifty yards, I reckon.'

The man called Jake looked away with disgust. He loathed his brother-in-law. The other was strong. He was weak. His wife and brother ruled him mercilessly. 'Yes,' he said quietly. 'About a hundred and fifty.'

'Itchin' to get me a grizzly,' grinned The Beard. Noticing Jake's disinterest: 'You'd better get to like huntin',' he hissed. ''Cause Wilma likes her coats, an' I like the greenbacks. Now get yer ass in gear, boy.'

Jake frowned. 'What the hell's that!' turning to the high ground.

The hunters were horror-stricken as the he-bear stormed down the slope below the forest at almost thirty miles an hour.

Four hundred yards away, thought The Beard, the grizzly would be on them in under thirty seconds, his formidable fangs eager to tear them to pieces.

Ashen faced, he stared in disbelief: males left after mating. But this was no ordinary varmint. No siree! He had to be the one all Colorado talked about. Few had seen the grizzly of Devil Mountain. Most had been scared off by the stories surrounding the place.

'Jesus H. Christ, Jake,' he gulped, 'it's 'im. Gotta be! Let'm get to two hundred, then blast the bastard. There's a fortune on his hide. I'll take the old lady. We'll get both while the goin's good. Don't screw this one up. It's yer chance for immortality.'

Jake swung his weapon on to the he-bear, his hands shaking badly. His brow, lathering with fear-sweat, fogged his vision. Why me? he thought. I don't want this thing. Damn it to hell! 'Oh God, please don't let me miss,' he prayed.

The Beard cackled to himself, as the power of the kill rose full in him: saliva dribbled from the corners of his mouth; his eyes, cold and bloodshot, slitted viciously. Aware of his brother-in-law's aversion for blood sport, he licked his lips with satisfaction. One day, he'll

10

meet with an accident, he thought. What the hell Wilma married him fer, I'll never know.

The female rose to her full height, her small eyes recognising the male leaping down the slope; he who had given life to her cubs with his seed.

Too late, instinct told her that danger was nearby.

Bounding on to windline, she sniffed the wind. Man! Shock preceded fear – then anger. Enjoying the cubs, she had forgotten the one law of the wild: survival. Afraid and vulnerable, she beckoned her young as they ran about helpless, sensing her distress.

The bullet silenced her growls, knocking the she-bear on to her rump as it gouged deep inside her chest. Tenderly, she touched the fatal wound, her long claws sticky with bloodied fur.

Fright of the man-noise, confused by their mother's affliction, the cubs instinctively licked her wound, pawed her face.

She cried out in agony. Man with his noise of death had found her. Finally. For many summers, she suffered from this fear. The cubs were two springs old, could survive if they hid well enough, long enough. Food was plentiful in the valley. But only if she could fight off her attackers.

She knew it was hopeless, that her mate, too, was helpless against man-noise. Heavy with pain, she could not see him as her eyes clouded like a river mist. But she could make out his mountain where he had loved her, and somehow, that gave her strength.

The wound burnt hotter than childbirth as she struggled back onto her hindlegs, her defiant roar stifled by the hole in her lung. Weak through bloodloss, she pushed the cubs behind and stoically awaited the enemy.

Her time was near, and she would give of her best: for her young and her mate.

The he-bear's battle cry cut the valley as he charged at the hunters. Springing sideways, his great bounds propelled him closer to the enemy, the obnoxious smell driving him to the heights of insanity.

Man, the supreme enemy; the violator; the destroyer.

Hearing the man-noise, he had seen his mate slump to the ground, then stumbled as Jake's bullet smashed through muscle and sinew, creating a fire of pain in his shoulder. He saw sky and earth as he rocked to his knees: a deep sadness engulfed him for her and the young. His family.

Anger welled again, the anger of an animal incapable of hatred. Charging on, his death roar boomed into the Colorado morning.

A second bullet spat chunks of rock into his face, and the anger turned to fear as he fled for the sanctuary of higher ground. Afraid to look back, he charged over rocks and broken timber: forever onward away from Man and away from her and his offspring.

Stopping to lick his wound, he moaned out in anguish before continuing his climb.

'I wounded him,' Jake's relief surpassing the loss of a kill.

'He's alive,' The Beard's face dark. 'You're happy about that? He'll be one dangerous . . .'

'Hell, we was going one way!' Jake's face terror white. 'You know how I feel about this. Yeah, I'm pleased about it. Glad I didn't kill him. You didn't do any better, I see.'

The Beard cursed and struck his brother-in-law. 'You cowardly bastard. You didn't try! I nailed mine good enough. She's goin' nowhere. I suppose I'll have to settle fer the cubs as well.' Moving closer: 'You foul up again, an' I'll forget we're related.'

Jake swallowed. His body felt cold. There was something wrong about this trip, he thought. Moving cautiously through the scrub, his senses were honed for signs of attack. I shouldn't have hit that he-bear . . . But what could I do? God, this man is evil.

'I can smell 'er,' said The Beard. 'It won't be long now.'

She stood erect as they emerged from a dip in the land. Summoning a final effort, she bared her fangs and lunged forward. But her knees buckled after the first stride and she fell to her knees. Coughing blood, once more she gurgled defiance, but strength, like the mountain, was almost a memory.

She never felt the second bullet shatter her skull. In life, she was sublime, in death, the embodiment of beauty; simple, moving and utterly tragic.

Petrified, the cubs pawed at her lifeless hulk.

Two shots from The Beard's rifle, and they, too, joined their mother in eternity.

Jake fell to his knees, vomit spraying the ground.

Unnoticed, the small figure of the grizzly moved along the high ground.

'You cowardly bastard,' The Beard spitting at his brother-in-law. 'Get off yer knees. Yer not a goddamned woman. Jesus H. Christ, yer not even a child.'

Painfully, the he-bear heaved himself over a tall rock balancing on the slope. The pine forest shook behind as if protesting the genocide, the wind strengthening the smell of his dead family. Proud, impotent and humiliated in defeat, he jumped up and down, thrashing his paws as if he could still prevent the massacre.

He had seen her push aside the cubs and face her attackers. But the man-noise had cracked and he had groaned, thumping his chest as she slid away from him. He knew her seasons had ended.

He had gagged as his offspring were slaughtered.

Heartbroken, he now watched as The Beard danced around his family.

Elated, the hunter gave a loud war-whoop and jigged another circle around the mound of corpses, the prospect of a good price for the skins shading his disgust for Jake's weakness. He was happy. He could afford to be condescending. 'Sorry about the holes in the skin, pardner, but Wilma'll understand,' he guffawed. 'Pity about the big fella, though. Should've taken him myself. Still, this makes up fer it. Tomorrow's another day.'

Glassy eyed from retching, his brother-in-law's curses still ringing in his ears, Jake saw the he-bear lumbering along the edge of the pine forest towards Devil Mountain, stop a moment, then continue. 'If they ... if they belonged to him,' he choked, 'and they might, no matter what they say about bears parting after a month or so ... then we killed his whole family.'

'Hell,' snarled The Beard, 'this ain't no time to get sentimental over no bears. They'd have killed us. So what, if they do get together after matin'. Who cares! They ain't got no feelings like you 'n' me. C'mon, help me skin these critters before the cats come callin'. Jesus H. Christ, this calls for one dang of a celebration.'

The Beard tugged a bottle of whisky from his pack and glugged greedily. Eventually, he set about his gruesome task. Drunk with power, he skilfully severed the bears' heads and cut away the skins, singing raucously across the scrub.

Jake drank to calm his nerves, sickened by his brother-in-law's depravity. What makes a man sick like that? he thought. One day, Wilma will have to choose between him and I. But he knew full well that she never would. How thick has blood got to be?

As The Beard finished, the sun hottened overhead and the flies, too, drank of their prize.

High overhead the female eagle circled the valley, hovered a moment before disappearing among the fortress of rock.

Lethargically, the he-bear climbed his mountain. Despair rose from grief and his wound, something humans experience before spiritual awareness. Occasionally, he stopped to lick his aching shoulder. It felt worse than the bite when he'd fought for the female. He had defeated the other bear. But what could he do against man-noise? Man hid behind a destructive sound to strip him of his coat. For what, he didn't know.

It was beyond him.

Up he went, higher and higher, passing through the forested lower slopes and pressing on above the timberline. He ignored the deer and elk and the mountain lions he knew would be gloating from a distance.

Soon, he entered a desolate expanse of surging rock; windswept places that offered refuge, a fortification in the clouds where he could pine to the heavens. The air was thinner here, and colder, and he *looked back a fleeting moment at the small valley below shadowing with cloud. Weak-sighted, he gazed at the land holding his family to its breast. Then he turned and was lost, a lonely speck on the roof of the world.*

Returning to the eyrie, the female eagle flew over the corpses; hovered a moment far above the he-bear. Then, like the wind, she disappeared into the firmament.

CHAPTER 1

Winter; Liverpool:

Benjamin Thompson was a frustrated writer, whose world had crashed in his fortieth year.

He stared through the high-rise window at an opaque sky, pregnant with snow. It was Christmas Eve. That morning he had been fired as the political correspondent on the Liverpool Echo; three hours ago he had been served with divorce papers.

Numb with shock, his eyes drifted once more across the notice, the dispassionate legal jargon stabbing at his heart with every word. Somewhere between the 'party of the first parts' and the 'party of the second parts', his tangled brain registered the final hammer blow: his wife Rosemary was suing on grounds of mental cruelty. The four year on-off marriage had finally plunged into the abyss.

A combination of turbulent rows and dogged determination to pursue their careers had eventually driven Benjamin from the lavish country cottage to the sparse bachelor apartment high above the waterfront. Discordant views of the dirty river, a dismal dockside street where the houses appeared to be crumbling into the Mersey, reflected his grim mood.

Shivering, his steamy breath fogged the gloomy shadows. He had forgotten to feed the electricity meter. Daylight struggled through salt rimed windows, glinted dully off a cracked wall mirror. Tossing the divorce notice onto the bed, he caught his reflection: the haggard stranger with burning eyes shocked him. Was this the man they saw at the office? He remembered the stolen glances; whispers in the corridors. *Oh God!*

Slim, of medium height, his carbon black hair was brushed severely back from a high forehead; a streak of grey shot from a widow's peak. A sad face, gaunt and punctuated with high cheekbones and cinammon brown eyes, hinted some weighty decision in the making.

Now you've lost everything, Ben, he thought. It's all been a waste; a damn waste. What the hell was it all for? Where did we lose it?

He searched the cluttered table for hope; half a loaf, some margarine and an unwashed coffee cup stared back: so too, Dickens, Tolstoy and Hemingway and three cardboard boxes containing unsuccessful manuscripts. A publisher's rejection letter lay crumpled on a dinner plate. There was no hope. He screwed up the notice and threw it onto the bed.

He sat thinking by the window as night closed in. Chainsmoking, the thoughts depressed him as he drew the smoke deep inside his lungs. Scanning the room, everything felt suddenly strange. He put it down to his mood. Like the strange cottage and a stranger for a wife and her world of strange nothing people existing in a financial vacuum he could never come to terms with.

Damn it, he thought, I've been living a lie. The greatest lie of all time. Rosemary and the newspaper have seen to that! Damn them all ... *But there was still his writing.*

Yet, three hours ago, against every emotion he understood, Benjamin had decided to make a fight of it. He would find a less demanding job, and, if Rosemary could put her marriage before the fashion house, there was hope among the ashes. But the sight of the pimply faced man holding the divorce notice had crushed him. It was over. Only the lawyer had won. Breaking down, his tears had glistened like slivers of ice in the cold December sun.

Through the door, he heard people singing in the festivities. Unconsciously, he stared down at the river ablaze with harbour lights; three tankers shone like Christmas trees through the night. Car horns honked by the Pier Head. The celebrations were in full sway.

He opened the window slightly, wanting, needing to be part of it all. Something wet hit his face. It would be a white Christmas after all. But the snow only aggravated his loneliness. He closed the window. For no accountable reason, his mind flashed back to a feverish search for background in a badly written novel. He had compared his hero's marriage to the weakening blips on a hospital life-support machine. Unwittingly, he had described his own dilemma.

Mercifully, there had been no children. Rosemary's world had even denied him fatherhood. Yet he had been equally to blame, forever chasing deadlines, endlessly disgorging copy for unmerciful editors. Angrily, he stubbed the cigarette and threw on his overcoat. 'Christ,' he blurted, 'I need a drink.' Banging the door, he turned the key. Ignoring several well-wishers, he took the lift and hurried out into the snow.

The block attendant lurched across the pavement, clutching a bottle of wine. 'Doesn't he know ish Chrishmash,' he burbled to Benjamin's back.

Benjamin did not see him collapse over the threshold; fall asleep instantly.

The Paradise was a docker's pub squatting among the blackened monstrosities of the dock road. It was jammed solid with fiercely drinking men and over-painted women. Like its clientele, it weathered on under a permanent tobacco and alcoholic haze; both were big and dirty and stank of sweat, grease and beer.

The bedlam suited Benjamin's mood; a peculiar release from the sedate trappings of his former watering hole.

Fighting his way to the bar, he grinned at a sign above the counter: Drink is a man's right – anything else is God's mercy. GO in peace or don't COME back. Shouting to the barman, he bought a double whisky. A television caught his eye; the newscaster miming police brutality in South Africa; outside cameras telling the story in pictures.

Violence sickened Benjamin; grateful the sound was killed by the Paradise faithful. Still, he seethed at the sjambokked bodies cluttering the screen. That's not a reasonable act, committed by reasonable people, he thought. When did we ever lose Christmas?

A docker knocked him off balance as a news report showed a dramatic aerial rescue in the Colorado chain of the Rocky Mountains.

'Sorry,' the man's voice rich with rum. Looking mistrustfully at Benjamin's handmade overcoat, he yelled for a refill.

Benjamin squinted through the smoke fog. He's got my number, he mused. He's right: I've become a snob. Nobody I know would be seen dead in this dump. And I'd be too proud to let on I'd been here. Pride the Class Distinctioner; Pride the Rapist of Institutionalised Man: above all, Pride the Hypocrite. Mr-High-and-Mighty-Proud-Thompson confesses to hypocrisy. I am a socially diseased prisoner: Rosemary's world has judged and condemned me and the dockers are my gaolers. *How bloody pathetic!* He ordered another double.

'Now there's a wonderful thing for you,' said the docker.

'What?' Benjamin straining to hear.

'Why, that mountain rescue,' replied the man. 'Holy Jaysus, to think they found him up there in all that rock and snow. Freeze the balls off dear old Saint Patrick himself, so it would. 'Tis nothin' short of a bloody miracle, sure it is.'

Benjamin looked up. The report had almost finished as the cameraman inside a United States Air Force helicopter zoomed in on the craggy rock face. The rescuers were attaching the survivor to a steel cable hanging from the craft. Slowly, the man swung upwards and away from a towering ice plateau looming above the hovering machine, and, as it flew off, the camera captured the horror and splendour of the vast desolation.

Benjamin was stunned: swallowed by time and space; transfixed by naked beauty. God! he thought. *God!*

The docker explained how a Denver radio ham had picked up the stranded man's signal and alerted the rescue service. 'Said he'd have missed the poor bloke if he hadn't stopped at home. It was the daughter's wedding anniversary, but his wife caught the 'flu so he went back to his radio. *A bloody miracle, so it is.*

'How do you know?' Benjamin pointing to his ear.

19

The man laughed. 'Picked it up on an earlier bulletin. Might as well be deaf for all the good it does listenin' in this place. Go well, now. Merry Christmas.'

Benjamin nodded and ordered another double. He had been moved; stirred deep inside. He had seen hundreds of mountains, but this one had beckoned, no, summoned him, from halfway across the globe. He had been meant to see that newscast. *Ridiculous!* Could he really accept that he had been issued divorce papers, dismissed by the editor to be summoned by a lump of rock? It must be the whisky.

Then why is my heart still pounding? throwing the drink down in one.

Drinking heavily until closing time, his head spun and his empty stomach felt as if someone were scraping a steel comb across its lining. A blast of cold air stung his face as he shuffled over-corrected sidesteps out into the driving snow. The whisky changed his mood constantly; happy-sad, happy-sad. He began arguing with himself about the prospect of living on a mountain; at first, gentle and subtle, then harsh and callous.

'I'd be free of responsibility,' he mumbled towards a passing family. 'Yet total disregard for responsibility is unthinkable. On the other hand, relief from Institutionalised Man and his bureaucratic bungling has definite appeal.' Kicking a newspaper, he cried out: 'To hell with polarised politics, religion and test tube marriages that say little when you get right down to it. Pride versus Ben Thompson,' he shouted at a street lamp. The television mountain or civilisation, what do you think, Mr Lamp? What, what's that, you say? Let the questions be damned and get on with the game. Thank you Mr Lamp, I've been crucified long enough!'

Christ, he thought, I'm drunk.

He began laughing outrageously, waving his arms like an orchestra conductor; threading his life in words to the rhythm of his hands. With his writer's passion, he told the lamp about life under the Jesuits in the children's home; how he ran away from the beatings to sell newspapers by day, beg from drunken sailors by night. Weeping, he recalled sleeping rough when Sundays were the loneliest days of all; eluding the authorities and finishing his education at an evening institute . . . and then journalism, love of the written word . . . And then Rosemary . . . And now nothing . . .

Seeing double, he clung to the lamp and spoke reverently about the mountain, his mood shifting once more as he became moved by his own words.

'I can see the headlines now,' he said to the light. "Hack writer leaves for unknown US mountain".' He told the story about life in a cloud covered cabin, drawing on his resources and altering the text according to his mood changes; emotionally charged one minute, full of depression and humiliation the next. He built and nurtured, moulded and improved in preparation for the meaty impact that would burst and leave the reader breathless. But he became too melancholy, and the ending escaped him as he slid tearfully to the ground, his voice a pathetic croak among the blasting music and peals of laughter behind closed doors.

The snow thickened, painting a white dust over Benjamin. Lying on his back, he squinted up at the double yellow light. 'Inspired by TV newscast,' he sobbed, 'author dies for writing. Pride denied his rescue so the world couldn't gloat at his downfall over its fish and chips before its soap operas and equally obnoxious soap adverts. A fool who lost himself in the telling of his own story.'

Struggling to his knees, he spat: 'No docker's miracle for me, and no damned helicopter. Anyway, they'd all be too far gone in the Paradise to read the newscaster's lips as they bundled me off to a pauper's grave at the back of a gas factory . . . Oh, the bastards, the rotten bastards. *Rosemary, what went wrong with us?* With everything? I'm sorry about the mountain, my darling. It was only a dream, an anaesthetic to kill the lawyer's words . . . only a dream . . .'

Heartbroken, he beat the snow with his fists.

Eventually, he slithered back to the apartment block. His mood changed once more and he was deliciously happy.

Someone had removed the attendant from the threshold, but Benjamin's feet found the man's wine bottle.

Gingerly, he groped towards the lift; stopped as a crooner oozed about dreams. 'Ah sir,' he hiccupped, one hand on lapel in lawyer fashion. 'Your dream is unconvincing. Your words serve a particular purpose for a specific audience. Forgive the pun, but you sell dreams. In reality, a man who can dream has everything and is content. A man who cannot, has nothing and is no wiser. But a man who dreams unconvincingly as your audience, or they wouldn't have to buy yours, dies in a living hell. Merry Christmas to you.'

Satisfied with himself, he staggered off.

The attendant crawled along the hallway. 'Bloody dribble! You're pished Mr Thompson.'

'Pleb,' retorted Benjamin haughtily.

'You sheen my wine?'

Benjamin glared down at the man. 'I've sheen no wine, only mountains.'

The lift door closed and the man renewed his search for the bottle.

Locking the apartment door, Benjamin flopped onto the bed. Fully clothed, he slept fitfully, never knowing if the blurred images racing through his confused mind, belonged to Rosemary or the mountain. Shortly before Christmas Day, he dreamt that he had both, but, on waking, knew that he had neither.

Picking up the divorce notice, he folded it neatly and replaced it in its envelope. Head thumping, he moved to the window. Rubbing the glass, he stared at the white ships aground in the ice covered river. 'There are things to be done in my life,' he said quietly. 'And it's about time that I did them.'

★ ★ ★ ★ ★

Summer; Buffalo Creek:

The bartender of the Buffalo Creek Motel polished a beer glass and held it up to the light for inspection. Normally, it was only a dip and dry, but, with the funeral, there were only four customers, all of whom were engrossed in five card stud.

Hardly a word had been exchanged since their arrival.

It was a long bar, low ceilinged and adorned with hunting trophies, together with the framed smiles of their victors. Pine tables yellowed from the afternoon sun streaming through the front window. Cigarette butts untidied the timber floor.

The card players pondered their chances at a corner table; a pile of bills were ringed by beer glasses. The Beard and Jake sat opposite one another.

'See you,' grunted a sallow faced individual.

'Hell, you drunk, Merl?' groaned Eb, a bald headed barrel of a man with furtive, wide spaced eyes. 'I ain't *raised* 'im yet.'

'Now, now, boys,' the bartender thankful for the break in silence. 'No arguin' today. You should've been at old Bob's funeral 'stead of playin' five card.'

'You feel so righteous, why didn't *you*,' stabbed The Beard, winking at Eb.

'Maybe we should've. Bob was OK,' remarked Jake, avoiding the uncomfortable glances of the players.

'Told you before,' snarled The Beard, 'to keep that kind of shit to yerself. Another round, barten'.

The man brought the drinks. 'Hey, here comes the hearse! Must've been thirsty work.'

The men stared through the window as a huge top hatted man braked the car in a cloud of dust and strode towards the bar.

'It's that bloody Irish Mick,' Eb throwing down his cards. 'Madman, if you ask me.'

'Nobody did,' The Beard concentrating on his hand.

Heavy footfalls preceded the slamming of the door as the Irishman stormed to the counter. *'Whisky! Double!'*

Paddy Martin missed his beloved Ireland almost as much as he hated the English. A Kerry man, he was six feet seven tall. Two hundred and fifty pounds of seasoned muscle was topped by carrot red spiky hair, exploding like porcupine quills beneath his hat. A large granite face, hewn by humble origins and the misfortunes of his political convictions, was forested by a wild outcrop of beard. The man was seldom given to emotion.

A staunch republican, Paddy had been an active cell member of the Provisional Irish Republican Army, fighting the cause for many years in England. An informer had ended his activities the previous year, and the organisation had promptly flown him across the Atlantic with funds paid by Noraid, the army fund raising organisation in New York.

Disgruntled over his enforced stay, he had drifted from state to state, venting his wrath on all in his way, often provoking the unfortunate victims. His sole friend was Mona, a battered shillelagh named after his dead mother. When you fought Paddy, you fought them both. Despite his size, the Irishman felt no qualms about using Mona.

A man of few words, he kept his own counsel. He trusted nobody.

'How'd it go?' enquired the bartender. All but The Beard studied their cards. The Irishman's reputation was legend.

'As they always do. A man was buried while his friends drank.' Sinking the whisky: 'Same.' Drinking fast, he turned to leave.

'Can't take the pace, eh, Irish.' taunted The Beard, angry at the implication of the man's words.

Keeping his back to the hunter, Paddy removed the top hat, opened the funeral coat. 'A wise man knows his limits, Yank.'

The ensuing silence was broken by the scraping of The Beard's chair. 'Meanin?' pulling a skinning knife from the top of his boot.

Still with his back to the hunter: 'I respect a man's ways, not a fool's.'

Before The Beard could cross the room, Mona appeared in Paddy's hand; a moment later, he lay unconscious, his blood pooling on the wooden boards and the fallen knife.

Just then, eight morners entered the bar. Seeing Paddy standing over The Beard, they rushed at the big Irishman, calling to the card players.

Mona cleaved the air in devastating fashion; shrieks, curses and breaking bone reduced the place to pandemonium.

With two men clinging to his legs, Paddy called out in Gaelic as he dealt out fast and furious punishment. Oblivious to danger, he waged war around the bar as tables and chairs flew with alarming accuracy. The front window shattered as two mourners sailed out into the driveway.

Hardened hunters, the attackers fought ferociously, finally wearing down the raging Irishman. Among fallen bodies entangled in the broken furniture, four remaining men battered Paddy's face to a pulp; finally subduing him with a dismembered chair leg. Dragging him outside, they threw him among the trash cans.

Inside the wrecked bar, the bartender talked rapidly to himself.

Regaining consciousness, Paddy sluiced his blood-caked face from a wall tap. Holding his ribs, he retrieved Mona from the carnage and hobbled to the hearse.

Swearing profusely at the broken windows and slashed tyres, he spat globules of blood into the dirt. 'No different from the English!' he gasped. 'This is the fourth town, Paddy me boyo, in almost as many weeks. You're running out of welcome.'

Painfully, he walked to the freeway, wheezing from cracked ribs. 'No sense in waiting for the police. *People! Bloody people!*'

A northbound truck picked him up two miles out of Buffalo Creek. When the driver asked his destination, Paddy growled: 'Away from civilisation.'

CHAPTER 2

Mid-summer; Cascade, Denver:

Young Hank Miller hated chores. Moreso, the freckle faced Coloradan loathed errands. But when his father had told him to pick up an 'old journalist pal' from Stapleton International, he had jumped at the chance of driving to the airport.

His reward for the trip was possession of the pick-up for the rest of the day. Pop's broken leg has come in useful, he thought, scanning the arrival lounge now filling with tired travellers. After dropping the Limey, Thompson, back home, I'll take Myra Broadbent up to the shack for the afternoon.

Whistling tunelessly near the enquiry desk, he heard his request paged for the Englishman. Taking out the dog-eared snapshot of his father and the man toasting in some bygone New Year, he muttered: 'Serious looking guy! Wonder how much he's changed?'

Seeing a dark haired man approach the desk, Hank recognised the journalist and introduced himself. 'Is it Ben or Benjamin?' taking one of the suitcases.

'Better make it Ben. Benjamin doesn't sound Americanese. Where's your father, Harry?'

The young man laughed. 'Since he wrote you in England, he broke his leg fishing Eagle River. Nothing was biting, so he tried his hand climbing Mount Evans. Just the bottom bit!' Seeing Benjamin's concern: 'He's OK, though. Tough cookie, is Pop!'

Benjamin smiled. 'That sounds like Harry,' he said, moving towards the exit doors.

'Mom's plain mad with him sitting there all day using the place as an office. Papers everywhere! I reckon that editor of his'll keep calling when Pop's pushing up daisies. Are all you journalists like that?'

'Mostly,' grinned Benjamin. 'All papers and calls and gastric ulcers.'

Stopping at the pick-up, Hank piled the suitcases into the back and roared onto the freeway. 'About an hour to Cascade. You'll get used to driving on the wrong side over here. Met Pop when he was with Time, didn't you?'

Benjamin nodded. 'We met in London in '68. His letters were full of you and your sister, Annie.'

'She's OK, I suppose. Until she opens her mouth. Heck, can she talk!'

Benjamin fell silent. The long flight and the months following the divorce, suddenly took their toll. Nodding off, he was jolted forward as Hank swerved to miss a biker weaving through the traffic.

'Idiot! I guess you've got them in Liverpool, huh?'

'Yes, we have,' blearily watching the open country as the pick-up cruised through the Columbine Valley. It was hot and the windows were closed. He half listened as Hank pointed out Douglas and Cherry Creek. Exhausted, he failed to appreciate the Pike National Forest billowing along the South Platte River.

Rolling down the window, Benjamin smelt mountain country. 'Where's Mount Evans? Is it near Devil Mountain?'

'You mean Pop's Folly,' chuckled Hank. 'About thirty miles back. Not sure about the other one, but Evans is on the east side. There are five ranges. Pop showed me your letters. Looking for a mountain, huh!'

'I suppose you could say that. I've just...'

'Hey, no sweat, Ben. Pop told me all about the divorce and the job. Sorry.' Leaving the Englishman to his thoughts, he pictured

Myra Broadbent waiting at the roadhouse. Not a bad day, Hank, he mused. Not bad at all!

Benjamin slipped back into his reverie as the pick-up raced southwards along the sunlit freeway. Still unable to hold the Colorado beauty, he thought of Rosemary's bombshell six months before when life had almost stopped. Existing in a cocoon, he had drifted like a ghost through the sordid affair. By him not contesting the case, they had been spared the humiliation of dirty linen bandied about the courtroom. But the pain had remained ... *and the misery of four wasted years spent loving an enigma.*

After New Year, he had left Liverpool to work in a London provincial. The job paid the rent, kept his car on the road, but precious little else. Vague offers of improvement were made over drinks, but nothing concrete. He had been deeply touched by Rosemary's gift of half their savings, together with her love and wishes for the future. *'Find yourself, Bengy,'* she had written. *'Don't lose yourself in the telling of your own stories.'*

So like her, he thought as they approached the outskirts of Springs. Concise and so correct. Haunted by the mountain rescue, he had studied Colorado and its giant range slicing America like a huge abdominal scar. He remembered the surge of excitement on learning that Harry Miller was the political editor on the Colorado Springs Sun.

That was a chunk of coincidence, he mused as Hank slowed the vehicle past the Garden of the Gods; moved it along a tree-lined cul-de-sac fronting sedate brownstones and manicured lawns on the northern perimeter of Cascade.

He smiled to himself at Harry's initial letter: 'Come over, Ben, and sort out that problem.' Typical, he thought. Ebullient as ever.

Swinging the pick-up into an underground garage, Hank toppled a trash can as a pocket Venus of a woman in her late forties glowered from the open front door. 'Home, sweet home, Ben,' he cried.

'It won't be while you continue to drive like a lunatic,' snapped Helen Miller. 'Get those cases into Ben's room and be about your business. And listen, young man, if I smell so much as a whiff of Myra Broadbent in the pick-up when you return, you're for the high jump.'

Hank began to demonstrate, but a stern finger indicated swift departure. 'Kids,' she said, breaking into a smile. 'I'm Helen. You must be dead on your feet, Ben. Come inside, the old warrior's been counting the days. Just remember, stay as long as you like. We understand what you've been through.'

'Thanks Helen. I'm er ... a trifle embarrassed about...'

'Nonsense! It may be a long time since you two invaded the bars in Fleet Street, but friendship is friendship. We're a muddled household, but you'll survive.'

She led the way along a pictured hallway, the air rich with a Beethoven sonata. Benjamin followed her into a large open-planned living room crowded with divans and easy chairs. Three walls were dedicated to prints of the early American West, while the carpet had lost a battle with two typewriters, numerous reference books and a mass of paper balls that had rebounded off a wicker basket. A television set faced the wall.

'We don't encourage the monster,' said Helen, touching his arm. 'Television is an anti-social disease.'

With one leg in plaster, a red faced, jovial man with sparse grey hair, lay sprawled on a divan, as if eulogising the untidy correctness of the place. Glasses slipped off the end of his nose as he dropped a piece of paper onto the floor. 'Ben,' yelled Harry Miller. 'Oh Ben, come here and let's take a look at you!'

The two men shook hands. They hugged each other.

Helen smiled and left the room.

Harry beamed through wet eyes. Pointing to his broken leg, he said: 'Got a bit ambitious. You know me!'

'I know you, Harry,' Benjamin eyeing a lewd comment on the plaster.

'Courtesy of my editor, would you believe! God, but it's good to see you again, you old newshound.'

They sat in awkward silence before embracing again. Finally, Benjamin said huskily: 'I don't want to go back, Harry. There are too many memories.'

'I understand, old buddy. We'll talk later.' He looked up as a young girl in a flowing kaftan pushed a drink trolley through the doorway. 'Right now, we celebrate. This is Annie, my second favourite gal!'

Embarrassed, Annie shook hands and ran into the hallway.

'Cute kid, isn't she! She's like that first time with everyone. Get

29

to know her, and she's Helen all over: boss lady. Hank's alright too . . . when you can grab his ass fast enough. He's making hay with my leg, but I'll rump him for the trash can when the plaster comes off.'

Benjamin offered a cigarette pack. Inhaling, Harry said: 'Helen'll show you your room after. Full of back issues of the Sun. Otherwise it's habitable. Hell, letters out of the blue, and now you're here!'

'I'm still catching my breath,' Benjamin raising his glass.

'Like I said, we'll talk later. A few weeks later. Relax and enjoy America. Let the mud settle in the pond and you'll see it all the clearer, old buddy.'

Benjamin fidgeted nervously with his glass as shafts of sunlight blazed across the room. Gazing into his friend's eyes, he wondered what the man thought about his plan to live on Devil Mountain. He felt uncomfortable. They must think I'm crazy; over the edge after all that's happened. Maybe Harry was right: I'll see things differently after a rest. I doubt it.

The two men drank recalling the days; mellowed with remembrance.

For the umpteenth time, Harry swatted at the fly assaulting his peeling nose, burnt by the scorching July sun. Discussing the ramifications of American nuclear missiles stockpiled in Britain, periodically, he poked a knitting needle inside the plaster to relieve the itch. Coming to a temporary lull in the conversation, he studied Benjamin's tanned features. Five weeks, he thought, and he looks a new man. It's time he spoke about that goddamn mountain of his.

Fit from hiking in the Colorado valleys, Benjamin looked at the unopened cigarette pack on the garden table. He had not smoked for a month. He was mulling over Harry's last question regarding nuclear power as a deterrent.

'Deep inside, I don't agree. As a person,' aware of Harry's intense gaze. 'As a pragmatist, however, I concur. But we need statesmanship, not brinkmanship. It's Institutionalised Man at his worst. The solution lies elsewhere, but sadly, the human race hasn't achieved that level of intelligence yet . . . I wonder if it ever will.'

He began walking around the garden, talking over his shoulder.

'As much as I admire Reagan, his administration is only the legacy of former power bases. All we've achieved is the colossal goal of legalising bloodshed with a flourish of the political pen; a paranoic right to destroy if it's on paper.'

He moved towards Harry as the man made another unsuccessful swipe at the fly attacking his nose. 'We're conditioned by our own invention: bureaucratic madness. Bureaucracy creates imbalance. Rosemary said I stood to lose myself in the telling of my own stories, but isn't that also true of a government's decision?'

'Bureaucratic or not, Ben, war is a necessary evil. Grotesque, but it's *all* we've got. Like you said, us mere mortals haven't attained that higher level of intelligence.'

Harry raised an eyebrow; his way of leading up to a question. The act was not lost on Benjamin. 'But I sense you didn't invite me into the garden to talk about politics,' his face regaining its solemn mask. 'Out with it, Harry!'

Harry poured two beers. 'Sit down, for Chrissake. You're like a general before a battle.' Sipping his drink: 'Play-it-straight-Harry, that's me. That's what they call me in the office. It isn't easy, but here goes, old buddy. You're looking damned fine. Not the man who crawled out of England six weeks ago. Is this mountain thing, right?'

Benjamin shifted, his face shadowing. 'I think so,' he replied softly. 'No disrespect to you and Helen and the children, but it's all I have. And in a peculiar, I suppose you'd call it a sadistic way, all I want. I can't really explain it. It's something I have to do. I don't mean to use cliches, but I know what I've had. It sounds childish, crazy, a middle-aged political correspondent who has to find himself. I know I've only seen it on television – for a few moments – but I'm hooked on that mountain. How long does it take to fall in love? This isn't love, but it's just as powerful. Possibly more so.'

Harry sat shaking his head as Benjamin re-commenced his stroll of the garden. Stabbing the needle back inside the plaster, he said: 'Look, for what it's worth, I've spoken to my chief. Gabass, I call him. A man of a thousand words, but an OK type. And he understands journalists. I've got some pull with immigration: if I can square things with them, he'll hire you.' He sighed. 'What I'm saying is, Ben, go up your mountain. Just don't come down with your marbles crushed. High places do things to a man's mind.'

'There's more, isn't there,' said Benjamin gravely.

'You bet your ass, Daniel Boone,' Harry lighting a fresh filter from a half-smoked cigarette. 'Far more. I've seen better men than you, younger men, thrown in padded cells because they overstayed their welcome up there. Moderation's fine, but prolonged, mountains kick like a mule. Ready for the bottom line?'

Benjamin breathed deeply, opened a beer can.

'For starters, it's difficult acclimatising to that rare atmosphere. Takes about three months. But remember, we're in the eighties down here – with not much summer left. Winter up there's been known to drop to fifty below. Assuming you find yourself before the big freeze-up – which I doubt – you might go and lose yourself in all that desolation. Remember, you're a city boy.'

Benjamin sat down next to his friend. He had studied books on the mountains and the hunters who craved their solitude, but Harry's brand of matter-of-fact practicality was getting to him.

'Let's assume you don't go bananas,' continued the American. 'But you've still got two enemies almost as big: the elements and wild animals. Both are killers. Apart from sub-zero temperatures, the Rockies get gale force winds – and stronger. The wind-chill factor freezes a man faster than he can breathe. Snow blizzards on the mountains are frequent, and the hail is as big as your fist. Underfoot, it's slipperier than a politician's tongue, so stay clear of the edge. The warm chinook winds from the eastern slopes heat us up fast down here, but they're no good to you up there in the clouds. There's a prairie load more to it, but that'll do for the elements just now.'

Benjamin held Harry's eye as the American searched for the words to dissuade him of his decision.

I'm trying to be a friend, thought Harry, but he's got that vacant look I've seen in madmen. Christ, he's been hurt! For all the good it will do going up there, he might as well walk off the Empire State. Damn that fly!

'OK,' he said, pulling on his beer. 'If you think you've got no problems up to now, Mr Boone, here they come: mountain lion, bobcats and rattlers to name just a few. You don't have to understand them like the weather. It's suffice to know they don't like humans: period. And there's a certain grizzly prowling around where you're going, who isn't too crazy about man, either. I'll tell you about him later. It's their town and they don't hand out invites.'

Benjamin had started drumming his fingers on the table, trying to picture winter on Devil Mountain. Like peace, it was beyond him.

'Oh, did I forget Rocky Mountain spotted fever, compliments of a tick that's as close to typhus as you don't want to be! There's no drug store near the Happy Hunting Grounds. And you'll have to learn to shoot, fish, hunt and read the stars – if you can't read a map or lose it hightailing it from that grizzly – and know your cloud formations because the weather up there changes like a woman's mind on sale day. You'll have to track, know the signs, just to stay alive.'

Benjamin remained silent. Staring at his drink, he was wondering about the bear. Was there just one, or were there more? Recalling an old movie on grizzlies, the prospect of meeting one on a mountain held grim fascination.

Harry put an arm round his shoulder. 'I'm not trying to sway you, Ben, believe me. But right now, you need a friend more than you've ever done. I wouldn't be that if I didn't present the dangers of your venture.'

To Harry's amazement, Benjamin began to smile recklessly. Jeese, he thought, that's a side I didn't know about. 'Alright,' he shouted angrily. 'You're not Daniel Boone yet, and you can't walk on water, either. You're only one man, Benjamin Thompson. How the hell will you build your five star cabin? You can't exist in the open. How will you get your supplies up there? Got a delivery service, have you!'

'I'll find a way,' hissed Benjamin, his face cold, eyes penetrating. 'If I have to crawl every inch, I'll do it – despite your lions or bears or whatever. I'll do it, because I have to. *There's nothing else.*'

Sadly, Harry stubbed his cigarette and sighed. 'OK, have it your own way. Basically, that's the bottom line, but there's a prairie load more as I said. If you can survive all that, then there's a desk waiting for you at the Sun.' Emotion cracked his voice. 'I'll write your story, Ben. It'll make good copy, middle page news on a weekend supplement for the breakfast table, maybe . . . But I'll be damned if I'll write your obituary.'

Hesitantly, Benjamin rose. He had no right to hurt Harry. The man was like the brother he had never had. Am I going insane? Already there? I can see the logic of his words, but the mountain keeps coming through. Why? For Christ's sake, why? Even if I do live to find myself, I might not like what I find. It's like knowing the future: we're not meant to know. But surely we are allowed to know ourselves!

More puzzled than ever, he spoke quietly. 'Harry, dear Harry. Right now, there's more chance of losing my sanity down here to civilisation, than up there. I'll take my chances. After all, I am free of responsibility. I know I'm not being responsible to myself, so spare the lecture. I love you and Helen. You've both done so much, and the children. You're my future. Just let me do this thing. I know you would in my place. Please! And whatever you think, I'm not running away. It's the exact opposite.'

'I know, old buddy. I know.' There were tears in Harry's eyes. Finally, squashing the fly, he said: 'I'll tell you about Devil Mountain, and that survivor you asked me to trace from the TV newscast. Incidentally, that grizzly hampered the rescuers. Remember this: always. Psyche your mind and body to perfection – or as near as you can get at your age. Humble yourself before the mountain; respect it. It doesn't belong to you; it's not your home, Ben. Your place is down here with the rest of us goofballs. *Learn, find and leave.'*

Benjamin stared into space, his heart heavy for Harry.

'Now go and get the snack tray from the kitchen. And bring the bourbon. I need a stiff one.'

The man shook his head as Benjamin moved towards the house. A bloody waste, he thought. Those damned Jesuits screwed him up. He's never really got over the beatings, enforced fasting and catholicism being rammed down his throat. No wonder he isolated himself from people by hiding in his work. He's lost before he starts. How can he find what was never there in the first place? Forward is his only way, and maybe that's too late.

Lighting another cigarette, he cursed the broken leg. If only I could go with him. But he has to do it alone . . . Then there's Helen and the kids: the job to pay the mortgage and insurance and the kids' education and all the rest of life's little bills. Shit, in a strange way, I envy him.

Helen Miller's intelligence complemented her good looks. She had adjusted to middle-age better than most women at the PTA, her only outside activity apart from Saturday morning library.

She had just returned from her weekly tryst with literature when Annie dashed flush-faced into the kitchen. 'Hey Mom,' she blurted. 'He's done it again! Lit out of the home.'

'Who has?' Helen rounding on her daughter.

'Why Sam Fynn, of course. Who else! Seems like he's really foxed them this time. Stole a hundred dollars from the reverend's drawer and pushed off.'

Helen Miller recalled the reports in the Sun, dramatising the young orphan's numerous escapes from the home. His name usually cropped up at the PTA one way or another. She had spoken to Sally Brown, the chief welfare worker, about the boy, who was repeatedly at her wits' end.

'Seems he left two nights ago,' continued Annie in a torrent of words. 'He's been on the radio: a truck driver who gave him a lift to Loveland, caught the bulletin and called the cops. But Sam was long gone by then. What'll they do to him? He's only ten!'

The mother sighed and pushed the hair from her daughter's eyes. 'He'll be caught. I just hope he's alright. Hitching can be dangerous, especially for a child.'

'I'm not a child, and I'm only two years older than him,' came the indignant reply.

Helen smiled. 'No matter how old you are, you'll always be a child to me and your father. So will Hank. Speaking of whom, what's he up to? It's too quiet around here.'

'Aw, he's out pumping iron; showing off in front of that Myra Broadbent. You know, the one with the big boobs.'

'I beg your pardon, young lady! That will be all.'

But Annie was grinning as she helped herself to a sandwich from the lunch tray. 'He doesn't like weights any more than we do. Myra's a macho nut and a first class...'

'Not with your mouth full! I've warned you about that kind of language. Your father doesn't pay good money for schoolyard expletives.'

Glancing through the window, she saw Harry with Benjamin

moving towards the house after another of their long talks. Why is it always so difficult for men, she thought, her forehead creasing. And now Hank had discovered women.

Annie began setting the lunch table, imagining Sam Fynn being hunted by the authorities, alone and frightened in some lonely place, while her mother worried over Hank and what to do about Myra of the big boobs.

The telephone rang. It was Hank. He was skipping lunch.

★ ★ ★ ★ ★

Sam Fynn was a ten year old orphan who had stolen a hundred dollars. On hearing his description on the radio, he had fled into the forests before continuing his journey north. After a month of rough living through Wyoming and Montana, his young world had been ravaged by fear, hunger and desperation.

Since running away from the home in Colorado Springs, he had hitched and walked two thousand miles. Sleeping on the prairie or the alleyways of towns, he took food where he found it. High prices had gobbled the reverend's money: stealing was a necessity. Dreaming of the Colorado mountain country, he had finally dragged himself from the boondocks of Atlantic City and drifted back south. Resting for a few days in Laramie and Cheyenne, his spirit had strengthened as he began the long haul to Grand Lake in the mountain districts.

Fair haired with impish blue eyes, Sam was small for his age. Thin boned, he possessed an open face, firm jaw and a determined mind. His small rucksack contained a fishing line and clasp knife from a Rockport junk store, a change of clothes stolen from a church bazaar, and, among an assortment of boy's things, a worn out photograph of his dead mother.

At two o'clock one grim morning, a farmer's wagon dropped him at Grand Lake. Thanking the driver, he trudged through a heavy drizzle as a biting wind moaned in off the mountains.

Shivering the final night hours in a disused cowshed, he set off before dawn for the Arapahoe National Forest. Wary of game rangers, he plodded through hoar frosted valleys and gloomy passages of timber, oranging with the merging day. His sodden clothes smoked as the sun broke over the mountains.

He watched as the female eagle glided over the valley; become lost in the treetops.

Reunited with the big country, his heart hammered joyfully: he was truly free as his miserable past crumbled before the towering magnificence marching stoically into the sky. At least, for the moment, he was free! He knew of an exclusive hunting lodge near Longs Peak, some distance along a wide dirt track. He smiled expectantly: the lodge meant food, and weekend hunters never started until well after sun-up; never without picnic hampers.

Leaving the rucksack near a giant sequoia tree close to an isolated dam, he set out for the lodge. After an hour, he was hiding behind a rhododendron bush as gaily clad hunters gossiped near the vehicles being loaded with the food baskets.

Sam's stomach growled as cooking smells wafted from an open door. He waited with baited breath as, at last, the vehicles crunched dirt and sped off along the track. Slinking to the kitchen, he struck: fast, organised; efficient.

Lungs close to bursting, he zig-zagged through the forest back to the sequoia. Heart beating in his ears, he waited for sounds of being followed. After agonising for several minutes, he walked the short distance to the water's edge. Grinning broadly, he tore open the hamper. His eyes bulged at the neatly packed lunch: chicken, eggs and bread; a flask of coffee and quart of milk with telescoped plastic cups, knives and forks.

'Speed and dare, Sam,' he exclaimed, tearing the meat and stuffing it into his mouth. Pouring coffee, he guzzled and slurped until his contracted stomach groaned in defeat.

Deciding on a paddle, he moved into the shallows; laughing merrily at the sky on the dancing water, he felt the tension cruise deliciously from his body. Returning to the hamper, he was stopped in his tracks by food scraps in the grass.

'I didn't do that,' he puzzled out loud. A scratching sound made his neck hairs bristle. He relaxed as two tiny ears appeared over the top of the hamper, followed by a black face; whiskers heavy with chicken morsels.

Sam smiled as the kitten pawed the lid, struggling to get inside the hamper. 'So you're the thief,' stroking the cat's head. 'I guess we're two of a kind: a long way from home and a mile between meals.'

The kitten sniffed his face, miaowed and continued its battle with the hamper lid.

'You've sure got belly time, cat!' pouring some milk into a cup. Sitting down, he watched the animal finish the drink; grinned as it climbed onto his lap. Cleaning itself, the kitten's purrs soon changed to shallow breathing. It was asleep.

'Wonder where you're from, cat?' talking quietly to the sleeping kitten. 'You're a scrawny runt! Should be suckling off your Ma, not roughing it out here in the big country. Don't tell me you ain't got a Ma; all cats have mothers. Only kids like me ain't got a Ma because grown-ups do the darndest things. Mind you, it isn't so bad after a while, being on your ownsome. A guy gets used to it.'

Memories since running from the home flooded back: survival in the city backstreets; the haunting fear of being returned to polished dormitories, carbolic floors, and the nightly weeping of lonely boys.

'You don't get used to it, Sam,' he muttered, as the kitten stirred. 'And you know it. But you don't want to hear my troubles, cat! Got enough of your own, huh.'

The kitten stretched and curled back into a ball.

'Heck, you're a neat cat! But I can't keep calling you 'cat'. It'll have to be a temporary name, because you can't stay with me. Life would be too tough for a little guy like you, what with me on the lam and everything. How about Boogaloo? I'll sneak you up to the lodge after dark.'

Tenderly, he touched the kitten's head: 'My first real friend.' The sequoias creaked as the boy entered into a disturbed sleep. Boogaloo crept onto his chest, rising and falling in rhythm with the lapping dam water.

At five, Samuel Fynn had been taken from his alcoholic mother, two days before the haemorrhage that had severed her life. After the court had placed him in the orphanage, his only recollections of home had been the alternating cries of pleasure and pain as his mother clung to her clients in order to supplement the low income. Never knowing the boy's father, she had named him after Uncle

Sam in the vain hope he would one day shine where she had fallen. From the age of seven, however, Sam had become a legend in other spheres; notably running from the Colorado Spring home on eleven occasions. A quick mind and indomitable spirit, the boy lived to escape.

Sam Fynn's bastardy had created a fighter and rebellious loner: a scared man-child searching for the love he'd never received.

★　★　★　★　★

With a full belly, the he-bear moved better since the spring when the man-noise had wounded him; killed his family. As the hurt had diminished, he slowly progressed down the mountain to the timberline. It was time to live again. He belched loudly, the feel of goat heavy in his gut.

Overhead, the sky was a cloudless blue; below, the valley footing the timberline shimmered a thousand shades of green in the heat haze.

Satisfied, the he-bear would once more secure the territory around his mountain. He knew there would be fighting with other bears before his dominance was reasserted; that the male lion would be waiting.

With renewed spirit, he burst into the forest. Galloping recklessly down the lower slopes, he roared out loud, filling the valley with his presence. Ignoring the scrub with the sun-bleached bones of his family, he stormed northwards. At full speed, his great bulk swept over buffalo grass, pulverised bush and sapling; splashed through rivers, bounded over tall rocks . . . calling, forever calling his return.

The other animals hid in fear as his triumphant cries echoed through the valley.

Eventually, choosing a meadow loud with bird and stream, he rolled, leapt and grunted his delight. Scratching against a pine, he slid slowly down its trunk. The prospect of another mate dropped him into a deep and contented sleep.

Back to the tree, legs sprawled out in front, his snores mixed with the peaceful sounds of the meadow.

A fleeting shadow crossed his face as the female eagle flew past the sun.

CHAPTER 3

Downtown; Denver:

Like most women, Sally Brown was disenchanted with her age. At mid-fortyish, she claimed that her's was the wrong profession: for marriage. Working with deprived children for twenty-five years, she had, albeit unintentionally, denied herself motherhood.

Heating the coffee pot, she poured and flopped wearily into an easy chair, thinking about her latest meeting with the Cascade PTA. Sometimes, she thought, I think they only play at caring for orphans. Yet, in the real world, who can blame them? They have family problems of their own.

She frowned as a familiar, unwelcome face surged to the forefront of her mind. 'Can I *ever* escape from you, Sam Fynn?' she muttered out loud. 'Lord knows, I've tried everything to help you settle, but you just carry on disregarding authority in your own inimitable style. But this time, you've gone too far, my lad. Now you're a thief to boot!'

Scolding herself for talking to the coffee pot, she sighed as the doorbell rang. It was her elder sister, Sonia.

The Brown sisters, despite a six year age gap, were often mistaken for twins. Slightly sweeter than plain and a stocking thickness above five feet, they both wore straw coloured hair tied at the nape of the neck, emblazoning the Slavic side of their great-grandmother. Sonia had spread with childbirth; Sally remained firm and trim.

They talked family before Sonia broached her sister's spinsterhood.

'Really Sis,' exclaimed Sally. 'You'd think I was Eleanor Rigby. I'm only forty-five. There's time. If it's kids you're worrying about, don't you think I get enough of them in the job?'

But Sonia was having none of it. 'I know you too well, Sal. You don't fool me for a minute. Every woman needs a man sometime in her life – even though most of them are complete idiots by the time they reach fifty. Still, you're not a nun: give yourself a chance. They take advantage of you at the office: 'Don't worry, Sally Brown will cover for you; she's doing nothing tonight, or tomorrow or next week or whenever in her life.' For heaven's sake, my girl, it wouldn't do any harm to say 'no' for a change. Don't look at me with that hurt expression; you know I'm right.'

Sally refilled the coffee cups. 'And you'd rather I went home to a husband every night, instead of my books and the job? I haven't met Mr Right yet – and I have had one or two discreet flings. I enjoy myself in my own peculiar way, believe it or not, Sis. I'm beginning to resent these intrusions on my sex or lack of sex life. Hell, I don't invade your marriage bed!'

'You're *missing* the point,' Sonia said heatedly. 'They're already *talking* about you, Sal. You *know* I pay *no* attention to gossip, but I overheard someone in the supermarket saying you were . . . well, odd. *Naturally,* I gave them a piece of my mind, but it still remains that you're leaving it a bit late to catch a man.' Putting an arm around her sister's shoulder: 'I don't mean to interfere, honey, but I just worry about my little sister, that's all. Don't blame me for that.'

Sally stood up, nonplussed by Sonia's outburst. Gratefully, she picked up the receiver as the telephone broke the uneasy silence. Answering in a clipped business tone, she replaced the handset and announced that she was going back to the office. 'Something's come up in the Fynn case.'

'It's Friday evening, for God's sake,' blurted Sonia. 'I was going to ask you over to make a foursome at bridge. Anyway, who's Fynn? Not that ungrateful little urchin who keeps climbing over the wall!'

'That's one way to put it,' returned Sally, her face flushing angrily. Throwing on her coat: 'That kid needs my help more than I need bridge or your matchmaking. I better hadn't find out who's talking about me in the supermarket. Because if I do, my heavens, I'll . . . Why I'll given them a piece of my mind. You can let yourself out, Sis.'

Sonia stared as the door closed behind her sister. Well, that didn't do much good, did it? she thought, putting the cups in the drier. I've tried every which way with her and I'm still wasting my time.

Picking up the phone she dialled home. 'Put Larry off, sweetie! Sis has flown the coop again . . . *What do you mean!* Of course I know what's best for my own flesh and blood. I'll be home in fifteen minutes. Be sure and clean up any mess you've created since I've been gone.'

Letting herself out, Sonia walked to the car lot, mentally cursing her sister's defiant stance against marriage.

Driving through the evening traffic, Sally thought over Sonia's words. Have I left it too late? One day, I won't have the job: what then? Yikes!

Stopping at a pedestrian light, she recalled the short message from the office: Fynn had been seen in the Grand Lake area. Help, he's all over the place. And now the mountains! If anyone needs a family, he does. It would certainly put an end to his rebelliousness; someone to look up to. But I don't think the right people for him have been invented yet. I suppose in a way, he's like me. Does his own thing. And then she chastised herself for condoning the boy's activities.

'Heavens,' she said to herself, 'I'd take him on if the committee would waive my age. After all, I'm an expert on Sam Fynn.' Changing into second, she mentally criticised herself. I don't want a man, and I definitely don't want Sam Fynn. *Oh dear, what in the name of heaven do I want?*

Pulling into the kerb, she locked up and walked briskly across the sidewalk. Work, she thought. Work keeps life's little problems – and the big ones – at bay. Opening a glass swing door, she nodded to the security man and made for her office.

★ ★ ★ ★ ★

Sam studied Boogaloo and knew he couldn't part with the kitten.

'Anyway,' he shrugged, 'it might be too risky going back to the hunting lodge. No, the little fella will have to travel in my pack. Shouldn't bother him, he likes sleeping.'

He had remembered one of the boys at the home talking about Devil Mountain: 'Nobody goes there: too spooky.' I reckon I'll fish the Colorado for a few days, see how things go. Weather's okay! I can trade my catch for food and money. Then I'll head for that creek near the mountain – if his memory served him right – that had plenty of beaver and more fish. Yes, maybe I'll give that mountain valley a try.

The cat nuzzled his face. 'You agree little fella, huh! That's settled then. We'll lit out at first light.' Snacking off cold chicken, afraid of the dangers a campfire would bring, he slept beneath the towering sequoias. At daybreak, he walked west into the mountains, Boogaloo snoozing inside the pack. Happily wandering through the valleys, he lived off his catch; revelled in the warm nights: rustling leaves, campfire smells and the kitten on his chest.

On the fourth day, Boogaloo saved his life.

Missing a forest track, he was hiking through dense timber lining a gradual rise between two valleys. About to strike off at an angle to bypass a cluster of trees, the kitten suddenly sprang onto his shoulder, its tiny cries stopping him beside a tall pine.

'What's up, Boogie?' stroking the animal's head.

Jumping to the ground, the cat sniffed a leafy hump near the tree. Gently, it pawed the leaves; miaowed, tail fluffed.

Edging closer, Sam said: 'What have you found, little fella?' He stared alarmingly as the kitten pulled away at leaves and twigs, revealing a rusty length of chain tied to the tree and attached to a

44

bloodstained length of steel. His mouth went dry as he gingerly pulled the cat away from the open bear trap. Taking off the pack, he found a long stick and sent the lethal teeth snapping together with a hideous clang.

Shaking, he picked up the pack and retraced his footsteps, his mind a prey to the dangers of man.

After a week of avoiding the forests and camping beside creeks, he arrived at a hill some miles to the south of Devil Mountain. Finding a red box canyon abutting the valley below the great rock, he made camp for the night. Just before sunset, he bolted upright at the eerie sound of a distant echo, followed by several more cries ghosting through the night air.

'That's no animal,' he stuttered into the fire. Holding onto the kitten, he stared fearfully through the river mist into the canyon.

Boogaloo pawed at his chest, yawned and went back to sleep.

I'm not alone in the mountains, thought Sam. There's somebody else. Who? It can't be anyone after me; I've covered my tracks well. Haven't I? Anyway, if they were on to me, they wouldn't advertise themselves by calling through the canyons!

Sleep came with difficulty.

★ ★ ★ ★ ★

The Millers waved furiously to Benjamin standing beside his heavy rucksack. And then he was alone as the pick-up bounced back along the track, its engine drowned by the nearby Colorado.

Perfectly still, like a penitent in a cathedral, Benjamin suffered his first attack of isolation as the adrenalin pumped from his body: the divorce and sacking, the flight from England and the Miller hospitality, followed by the gruelling weeks of physical training and study was now over. Despair suddenly pervaded him as he took stock of his surroundings. A single, dominant thought, detonated inside his head: everything is so ... *Big.*

He blew on his hands for warmth as a cold, post dawn snap, breathed heavily onto the hazy banks of the river, the misty fingers eddying above miniature whitecaps slapping in midstream. Everywhere, silver cobwebs littered moss covered hills as soaring

45

blue spruce and ponderosa pine marched steeply away from the riverbank; a mosaic of columbine and fairy slipper rippled at their feet.

Awed, Benjamin drank in the narcotic aroma of crushed vegetation and the contagious smell of the mountains. Dull shafts of sleepy light splashed all round; filtered to the forest floor already awake with a myriad insects.

He looked downstream to where the Colorado snaked, its width trimmed by fallen timber and rock forming a natural ford that led to a track curling up through the forest.

'Take that one, Ben,' Harry had said. *'Often use it on my fishing trips. Keep west; head two-seventy on the compass and the Rockies are only a prairie away. Watch out for hunters popping off out of the woodwork. You'll make plenty of mistakes, but just believe in yourself and you're past first base.'*

Glaring at the ninety pound pack, he growled: 'Let's be having you. Now is when it begins.'

He arrived at the river bend flushed and sucking for air; his legs were buckling under the heavy load. Wriggling free of the harness, he recognised his first mistake: he had trained light. Laying the pack across the ford, he massaged his burning shoulders. Over ambition sparked the second mistake as he became transfixed by a large trout finning in the shallows.

Eyes adjusting to the grey depths, he spotted a shoal of black spotted fish resting beneath an overhand in the bank. Trying to emulate the stories of Indians fishing with their hands, he was oblivious of a beaver surfacing near his pack. As he delicately toed his way towards the shoal, the original trout shot between his legs, sending him pitchpoling forward into the freezing river. Ejaculating uncharacteristic English, he bumbled about stubbornly for half an hour before capitulating.

Teeth chattering, he stared in disbelief as the rucksack began skating across the ford. Running forward, he was stopped in his tracks by the wet head of the beaver, its teeth firmly embedded in the pack. He lunged forward unsuccessfully as his belongings disappeared over the edge with an ignoble ploosh; the beaver staring back defiantly before diving below the surface.

His third mistake materialised when two beaver pups popped up to see the cause of their parent's anger: the heavy pack had snagged a log, pushing it across the canal entrance to the family underwater lodge. Nature and bad temper had taken its course.

Dragging the sodden pack onto the ford, Benjamin moved back to the bank; miserably hung the wet contents to dry on tree branches and rocks. By late morning, he walked up Harry's fishing track into the forest. After five miles, he was sweating profusely; on losing the track through fallen trees and heavy foliage, he began to wander. Cursing and trudging a circuitous route march around the Arapahoe National Forest, he grimaced as hill followed tortuous hill, until, by early afternoon, he was exhausted. He was also lost.

A combination of pain and a succession of mistakes fuelled the fires of his mind: he became bad tempered; irrational; careless.

Snapping open the map, he glowered at the neat and orderly contour lines with their coloured symbols. He reflected dismally over his tired condition, when, after training, he had always nodded off during Harry's map reading lessons.

'Damn it,' he spluttered, 'I've followed the compass west. Bloody sure I've seen the same trees. According to Harry, the sun should be at my back: I can't see anything for these blessed trees! The Colorado should be somewhere over . . . Shit! And how the hell can anyone lose the Rockies, for Christ's sake!' Bitterly: 'Because I have. Benjamin Bloody Thompson has lost his temper, and in so doing, has managed to sever from mankind the entire North American length of the Rocky Mountains. If it wasn't so damn stupid, it would be pathetic! Laugh, that's what I should be doing; things will look clearer, according to the gospel of Saint Harry. I wonder if Daniel Boone ever got lost?'

Stretching his aching limbs, he watched idly as a red squirrel darted from tree to tree. Success dawned: I need height. Standing on the pack, he launched himself at a lower branch, but his hands gripped fresh air as he returned painfully to the forest floor. Cut and bruised, after two more attempts, he was shinning up the pine tree. From a perilous position some fifty feet up in the creaking boughs, he spied the red box canyon frequently mentioned by Harry when reminiscing his fishing exploits.

Climbing back to the pack, he caught the squirrel give him a queer look before vanishing amid a series of whistles and chirps. 'He'll know where the sodding mountains are,' opening a soggy packet of sandwiches. Ill tempered, he threw down the bread and took a long pull from the coffee flask. Good old Harry, he thought. Napoleon five star to the rescue.

About to continue, his eye fell on a tiny movement around the discarded sandwiches. He became intrigued as an orderly column of ants began transporting crumbs across to a decayed tree stump. We learnt a few military tactics from the little buggers, he mused. So strong for their size! One leaf cutter constantly fell under its load, and Benjamin offered words of encouragement until it finally arrived at the nest. 'If you can do it, old son, there's hope for Thompson,' he beamed.

With a surge of fresh confidence, he fathomed the mysteries of his wayward compass: when held close to the pack, the needle moved erratically around the dial; away, it pointed to true north. The variety of food cans were responsible for his enforced forest rambles.

With a lighter heart, he strode off on a true bearing. Within an hour, he had crossed the first of three valleys standing between him and Devil Mountain. By late afternoon, legs quivering from an agonising ascent up a forested re-entrant, he gained the high country: collapsed on a polished mesa overlooking a long, narrow plain; scrub sliced by a meandering creek and sprinkled with boulders.

Wracked with pain, Benjamin was jubilant as he stared at the vast expanse of rock calling from across the valley: bedecked in pine, a confusion of peaks and sun-dappled labyrinths thrusting through the clouds, the Colorado Rockies stood before him in turbulent majesty.

But even this awesome presence was dwarfed as he focussed on one mountain, its fourteen thousand feet twin peaks obscured by scudding cumulus. Speaking quietly, as if to an old and sacred friend, a confidant of his most innermost secrets, he said: 'Devil Mountain, I've come home for the first time in my life.'

His first moment with the mountain was ended by a roaring crescendo of joy, his screams cut the valley again and again, their echoes mingled, swept on the wind and rushed to the lofty wastes of the sky.

Benjamin Thompson had arrived at his mountain. His heart exploded for the future.

During his first night on the mesa, he was kept company by a nagging wind, frosty stars and a riding, full moon. A crosslegged figure in a sleeping bag, he willed himself into the silhouette of Devil Mountain; released his past and entire being into its desolate and terrible spaces. Like a knight preparing for holy battle, he confessed his heart to the mountain: exposed a life of weakness and shame in a man incapable of resolving even the simplest of truths. Without exception, he bared his soul to the mighty chasms of rock until he felt a great calm as the sounds and ink of night subsided for the noises and grey of dawn: his vigil was over; his baptism solemnised.

He smiled like a woman after childbirth as the sunrise painted Colorado with slashes of pink and gold, informing the big country that the day was here. Moving to the edge of the mesa, he was engulfed by a fortitude he had never known.

Paddy Martin hit Cripple Creek like a hurricane in search of fresh wind. The following morning, he awoke behind bars. Writhing on the cot, his battered body laid testimony to the latest bar brawl, while a throbbing head joined forces with a broken nose.

Head in hands, he groaned as a police sergeant rattled a tin mug against the bars. 'Holy Jaysus, don't you Yanks believe in letting a man die quietly!'

'You wanna break my town, asshole; I'll break you! You've got a visitor. Five minutes, pal,' he said to the man clanging the cell door.

Paddy studied the pencil of a man in Levis commence strutting around the cell. He did not like his silence, or his refusal to shake hands. On being curtly told to 'sit down, boyo', his anger erupted. 'Who the hell are you, you walking toothbrush?'

The man froze in mid-stride; eyes devouring the big Irishman. 'I won't repeat myself after this, Martin,' he spat. 'Now if you know what's good for you, sit down. My name's McAvoy and you're in trouble. I saw your fine performance last night, the likes of which I hope never to see again for many a day – from one of our own. Get my meaning, Paddy? Obviously not, judging by the stupid look on your face. You broke security for the last time. *Savvy?'*

Paddy grunted something and took out a crumpled pack of cheroots. Manoeuvring his numb lips apart, he lit the cigar and wheezed: 'Get to the point, McAvoy. Life's passing me by while you think of idle words.'

'We'll see about that,' the man checking the sergeant was out of earshot. 'Let's get this over with quick. I think you're something the cow dropped, and I couldn't give a Limerick fart what your idea is of me, so listen carefully, because Cripple Creek isn't exactly on my circuit.'

Trying hard to concentrate through the pain, Paddy remained silent as McAvoy explained that he worked for Noraid, the IRA fund raising organisation. He had been present, albeit in the background, when the Irishman had arrived in America and had kept a distant eye on him ever since. Unfortunately, Paddy's bar room battles were embarrassing the Noraid hierarchy in New York; too many people had to be paid off. It was time to cool it or else . . .

'You're a walking disaster, Martin,' the man hissed, moving closer to the cot. 'You can't go round thumping up the people who are funding us. Jaysus, I feel sorry for the poor Yanks. Most of us have lost someone to graveyards or prisons, but we don't go to pieces like you. I can't go back, either. The only reason I'm here and not your executioner, is because I know you were good in London.' Even as Paddy raised himself from the cot, the man drew a pistol, ramming it hard against the prisoner's head. 'Next time, I'll pull,' his face devoid of feeling.

Paddy heard how his previous night's exploits had been settled by fifteen hundred dollars; three victims and the police sergeant's silence. Helpless, he nodded mechanically to the 'request' to 'go and lose yourself' until you're 'sent for'. But when, was the question. When could he return to active service in England or Ireland? He didn't care where, so long as he could kill Englishmen.

'Not for another year at least,' replied McAvoy. 'You blew that informant's head off in church, Paddy. *During the service!* People remember that kind of thing. Get a job on a farm, anything, but stay out of trouble. We'll keep in touch. We look after our own, you know that. You should also know that we look after those who can't look after themselves. Twelve, maybe eighteen months, then you can go home.'

'Seems like I have no choice. I'll need money. I lost a bundle . . . I was robbed last night. You say you were there; I don't suppose you saw what happened to my shillelagh during the shindig?'

The man smiled thinly. 'Word has it there's a thing between you and that stick. Lucky for you I found it before the cops moved in. Bad evidence, that. I'll return it as you're leaving on the bus. No more trouble, Paddy. I want your hand on it.'

Paddy scowled through bloodied lips. 'You got it, McAvoy. Where I've a mind going, you won't hear a peep from me until it's time to go back to the war.' Silently, he wrote McAvoy's death warrant. Time was all it took, and he had plenty of that.

McAvoy nodded gravely. 'Sergeant.'

The cell door opened with another clang. 'You sorted that asshole out?'

Paddy made a mental note to repay the policeman's hospitality.

Too excited to cook, Benjamin heated water for coffee; ate half a slab of chocolate. Opening the pack, he refilled the water flask; replaced the gas stove in a side pouch and changed shirt and socks. *'Feet are all you've got up there,'* Harry had said. *'Most things, you'll cope with: but not wet feet. Bugger them, and you bugger yourself. Clean socks every day: hygiene and all the little things you do in captivity are more important up there than down here. Every day discipline becomes deadlier-than-you-never-thought-it-could-be-survival.'*

Through Harry's old service binoculars, he studied the timberline where he proposed to build his cabin. Choosing four possible lines of approach, he disregarded access from the west within the mountains.

The southern route held promise; the gradual incline where Devil Mountain joined the lower peaks, comprised few rocky outcrops and sparse timber. Unfortunately, the final leg was hampered by dangerous chunks of rock, too large to negotiate with the heavy pack. A similar ploy from the north east too, initially offered little rock, but ascent through acres of steep forested area

51

was only possible after a long trudge from the far end of the valley. The easterly passage, however, held the shortest route. It was also the steepest and most perilous.

Reconsidering the north east approach, a natural dish scalloped from the rock slightly south, it curved gently upwards and swung left, skirting much of the pine. The final hundred and fifty yards, though a jumble of jagged rock, was smaller than the higher route and could be negotiated by climbing a portion of the forest and cutting through the latter slopes petering at the timberline.

Benjamin decided on the fourth route.

Today, he would reconnoitre the valley in easy stages; the previous day's stiffness was firing his limbs. Before first light tomorrow, he would begin the long climb to his new home.

Squatting, he threaded his arms through the pack straps and pushed up onto his feet. Gathering breath for his effort, he tackled a kind slope spiralling to the valley floor.

Stumbling occasionally, he descended from the mesa and hobbled across the scrub to the creek. Puffing, he recalled how much closer, easier, his goal had seemed from above. Throwing off his dusty clothes, he bathed in the shallows; savoured the breeze on his naked body. As the cold water sucked away a multitude of cramps, he closed his eyes, imagining when he was back in England dreaming about Colorado: opening them, he laughed uproariously, splashed and whooped with joy. 'Now I'm here,' he yelled at the top of his voice. 'I'm bloodywell here.'

The moment of release passed, he gazed at the vastness all around; felt insignificant among this extravaganza of giants. Draping his wet things over a boulder, he drank coffee and finished the chocolate. Dressing, he left the pack and went off to explore.

Eight miles long and one wide, the valley ran from north to south. Sloping from Devil Mountain, the ground resembled a lumpy mattress; red rocks and boulders littered like leaves in some gargantuan prehistoric autumn. The scrub where the she-bear and her cubs had died, bordered the foothills off to Benjamin's left, separated by the steep rise where the male had made his futile charge from the forest. The creek divided the valley in half; a beaver dam had been constructed downstream, south of the mountain. A natural dam sparkled at the base of the mesa where Benjamin had slept. Patchworks of wild flowers carpeted the valley; a variety of bush and tree hugged the banks of the creek. Cactus sprouted everywhere.

With his forest ramblings still hurtful for thought, Benjamin spent most of the day observing the ground. He drew his own map; picture reference points of tall trees, odd shaped bushes and boulders. He noticed that there were trout in the creek, prolific bird life all round; that the cottontail rabbit preferred the lush meadows at the valley ends and the grey-green buffalo grass ringing the dam.

By early afternoon, the sun punished overhead. Glaring from rock and water, it changed the valley into a natural oven.

After cooling off in the dam, Benjamin amused himself with a stick, poking it in all manner of places. He was amused when a large eared harvest mouse darted from the cover of a bush; grinned robustly as he prodded a peculiar shaped rock beneath a cactus plant, only to retreat smartly as, to his horror, the rock emitted a rattling sound. Fortunately, the snake had been sleeping in the strong sun.

Cautious now, he made for the centre of the scrub. Studying the different animal tracks in the dust and along the muddy banks of the creek, he associated large areas of flattened scrub with passing tourists and hunters; broken branches and scuffed bark with past storms.

'No sign of large animals, here,' he observed. The habit of talking to himself in wide spaces had come naturally.

A grassy mount teemed with ants, and he recalled the workers storing his wet lunch in the forest. Prudently, this time, he parted the green stalks: he was shocked by the skeletal remains of an enormous beast. He had stumbled across the crude burial mound of the she-bear and her three cubs. While examining her skull, a piece of lead fell from an eyesocket. Kneeling, he picked up the flattened bullet. Brow creasing, he recalled reading Harry's newspaper clippings concerning the mountain region: a man with a beard had boasted of the killing. He had stated that the she-bear had attacked him and his brother-in-law while they fished the Colorado; had said that he had shot the grizzly through the chest in self defence. No cubs were mentioned.

Some chest shot, he thought. And nowhere near the Colorado! The bastard conveniently forgot the over-kill, taking in the smaller bones. Venom surfaced. '*He killed her young. The heathen, bloody bastard, massacred the entire family.'*

He walked slowly back to the creek as the last splurge of orange engulfed the mountains. As his fry-up sizzled, he mulled over the morning route to the timberline on Devil Mountain. But, despite concentration, his mind kept returning to the pathetic mound of bones.

Now, like God and peace, Benjamin knew that even Man was beyond him.

CHAPTER 4

The grizzly sat on the timberline munching blueberries. His stained claws picked delicately from a torn branch at his feet. The he-bear's thick fur rippled like a wheat field on the mountain breeze; shone from a brassy sun.

For almost a week, he had plundered his territory for food. Starting with the trout rapids in the red box canyon, he had then caught a stray beaver pup before meandering up to the high forests. There he had dug for insects, roots and grubs. Sleeping, capering on the timbered hills, he had raced back down to the grassy meadows plentiful in berries, honey, nuts and more fish.

Comfortable from the days of the hunt, he belched contentedly; became frisky. He had seen another female roaming near the beaver dam. Rolling on the ground, he suddenly bounded the fifty yards between the pine and mountain; loped back again and vaulted into a tree. Vigorously scratching his chest, he then lunged back onto the ground and dashed in circles before lying on his back licking the rock face.

For a moment, he forgot the female; remembered the lion smell and her new mate on the morning mist. Recapturing his territory, he had killed the old male lion. But he felt no sorrow for her, for that was the way of things in their world: survive or succumb. He welcomed it. At least there was no man-noise. But even now, he sensed the lioness' vengeance: she would try, he knew; soon, with her new young mate.

Again, thinking of the she-bear, his body tingled with anticipation.

★ ★ ★ ★ ★

She was a large cat; two hundred pounds of raw muscle sprawled motionless along a low branch. Ebony black, the small headed lioness killed the grizzly with cold, hypnotic eyes.

Lost in the foliage above, her new mate contemplated the short charge across the timberline. Off windline, like her, he gauged the arch-enemy's deceptive but swift reflexes and powerful body.

With slow, co-ordinated movements, the lioness slunk head first down the tree. Lying flat, a slight tail twitch signalled him alongside.

Ears pinned back, both pairs of eyes locked onto their quarry. Above, the timber swished as the breeze subsided. Nostrils flared: ears and tails now rigid; haunches raised for the strike. Then madness in unison as they streaked through the sunlight towards their prey.

★ ★ ★ ★ ★

Benjamin had slept fitfully, frequently aroused by the nocturnal ramblings of the valley inhabitants. His blood had chilled at the thought of a snake sharing his warmth inside the sleeping bag. Wide-eyed half asleep, the pack straps again burning channels in his flesh, he dragged himself from the camp site and began the ascent to the timberline.

Like an untidy tortoise, he slogged up the lunarscape of rock in the half light. Cold, the previous day's exertions sent familiar aches tearing at every fibre of his body. Ruthlessly punishing himself, resting ten minutes to the hour, his brain forged upwards, dragging him on behind.

When the sun fired the treetops, he collapsed a thousand feet below the timberline.

Now, weakened by altitude, his breast heaved as he gulped for air. His heart thumped like a jackhammer; ears popped with decreased atmospheric pressure. Lathered with dust and sweat, he scanned the opposite slopes of waving timber; a vast canvas changing with the lights and shadows of dawn. Craning his neck, he gazed up at the monstrous wall of rock towering miles overhead. Smiling grimly, he imagined the mountain gripped in winter white; ravaged by storm and blizzard. It was indeed, a terrifying thought.

Drinking water sparingly, his mind suddenly centered on the cool liquid: or more precisely, the lack of it on a mountain. That posed a very real threat. In winter he could trap rain and melt snow: it was a long way down to the creek in summer. Heavy, sloppy water! Did Harry mention something about a lake up here? Damn ... Damn ... Damn...

Unnerved by the water question, attacked by flies and exhausted from the climb, he experienced a growing depression that robbed him of reality; changed each minor challenge into insurmoutable feats requiring Herculean strength. He became intolerant and moody, continually losing his temper: argued with himself about insignificant points of history. One minute, he was the pedantic purist questioning Danton's loyalty to the Directory; the next, he waged dialectic war against the Thatcherites in support of a return to a Cromwellian England.

Addressing the sweat-stained pack, he gasped: 'Your bloody weight doesn't help. I can see two or three days ahead – and they all go up! I'm not a mountain goat. Heck, my shoulders are in hell, my back's half way there and my legs are raising the white flag. *Oh shit, I feel sick!*'

Looking down into the valley, he began chuckling to himself. 'That's it; that's it exactly. I feel like Christ when Satan offered the kingdoms of the earth if he would jump off the mount. Is this my turning point? Maybe I haven't got the guts after all. The little things are crucifying me, when all I should be concentrating on is getting up to the timberline.'

His head dropped; hair rat-tailed in the rising wind. The sun toasted the mountain as he waged a desperately lonely battle within himself.

What would I have done, he thought, if I hadn't gone to the Paradise last Christmas Eve and seen that television rescue? Whatever, I wouldn't have been standing knackered, Christ knows how many thousand feet up in the air with a ninety pound rucksack for company! Institutionalised Man: do I really loathe him so much? Of course I do. But where's all last night's mountain philosophy gone, tell me that? Right now, I'm forty-one and out of steam. Who the hell do I think I am? Some Twentieth Century pioneer who's found something all America overlooked!

Loudly, he theorised with half constructed solutions while his temper matched the scorching sun. Eventually, remembering the worker ant, he built an intricate mental reservoir rich in literature with which he could assault the final approaches to the timberline.

Punching his arms through the shoulder straps, he half stood before falling onto his back. Squirming like an overturned crab, he laughed out loud, got up and resolutely continued his climb.

Within minutes, every muscle in his body screamed for release as the incline steepened. Reciting poetry, old headlines and short story extracts, anything with which to fight the maelstrom of pain and fatigue, he fought doggedly onward, higher and higher, until his mind pushed him through the pain barrier and among the pathway of rocks bending towards the timberline.

Falling to his knees, his tongue was a dried-up board: except to retch, he could hardly move. Yet Benjamin was in raptures. After several minutes, he recovered his breath and decided to deviate from his plan to climb the forest slope: instead, he weaved through the necklace of rocks.

He closed on the timberline as the lions' death roars demolished the stillness like some wild thing in pain. Frozen with terror, he stared as the twin menace flashed from the timber towards the he-bear lying against the rock face. The primitive, bestial sounds of the fight, sickened him. He cringed as the two cats hung from the he-bear's neck and chest. If I'd gone the forest route, I'd have walked into that! *The broken branches in the valley . . . The scuffed tree trunks . . .* And here he was in the flesh, the he-bear of Devil

Mountain: the one who doesn't like man; whose family remains I held in my hands. Christ, did I ever listen to Harry?

Inside the pack, Benjamin had one of his friend's stripped down rifles, but he knew his best weapon was luck combined with being off windline: if luck ran out and one of the raging beasts came across him, there was no time to assemble the rifle. He prayed as the frightful contest came to its brutal conclusion not fifty yards to his front.

After the lions had hit the grizzly in lightening succession, they had torn at his throat and chest with blind fury. Bear and cats now savaged; fangs flashed, claws scythed and blood spurted, all ripping and roaring on the hot earth.

Forced against the mountain, the he-bear clubbed viciously with his huge paws until the male lion finally crumpled, its skull smashed to a pulp. Saliva mixed with his blood, the grizzly turned his attentions to the female cat, now lashing frantically at his face.

With the grizzly's front legs wrapped tightly around the lioness' body, the combatants fell to the ground in a terrible death grip: cat tearing with the back legs; grizzly crushing unmercifully. There could only be one outcome, as, with hideous wheezing sounds escaping from gaping jaws, the lioness' strength ebbed; ribs cracked like egg shells; head blacked as her death throes began.

When it was finished, he pulverised her corpse; then that of her mate. Giving vent to his fury, flesh and bone were scattered across the timberline; blood coagulated on the blueberry juice at the spot where the he-bear had been attacked.

Licking his wounds, he moaned painfully to the forest; then, a full throated victory call consumed the timberline as he moved down to the creek to bathe his torn coat.

Stupefied, Benjamin emerged from the rock pile. Assembling the weapon, he left the pack and moved carefully towards the corpses, already alive with flies. Still disbelieving, the gruesome chunks of meat, fur and bloodied bone sent a shaft of sadness through his breast. At least they hunt without evil in their hearts, he thought. They kill to live, not like some of us, the other way round.

Constantly fearing the grizzly's return, he collected the pack and moved into the forest: dead and rotting meat would bring the scavengers. Shock and exhaustion threw him into a troubled whirlpool of sleep, until, like some thief, silence broke into Benjamin's troubled slumbers; stole him into a purpling dawn, a shadow before the sun soaked the timberline with day.

Knuckling his eyes, he yawned foggy breath; fingered the stubble on his face. Before breakfast, he ran on the spot to ease the previous day's exertions. The sleeping bag was left to air on a branch. He ate a little, his mind still heavy over the grizzly's annihilation of the lions. And the long night had been filled with the gruesome squabbling of wolves over the torn carcasses.

Scrubbing the tinplate with earth, he poured coffee and sauntered to the forest's edge. Enjoying the misty valley and the moment of living, all sense of danger vanished. Mind you, Ben, he mused, that Dickens will have to be watched.

During the night, he had christened the he-bear after the English novelist.

Finishing the coffee, he conditioned himself for work. Before constructing the cabin, it was vital he set up a crude, but effective alarm system around the camp site. A motley assortment of empty tin cans were soon strung along the timberline as he scouted for his cabin space.

He soon settled for the south east corner of the timberline with its views across the valley and down into the red box canyon: although outside the forest, and exposed to high winds, rain and blizzards, inside the trees, the cabin would be far colder and the light poor.

Taking out a diagram copied from one of Harry's old pioneering books, he studied the drawing closely before turning his attention to the thinner end pine, its growth stunted by rockier ground. 'Twelve by nine and eight high,' he muttered out loud. 'Should do the job. Fitted notches for tight end joints; half planked roof members split by driving a wedge at equal distances along the log. Hmm, won't be easy.' On completion, the nine hundred feet of six inch pine would have to be chinked with mud, moss and stripped bark; every hole and crack filled to defy winter's menace. A single door, two windows and a fire breast would be the final touches to his new home.

He estimated a fortnight's work, with one day in three for water collection and odd trips to the Indian trading post two miles east of the box canyon.

The sun glinted off the axe head as he went to work; the melodic tones of the timberline became bludgeoned by the clunk of metal on wood, the eerie rattling of the alarm system and Benjamin's imaginative language.

It was hot, gruellingly savage work: *swing, cut, pain; swing, cut, pain.* Blisters egged on his soft skin; bare chest became painted with sawdust and blood as he attacked the pine; swinging, cutting and hurting until he had toppled nine trees by late afternoon. Shaking from fatigue, bloodied hands cramped and useless, he forgot about food. Crawling into his sleeping bag, his snores rose with the sinking sun.

He awoke to a deep burning sensation; stiff limbs groaned when he began his daily limbering up process. Back to work. Gritting his teeth, he cursed loudly as, once more, his face and chest were lascerated by falling branches as he swung at the timber.

He was soon in agony as every bone jarred with each contact with the axe. Again: *swing, cut, pain; swing, cut, pain.*

When the first tree groaned away its life, the falling trunk nearly decapitated Benjamin. He jumped aside as a stout branch catapulted a hair's breadth above his head. The second, a soaring eighty footer, toppled with a resounding crack, only to crash onto the rocks, toboggan down the slope and lurch into the lower forest.

'That wasn't very clever, mister,' a young voice mocked from behind.

Benjamin spun, his shadow covering a blue eyed boy in rags. The youngster wore a greasy stetson and carried a pack, the flap of which bulged periodically.

'Aren't you a long way from home?' Benjamin said acidly, angry at the remark, but curious over the moving bulge.

Sam gaped at the man's bloodied chest. 'Home's where I am, no place else.' Sitting on a tree stump: 'Heard you calling out a few nights back. It *was* you, *wasn't* it?'

Benjamin licked his cracked lips, palmed sweat from his brow. 'Yes,' he replied irritably, 'I was on the mesa,' pointing across the valley. What the hell's he doing up here? he thought. No more than eleven; could be younger and small for his age. He's in bad shape and scared. Damn it, I suppose I'll have to make him a meal before sending him on his way. What the devil is moving in that pack?

'I'm Ben Thompson,' reluctantly extending a hand. 'Who are you?'

Sam fidgeted; looked around the timberline.

'Never mind, a name's not important up here ... but your handshake is. You've nothing to fear from me, boy.'

Slowly, Sam took the man's blistered hand. 'You're a Lim ... an Englishman, aren't you?'

Benjamin nodded, scrutinising the boy now shuffling awkwardly; brow creased as the bulge moved back and forth inside the pack.

Sam was confused by the man. Everything about him was different. He didn't fit up here in the mountains. He'd read about crazy Limies who wandered around the world doing odd things in even odder places. He didn't trust him. 'Your hand looks sore,' he said. 'Does it hurt?'

'Hungry?' Benjamin slamming the axe blade into a fallen tree. 'Don't feel bad about it, I missed breakfast. The hotel's over here,' striding off towards his own pack leaning against the pine. Talking over his shoulder: 'What have you got in there that keeps moving about?'

'Oh, that's Boogaloo. I guess he wants out.'

'Booga ... who? Now just a minute, young man,' frowning as the kitten jumped into the timber. 'You've no right travelling up here with a kitten. It needs its mother.'

'I'm all the family he needs,' said the boy defiantly. 'He saved me from a bear trap the other day. I met him in the Arapahoe Forest. No siree, Mr Ben Thompson, I ain't shacking up Boogie, no ways. He likes it up here. Are you ... ?'

'I'm not a hunter,' rapped Benjamin. 'I've seen some of their work already down in the valley.' Taking the gaunt face and holed, dusty boots, he grimaced. He's hiding from something or someone, he thought. Unsure if it was a trick of the sun, for a moment he saw his own young face staring up at him: the half starved face of another child, begging his bread from drunken Liverpool sailors. Christ, that's all I need! He looks the part. Why else would he be up here? 'Take what you need,' he said angrily. 'There's powdered milk for the cat. I'll make the fire.'

Sam felt decidedly uncomfortable with the man. It's plain as the nose on my face, I'm not welcome, he thought. Still, I'll eat his food and lit out.

Stuffing himself greedily, the boy shared his plate with Boogaloo; the kitten raiding Benjamin's food with indecent arrogance while the man studied the rock face.

'You don't plan climbing that, do you? Only a fool would try it. Heard tell a while back about a . . .'

'I'm not interested in your prattle, boy,' barked Benjamin. 'Just eat and go back where you came from . . . or are going to.'

'I was just making conversation,' Sam now wary of the man. He could be the physical type, he thought; the kind who beats up on kids. But he was astounded by the Englishman's reply.

'I'm sorry! I didn't mean to take it out on you, young man, but I've a lot on my mind just now . . . And I . . .'

'Didn't count on a boy and his cat gatecrashin' huh! Well, don't worry Mr Thompson, me and Boogie'll be on our way just as soon as we've eaten.'

Embarrassed, Benjamin poured more coffee. 'In answer to your question, Sam: yes, I will be climbing the mountain. But not yet. My first priority is water. There's plenty below in the creek, but it's a long haul. I'm hoping there's a mountain lake somewhere nearby. Maybe I'll take a break from cutting trees and have a look.'

'A guy once told me about a hunter who slept out in the spring when a mountain lake overflowed and drowned him in a gulley. He was washed down the mountain like a . . .'

'You've made your point . . . I'm still waiting for a name, boy?'

'Sam . . . Fynn,' came the hesitant reply.

'Wasn't so hard, was it! People may have heard about you down there, but I haven't up here.' Standing, he half-smiled: 'You'll be gone when I get back. I'll say goodbye. Go safely, now.'

Puzzled, Sam watched the man move clumsily over the timberline; Boogaloo had dozed off under the pack flap. Where before the Englishman had scared him, now he felt at ease, experienced a strange attraction for the figure in the distance. He's got to be mad, he thought. Climb Devil Mountain! 'But he doesn't ask questions, Boogie,' stroking the kitten. 'You stay here and finish off your nap, while I keep an eye on Ben. He ain't used to the mountains.'

'Hey,' he called, and dashed after Benjamin. 'Don't worry, I'll move on after we find your lake. You don't really mind, do you? A couple of hours'll do no harm.'

Benjamin scowled. What could he do, anyway? If he had judged Sam Fynn correctly, the entire British Army would fail to harness the boy. 'Very well,' he shrugged. 'But mind how you go. I'm not too good at fixing broken legs.'

Sam grinned. 'Listen who's talking,' he grinned, as Benjamin tripped over a fallen branch.

Juggling around, they clambered up a narrow shelf winding past a scar on the rock face. It was a bleak, chilly place. Strong gusts stung their faces, tugged at clothing; dust blew up their trouser legs. The shelf gradually looped back on itself, ran off at right angles, before climbing steeply across the scar and into a gaping cavern, the entrance to which, was strewn with flattened rock, weathered through aeons of ice and heat.

'I'll get the torch,' exclaimed Benjamin peering into the blackness. 'Stay here, Sam. There may be potholes inside.' Returning breathless, he snapped on the light and led the way inside.

Dank and cold, the cavern stank of decay as if some archaic denizen had been partially preserved in the labyrinth of rock.

'How far do you think it goes, Ben?' Sam's voice rebounding off the walls before dying in some forsaken cavity deep in the bowels of the mountain.

'Difficult to tell,' sliding the beam across the floor and ceiling; droplets of water twinkling in the fissures of rock. 'It's about fifteen feet wide and ten high. Could be anything! It gets more saturated the further we go.'

They struggled for balance on the slippery ground as it cut deep into the mountain. Odd shaped puddles materialised in the torchlight; walls dripped incessantly with a crude drumbeat of recurring plops as the temperature plummeted. After a series of bends, the floor levelled and they found themselves in a straight corridor. Smaller tunnels splayed off like monstrous tentacles, accompanied by more plopping and gurgling into the loneliest depths of their subterranean world. Here, the walls ran freely with water; hideous trickling sounds echoed towards infinity.

'There *has* to be a lake up there somewhere,' Benjamin's voice punctuated by excitement. His teeth chattered as he tried to calculate the distance from the entrance.

'It's p . . . possible there's one up there,' Sam rubbing his arms to restore the circulation.

'We'll turn back if it gets colder. No sense in freezing. But water has to be here somewhere,' his hopes dashed as they came to a dead end.

Eager to return to the warm fresh air of the timberline, Sam started back.

'Just a minute,' Benjamin's torch produced liquid diamonds rolling and falling from protruding knuckles in the wall: an oblong recess two feet from the floor, threw an inky grin into the pathway of the light.

Thrusting the torch into the void, Benjamin ordered Sam to remain while he squirmed along the narrow passage. After several yards, the recess angled off and the torch beam was killed by merging daylight silvering round a distant corner.

'Eureka,' he muttered. But his elation was cut short by sobbing sounds emitting from the main passage. Slithering backwards, he found the boy crying in the dark. 'What is it? Not afraid of the dark, are we!'

Sam's wet face cut him through the torchlight.

'They . . . they used to lock me under the stairs when I ran from the foster home. They beat me and left me in the dark all night. I . . . I'm sorry, but I can't get used to confined places – not on my own.'

Shit! thought Benjamin. What the heck have I got here? I'll be gentle until we get back: but then he goes, cat and all! 'It's only a few yards to the outside,' patting the boy's shoulder. 'Think you can make it?'

Sam nodded and they wormed through the tunnel, their eyes paining as the light blasted through the jagged opening.

Scuffling onto a ledge above the lake, they squinted at its placid surface darkened by a sheer mass of rock corkscrewing thousands of feet into the clouds.

'Holy . . .' Benjamin's breath stifled by the raw grandeur.

'That's real mountain high, Sam shading his eyes. 'Gets to you,

doesn't it!'

Benjamin blinked to relive the second of discovery. I wonder if anyone else has stood on this very spot? I feel insignificant; totally so. But in a lonely, beautiful kind of way.

He watched as Sam bounced stones across the water with deft flicks of his wrist. How do I tap this lot? joining the boy in the shallows.

A natural reservoir, the water was trapped by the rock strata; snow and rain stayed here after the violent seasons. An elasticated semi-circle, the lake had eaten into the mountain, letterboxing above the cavern ceiling. Sixty yards wide, black-grey boulders gaped through the clear depths from the lake bed. Grotesque sentinels of knarled rock grew from the banks like giant tree roots, twisting, pushing upwards in a race for the sky.

Benjamin scratched his chin. He could see no practical method in which to sluice the lake. 'Let's see where that goes,' wagging his head at the half submerged letterbox.

Using the rock face, they sploshed towards an outcrop resembling a dead man's teeth; ugly, slimed stumps gapped in a jawline screaming to the heavens. Passing in single file, they walked along a truncated gulley, the ground saucering until it stopped directly above the scar and the narrow shelf.

'Back where we started!' Sam craning over the edge.

But Benjamin was concentrating on a smooth pan of water filled from the letterbox and lipping into a shallow trough of stones. 'There's my tap – and filter, too,' he muttered. Summer had evaporated much of its contents, but nevertheless, he imagined the winter deluge: countless thousands of tons of precipitated rain, snow and ice hurtling through the letterbox, foaming along the trough and creaming down the scar onto the timberline.

'Nature's a powerful instrument, Sam,' scooping a handful of water. 'Ah, delicious! just think, it's taken millions of years to percolate through the rock and into the cavern; carve out all those other tunnels. All that energy and all I want is a tap flow.'

Sam became caught up in Benjamin's enthusiasm to trap water. 'How will you do it?'

By way of explanation, Benjamin calculated out loud lengths of pipe run, the head of water and estimated construction time. His pipeline of hollowed logs would be almost a hundred and eighty feet to the timberline. The head was a good sixty; three feet for every foot in drop. A ladder to the water pan would eliminate the cavern; caverns could flood. Cutting the timber was simple compared to the hollowing out process.

'If it floods in winter, I can't stop it with my finger like the Dutch boy. I'll just have to remove the first log by the pan and let nature take her course. There'll be plenty of water around by then anyway! I'll replace the log in summer and dam the lake here at the pan when the level subsides. It's just something I have to do for myself, Sam. I don't expect you to understand. It'll be tough, but the mountain will collapse before I give in.'

The boy pulled a face. The fool could have built his cabin down by the creek. Why in tarnation he wants to build it – and a pipeline – half way up a mountain for, I don't know! He's got to be loco.

Filling up two empty water bottles he'd brought, Benjamin led the way back through the discordant utterings of the cavern, his tuneless whistle keeping time with his falling shadow.

'How can you call a grizzly, *Dickens*!' Sam's face flickering in the firelight. He had promised Benjamin that he would be gone by first light the following morning.

'*Boogaloo* doesn't sound too clever, when you think about it,' Benjamin enjoying the smell of woodsmoke and the scarleting valley washed in sunset. He had resumed with the axe in the afternoon; sixteen trees now lay scattered in a wild entanglement of branches, trunks and belongings. The boy had assisted in trimming the timber; his cat had dribbled pine cones around the stumps.

'If I thought of the bear as a man-eater,' Benjamin yawning in mid-sentence, 'I'd be petrified. For the most part, they're inquisitive creatures – and I know you can't rely on them. Rather like us humans, don't you think! I'll respect him if he respects me. Anyway, it's his home. By giving him a name, it helps me: rather like a picture book helps children with their learning. I'll watch him; he'll watch me. We'll get along. It's called coexistence.'

Sam shook his head slowly. The Englishman sure had the darndest ideas about things out here in the big country. He wouldn't make the fall, let alone winter.

Benjamin stared at the cat snuggling into the boy's side. 'When they catch you – and they will – he'll have to go. Animals are nice people. Don't hurt him; let him go. Hand him in at the lodge you spoke about earlier.'

Sam looked longingly into the glowing fire. Why couldn't life always be like this? Why has it got to be running away and getting beaten; never knowing from one day to the next where I'll be? 'You really care about all this rock and stuff, don't you!' changing the subject. 'You're not like the adults I've met: they're too busy doing other things when you need them. But you ... you just bumble along as if nothing ever got to you.'

Benjamin smiled thinly and threw more logs onto the fire. 'It gets to me, Sam. I guess I've become adept at hiding the upsets and the calamities of my life.' He stopped as a wolf howled in the forest. 'I'll tell you my story, if you'll tell me your's. We'll never meet again, so we've nothing to hide.'

They talked far into the night below a tapestry of stars, while the wind moaned among the crevices, scampered across the plateaus like an invisible demon seeking peace.

Slipping into his sleeping bag, Sam recalled the Englishman's final words: *'Find yourself another mountain, boy. This one's been claimed.'*

Benjamin failed to notice a small rat nibbling at food scraps as he drifted into an uneasy doze.

Only Boogaloo saw Dickens' giant form silhouetted against the Milky Way, as the grizzly stopped to watch the sleepers before ghosting back into the mountain.

When Benjamin awoke, the boy and his cat were gone.

CHAPTER 5

The beginning of August heralded Benjamin's fourth week on Devil Mountain. Cautiously optimistic, he went about his chores with fastidious deliberation; became fitter and more at ease with life on the timberline. But while the continued absence of Dickens had alleviated his problems somewhat, Sam Fynn's category of mysterious arrivals and departures angered him: the boy flatly refused to leave.

For all kinds of reasons, he wanted Sam off the timberline, not the least of which was the solitude to plan his future. Of all things, he had not counted on a runaway child arriving on his mountain. Temper fraying, he had finally lost patience and told the youngster that he would take him to the Indian trading post on completion of the cabin to await the arrival of the authorities.

Today was that day.

Benjamin's face creased with strain as he hauled the final log into position. His wiry frame, now dark from sun and wind, shook with fatigue; wood shavings fell from shoulder length hair and straggly beard.

Scowling at the kitten cleaning itself on the ridge: 'You're no ratter, that's for sure,' he muttered, recalling his discovery of the torn food packs. He turned his attention to Sam who was carrying rocks for the chimney breast. Like it or not, the bugger goes today! he thought. And his useless cat!

'Almost time,' he shouted. 'Round up the moggy and get ready. You're not doing another Houdini on me! I called the authorities from Indian John's trading post. I'm a guest in your country: if immigration found out about you, I'd be shipped out with a don't-come-back note.'

Downhearted, Sam toyed with a button; Boogaloo raced off the roof and dribbled a pine cone at the boy's feet.

Talking to the top of Sam's stetson: 'Like it or not, young man, you belong to Denver Welfare. A Miss Sally Brown wants to see you. If you're worried about the money you took, I, er, I told my friend Harry in Cascade to tell the priest that you've still got his hundred dollars. What you've done around here on and off comes to about that. It er, might stand for you.'

Sam's eyes were moist. 'I like it up here, Ben. So's Boogie! You'd be putting us both in prison. I . . .'

Benjamin grabbed his shirtfront. 'You've got to talk to people, you little shit!' his voice raspy. 'Tell the priest how you feel, really feel about things. Especially about that room you're afraid of. My guess is that you've twisted everything, blown it out of proportion by your silence.' Grinning slightly: 'And there's a bit of the rebel about you, Sam Fynn.'

Sam's face became alive with the old fear. 'They'll lock me up again,' he blurted. 'You're just like them: you don't understand. I thought I could trust you: you said we were partners!'

Benjamin hid his feelings. It had been difficult not to grow fond of the boy and his cat. 'Look,' he said softly, 'thousands of kids have to face up to your problem, and they shape up to it. Have you ever stopped to think how the masters or the other kids worry about you each time you break loose? Do you really care about them staring at your empty bed night after night? Don't kid yourself, they don't regard you as a hero for running away! I ran once, and I'm not proud of it. But the circumstances were different.'

Sam shrank from Benjamin's glare.

'Look at me, damn it! You were intended to live and your

70

mother die. That's all a part of life. It stinks, but that's the way it is, and we have no say in the matter. You can't go around condemning everyone for something they didn't do.' His voice hardened as the boy thrust out his chin in defiance. 'Get that chip off your shoulder, Sam, and learn to live among decent people or get off my mountain and go back to the hobos where you belong!'

Hating himself, Benjamin walked to the rock face. I had to say it, he thought. Anyway, what the hell, he's none of my concern: just another kid bursting for freedom. Mind you, I should have got rid of him the day he arrived. He turned at the footfalls behind.

'Can I name your cabin, Ben?' The boy handed him a cold beer. 'There's still a few left in the water pan from the last trip to Indian John's. I'll go down after I name it.'

'You didn't bring a rat up here from the trading post, did you; I've seen its droppings.'

'A rat! Up here!'

Benjamin recalled the night after supper, agreeing to let Sam christen his home. 'Everything as well as everyone, should belong, Ben,' he had said. 'Sure,' he replied. What have you decided on?'

'Virginia, after your virgin queen, Elizabeth the First. We nicknamed the state, the Mother of Presidents.'

'Eight of them, I believe,' Benjamin opening the beer. Lord Cornwallis surrendered the British Jack at Yorktown and your Civil War ended at Appomattox. Yes, I'd say Virginia's a grand name, Sam.'

They walked back to the cabin, Boogaloo ceased playing football with the pine cone and scampered back onto the roof. Man and boy clambered up after the kitten before Benjamin announced: 'Virginia, you said. Virginia,' they chorused. The cat moved out of range as the roof was sprayed with beer.

'By the holy Mother of God, what have we here!' a deep voice rang out.

Man and boy shielded their eyes as a fiery-headed giant stepped from the forest into the strong sunlight.

Paddy Martin stared up in bewilderment. 'I knew things were different in America, now, but wasting good beer beats the lot,' he grinned. 'Paddy Martin's the name. I heard from the Indian trading post that someone was up here. Thought I'd take a look.'

Benjamin climbed down and offered his hand. 'Thompson. Ben

Thompson. I er... we've just about finished building it,' feeling silly caught christening a cabin by a stranger half way up a mountain.

The Irishman merely shrugged his great shoulders. 'English by the sound of it,' his voice turned flinty; eyes suddenly showed mistrust.

Benjamin recognised the big man's enmity; met his eye. 'I have no fight with your country,' he said. The '98 Rebellion's where it should be: in the history books.'

Gauging his man, Paddy threw his pack against the cabin. Smiling, he said: 'There are those of us who see it differently. And as Ireland was ours in the first place, it's an uprising to us. Your boy?' indicating Sam.

'No. Like you, he's passing through.'

'You're a Scouser, Thompson. I've fond memories of your city. The boy?'

'Around here,' replied Benjamin. 'He's just about to go home. A beer before you leave, Martin?'

Paddy nodded and Sam moved off to the water pan, Boogaloo close behind.

The Irishman lit a cheroot. 'You had words. I waited.'

Benjamin smiled thinly. 'He makes a habit of running from the orphanage. His heart's in the right place, just a little out of practice. He's going back today.'

'Nice country,' Paddy sweeping his hand over the valley. 'Must be a few thousand feet up here!'

'Six,' Benjamin eyeing the shillelagh. 'Where are you headed? he asked coldly.

'I'm just wandering, Thompson. Biding my time and wandering.' Catching Benjamin's icy tone and quick glance at Mona: 'An old friend.'

Sam returned from the water pan and Benjamin waved him to hurry.

'You won't make it before last light if you take him down now,' Paddy stripping to the waist. Hot walk up here!'

Angry he had let time slip by, Benjamin's face darkened. First the boy and now the Irishman, he thought. He sipped his beer moodily.

'What's your line, Thompson?' Paddy opening his can and

watching the boy's face. Now there's a true rebel for you, Paddy, me boy! Pity he's a Yank. A bit highbrow, Thompson, but he hasn't got the mark of other Englishmen.

'Journalist,' Benjamin replied. 'I use the pen, Martin. What do you use?'

'Anything.' Tilting his can: 'To your cabin.'

Benjamin drank uneasily. The man wreaked of violence. Still, I'll be shot of the boy tomorrow, he reflected. Hopefully this one won't overstay his welcome.

'By the by: my cooking's passable,' exclaimed the Irishman. 'And I can hunt,' pointing a thumb at a gleaming rifle barrel protruding from his backpack.

Benjamin half smiled and finished his beer.

Paddy Martin loved potatoes: any way, including raw. He was preparing a monstrous concoction of his 'beloved spuds' for the evening meal in two pans. He had shot a small deer and jerked the carcass in Indian fashion to preserve the meat. Chopping vegetables for the stew, he said: 'Not as good as my dear old Ma's, God rest her soul, but it'll do. By the way, something's been at my spuds!'

'A rat,' Benjamin engrossed in a book of poetry.

Paddy rolled his eyes. The campfire daubed his massive hulk across the timberline and onto the rock face. His wild looks resembled an ageless Hibernian warrior as he watched his stew bubble and spit.

Afraid of the Irishman, Sam sat close to Benjamin. Conversation was stilted: the boy was leaving; the Irishman was intruding.

Paddy began singing into his beard, his deep bass sad as it painted a nation's struggle:

> *'At the siege of Ross did my father fall,*
> *And at Gorey my loving brothers all,*
> *I alone am left of my name and race,*
> *I will go to Wexford and take their place . . .'*

'What's that sad song?' Sam dipping a finger into the stew.

'The Croppy Boy! Oh, it's just a silly Irishman's dream, me

73

bucko.' Looking at the boy, but his comments aimed at Benjamin, he continued: 'We weren't enough like you Yanks to throw off John Bull's yoke. Ireland is to Britain as Cuba is to your country – too close for comfort, depending on your colours.'

'Why doesn't Britain leave Ireland alone?' Sam licking his finger.

Benjamin looked over the top of his book. Oh God, here we go, he thought. The Fenians and the foe. I've heard it how many thousand times. What new twist will Martin give it?

Paddy dished up. Relaxed by the grandeur of the Rockies, he spoke about his home as he had never done before, tranquilised by the vortex of a Coloradan sunset. 'Historians, politicians, they all say it's a religious thing. The Catholic Church has been the scapegoat for successive English land barons over the centuries to further their lot. We were quite happy fighting each other before the English festered my homeland.' Looking at the boy: 'Simply put, Sam: Mr Thompson's England needs the utilisation of our northern docks in the Six Counties, and is jealous should an alien country try to use the Six Counties as a springboard onto the British mainland. But more than that, much, much more, we Irishmen need our land and the freedom it gives our soul. That's what they've taken from us and the reason why John Bull can never understand why we hurt the way we do.'

'Six Counties?' Sam poking the fire.

Paddy shovelled a mouthful of stew before replying. 'Your English friend calls them Northern Ireland – the name you read in the newspapers. The truth is that England partitioned us pretty much like you threw the redskins into the reservations. We have thirty-two counties like your fifty states. Apart from sheer English bigotry and arrogance, the present situation is much a domestic security situation should we make the wrong friends.'

'Like Wolfe Tone and his United Irishmen's marriage of convenience with Napoleon,' fenced Benjamin, referring to the Irish Rebellion of 1798.

Paddy checked his temper. 'Bad easterlies prevented the French landings at Bantry Bay two years before. We lost, waiting for that French idiot General Hoche to elude your blockade of Brest. The wind came up and that was that. Otherwise, you had your pants down, what with the troubles with France and the neverending policing of your so-called dominions around the globe. Tone was correct: it was England's greatest escape since the Spanish Armada.'

Sam fed Boogaloo some meat as the two men stared at one another across the fire.

Well versed in the 'Irish Problem' in his native Liverpool, Benjamin was aware of the dismal modern-day political ramifications pervading the unfortunate isle long since the fourth century BC when the Celts had arrived from Gaul to subdue the inhabitants and establish a Gaelic civilisation. 'Ireland's tragedy,' he said, closing his book, 'are the combined sins of parricide and fratricide and mothers lose all. Tone couldn't have had in mind the blowing up of innocent children. The present generation seem to be turning that dream you were singing about into a nightmare – for everyone.'

Paddy loaded more stew onto his plate. 'There are those who would disagree strongly for far less,' he hissed. 'In a sense, you are right: only a madman enjoys killing. Especially his own countrymen. You English can't understand; Irish blood does not flow in your veins. That's our great national tragedy: our hot Irish blood, handed down from the great clan chieftains. Both sides have much to be sorry for, but a soldier cannot afford the luxury of idealism like journalists frequently indulge themselves. He can, however, regain another inch of his own soil.'

The fire crackled as Sam piled on more logs; the three silhouettes on the timberline ate in reflective silence.

Benjamin poured the coffees and studied the Irishman. He speaks from the heart, he thought. But a violent one, nevertheless. What would I be in his place: writer or fighter?

Paddy's face danced in the firelight like a man-devil from hell. Belching loudly, he washed his plate and lit a cheroot.

'Turn in, Sam,' said Benjamin. 'Early start in the morning.'

Paddy nodded to the boy as he moved reluctantly inside the cabin. Quite unexpectedly, he said: 'Do you believe in the existence of God? Most writers don't normally, do they?'

'Some do; others search. It's like the Holy Grail to them. No one has ever proved he exists. The Bible is little more than exceptionally bad sensational journalism. I accept that something happened in the beginning, otherwise we wouldn't be here.

Probably the Big Bang theory comes closest to it all. God, Allah or whoever, confuses me: they allowed us all to fall into our present impasse – if they exist. Basically, I think all gods are the end product of Man's own invention; a necessary formula invented by a handful of plutocrats to control the masses of the planet. If He exists, God, like peace, is beyond man.'

Benjamin refilled the coffee mugs. 'Being a republican you'll be a papist no doubt. It's pure faith born out of Rome. Your brand of faith keeps the flock subservient while paying the Vatican's running costs. The papacy has turned Christ into a Midas. Its fight against birth control, for instance, is not based solely on spiritual issues, but to increase the Sunday plate to support its vast conglomerates. I can't believe in a so-called piety that condemns millions to a life of ignorance and poverty on one man's say-so. The higher the income bracket, the lower the birthrate. Contraception is a rich man's luxury bought by his gold: it both appeases his conscience over the lapse of religious dogma and keeps the clerics in the best brandy. I know one man personally who paid his priest in Scotch as a price for using condoms. I ask you: who has found this Christ-god – rich man or poor man?'

Paddy swirled his coffee. 'There's a substance of truth in what you say. I suppose I'd have to put you down as an atheist, although I dare say you do believe in something sometimes, even if it be a beetle or a slug. But forget the type of religion: isn't God part of the reason you're here? I mean, what middle-aged man – an intelligent one at that – ups and plants himself half-way up a mountain. If I'm intruding, tell me so.'

Benjamin shook his head. 'I've nothing to hide. I had a marriage break-up; lost my job. I decided to try my luck out here. I'm on the mountain because I . . . I have to find myself. And I don't think any of your religions or gods will help me. But if I happen to stumble on Him, come to terms, I'll accept Him. There's no blood on my conscience. Pardon me, but from the way you talk, for someone who advocates power through the barrel of a gun, you make a strange bedfellow with your god.'

Paddy looked up at the mountain silhouetted against the sky. 'That'd be a turn-up for the book: a writer finding God on Devil Mountain!' His manner became grave as he walked around the fire to stand above Benjamin. 'Conscience, Thompson, is like the soul:

76

it knows right from wrong. If a man can't recognise his worldly struggle – and I have made mistakes – there's little hope of acquittal when the time comes. I enjoyed the fire talk. Good night.'

Alone, Benjamin let his mind fall into the stars. He wondered why the Christian god didn't spend his rest time improving the humility men should live by. If he could manufacture the universe . . .

Turned in some distance from the cabin, Paddy Martin also gazed up at the stars: but his mind was a captive to things other than Christianity; the setting for his thoughts was a small church on the outskirts of Tralee on Ireland's west coast. He remembered as if it were yesterday as he stood in the November rain listening to the congregation singing through the open door . . .

'You'll be goin' yourself!' gasped a latecomer, saturated to the skin. 'Bloody weather! Don't be shy 'cause you're a stranger,' continued the man. 'Just get in out of this rain.

Paddy smiled and followed the man into the tiny porch that led to the nave of the church. But his smile didn't match his mood. He hadn't wanted to be seen close up. Not for what he had to do. Dipping his fingers into the water font, he crossed himself, genuflected and moved into the aisle.

He had memorised the informer's face from the photograph provided by the local IRA commander. 'He'll be six pews down on the left, four parishioners in,' the man had said. 'A space will be left directly behind the target. Our men will be all around to make sure you get the right one. You'll only get a side profile as you enter the pew from behind. You might be lucky if he turns at your late arrival. The rest is up to you.'

His heavy boots clumped on the timber boards, but the singing drowned his arrival. Gripping the sawn-off shotgun beneath the raincoat, he counted the pews; stopped at the sixth, knelt again, crossed himself and moved into the empty space. The victim didn't turn round as Paddy took out the shotgun, pointed it at his head and pulled the trigger. Before anyone could move, he was back out in the rain and running for his hire car parked in a nearby lane . . .

After a tense period of safe houses in Dublin and London, he had been flown out to New York where he stayed with Noraid members. Finally, it was decided that he should lose himself in the Rockies until the call came to return to Ireland. The hearse driver's job had been a mistake; so too the brawl in Cripple Creek and the confrontation with McAvoy.

I won't forget that son-of-a-bitch, he thought as a shooting star raced overhead. Aye, and I won't forget you either, Devil Mountain, with your curious Englishman and runaway orphan. For some unaccountable reason, he remembered seeing an eagle shortly before meeting the Englishman and the boy. And he'd heard talk of a killer grizzly at the Indian trading post. 'Humph, there's all kinds up here, Paddy!' he muttered. Smiling, he drifted into sleep.

Dawn came fast, accompanying a fusillade of rifle shots from the forest. The two men rushed from their sleeping bags; the boy sat up with horror as several bullets thumped into the cabin walls.

'It's me they want,' barked Paddy, quickly explaining the bar fight in Buffalo Creek. I almost bumped into the bearded bastard the day before yesterday. I thought he hadn't seen me. There's three of them. I'm sorry, they must've tracked me up here. Look after the boy, I'll sort it out in my own way.'

'You can't go out there; they'll kill you!' Benjamin rapidly unpacking Harry's hunting rifle. 'You'd know more about this than I,' handing the weapon to Paddy.

But the Irishman ignored him and walked out onto the mist-covered timberline. The firing stopped and he was surrounded by the hunters.

'What's happening?' Sam staring through the open doorway. 'Who are they?'

'Stay where you are,' ordered Benjamin. 'It's none of our concern.'

Just then, The Beard's voice echoed across the timberline. 'Whoever you are, mister, we ain't got no fight with you. Stay put. Our fight's with the Mick.'

A gentle wind rolled down the mountain, blowing mist around Paddy and the three hunters.

78

'They'll kill him!' said Sam, clutching the cat. 'What are you going to do?'

'I got the impression you didn't like him,' replied Benjamin, staring through the window opening. 'Anyway, I think Mr Martin is well able to take care of himself. He refused the rifle.' Shit, he thought, I chose the wrong mountain! Orphans, IRA hard men and now hunters.

'You can't leave him on his own, Ben,' Sam cried. 'He's done us no harm! He could've fought here and put us in danger, but he didn't.'

'Now listen you . . .' he stopped as The Beard clubbed Paddy to the ground with his rifle. He felt sick as Eb, the bald headed card player, kicked the Irishman in the groin. The third man, Jake, remained still, his rifle limp in his hands.

Something snapped inside Benjamin's mind and he rushed out onto the timberline. Ignoring The Beard's warning, he marched up to the hunters and demanded they leave the mountain.

Paddy laughed cruelly. 'Get the hell out of here, you idiot! They wouldn't think twice about killing you too. Get back to the kid.'

'What kid?' spat The Beard.

'The one in the cabin,' Benjamin edging closer to the lead hunter.

'That's far enough, Limey,' Eb coming up on aim.

'So you're the crazy they're talkin' about back at Indian John's tradin' post. Freaked out by mountains, huh!' Glancing at his comrades: 'I wonder if he's for real,' sending Benjamin to the ground with a vicious kick to the stomach.

'Just a no-good Limey asshole,' guffawed the bald man, prodding his rifle barrel into Benjamin's neck.

'Put a few feathers on that skull of yours,' said Benjamin, 'and you'd double for the national emblem.'

This time, the rifle barrel struck his cheek, the sights tearing skin to the bone.

'I warned you, Thompson,' hissed Paddy. Scowling at The Beard: 'Leave him alone. He doesn't fight your way.'

'Oh, and what way is that! He gonna kiss us to death,' laughed The Beard, turning as he caught a movement on the roof. It was Boogaloo.

'It's the kid's,' growled Paddy. 'For Christ's sake!'

'OK,' rapped The Beard, 'that's enough wet nursin'. Into the forest, Irish.'

Jake had moved across to Benjamin, still sprawled on the ground. 'Look pal, do as your friend says. This guy's ruthless. He'd kill the kid if he had to.'

'You're not like them! Why?'

'Skip it. Just get inside.'

'Hey,' called Eb. 'I wanna pot that cat on the roof.' The rifle bucked in his shoulder as the report filled the timberline. Boogaloo disappeared from the roof. 'Got the critter,' he chuckled.

'You killed Boogie!' cried Sam as he raced from the cabin. Charging at the hunter, his fists were bunched to hit.

'Push off,' Eb back-handing the boy. 'Ain't you got no home to go to.'

Paddy was too late as Benjamin lunged at the man, kicking and punching him to the ground. Despite Eb's howls, his attacker bit and scratched, pummelled and head-butted until he was half unconscious and bleeding badly around the face.

The Beard discharged a shot into the air. 'On your feet, Limey. You asked for it! Eb, get your ass up, boy. Jake, keep the Mick covered. If he moves, plug 'im. This snotty-nosed Englishman needs a lesson in manners from real mountain men.'

Paddy went cold as the two men mercilessly beat Benjamin to a pulp.

Sam, grabbed his arm. 'Help him,' he sobbed. 'He tried to help you, and now he's being beaten for Boogie.'

'Get back inside,' roared Paddy. 'GET BACK.' As the boy retreated, he grabbed Jake's rifle and advanced on Benjamin's attackers. Laying the bald hunter out with a terrible crack to the man's temple, he rounded on The Beard, cocking the weapon and coming on aim.

'N . . . no,' gasped Benjamin, the words hardly audible through bloodied lips.

'On your knees, asshole. Now!'

Dropping his own weapon, The Beard did as he was told; gagged as the Irishman rammed his rifle barrel into his mouth, breaking several teeth and cutting his tongue.

'Now pray, you bastard,' Paddy's trigger finger tightening slightly.

Fear shone in The Beard's eyes as death loomed in the Irishman's eyes.

Benjamin dragged himself alongside the Irishman; tugged at his trouser leg and shook his head. 'No,' he said weakly. 'Not on my mountain. Not even you came here for that.'

Paddy cursed as Benjamin struggled to his feet, blinked as something moved behind a rock outcrop along the timberline. 'Up,' he hissed to The Beard. 'Collect your scum and get the hell out of here before I change my mind.'

Benjamin turned on The Beard as Sam ran back towards them, pointing at the mountain. Ignoring him, Benjamin choked: 'So it's true: all the good ones died at the Alamo,' his cinnamon eyes pitiless. Now rounding on Eb as the man came round: 'Kill a boy's cat, would you...' all further action froze as a terrifying roar echoed from the mountain as Dickens galloped towards them.

The Beard, who had heeded Sam's warning, picked up Eb's rifle and turned to fire, but was rugby tackled by Benjamin; the rifle cracked harmlessly into the air.

'You'll die doin' that one day,' snarled the hunter as he sprinted after Jake into the forest.

Throwing The Beard's rifle into the pine, Benjamin walked slowly into the centre of the timberline, quite unable to resist the delicious moment of insanity to face the charging wildness now storming towards him.

Paddy groaned something under his breath, grabbed Sam and raced for the cabin. Going straight to his pack, he pulled out his rifle. 'I should have done this before,' he muttered angrily. 'But they wouldn't have killed anyone; just a beating.'

'What?' said Sam.

'Shut up!'

Dickens had groaned loudly as the cold creek bit into his torn flesh after his fight with the lions. Afterwards, he had roamed the valleys, searching for the new female whose scent he had found near the beaver dam before the fight.

81

Resting on the mesa, he had prowled irritably in the high timber looking for her. Returning to the mountain, he had smelt a man-smell, other than the hunters', sleeping with his cub and a rat-like creature on the timberline.

From a plateau, he had watched the man rise with the mountain fog, jerk himself up and down before emitting strange battle noises while hitting the trees; then crawl into the forest to sleep. And he never mated with his large, red haired mate! He was odd.

Dickens was confused, for the man never hunted like the others; instead, took his food from a headless, scentless animal he sometimes carried on his back. And he would walk alone in the moon's path while his cub and the rat-like creature slept on the belly of the headless animal.

He was very odd, indeed.

But today, things had been different. The hunters had brought their man-noise to the timberline. He had seen the hairy-faced killer of his family attack the odd one and his red haired mate; destroy the rat-like creature. Confusion had exploded into white anger: he attacked.

★　★　★　★　★

Sam was hysterical; Paddy beat the wall in frustration, yelling out to Benjamin, but the man maintained his ground in front of the advancing grizzly. Closing his eyes as the beast bore down on the Englishman, he recited a short prayer before looking up in disbelief: *'He's talking to the bloody thing!* I see it, but it can't be true. He's alive and having a bloody conversation with the bear!'

Sam joined him at the open doorway. 'He's letting it sniff his face! It'll bite his head off! Can't you shoot it?'

Paddy chuckled: 'If I shot that animal, me bucko, I think Mr Thompson would shoot me. I'm just beginning to appreciate that man.'

Dickens' roar reverberated off the rock face as he loped back up the mountain; vanished in a mist halo beneath his plateau.

'OK mountain man,' Paddy growled, 'that's enough heroics for one day. You alright?'

'Yes, I think so. I don't know why I did that. Quite strange, really. Something queer came over me.'

'Let me know when you feel another attack coming on,' said Paddy, 'and I'll make myself scarce.'

'I'm sorry about Boogaloo, Sam,' as the boy came to greet him.

'Let's get you inside and sort out your face: what a mess!' Paddy examining Benjamin's cracked nose and badly cut and swollen face. He was concerned about the broken ribs.

Bathing the wounds with salt, he tore one of Benjamin's shirts into strips and bandaged his ribs. 'Don't want your lungs to get punctured, do we!'

Benjamin could hardly breathe. He nodded his thanks.

'I suggest you get someone to improve your boxing style before round two comes along.'

'You think they'll be back?' wheezed Benjamin.

'No doubt of it. If not here, somewhere else. You have got to go down sometime. Talking of that, I guess I'd better get packed. Want me to drop the youngster off at Indian John's place?'

'Would you mind. You don't have to go so soon. I mean ... Well, come on back here whenever you like. Shake on it?'

Paddy smiled and took Benjamin's hand. 'Yeah, why not. Hey, that bloody rat's been at my spuds again!'

Just then, Sam burst in the door, Boogaloo in his arms. 'I found him in the rocks,' he said gleefully. 'They missed him.'

The two men looked at one another in dismay: The animal would not be allowed in the home.

The sun hottened on Sam's back as he crouched behind a rock. The thought of polished dormitories, men's echoes along green corridors had induced panic. Once more, he ran. But this time, he had wanted to stay. Clutching Boogaloo, he moved from the timberline and scrambled down the rocky dish: panting; sobbing; running downwards. Running away ... Away ... Away...

Slipping, he lurched sideways and tumbled into a hollow and cannoned off a lightning stump. Dazed, he heard heavy breathing nearby. He fainted as Dickens popped his giant head above a fallen tree where he had been sleeping off a large marmot.

Boogaloo jumped onto Sam's chest and spat at the grizzly; back arched, tail fluffed.

Dickens yawned and rolled over to continue his sleep. The odd one had saved him from the man-noise: his cub should live. He wasn't so sure about the rat-like creature. Yet close up, it wasn't a rat! A shadow crossed his face and he looked up as the female eagle glided overhead. One day he would take her from the sky.

CHAPTER 6

Winter struck ruthlessly as Colorado was plunged into chaos. Unfriendly skies, ravaged by black hammer-head nimbus, shot steel sheeted rain at the earth: pummelled mountains and valleys; swelled rivers and creeks. The temperature plummeted alarmingly as gale force winds screeched across the lowlands and tall country. When the snow blizzards arrived, the Centennial State was frozen into a rigid ice tomb of swirling white.

Devil Mountain stood in the centre of this natural bedlam.

Benjamin had been snowed in for three weeks. Using Indian John's trading post as a relay station, he kept in close touch with the rangers, assuring them of his safety, despite their urges to leave the timberline. Utilising the time to write some poetry and pursue the blurred outline of a novel, he made regular entries in his diary, a record kept since his first night on the mesa three months ago.

Having just made another entry, he stopped to take stock of his position. Only a small scar above one eye remained from the hunters' brutal attack. His ribs still ached, but were almost mended thanks to Paddy's crude, but effective nursing. He had not heard from the boy since that day; the Irishman himself had continued his wanderings a week later.

Sifting his thoughts, he stared at the neat rows of boxes filling half the cabin space: reading material, food; essentials and heavy clothing for the mammoth freeze-up. His savings had dwindled drastically.

The fire crackled while wind lamented in the chimney. Content with his isolation, he rummaged for a can of beans. Opening it, he heated the food on a metal plate over the flames. Thank God the Irishman was around to help carry this lot up, he thought, recalling the tortuous trips from Indian John's up to the timberline. But a more strenuous month had been spent constructing the now defunct, ice-laden pipeline.

Their friendship was cemented through hard labour by day, and long nights spent talking, tolerating and learning; two men on a mountain.

Having left before the rains, Paddy had not visited since the first fall of snow.

Benjamin thought of the unsettled Goliath, roaming from town to town with Mona. He had his cause, too. I have literature. The shillelagh is symbolical of love, so too, in his way, the Irish cause. My writing isn't really symbolical of anything that close. Who's the winner?

Grinning at himself, he gazed through the window slats at the sugar coated valley. Yikes, it's morning! I must have worked all night on that chapter. *Bloody hell!*

His thoughts turned to the boy. Why did he do it: run away again? I thought I had talked him out of it. It's nearly a month! I hope he's keeping warm. But he is a rebel, and in a strange way, I miss him and his runt of a cat.

Finishing the beans, he opened the door. The day smacked his face; blew away the mental cobwebs. He stared as the mist appeared to move the rocks around like fog bound ships; hoar-frosted trees sparkled from a watery sun as they swept down to the valley.

'Not a bad back garden,' he chuckled. Completing his daily exercise routine, he returned to his diary. Rearranging the jumble of words in his head, he wrote:

Colorado winter is severe. It leaves nothing

> untouched. I study the animals: It is I who suffers. The
> boy and his cat are still missing and Paddy continues
> running from himself. His visits are less frequent . . . In
> truth, are they any different from me, or I from them?
> That question is one of my great imponderables.

His breath tumbled across the cabin in long grey clouds as he heated another can of beans. Eating and thinking, he gazed into the fire until Paddy came back into focus. Essentially, the man is a mystery, he thought. Comes and goes like the wind. In and out of my life like an unlaid ghost afraid of Judgement Day. That would fit, despite what he said about acquittal when the time came. Lord knows what he does? Why he goes to the towns is beyond me. It's as though some persecution complex drives him to atone for some past guilt. He's a secret one, too.

Sighing, he went back to the diary:

> Dickens has grown hostile of late. Maybe he expects
> too much from his new mate. He didn't get enough
> food for winter . . . or still pines for his old mate. I must
> reply to Rosemary. Harry, too. The Millers have been
> a blessing. I'm dreading the trip to Indian John's post
> box . . .

A week before the first snow, Harry had forwarded Rosemary's letter to the trading post. Benjamin's ex-wife had been distressed about his new venture, adding: *'I have a boy-friend, Bengy, but nothing serious. Life goes on and I pray that you, too, will find more attractive friendships than the cohabitants of that horrid place . . . Really, Bengy, a mountain of all things. In the American wilderness!*

His eyes laughed, deepening the crow's feet. 'Just as well I didn't mention Dickens,' imagining the panic. Harry had written sternly on the subject of the bear.

The Millers had seen the priest and told him about Sam. *'If her returns,'* wrote Harry, *'Hogtie him until they can get someone up to you. The weather's closing in, so it could take some time. Even choppers find it difficult to operate in that turbulence.'* He had added a PS: *'That blonde, Sally Brown, asked a lot of questions after she met you at "Virginia" after Fynn disappeared. Strikes me, she's keen.'*

Benjamin pictured the woman as she arrived flushed and breathless from the climb several days after his fight with the hunters. He, of course, had looked far from his best, but they had gotten on well enough in a professional capacity. He had noticed the bare wedding finger.

She had explained more or less what Benjamin had found out for himself: That 'Sam had a chip on his shoulder the size of Pikes Peak. Underneath lives a beautiful, but lonely person. But, we have to be practical. I had to meet you myself. The priest is too old to climb mountains. The boy seems to look up to you. I'll keep calling the Indian trading post – just in case. It must be difficult managing up here...'

Benjamin found himself smiling. You've only been up here a few months, he scolded himself. Yet his thoughts were not entirely sexual. He hoped she had left a message with Indian John.

Glancing outside, he watched the valley being whited out by heavy sleet.

His nose dribbled. Going back to the diary, he expressed his foremost fear – guns:

> Anything is possible in this big country. If this cabin
> were destroyed by a storm or avalanche – God forbid –
> I would be forced to make one of two choices: leave, or
> stay... Steel myself to kill to live. It is another of my
> great imponderables: Guns...

Snapping the diary shut, he made coffee. Admiring the view, he jumped at a sharp crack as an icicle fell from the roof into the snowdrift, now almost at window height. That was another imponderable: rising snow. He could be frozen in. Donning a parka, he put on a broad rimmed hat, tied a scarf over the top to cover his ears and went outside to shovel away the mound.

In seconds, his face and beard were rimed with ice crystals. Finally, his work complete, he decided to inspect the pipeline. Crunching across the timberline, he began sweeping the snow build-up from the hollowed logs. Fortunately, the ice present was insufficient to topple the line. Humming, he examined the supports, working his way towards the ladder at the foot of the water pan.

A rising wind threw sleet into his face as the temperature dropped alarmingly. Cold ate through the heavy clothing as he worked faster. Soon, he was numb and breathless.

The blizzard came in seconds, mummifying mountain and

forest. The wind thundered deafeningly, blasting off rock and whooshing through the trees. The wind-chill factor plummeted the temperature to minus twenty Fahrenheit. Visibility was nil.

Benjamin fought blindly in the direction of the cabin, twice bumping into the rock face. Hammered by the powerful thrusts of the wind, his body became emaciated with extreme cold.

After ten arduous minutes he found the cabin door and forced it open. Thawing out in front of the fire, he felt the ice devil slip away as his heart pumped furiously, making him feel dizzy. He made more coffee.

The blizzard raged for two days and nights, blowing itself out on the third morning. Roof-high drifts had continually doused the fire, making Benjamin's life a misery. Digging himself out, he looked forlornly at the sky, opaque and pregnant with more white sickness: a dispassionate yardstick.

Looking down into the valley, the dawn stirred him: a formless white desert, blued beneath a sliver of an unseen moon. The creek gouged the snow like spooned ice cream while the mesa grinned white coated icicles. All trace of madness gone, the wind now fluttered and the cold was almost bearable. But the sky...

Stomping to the half-submerged pipeline, he cheerfully busied himself, once more clearing the line back to the water pan. If the weather holds out for a few days, he thought, I'll try and find a way to Indian John's.

He was thinking of Sally Brown. Missing a murmur on the ice plateau, he began singing and throwing snowballs at a protruding nib of rock on the scar beneath the water pan where snow and ice formed a caricature of a one eyed walrus. Engrossed in his new-found sport, the cushioned rumble high overhead went unheard.

The explosion stopped his heartbeat.

Awestruck, he stared at the mushrooming cloud of snow powder five hundred feet above, racing down the mountain. Mesmerised, he gasped as a growing rumble erupted into a rolling boom and a mammoth tonnage of black rock shot through the cloud: bouncing and gathering momentum, it blitzed over the rock face to hurtle like a meteorite across the timberline.

Benjamin's heart sank as Virginia was demolished. Tears froze on his face as he ploughed back to the remains of his cabin. Cruelly, the snow cloud scattered on the breeze: only muted echoes in the valley told of the catastrophe.

'You accursed whore-devil,' he screamed, wringing his hands at the towering rock face. 'Damn you too, Christ, you pitiless bastard,' as the chimney collapsed into the drifts. 'Oh Virginia!' he cried, falling to his knees and pounding the snow.

Like some angry demon, the wind rushed howling over Devil Mountain as the sky fell. The rising blizzard gripped Benjamin in a deadly paralysis as it leant a timeless quality to the wrecked cabin and drowned the timberline in a sea of white lunacy.

Death beckoned with every wind gust, each freezing snowflake as Benjamin tore frantically among the debris for his sleeping bag. Disentangling it from the mangled bed he pushed himself deep into the snow, insulating himself against the raging blizzard. Inside the drift, rubbing himself for the heat, he lay like a foetus in the growing womb of snow. In the blackness, he found himself praying to the god he never accepted, clinging to life beyond endurance.

Shortly before the blizzard strangled itself in the late afternoon, Benjamin met the rat: the large brown rodent crawled into the sleeping bag to share his body heat.

Fear-sweat turned to ice rime on his face after rapidly bludgeoning himself back into the freezing atmosphere. He belaboured the bag until the rat waddled off in the direction of the forest.

Cold enveloped like a death shroud as he exercised rigorously for blessed warmth: it was too late to shelter at Indian John's. Like the daylight, the trails had vanished; the valley and box canyon impassable. Partially flooded, the cavern beneath the lake presented a fiendish trap in return for protection from the blizzards: the horrors of drowning or disappearing down a pothole into the sub-arctic underworld.

Salvaging what few stores and clothing that he could, Benjamin stashed everything in the forest, using the timber as a natural wind-break. After constructing half shelter, half grave – again employing snow as a thermal insulation medium – he ferreted around the demolished cabin for his pack. Pulling on three more sweaters, he bit into a slab of chocolate: recoiling from the shock to his teeth. Preparing for the night, he slipped and snapped off part of his beard.

Cowering like a wild animal, he let his brain fantasise to bolster his ailing spirit; hyper-active, it also explored the lurid realms of depression.

He endured the night.

Morning spilled over the timberline with ghostly, spindly shadows and he smiled grimly: shadows meant sun and a pauper's bowl of warmth.

Rejuvenated by his night's sleep, systematically he sifted through the debris. Salvaging the winter clothing, most of the food, however, was crushed into the ground. Miraculously, his two oil lamps remained intact, and the coffee had survived.

Completely cut off, there was a week's frugal eating. After that . . .

Benjamin began thinking about the unpacked rifle . . . *steel myself to kill to live* . . . Hell, I wrote this disaster into my life . . . *if this cabin were destroyed by storm or avalanche* . . . Bloody hell!

Gloomily, he assessed the structural damage to Virginia. Eight more trees were required to replace side and end logs; most of the roof members were gone. Rapid weather changes, along with the chronic food supplies, demanded a speedy rebuilding programme before his strength collapsed. He considered starvation next to a fire tolerable when confronted with the bitter alternative. All in all, he just had to get on as best he could.

Almost despairing, he began to rebuild Virginia.

The days grew insufferably colder as the weather worsened by the hour. Devil Mountain became a freezing prison fortress: Benjamin could not leave and nobody could enter.

Constant hunger hampered the work: a thin slice of bread, some beans and one of Paddy's seeding potatoes, a meagre daily reward. Sleep, like the coffee, was plentiful. His body felt like sheet ice; stamina ebbed and his working day shortened. After three weeks of intense struggle, he was on the verge of breakdown. At times, he would whimper like a child, at others, rage like a madman; he hallucinated and argued irrationally with himself.

Some days, he became obsessed with insanity, unable to free himself from the condition that fed off his acute dilemma. During

91

an excessively violent snowstorm, he convinced himself that he was insane and that the blizzard was entering its third day. In fact, it had lasted just two hours: mentally, he really arrived at the edge of insanity.

Benjamin's life was draining: he needed more food, more warmth. And more than both, a miracle.

Finally, the food ran out, pitching him into a headlong battle of dour survival. Sheer physical weakness prevented him from hunting in the nearby forest. As before with his obsession for insanity, he now experienced a powerful craving for food that surpassed all other hardships. If he couldn't catch food he would eat the only source available: himself. Revolted by cannibalism, despite his longing, a deep nausea pitted his stomach and a profound sadness engulfed him as he considered the least operative and required part of his body. Something small, so that if the miracle occurred, it wouldn't be missed. He chose the little finger of his left hand.

The decision made, Benjamin froze the limb until it turned purple. Taking his knife, he closed his eyes as the blade cut through the skin, grating sickeningly on the small bone. Fighting back the bile, he broke the finger in order to sever it from his hand. Then he sat idiotically contemplating his act: he felt like a murderer.

Eventually summoning the courage, he bit into the finger, but fainted and slipped into delirium.

Two days later during a blustery, snow-blown morning, he groped lethargically for a fallen nail with which to refix part of his shelter-grave. Instead, he found a wedge of bread and a hunk of cheese.

Hope was suddenly rekindled as he gnawed the frozen food, and with it the beginnings of an idea. Before, like the now discarded finger, it would have disgusted him. Now, however, it seemed the most natural thing in the world to do.

Clearing a pathway to the timberline, he scooped three holes in the snow, each eighteen inches deep and twelve in diameter. Across each hole, he balanced three thin sticks forming a Y, at the junction of which, a portion of cheese was delicately placed. Crumbing a trail of bread from the shelter to the holes, he scattered morsels around the three traps.

When he had finished, he smiled to himself. 'Now, Mr Rat,' he cackled, 'get your arse out here and do what you always do – eat. Then I'll eat you! Get my own food back. Stand on the sticks and fall into a hole you fat little bugger, and that will be that. *Voila!* Dinner a la rat.'

Benjamin's broken beard and burning eyes gave him a heinous appearance as he licked his chapped lips in anticipation. In high spirits, he crouched behind a thick pine to await the crafty rodent. But as the hours dragged with no sign of the rat, he slipped gloomily into a frozen half-sleep. Awoken by a fall of snow from a low branch, he continued his vigil. Constantly wiping the snow mask from his face, he willed the rodent to take the bait.

On the point of capitulating, he disbelieved his eyes as the rat eventually trundled into view and began eating the trail of bread crumbs. Sitting up, his watery, bloodshot eyes executed their victim.

'Come, sweet rat, come,' he breathed, panicking as the rat waddled back towards the trees. *'No, no, please go back!'* he agonised. Slowly, it scratched around before continuing to nibble its way across the timberline. Standing close to the three holes, the rat seemed to be deciding about which piece of cheese to tackle first.

'Yes, yes, that's right!' whispered Benjamin. 'It doesn't matter which. Just go on, please, *Please . . .*'

Angry, the female was a big bald eagle; twelve pounds with a wingspan of nearly seven feet. She was irritable with her mate for being overdue with the catch as the young were acting up. But wasn't he always late nowadays, wandering the skies and performing his fancy feats for the young female in the red box canyon. Carried away, he sometimes returned empty handed. In their eight summers together, often they had flapped wings over his galavanting! One day, she would sort him out – *and her from the red box canyon.*

As she beaked the two month old eaglets, they ruffled their new dark brown feathers with impatience; heads and mouths, a contortion of movement. Her sharp eyes scanned the approaches to the valley far below the eerie, traced the he-bear's snow mountain, ice silvered forests and creek. The breeze told her he would be very late: the thermals confirmed it.

As she expected, he dropped from the sky above the box canyon: a solitary speck jaunting, impressing the young female on the hill. Angrily, she turned away. There would be more flapping of wings before nightfall. But not now.

With an ostentatious manoeuvre high overhead, he hovered before rocketing through six hundred feet and levelled off with an affected splay of wings. Floating lazily onto a nearby branch, he gave a haughty flick of his talons and a fish shot into the eerie. Leaving her to feed the young, he turned his tail feathers and viewed the day. Feeding bored him.

Snatching up the fish, she fed the eaglets. Afterwards, still annoyed, she beat her wings and shot above the murk into the blue void; calmed herself on smooth passages of wind. This was her world: space and air; freedom of the skies. Let him wait. For a change.

Seeing her younger rival performing graceful sweeps far below through the cloud hillocks, she dipped one wing and dived into the eggshell fog. Banking sharply, she arrowed across the other bird's path and continued her journey above the snow clouds. Exhilarated by sun kisses and the cooler air stroking her belly, she allowed herself to be carried along in mile-long arcs; gliding, rising, falling. Aimless, joyful, slicing through pristine, vacuous space.

Reluctantly, thoughts turned to the hungry brood. Streamlining her body, she dived like quicksliver; over a hundred miles an hour closing on the lower world rigid with winter. Planing between the snow-misted horns of Devil Mountain, she raked the glaciers and crevices, scoured the awesome rock for signs of prey: normally fish, today's anger had brought on change.

Cruising through a flurry of sleet, she saw the he-bear dragging a deer onto the ice-plateau; noted the man sitting in the pine watching something. But no prey. Dropping to a hundred feet, she flew over the tree-tops; sped through the valley and the red box canyon enjoying the updraughts on her wingtips. Still nothing! Only the beaver family working at their dam. Gaining altitude again, she skimmed towards the mesa facing the he-bear's mountain. Resting, she surveyed the valley as the weather deteriorated.

The kill must come soon.

Taking off, she rode into the growing storm. A lightning upsurge altered her glidepath and she dropped altitude slightly to correct her stability. Slipping effortlessly onto a thermal, she found herself floating over the timberline.

She saw the rat; now knew what the man was watching.

Streaking to five hundred feet, she hovered, studying man and rat. The he-bear was still on the ice-plateau. She sped invisibly higher until her back touched the ice crystals before they were snow. Two thousand feet above her victim, she swooped. Arrowing her body, she scythed downwards as wind blasted her face: mist, snow, then air as the timberline rushed towards her. Faster ... Faster ... her talons dropped for the kill.

Frustrated, weeping from cold and oblivious of his feathered rival, Benjamin silently urged the rat onwards.

With a final sniff of the air, the rat chose the centre trap. Gingerly, it balanced precariously on the thin sticks.

'Got you,' whispered Benjamin. 'Fall, you bastard, fall!' He could smell the meaty fragrance, taste the succulent flesh falling from the bone. *'My God, come on ... come on...'*

The rodent inched to the point of no return at the junction of the Y and looked upwards. Sensing danger too late, it squeaked loudly as swift death struck from above.

Too late, Benjamin saw the female eagle. *'No, no, no,'* his voice a throaty warble. *'Get away from my rat.'* Stumbling towards the traps, he dived in desperation as the rat was snatched in the great bird's talons and whisked triumphantly back to the eerie.

Benjamin was devastated. 'Christ, you bastard,' he wept. 'You want me to die. WHYYYYYY!...'

Picking up the three pieces of cheese, he stumbled back to the shelter. Sitting with a vacant look in his eye, he nibbled the bait and mumbled incoherently to the rock face.

95

As it had promised, the weather closed rapidly, battering Devil Mountain with a ferocity that threatened to tear the colossus from the ground and fling it to the heavens.

Dawn brought the Irishman. Five days later, Virginia was rebuilt.

CHAPTER 7

For three weeks, Benjamin had fought for his life against pneumonia. The severe exposure had left his body weak and emaciated. Now, his fight for health over, he awaited Paddy's instruction in self defence, an aspect of his education thought lacking by the big Irishman. The finger still depressed and shamed him.

Apart from seeing to Benjamin's needs and rebuilding Virginia, Paddy had restored the damaged pipeline in between force-feeding his patient with regular servings of stew, vegetable soup and canned fruit. The man himself seemed immune to mountain weather. While on his wanderings, he camped in the boles of trees, between rocks or deep inside the forests away from the killer wind. A few days in each town, he would move to the next, drinking and looking and dreaming of going home. Nowadays, Mona remained inside his pack.

The snow had subsided to sporadic, gentle dustings. With no sign of blizzard, the wind still continued its onslaught, freezing the temperature in the minus thirties.

'September in England is usually warm,' Benjamin warming up for a boxing lesson. 'About the only month you can really rely on for good weather.'

'Forget that. Concentrate,' growled Paddy. 'You're standing like a pansy. Move on your toes, not like a pregnant duck. That's better! Now keep your guard up like I showed you, and probe with the other fist. That's right . . . No, no, no, you're flat footed again. Jaysus! Watch me.'

Benjamin rolled his eyes. Boxing: two hours every morning and one at night: sprints through the drifts, press-ups in deep snow. Grateful for sleep, he would rise to tortured muscles – but his style improved and his reflexes sharpened. However, he hated sparring with the Irish giant.

After the work-out, the two men cleared a track to the rocky dish near the water pan and stared at the perfect saucer of snow winding downwards past the forest. 'How you manage getting up that so easily, I'll never know,' Benjamin remarked. 'And still smoke that rubbish.'

'Brute strength and spuds,' came the reply. 'The tricky bit's knowing where the drifts are. No sense in falling into an ice-cream bath. I watch the wind. Pays your money, takes your chance.'

Benjamin returned the grin, his ears pricking up as something crunched snow in the forest. Paddy unslung his rifle. 'Your's isn't the only bear around here,' he muttered.

Suddenly, the new female grizzly from the box canyon rolled out of the timber into the dish some thirty yards away. Wallowing in the white mud, she smelt the two men and charged.

Paddy raised his weapon as Dickens joined his mate. But Benjamin pulled the Irishman backwards. 'That's his woman. We can make the cabin.'

Cursing, Paddy bounded after Benjamin towards Virginia as the grizzlies took up the chase. Paddy slammed the door as Dickens and his mate bashed themselves against the wall. The two men peered anxiously through the window slats as the beasts growled and thumped the cabin before moving off to continue their courting.

'You want certifying!' Paddy making the weapon safe. 'You want to kill yourself, that's fine, but leave me out.' Vehemently, he castigated Benjamin for his attitude towards the bears, now pounding up the ice plateau.

Arguing, the two men then sat quietly by the fire: Paddy smoked and drank; Benjamin read. Later that evening when tempers had subsided, they discussed the possibilities of Benjamin visiting Indian John's the next day. 'You're hung up on this woman, aren't you,' exclaimed Paddy angrily, pouring himself another stiff shot of bourbon. 'Been up here too long, so don't tell me you're concerned for the kid. You told me you don't even want him around.'

'I've only seen her once,' retorted Benjamin. 'What has it to do with you, anyway! You don't care either way. I promised I'd get in touch. Sure, I don't need Sam around, but I'm concerned. He's only a child.'

'Supposing the weather changes or you fall and break your stupid neck! I thought you had brains for breakfast . . . not fingers. At best, it'll take you half a day to get there and another back. For what! A three minute phone call. What if the lines are down? That'd be shit for luck.'

'I gave my word. I'm going! Since when has a little thing like the weather stopped you! Why should it stop me? I'm fine, now.'

'*He gave his word,*' grunted Paddy, waving an arm. 'Oh deary me. Your honour will kill you one day, mark my words.' Shaking his head, he passed the bottle.

They drank in angry silence. Eventually, Paddy said he would be moving on. 'Let me teach you to shoot before I go. Next time, the cabin mightn't be so convenient from Yogi and his missus.'

Though the dawn was once more windy and the cold excruciating, the sky held no promise of snow. Shouldering a small pack of emergency supplies, Benjamin slung Harry's rifle and moved outside.

'Go well', said Paddy, the familiar cheroot dangling from his lips.

Benjamin grimaced as the fireside sweat iced on his body. Adjusting his snow shoes he began the long trek down to the Indian trading post. The wind rose, throwing flurries of ground snow into his face.

Waist deep, he pushed himself down the dish, resting opposite the mesa two hours later. By late morning he arrived at the creek, walking over the frozen water to avoid the heavy snowdrifts hillocking the valley like a gigantic house of covered furniture. Pressing on through the box canyon to where the creek joined the

Colorado, he passed into the lower country: by early afternoon he strode into the stifling heat of the trading post.

Crammed with sporting gear and camping equipment, the place smelt of pipe tobacco, cooking smells and beer: it was the off-season. Muffled voices drifted from a back room; somewhere, a child was being smacked.

Indian John materialised from behind a stack of blankets. His leathery face cracked into a broad grin as he bared pink gums and a solitary yellow tooth in the centre of his mouth. His small eyes gave the impression of being privy to many secrets.

'How are you, John,' Benjamin shaking the old Arapahoe's hand. 'Youngest acting up again?' There was bawling behind a closed door.

'Grandchildren too much trouble, Bengymen,' he exclaimed. 'How's the mountain?'

'I think it gets bigger every day – or maybe I'm growing old.'

'Ah, bones break, rocks fall, what's the difference! The secret's in the heart. The Irishman told me about the cabin. Bad luck. He came for medicine when you were sick. Said you made friends with the Devil Mountain bear.'

The old Indian noticed the missing finger, but said nothing.

Benjamin frowned, picturing Paddy risking his life in the blizzard while he had slept. He hadn't said a word. 'Are there any messages, John? Sally Brown, the boy?'

'I don't know,' the Indian sensing his anticipation. 'I've been visiting my sick brother in Glenwood Springs. The children tell me nothing. Let me ask my granddaughter.' He opened the door and the crying stopped.

Benjamin moved irritably around the store. Until now, he had not been aware of the woman's presence in his mind.

Indian John returned, a letter in his gnarled hand. 'Came a week ago. I think it's the woman's handwriting, Bengymen. It's not like your friend's from Cascade.' Seeing the man's eagerness, he smiled softly to himself.

Eagerly, Benjamin tore open the envelope. The paper smelt of woman; feminine, exciting. His eyes raced across the single page, devouring every word and punctuation. Searching for the words that said she was coming, he read things that weren't there.

Dear Mr Thompson, or may I call you Benjamin,

100

*As yet there is no sign of Sam. I am deeply
concerned for his health and safety. It is a bad
winter. He has not been seen since he left you. I
hope he has had the sense to leave the mountains
. . . He's only a child and I look to you for his
safety should he return to Devil Mountain. As
soon as the weather permits, the police will
organise a search party with the game rangers.
But there's a limit to what they can do. Soon, it
will be impossible.*

*How are you keeping up there? I've read the
papers. The television and radio met. reports
aren't good. How do you do it? Really, you
shouldn't be up there, you know. If you don't
think it too forward, I would like to come out and
see you at Indian John's. The roads aren't too bad
if you take it easy. If you could let me know, I'd be
happy.*

Give my regards to Mr Martin (Paddy).
God bless you,
Sally Brown.

Mixed feelings burned inside Benjamin's breast: a growing
fondness for the woman; concern for the boy. She had given home
and office numbers . . . *If you could let me know, I'd be happy* . . . If
the lines were operating and she was at the office! The lines were,
and she was. In seconds he was describing the trip down to the
trading post; listening to her somewhat nervous, but concise
description of winter life in Denver. Yet all the time, just one
question seared in Benjamin's brain: when could she come? When
she told him she would drive out the following morning, his heart
found wings. They spoke for half an hour.

When he replaced the receiver, Indian John grinned: 'You
speak longer than daughters, Bengymen! I suppose you'll be
wanting to stay the night? You'll find all you need in there,'
pointing to a door behind the counter. 'It's a storeroom, but it's
warm. I'll tell the granddaughter we're one more for supper.'

Elated over the news, sleep eluded Benjamin.

Sally Brown slushed the automatic to a halt in front of the trading post. She smiled as Benjamin came out to meet her. They went inside, chatting nervously.

Indian John took them into the living room where he left the couple alone.

Sat before a blazing fire, they talked about Sam. But before long, spoke about their own lives with the infectious enthusiasm of children. He lied about the finger. Time flew cruelly, and, with the afternoon's fading light, they said silent and embarrassed farewells before Benjamin saw Sally to her car.

'Maybe,' she said softly, 'you can come to Denver and visit me.'

'I would like that very much.'

'So would I.'

The automatic pulled away. In seconds, it was gone.

Indian John stood in the doorway, his eyes smiling another secret.

Immediately, Benjamin found himself missing her. Maybe Paddy's right, he thought. I have been up there too long.

'You'll be all right in the storeroom again,' said Indian John. 'There'll be no snow tomorrow.'

Benjamin nodded and followed him back inside the trading post.

By mid-morning the box canyon sparkled beneath a streaky sun. The wind was stiff, but not harsh. Like spume-flecked wavelets, snow powder blew in silent confusion across the canyon floor.

Benjamin tramped the crusty layers of old snow on top of the iced creek. Enjoying the crunch and crackle under his boots, he felt like a teenager after his first date. He felt posivitely bubbly. So different from Rosemary. So ... different.

He was startled by two eagles as they shot overhead at tree height. He watched in amazement as they fought a running battle before streaking high above the canyon until the loser plummeted into the drifts. Following the female as she glided triumphantly back to the eerie and another flapping of wings: 'That was the bastard,' he hissed, 'who stole the rat!' Finding the dead mistress, he tied her to his pack. The carcass would be used for bait.

Passing through the valley, he stood in the lee of a snow mound and ate a sandwich; drank whiskied coffee. God, it's peaceful, he thought. Sometimes I wonder if I'll ever leave. If only we could exist here, I'd bring Sally . . . but that wouldn't work. Just then, he saw a white-tailed deer outlined by the dam near the mesa. Kneeling, he unslung the rifle, centering the scope hairs on the animal's head.

One day, I'll have to do it, he thought, marvelling at the magnified baby eyes and large pointed ears seven hundred yards away. He knew its winter-shed antlers would begin growing again in May. Deciding to stalk the animal and see how close he could get before alarming it, he moved upwind. At two hundred yards, the deer remained motionless, staring at the northern end of the valley.

At a hundred and fifty, Benjamin lay on a snow hump, studying the facing semi-colon tracks of the animal's dewclaws. Suddenly, his stomach lurched and he was thrown sideways as Dickens surfaced from beneath the snow. Fear-struck, he realised that he had been lying right on top of the grizzly's hibernation den. In disbelief, he stared up at the back of Dickens' head pointed in the direction of the deer.

Benjamin remained rooted to the spot as the grizzly charged across the valley after its unlucky prey. He had been saved by the animal's interest in the deer. He watched as the prey zigzagged in a pathetic bid to escape; heart stopped as it changed direction and headed straight towards him, Dickens snorting close behind.

Benjamin panicked. Standing up, he aimed the rifle and snatched at the trigger. Nothing! Bear and deer galloped closer. He remembered the safety catch. Fumbling, he knocked it to 'fire', but this time squeezed the trigger. Still nothing! In his anxiety he had forgotten to cock the weapon. Now it was too late.

Seeing him, the deer dashed off to the right, Dickens closing quickly. Intent on the kill, the grizzly had still not seen Benjamin.

Benjamin didn't wait. Standing no chance of climbing the mountain, he decided to run for the trees ringing the dam a hundred and fifty yards away. Sprinting for all his worth, he occasionally glanced over his shoulder. After covering half the distance, he groaned as again the deer changed flight.

This time, Dickens saw him. Believing that the odd one from the timberline had now come for him with his noise of death, he bounded after the figure running into the trees.

Benjamin arrived exhausted at the trees. Dizzy and sucking in air, he slung the rifle and dived hastily at a pine branch. Almost slipping with the thick gloves, he scrambled upwards as the tree swayed sickeningly over the ice covered dam.

Dickens hit the tree at the gallop, grunting, roaring and tearing through the branches in pursuit of his victim.

Benjamin cringed as Dickens' fangs came closer; his claws slashing the air inches from his head. Frantically, he tried to free the rifle, instead screamed out loud as, this time, Dickens gouged his face to the bone. Still unable to unsling the rifle in his cramped position, he pulled the trigger with the weapon on his back. Deafening him, the report frightened the grizzly into retreat, but not before clubbing Benjamin off-balance to send him crashing through the branches towards the icy surface of the dam.

His body pierced the thinner crust closer to the bank; the rifle skating in circles towards the centre of the dam.

Sensing victory, Dickens launched into space, his enormous bulk fountaining water and ice splinters into the air.

The powerful shock of the sub-zero water almost paralysed Benjamin. The heavy clothing and pack swiftly took him to the bottom. Removing the emergency supply pack, he struck out for the surface, only to crack his head on the ice crust. In terror, he searched for the hole in the ice, bubbles exploding from his mouth as his lungs neared bursting point. Blacking out, his limp form eddied against the jagged edge made by Dickens, now swimming off to the right in search of his prey.

Regaining consciousness, Benjamin vomited as he tried to claw his way onto the surface of the ice. The torn skin now flapped on his face; all pain mercifully frozen by the water. He emitted a hoarse scream as something touched his leg: Dickens! He relaxed as the pack surfaced, thrown up by entrapped oxygen. Lifting it onto the ice, he pulled out the hunting knife and made a hole in the crust. Using the hilt as a lever, he slowly eased himself out of the water. Almost there, the knife slipped and he fell back into the dam.

Crying with rage and cold, his numbed body no longer a part of him, Benjamin repeated the operation until he collapsed on the ice. The torn flesh spiked grotesquely through his beard; his clothes felt like concrete. But a growl galvanised him once more as Dickens' roar thundered across the dam.

Convulsing with icy spasms as the wind slashed through this clothing, he made the bank and stumbled off into the drifts, leaving the rifle far out on the ice. Moving off windline, he hid behind a snowhill and prayed. And then the pain burst from his mauled face as his body temperature rose.

Ten minutes later, Dickens gave up the hunt and bounded back to the den.

Now Benjamin fought a far deadlier enemy: exposure. Retrieving the rifle, he exercised to regain his circulation. And all the time the fire inside his face gripped him in a cocoon of pain. Taking out the Thermos, the whiskied coffee put fresh life into his innards, even though he shook violently from intense cold.

Keeping a wary eye out for Dickens, he slowly climbed back to the timberline. Now, he thought, I could easily kill the damned beast.

Making a fire, he drank whisky to dull the pain from his wound; resettled the torn skin as best he could. He knew it would leave a terrible scar from the eyebrow to his chin. Drunk, he passed out in front of the fire.

A week later, the blizzards returned. So did Sam Fynn. 'Ben,' he exclaimed, 'your hair is completely white! *Your face...*'

Sam had come to in the forest after Dickens had scared him following his fall. Boogaloo had licked his face, but there was no sign of the grizzly. Having checked that Benjamin and the Irishman had lost him, he hiked to the hunting lodge. Arriving in the early hours of the morning, he slept in the back of a delivery truck with a Denver registration. Hiding beneath a tarpaulin, he checked his position as the truck bumped through Brighton some twenty odd miles from the Coloradan capital. Reaching the city limits, he saw circus posters along the streets: his luck was in.

He found bit work, muckshifting and walking around with a sandwich board dressed as a clown for ten dollars a day and meals.

Lying that he was a local, he slept with the horses at night. The circus stayed for three weeks. When it moved to Loveland, so did Sam. This time he told them that his parents were in the process of moving to Loveland, and begged to stay. Boogaloo was confined to the make-up artist's caravan. The woman, who doubled as a fortune teller, adored cats and insisted the kitten become part of her act. In return for her patronage, Sam brought her trade.

When the circus closed until Christmas, Sam bid his friend an affectionate goodbye. Pushing a fifty dollar bill into his hand, she said: 'This ain't no life for a kid! Whoever it was before, give 'em a second chance.'

Three hundred dollars richer, he bought second-hand winter clothing and a new pack. Unsure if he would return to Devil Mountain, he once more took to the road, Boogaloo asleep inside the pack. Without really understanding why, knowing the welcome would be colder than December, he found himself hurrying to beat the blizzard forecast throughout the state. Like the weather, the reception had been icy.

The blizzard lasted four days and nights.

Benjamin continually updated the diary; forged on with his novel, often working through the night. It was a tragic love affair between two intelligence operatives working for opposite sides. Both were men. Driven to homosexuality through loyalty to their respective services, loneliness and sickness of their clandestine world, a mutual, almost apathetic regard changed to genuine feeling in Russian controlled East Germany.

He found it extremely difficult and painful getting inside his main characters: while their relationship repulsed him as a man, it excited him as a writer. Part fact, the story was loosely based on a retired SIS agent he had met while on assignment in Berlin. The man had become mentally disturbed after executing his lover at the Wall: he had been a double agent. The SIS operative had eventually thrown himself from the London Post Office Tower.

Comprehending their conflicting passions for country, their

desperate need for understanding moved him greatly: to Benjamin, their homosexuality made it a double tragedy. And that was where he continually fought with himself: what right did he have to judge their sexual preference? It wasn't something to be ashamed of or looked down upon, rather a fact of life. They couldn't help being what they were any more than he could help being what he was. Or could they? Imponderables, once more, whys and wherefores!

Still angry with Sam – although he was glad the boy had come to no harm – he kept him busy tending the fire, keeping Virginia spruce and making endless cups of coffee.

When the blizzard blew itself out over the valley, man and boy attacked the drifts around the cabin; remade the path across the timberline to the water pan, a fruitless chore Benjamin insisted be maintained as both symbolic and part of discipline. While the boy walked with Boogaloo in his rest periods, Benjamin practiced his shooting; stripped and assembled the rifle until he mastered it blindfold. He shadow-boxed morning and night.

But if Benjamin failed to register the radical change in many of his ways, Sam noticed with a child's perception. The long white hair and scarred face complemented the man's growing resentment of human contact in a macabre sort of way; the missing finger confirming some temporary imbalance. Sam had heard Benjamin talking in his sleep, recounting his ordeal in the snow and attempt to cannibalise himself. The man was becoming like the mountain itself: unreachable. The isolation was driving him insane. Yet Sam had heard him mutter to himself tenderly of a woman, but never mentioned her name. He noticed too that Benjamin grew increasingly moody in all manner of ways, especially where Dickens was concerned. He now believed that the grizzly was not fit to live on his mountain. Sam wondered if it all had anything to do with the writing or was he really flipping out?

'I've told you a thousand times,' snapped Benjamin one morning. 'I don't want your bloody cat sitting on my papers. If I catch it again, you'll end up wearing it for a hat.' Throwing on the parka, he picked up hat and rifle and banged the door.

He cursed to himself as he stamped along the path. His flare-ups were increasing and becoming more difficult to control. While despising himself for not harnessing the outbursts, he was delighted for the release that they brought. Christ, here's me writing about male lovers and I'm sitting on a mountain with a strange young boy! That'd make good copy for a scandal rag!

Looking down into the valley, he saw Dickens romping across the scrub. 'I will kill you next time,' he muttered. 'Paddy would have long ago! I wonder what he's up to? Probably gone back to Kerry as the local Godfather. His grin stretched the skin savagely across the scar from eyebrow to chin.

Feeling a sudden urge to inspect Dickens' ice plateau, he strode towards the ladder leading up to the water pan. Maybe there was a way up from the lake! Climbing cautiously up the ice rungs, he observed that the single tusked walrus stared boldly from the scar on the rock face. He derived an animal satisfaction by shooting it off, the rifle's power unlike anything he had ever experienced.

The lake and surrounding rock was an ice fantasy: a billion facets of refracted light. A slight wind moaned like a scared old woman among the crevices, ruffled surface snow in the declivities.

Crunching over the lake, his neck ached from looking up at the great ice tower. Impregnable for a mountaineer, he thought. But not Dickens! All the obvious routes were blocked by dangerous overhangs and vertical walls of sheet ice. He strolled to the far side of the lake where the mountain swept sharply downwards; where enormous jumbles of iced rock had spilled onto the higher slopes of the next mountain in an unholy communion of frozen mayhem. Here, a partially snow covered ledge twisted up to the main core that thrusted eight thousand feet to the tips of the devil horns. Proceeding carefully along the treacherous path, half an hour later he stood panting as he looked out across the vast plateau. It was a graveyard. Animal bones horrifically punctured the snowy wastes; lay scattered over the ice field in a windswept bareness of barbaric proportions.

So this is his lair, he thought. Looking down, a gigantic upsweep of ice obscured the timberline, but he could just make out the forest dropping away from the rim of the glistening plateau. One slip and he would plunge into this mesmerising picture of naked beauty. Shivering fearfully, he retraced his steps wondering if Dickens loved his mate among the ghosts of his victims.

★   ★   ★   ★   ★

Sonia Brown was exasperated with her younger sister. 'But Sal, you've only seen him twice!' she said. 'And the first time, hardly at all. You don't know anything about him.'

Since her meeting with Benjamin at Indian John's, Sally had been in raptures.

'How do you know Sis?' she replied hotly, brushing away a strand of grey hair. 'I'm old enough to weigh a man up. We did spend most of the day discussing each other. These things do happen you know. It's not always conventional.'

'Most of the day!' mocked Sonia. 'Big deal! He's an English divorcee, a journalist who dropped out to live on a mountain like a wild animal. And you become infatuated after only a day. Bloody hell, Sal! And you a responsible member of the community. Welfare, no less! Oh no, it's not good, not good enough by far.'

'That's quite enough, Sis,' Sally rising from her chair. 'You've got a short memory. You met George – long hair and all – on leave from Vietnam. He wasn't exactly sane either, and he was far wilder than Ben. You hardly knew him before you were married. Everyone was against it, except me. Remember? Anyway, you stuck by your guns and made it work – you both did. Why don't you let me sort out my own life?'

She crossed to the window seeing the early evening traffic stuttering through a fresh rain squall. Picturing Benjamin sitting in front of his fire, she said quietly: 'There have been men in my life. Not many, as you well know. You once called me a nun: discreet maybe, but never that! The length of courtship is unimportant, but what two people feel deep down. Everyone's the same. Some of us are more scared to accept it than others. I guess I'm one of them. But boy, when it happens, it happens! Believe me, I know what men are and what they need. What Ben needs! He hasn't found himself yet. His wife understood that, but never bothered to help him. He's so insecure in himself, hopelessly lost among his characters, he's like the Fourth of July without cranberry sauce and apple pie, like New York harbour without the Statue of Liberty. And that's dangerous. He's gone to the mountain to try and sort himself out, not become a wild animal. But I fear he may injure his mind if he stays up there too long. You know what they say about people and mountains. But I'll bring him down – slowly, but firmly.'

Ouch, thought Sonia. She's flying her battle flag. 'What if he changes, Sal?' she said solemnly. 'He's been up there three months already – straight off an aeroplane, or almost. Well, he may have appeared okay when you last saw him, but he mightn't be when he comes down.'

Sally caught sight of her reflection in the window among the traffic. Yes, she thought, but not admitting to her sister, the isolation and rare atmosphere can kill in their own way. Her thoughts were suddenly erased by the fleeting pictures of men she had known intimately, successful and homely men. And then came the distant view of a lonely cabin dwarfed by a mighty mountain caught in the depths of winter. Oh dear God, why him!

'When will you see him again?' Sonia standing and putting on her coat.

'He'll let me know through Indian John. Not long I hope.'

'George and I are worried about you, that's all. We are family!'

Sally embraced her sister. 'I know.' It was then that she realised Sam Fynn no longer dominated her thoughts. Please God, don't let my Ben get mountainmania.

CHAPTER 8

'What right has that asshole got to come to our country and shack up on one of our mountains?' Eb rubbing his bald pate and pouting angrily. A jagged scar ran across his temple where Paddy had clubbed him with the rifle. Left by the other two hunters, he had sneaked away into the forest after Dickens had left the timberline.

The Beard sipped beer through a straw. Wired, his jaw had been broken in three places. 'I'll kill 'em both,' he muttered over and over again.

"An we lost our goddamn rifles. *Our goddamn rifles for Chrissake!'*

Jake smiled inwardly as he watched the two men. His brother-in-law had been unbearable since the trip to Devil Mountain. Even Wilma had been incensed by events on the timberline. There had been talk of revenge ever since. But now that the weather had set in, he knew that there would be little chance of that until the spring, but hopefully the Englishman and his Irish friend would be gone by then. He suppressed a grin at the

Englishman's remark about Ed: The national emblem!

'Going for a leak,' he said, leaving the table.

As he left, The Beard said: 'Jaw'll be OK in a few weeks. He ain't comin'. Just you an' me. Stuff the weather; suits us. They won't find the Limey's body 'til the spring. The Mick...'

Eb grinned. 'Yeah, we'll do it to 'em good, this time,' his laugh brutal.

A large bosomed peroxide blonde strutted towards them in a tight fitting dress, turning the heads of several drinkers.

'Hi Wilma: what'll it be?' Eb striding to the bar.

'The usual, sweetie!' Sitting, she purposely revealed a well shaped thigh for the onlookers. 'Where is he?'

'The weasel's out back takin' a leak. You get those things on order like I told yer to?'

'On their way, big boy. You discussed what we talked about last night with Eb?'

The Beard nodded and winked. 'He's in. Told Jake nothin'. Hell, why'd you have to go and marry a wet rag like that fer!'

'Don't start again,' her face flushed with anger. 'You know he'll be worth money when that aunt of his snuffs it in Tennessee. Just be patient and you'll get that fishing boat. It ain't you who has to stomach him between the sheets.'

The Beard touched his sister's hand. 'Calm down, kid! I'm sure you don't go without altogether.'

'Filthy minded bum,' her grin cracking the heavy make-up. 'You shouldn't talk too much. Get better and shoot me some more fur coats, huh!'

The Beard smiled. 'You're one demandin' woman, Wilma.'

She smiled coquettishly: 'I know. Shit, here's Jake ... Hi darlin', she called.

Jake sat down moodily. He had seen smiles around the bar; noticed the over-raised dress. What are they hatching this time? he thought.

Dickens burrowed into the female's den in the red box canyon.

Enough was enough! It was time to love on the mountain. *She had been eager last time* . . . Normally, he would love in May or June and the cubs would arrive in the warmth of the hibernation period – but he wanted to love now before eating once more. Love had left him an empty belly for winter.

She allowed him to nuzzle her rump; tease her from the hibernation den and along the valley to the plateau of silver fire, the ice dazzling reflections from a sorry sun. She grunted as he began to take her. Surrendering, she moaned on the wind as they united, his seed bursting hot and deep inside.

They loved and roared and skated across the ice plateau before climaxing in a shattering crescendo that threatened to shake the mountain at its roots. Afterwards, on hind legs they called to the valleys: they had loved . . . loved . . . loved.

Benjamin had grown accustomed to shooting for the pot. His bag of small game comprised a healthy supply of meat. He loved the valleys and the forests. When not mending clothes, strengthening the pipeline or writing, he roamed for miles. Sometimes he would attempt the dangerous inclines above the ice plateau. One day, he meant to climb to the devil horns. Apart from Sally Brown, he found that life outside the mountains held little meaning; even Harry and his family had vanished into a mental mist of bygones. He was livid that Sam had blackmailed him with the weather to lengthen his stay on the timberline. He tolerated the boy and his cat like unwelcome relatives.

Although improved, the weather could prove ferocious; the glass falling alarmingly in minutes as the wind heralded in a fresh blizzard. But one snowstorm was much the same as the last to Benjamin, for he had become enveloped by the mountain. His soul moulded into the lofty wastes as he fell deeper into its frozen clutches. Virtually a recluse, he was becoming oblivious of his reason for being there. He knew the terrain like an animal; hunted and tracked like a woodsman and read the weather like one of his own chapters. He lived a dangerous fantasy world where even Sally became a Greek Goddess. He was suffering from anoxia: the rarified air had affected his brain.

Mountainmania was turning his mind, Devil Mountain his soul.

Today, he had spent most of his time noting the various animal spoor in the forest below the timberline. Standing on a steep rise overlooking the valley, he muttered to himself as a rain squall slashed across the valley from the mesa, pockmarking the drifts and transforming the mountain into shiny coal. He quickly retraced his footsteps to Virginia as loud rumbles shuddered the sky; lightning clicked around the peaks.

Moving up the dish, he imagined Sally waiting for him in the cabin: waiting to give herself to him completely. To the tune of Shenandoah, he began singing:

Sally Brown, oh Sally Bro-hown
You're the only girl in to-hown,
Who can ever make me see-ee
Always want your companeee,
Oh sweet Sally Bro-hown.

Seeing the oil lamp dim and flare between the slats as Sam moved around, he grimaced. Damn it! All I get for company is a runaway orphan and his mangy cat. Paddy's fine, but even he's a bloody hitman of some sort. 'Get the coffee on,' he bawled opening the door. 'Come on Sam, get . . .' The boy was not there. Boogaloo sat on a ledge next to the oil lamp. 'So it was you who moved,' he said in exasperation.

Putting a few more logs on the fire, he went back outside and called for the boy. No answer. He scowled as night drew in fast and rain pelted onto the timberline. Looking around, he saw Sam's rapidly disappearing footprints in the snow leading towards the ladder by the water pan.

Angrily, he strode through the slush yelling the boy's name. He goosepimpled at a second set of tracks partially obliterated by the driving rain. 'Mountain lion,' he breathed.

Rushing back for his torch and rifle, he quickly followed the tracks as they moved to the narrow ledge cuttting across the scar beneath the water pan. 'He's gone to the cavern,' he muttered. 'Oh Christ, it's pitch black in there! The cat's got night vision.'

Rifle barrel and torch in his left hand, the right gripping the stock, Benjamin slowly edged into the damp blackness; his fears aroused as a deep throated growl echoed ahead, reverberated off the cavern walls. A replusive picture flashed into focus of Sam's flesh being torn from chewed bone. How long has he been gone? he wondered. Damn it, I haven't seen any lion tracks lately!

Nerves screaming, he kept to the wall, all the time angling the beam at the centre of the tunnel: he was ready to fire in a milli-second. But that was still ample time for the cat to attack, he thought grimly. He stopped as a groan floated from somewhere below. *Oh dear Lord, he's fallen down a pothole!*

Moving quickly, he rounded a bend; stopped instantly as the cat's savage face glared at him in the torch beam. Lying by the edge of the hole, it now sprang to its feet, snarling at Benjamin.

He came on aim as the cat ran and launched itself in a blur of motion; pulled the trigger and prayed the bullet found its mark. Deafened by the awful bang, he was relieved as the lion's body slammed against the rock wall before rolling over to lie dead at his feet. Staring down at the lifeless eyes more terrible in death, his heart thumped crazily as breathing returned. *'Sam,'* he yelled. *'It's all right! The lion's dead. Where are you?'*

Sam had fallen some fifteen feet into a half flooded pothole: the water had broken his fall and the narrow diameter had allowed him to hang gamely onto a small ledge. Petrified, he had seen the terrible outline of the cat's head appear over the edge where he had fallen; endured the lion's ominous growls as it had pawed the air above its quarry. He had jumped in shock at the rifle shot, letting go his feeble fingerhold on the ledge. Now, he cried thankfully into Benjamin's torch light.

'Try and relax,' comforted Benjamin. 'I'll have you out in a jiffy.'

'M...my arm's bust!' the boy's teeth chattering from the cold water.

Unclipping the rifle sling, Benjamin made a loop and lowered the improvised rope to Sam. Hauling him to safety, he pummelled warmth back into the frozen limbs and hurriedly carried him back to Virginia. The boy had passed out before they arrived. Before splinting the injured arm, he stripped Sam; dried and wrapped him in blankets before lighting the prepared fire.

When the arm was splinted, Sam explained his misfortune. Bored, he had gone for a stroll. 'I was going to skate on the lake.

It was light, then. I heard the lion growl in the forest, but it was too late to turn back. I thought I'd hide in the cavern, but instead, I fell down the pothole. It must have stalked me. I'm sorry to have caused you so much trouble! Thanks for saving my life.'

Benjamin smiled softly. 'Forget it! How about that fear of the dark?'

'Strangely enough, I hadn't thought of it until now.' The kitten climbed onto his lap and nodded off.

The rain drummed on the cabin rood as a fresh wind howled down the chimney. Benjamin ate in silence, his marked face a devilish mask in the firelight. Boogaloo pestered him for some beans as he studied the sleeping boy. Pouring a stiff whisky, his thoughts centred on Sally Brown; then the Irishman; then Sam and his cat, before more odious recollections of Dickens dwarfed all else. He had another drink. Melancholy, he touched his scar. Suddenly, he realised that he was crying. 'Damn it!' he muttered. 'What are they doing to my life?' He fell asleep on the floor, his mind in turmoil.

With the dawn, steel sheeted rain beat a deafening tattoo on the roof as the wind groaned loudly across the timberline. Valley and forest were reduced to swirling mist clouds until the rainstorm reduced itself to a heavy drizzle by midday, slushing any remaining snow and icing the timberline. Under its new weight, the pipeline collapsed before dusk.

Benjamin was furious. Grumbling to himself, he paced about like a caged tiger. 'What's the bloody sense in it all?' he complained. 'Rebuilding and rebuilding!'

For something to do, Sam read on the bed. He had seen these moods rise before. Ben was best left to Ben. Boogaloo, stretched across his legs, cocked an ear in the angry man's direction. The boy knew if he spoke, another mouthful would fly across the room inviting him to 'take his cat' and 'disappear'. Benjamin wasn't the same man. The boy knew that. It was as though, feeling that he had no right to be on the mountain, he needed the place all the more badly. Devil Mountain was destroying him.

Constantly attacked by his devils, Benjamin fought bitterly within himself; more often than not, he confused fantasy with reality. Even now as the boy feigned interest in one of his poetry books, he wanted to offer the hand of friendship, but an invisible force, some perverse fragment of his remorseless crusade to find himself, combined with, yet another mood change, denied this; it was as if he had to shield himself with an invisible barrier to ward off personal contact while in search mode for the Thompson Holy Grail. And what of Sally Brown? Angrily, he walked out into the rain and complained to the sky. Soaked through, he returned subdued like a man blessed with a vision of God. Until the next time. Never was there a glimmer of acceptance of Sam and his cat.

And so it went on day after day after night after night.

★ ★ ★ ★ ★

Paddy Martin ate his meal listening to the banter of two men in the small hotel restaurant.

'. . . Talkin' of disasters,' a man from Maine was saying. 'What about that flash flood in Loveland back in '76! Killed over a hundred people. It swamped Route 34.'

'Yeah,' replied his lunch partner. 'Took my wife's eldest brother. Bad business! What about Rapid City in '72! South Dakota saw almost as many deaths with the same thing. You'd think all those government boffins would dream up some fancy scheme to control the floods!'

'See what you mean. Like the army blasts the mountain snow before it builds up into another mother of an avalanche.'

'Yeah, something like that. I can remember the time . . .'

Paddy screwed his eyes in thought . . . *One mother of an avalanche* . . . Paying the waitress, he walked out into the crowded Denver street. He had left his pack at the bus depot. Needing a drink, he stepped inside the Jolly Leprechaun. Ordering whisky, he lit a cheroot and eyed a woman feeding the jukebox. Like other down-at-heel characters with enquiring eyes and a handful of over-painted women nursing half-empty lipsticked glasses, the prostitude gave the Irishman the once over.

'Like a real good time?' she said, squeezing her nipples through the flimsy dress.

Paddy smiled. 'Not today, lady,' turning to his drink.

'At least give a girl a reason to hang on in this dump. Vodka!'

Paddy ordered. 'Either you should be in school, or the paintwork's a masterpiece!' Tossing two dollar bills onto the counter, he said: 'Play something Irish.'

Pulling a face for her friends' benefit, she moved towards the machine as another woman took her place at the bar. 'A bit out of the way for you, isn't it! This place has a reputation.'

Paddy stared at the vaguely familiar face.

'Sally Brown! We met on the timberline. I'm Sam Fynn's social conscience.'

'Oh right!' exclaimed Paddy. 'How are you? This isn't my normal. I can get worse.'

She laughed with him. 'I'm here on business,' indicating the prostitute. 'My job has its downside. This is her last chance: child abuse. There's also drugs and second stage syphilis. But I'm glad I bumped into you. I'd like to talk about Ben. How about my place, say six thirty?'

Paddy grinned broadly. 'Suits me!' reading the hastily scribbled address.

'From memory, you're a potato addict. Didn't a rat polish a few off for you?'

'Aye, the bugger . . . er sorry. Yes. It also pinched Ben's cheese when he . . .' he stopped, not wishing to hurt her feelings. He had seen how the two people had looked at one another.

'It's okay. Ben told me about the eagle. He would have died but for you.'

Paddy reddened. 'He's his own man.' Glancing over her shoulder at the prostitute: 'I think the er . . . lady, is coming back. Six thirty.'

Watching him take his leave, she turned on the woman.

'Help yourself to a drink,' Sally called from the kitchen. 'Dinner will be about another ten minutes.'

Paddy relaxed in an easy chair and studied the feminine apartment. A far cry from moonlit freeways, stinking police cells and violent men, he thought. Noticing a business file on a side table, he read the heading: Case No. 72327. Fynn, Samuel.

Sally observed him through the serving hatch. 'The bane of my

118

life! Ben has my sympathy – if he's gone back there. It sounds contradictory, but at least he'd be better off with Ben than ... wherever he's been.'

Paddy nodded thoughtfully. 'Can I help with anything?'

'No. Just help yourself to another drink. Dinner will be served in a jiffy. You haven't known Ben long, have you?'

'About a month, off and on.' He knew she needed to know more. 'He's just a man I met on a mountain. He's different from other men I've known. Certainly among *Englishmen*.'

Detecting his thinly veiled dislike of the English, she said: 'Not your favourite people, Paddy?'

He nodded somberly. 'But Ben sees things differently. I'm not so sure his kind is safe for society. He would certainly be unacceptable. He's too philosophical; all seeing. There are times he makes me uncomfortable, as if he's looking inside my soul.'

'But it must take courage to do what he is doing!'

'I'd agree if I knew just what it was he was doing,' grinned the Irishman. 'Oh, he doesn't lack for guts, I'll give him that.' He gave a diluted version of the fight with the hunters and the amazing climax with Dickens while everyone scurried for safety.

She then told him about her visit to Indian John's. 'Ben has high principles. Sometimes too high, I think. But you don't really think he's a misfit, do you? I mean, he is a journalist. He can't be that much of a recluse.'

'Something's burning him up. I wouldn't get too close if I were you – not wishing to put my nose where it's not wanted. He needs time and space. What happens after that is anyone's guess.' Getting off the subject: 'This stew's delicious. Reminds me of something my old Ma used to say: "If you don't make stew properly, you won't see people. To see them, you've got to look for the best in them". It took a few years to understand her. Good cooking brings out the best in people.' Reading her expression: 'People don't come easy to me,' he smiled. 'I wasn't blessed with a long fuse.'

Finishing the meal, Sally washed up and they settled down in the easy chairs. 'Sorry to keep on about him, but I'm ...'

'I know,' replied Paddy gently.

'He's writing a novel. Did you know that?'

'No. But it wouldn't surprise me. He's that way: full of quotations and things. My ma used to read Yeats to us. At heart,

119

the Irish are a romantic race, you know.'

Sally smiled and fished in her handbag. Producing a piece of paper: 'It's something he was working on. He let me write it down:

Like the snow, me heart is heavy;
Unsure of the future: friendless.
The mountain, too, hurts, a Calvary
For the Salvation we miss like ourselves
Until death screams the answer.'

Paddy inhaled on the cheroot. 'Not bad!'

'By 'friendless', he means spiritually. He sees mankind losing itself through greed; that by ignoring history we are all instrumental in our own downfall.'

'I suppose I'd go along with that, but I don't waste my life worrying about it.' Paddy smiled: 'But then, I'm another man.'

Sally stared deep into his eyes and saw nothing.

'I suppose he's trying to find himself up there: some literary knight in search of whatever literary knights search for. *If he isn't strong enough...'*

Sally bolted forward. 'He survived those terrible blizzards after his cabin was destroyed. Spring isn't all that far away,' she said prayer-like as if her words could help Benjamin against the cruelty of a mountain winter.

'I didn't mean physically,' Paddy mentally cursing himself. She's head over heels with him, he thought. Nevertheless, the facts had to be faced. 'He'll have been up there eight months by spring. The winter, the boy, the bear, me, you, the mountain – and biggest of all, Ben Thompson. Can one man handle all that? He's said little about himself, but happy Indians don't stay up mountains.'

Paddy's words reminded her of the heated discussion with Sonia over the possible state of Benjamin's mind when he came down. 'Maybe he won't wait till then,' she said, more to convince herself than make a point.

'Maybe,' came the matter-of-fact reply. He stubbed the cheroot. Christ, he mused, which is worse: loving a country, or a woman? And this one is *a woman!*

'Do you mind if I switch on to the news, Paddy? You see, you are fortunate. You carry your mother around with you in the shillelagh. I let the television carry Devil Mountain.'

The set pictured into life. '*And finally,'* said the newscaster, '*an*

120

Army spokesman said today that a new kind of dispersal bomb known as ADBA – Avalanche Destruction By Air – will be tested on the eastern slopes of Devil Mountain in the Front Range of the Rockies, next snow fall. If the bomb is successful, the operation will be repeated on Mount Evans and other peaks. It is hoped to eradicate expensive conventional ballistic methods to prevent snow build-up that leads to avalanches endangering life and property . . . And now for the main points again . . .'

Sally switched off the set and silently made coffee, her mind a prey to the worst.

Paddy thought back to the snippet of conversation in the restaurant . . . *Before it builds up into one mother of an avalanche* . . . The next fall could be any time. And Benjamin's small two-way radio had never worked since he'd arrived on the timberline. He even joked about it being the 'final failure of Man'. His only line of communication was the trading post, and the chances of his visiting there tonight were negligible. Suddenly, his eye fastened on the business file: the boy could be there, too!

Returning with the coffee, again Sally read his thoughts. 'I hope Sam isn't up there. How can we get word about this ADAB . . . ABAB . . . or whatever it's called? We have to do something!'

'First thing, get in touch with the Rangers. Call Indian John's. Ben may be there, you never know. He gets on with the old boy. Tell John we're on the way. While you're doing that, I'll nip across to the drugstore for some smokes. I'll drive.'

Picking up the phone, she said: 'Thank God for the Irishman.'

'Listen pal,' spat the prostitute inside the parked car. 'I told you that's her apartment block. *I should know!* She cost me a week's booze taking the Irishman away.'

Eb turned to The Beard. 'He's gotta come out sometime. Hell, am I looking forward to hitting this bastard!'

The hunters had come to Denver for equipment. By chance, they had seen the Irishman leaving the Jolly Leprechaun and had met the woman. A deal was soon struck.

The Beard nudged Eb as sparks flashed from Paddy's cheroot into the night. Turning the ignition, the hunter told the woman to leave before screeching the Chevvy away from the sidewalk.

The last thing that Paddy Martin saw were two bright balls of light streaking towards him: then pain; then blackness; then

121

nothing. The vehicle rounded a corner as his body landed in the street, face down in a pool of blood.

CHAPTER 9

S am stared apprehensively at the sky. The wind had dropped to a flutter.

⸱⸱'Looks like more snow, Boogie,' he said to the kitten, grinning as it scampered for the warmth of the cabin.

'Bloody cat!' muttered Benjamin losing balance. 'Come on, let's go. I want to bag something before the next fall.'

Sam smiled secretly as he adjusted the sling on his broken arm. Two weeks since his harrowing experience with the mountain lion, frequent outbreaks of foul weather had denied Benjamin the opportunity of returning the boy to the authorities. Instead, he had shared Indian John's advice as they hunted for the pot.

No longer squeamish or high minded about killing to survive, today, Benjamin had decided on a small deer.

He looked down as the cat decided to attack his foot. 'He's not getting very big, is he? In fact, he doesn't seem to grow at all! How old is he?'

'Only four months. Boogie's a runt; that's why he'd get cat 'flu or something in the city. His resistance would be low – not like up

123

here in the mountains. But come spring, he'll be strong enough, though.'

'You'll have to get him vaccinated all the same. You wouldn't want to lose him, would you?'

'You think they'll let me keep him, then? He did save my life from that bear trap . . . I know you've written to the priest.'

'I'm sure Sam Fynn will think of a way round that one. Yes, I've written to the priest, but he was non-committal about Boogaloo. Now put him inside and let's get on with it – we haven't much time.'

Slipping into newly made snow shoes, Sam asked: 'Going to try the northern end of the valley, Ben? Near that eagle's nest? You said you might.'

The man nodded and ruffled the boy's hair. Since the incident with the lion, he had grown somewhat tolerant towards Sam and Boogaloo. The cat had weaved its own spell.

I'm getting attached, he thought. Damn it! And I'm getting more enchanted by Sally Brown. They're both irrefutable facts: nothing to do with mood changes; as real as the mountain mist.

But what was a constant source of concern was a seemingly morbid and childish habit to over-care for everything. This, he knew, of course, emanated from a highly developed emotional condition in relation to his surroundings and a huge capacity to feel passionately for anything – good or bad – when the surge of inspiration electrified his whole being. He would mope over a crushed wild flower or pine for an injured animal or a tree blasted by lightning.

One day, he had even found himself weeping over the fallen pipeline, calling it 'Fred'. All in all, he accepted that as his life was totally out of context with the *status quo* and governed by the mountain – and to an extent by Dickens, of whom, he now respected as the rightful owner of Devil Mountain – and that his emotions were totally out of control as he had come to understand them, his one true goal was to study coexistence through the animal kingdom and take that knowledge down to Harry's world of 'goofballs' with the intention of, if not purifying society, then injecting it with a spark of hope.

Unwittingly, he had found religion of a kind.

Sam followed him down the dish. The going was easy up to

now as the drifts had been partially eaten by torrential overnight rain. Below, the valley squatted in frozen silence; above, the sky promised snow.

Benjamin stopped suddenly, his body rigid as a tree. Taking aim, he took a deer breaking from the forest. There was no sign of Dickens.

Sam helped cut the carcass.

'Hear anything?'

'Just a light wind in the drifts, Ben.'

'No. It was something else.' His eyes slitted in concentration. 'There it is again!' They looked upwards as the muffled drone of an aircraft penetrated through the sickly pall of the clouds.

'The Air Force Academy at Springs isn't too far from here,' Sam puffing from his exertions.

'Think we've got time for a rabbit before the sky drops on us?' Benjamin catching sight of a fluffy ball moving along a small ridge. 'Eastern cottontail,' he whispered. 'Must be hungry. He sleeps during the day. By that tail, he's about five pounds! Soup for us; meat for Boogaloo. Stay here.'

Sam watched him crouch-walk off windline; stalk the animal like a professional hunter. He smiled as the rifle crashed and Benjamin returned with the cottontail hanging from his belt.

'OK, let's vamoose.'

'That's an unusual word for you!'

Benjamin chuckled. 'I feel in an unusual mood. Let's have a party!'

Sam stood open-mouthed. 'A what! There're only two of us.'

'Wrong Sam. You're forgetting that black coated runt of yours.' He gave a deep belly laugh. 'Think I've lost my marbles, eh?'

Sam smiled with uncertainty, but it soon gave way to infectious laughter. 'What are we celebrating?'

'Friday! It's bloody Friday, Sam,' Benjamin enjoying his echoes through the valley. 'Won't take long to cook something. We'll liven old Devil Mountain up a bit!'

The boy listened excitedly as Benjamin explained all about his 'Friday' party.

'We'll have bean-can hats with chin strings and songs aplenty, my lad. Yahoooo: God save the Queen and the President of the

United States.'

I like this Ben Thompson, thought Sam. Not that raging wild man who scared the living hell out of me a while back. Maybe he's come to some kind of terms with himself.

The first flakes of snow fell as they crossed the timberline.

★ ★ ★ ★ ★

'I was half way through the box canyon when I heard the shots, Uncle,' explained Indian John's eldest nephew. 'They'd gone by the time I got there. I saw the animal tracks and blood spoor, but the snow started so I turned back.'

Indian John's face was grave. Sally Brown had called from a hospital pay phone: the big Irishman had been critically injured by a hit and run driver. And now, the Army was going to bomb Devil Mountain with some new-fangled air bomb.

'They'd gone!' his voice rose. 'There were two sets of tracks!'

'One was about the size of snow shoe track a kid would leave. I didn't know there were any . . .'

Indian John cursed and slammed the receiver. The lines were down. The boy had returned and was up there with Bengymen. He stared forlornly through the window: it was worse than the heavy snow storm that had claimed his wife ten years before in the box canyon. Hearing the aircraft overhead: God help them, he thought. Visibility is down to zero-minus. He rubbed the glass, picturing his wife after the wolves had finished with her two weeks after she had gone missing. 'God help you both,' he repeated.

★ ★ ★ ★ ★

Sally Brown looked at her brother-in-law George, arguing with the army sergeant over the phone. Her eyes had glassed, were red rimmed from crying. She had panicked on the night of Paddy's hit and run, forgetting to give Indian John her sister's number. Ever since, the lines had been down. And now George was getting no sense from Cheyenne Mountain Combat Headquarters to prevent the bombing: and still no sign of the boy.

'Shit!' cried George. 'You'd think with half the military on the moon, you could talk to an asshole in an army camp. I'm sorry Sal. Why don't you take a sedative, get some sleep? You've been up for the last thirty-six hours!'

'She didn't sleep much when you were away,' she replied, indicating Sonia. 'I think I'll go home, it's closer to the hospital. I want to drop in on Paddy in the morning. If the weather clears up . . .'

'Sis,' Sonia. jumping from her chair. 'You're not thinking of going out there. It's ridiculous. George, make her see sense!'

'Son's right, Sal. Why don't you bed down here. I'll stand by the phone, let you know the minute . . .'

'Thank you, no George. I would feel closer to him at the trading post. He . . . might even be there. You'd have gone to Nam, Sonia, along with millions of other women if they'd let you.' She got up to leave.

'You're being irresponsible, Sal.' Sonia stood defiantly in the doorway. 'I won't let you. We'll phone in the morning – the lines may be up then.'

'It may be too late. I want to be alone.' She put on her hat and coat. 'You can't stop me. I'll call as soon I hear anything.'

The following morning, Sally called: 'They bombed it, Sis,' her voice shaky. 'They said on the five o'clock news that millions of tons of rock and snow was dislodged. The Army called it a *successful operation*'. Then she broke down. 'Oh Sis, I . . . I loved him so much. More . . . more than I've ever done in my life . . .'

★ ★ ★ ★ ★

Benjamin threw a chunk of rabbit meat to Boogaloo near the fire. Drinking rum and sweating from the blast- furnace heat of the cabin, his head felt light. 'Come on, Sam,' his voice loud with drink. 'Give us Yankee Doodle again? I'm getting the knack of this,' rattling two spoons between finger and thumb against his thigh. The can hat wobbled on his head; an eagle's feather

127

sprouted from the top.

'I've sung it three times already,' the boy complained. His stomach ached through too much venison.

'It's got the right rhythm for the spoons, Sam. Just one more time for old Ben,' adjusting the hat that had fallen over an ear.

'OK, but you promise to do Rule Brittania with a *far-out* accent!'

'Done!'

'*Yankee Doodle had a pony . . .*'

The spoons rattled and Benjamin whooped and yelled until he was hoarse.

Boogaloo had stopped eating: ears pointed sharply as he looked at the door.

'*Yahooooo!* Bravo! Well done, Sam, Benjamin fighting for breath. 'Phew, it's hot in here.' He swayed towards the window. 'Heaven'll be asking for some of this snow back if it keep this up. Now, how about . . .'

'Rule Britannia,' cut in Sam.

Benjamin sighed in resignation. 'Just open the door a crack, I'm roasting alive. Aren't you?' He grinned as Boogaloo streaked outside. 'Wants to do his business,' topping up his drink.

'You don't have to make a thing about it, Boogie,' said Sam as the cat miaowed on the threshold, staring up at the sky.

'*Rule Brit-tan-yah, Brit-tan-yah rules the waves . . .*'

Sam conducted, strutting around the cabin and stamping his feet. Their voices cannoned off the walls as they strove to out-sing one another. They failed to hear the muted drone of an aircraft moving onto its bombing run high above the cabin.

'. . . *Brii-tohns, ne-voh, ne-voh, ne-voh will be slaaaves.*'

Benjamin flopped sideways on the bed. 'God, I haven't sung like that since I don't know when,' he croaked.

Sam had gone to the door. 'What's the matter, Boogie?' frowning as it scratched his knee. 'Too much noise for you, little one?'

'OK there?' Benjamin's head threatened to spin off its shoulders with the combined assaults from the heat, rum and singing.

'Something's wrong, Ben! I've seen him like this before. He knows when things aren't right.'

128

'Nonsense! He's a cat, not a clairvoyant. Dickens is off with his mate and there're no bobcats or lions around except your's.' Taking off the can hat: 'Close the door, it's getting cold in here all of a sudden.'

They heard it together.

Benjamin laughed. 'There's his problem: he doesn't like planes. Full marks for knowing it was there, though,' slipping to the floor. 'Now, what about . . .'

'I tell you, he's never wrong. The bear trap before I met you, the loose packed snow you would have drowned in last week and Dickens the other day. Sixth sense, call it what you will, but something's sure spooked him.'

Benjamin frowned, but it merited a quick look. 'Very well,' donning the parka and hat. 'I'll take a stroll, but it's white pea soup out there.' Grabbing the torch and rifle, he tumbled through the door.

The cold sobered him instantly. It was deathly quiet.

The snow was again knee high as he ploughed across the timber-line, unsure of what he was looking for. Suddenly, his nerves screamed in his ears for the danger that was about to strike through the drifting yellow-white wall in the torch beam. His heart stopped. That sound! There was no mistaking it. He urinated with fear. *Avalanche!* Looking, he knew, rather than saw, the giant snow cloud already mushrooming and hurtling its impregnable icy white death upon him. He didn't stop to think about the rocks that would be torn from the mountain side and thrown onto the timberline. 'Sam, get out of there. *Avalanche.*'

The boy grabbed his jacked, picked up Boogaloo and followed Benjamin's silhouette into the forest.

Bumping into the pine, they slipped and slid through the sloping timber as invisible snow and ice and rock whooshed and rumbled and crashed all around: bashed into trees and steamrollered past with a heart-beating sickening thundering and splintering and mangling of wood and ground of earthquake proportions.

Steeling himself, Benjamin led them to safety where the forest dipped sharply towards the valley. 'I think we're out of it,' he said breathlessly. 'Best to be sure, though! We'll head off left for the dish. It's out of range over there. Wait! It's that plane again.'

129

'Ben – they're bombing the mountain!'

'What! Who is? What are you talking about?'

'I remember Indian Join mentioning it a while back. They – the Army – do it every year to prevent snow build-up.'

'Then why no explosion?' Benjamin's face reflected stark terror. 'No! You must have misunderstood him. I know they play around with all kinds of devices nowadays – governments are keen on wasting the people's hard earned money – but you may be right. Assuming you are, that pilot up there mightn't have finished yet.'

'Maybe not,' Sam pushing Boogaloo's head back inside his jacket.

'The cavern! Hurry, before he buries us till spring.'

The awful mountain quiet had returned as the aircraft flew off for another run-in.

Drenched with snow, they fought through the morass, as, once more, the plane circled overhead in preparation for another bombing run. As they edged up the scar, they heard its engines grow louder and louder until it was directly above the the cavern. Fearful of a wrong footing, they inched along the snow-packed ledge until Benjamin's torch caught the bleary outline of the entrance. They rushed inside as the air bomb released another colossus of rock and ice onto the timberline.

Shaking violently from cold and fear and the terrible cacophony outside, they listened as the mountain exploded with earsplitting crescendos; reverberated as the rock strata was wrenched from the main core and ejected onto the lower regions with a terrible finality.

Benjamin couldn't help wondering what the pilot thought about as he dropped his infernal bombs from the safety of altitude. Damn him to hell, he thought. It's not his fault, but damn him to hell all the same.

In a short time, the timberline was obliterated.

Benjamin allowed a half hour to elapse before heading off back through the forest: the timberline was impassable. Struggling up the slope, they arrived back at the spot where they had entered the forest: there was no sign of Virginia; instead, an enormous half-frozen confusion of ice-rock squatted before them.

He suppressed his grief as they trudged through the night for warmth until the pale light of dawn cruelly enhanced the grim picture of destruction: broken trees and rocks lay scattered like the discarded and unwanted toys of a spoilt child. Silently, he stood alone by Virginia entombed in ice-rock. He didn't look for the pipeline. He knew what he would see.

'Maybe a rock didn't hit it, Ben,' Sam feeling for the man.

Benjamin didn't speak. This was just another mountain he had to climb, he told himself. You have to climb it or perish. You both will. It's as simple as that. The boy may be right, a rock may not have hit her, but all the time he was thinking about it the ice was forming a seal over his home; binding together snow and rock into a hideous glue that would not melt until spring, and would in all probability crush the walls like eggshells.

'We've got some digging to do,' he said at last. 'How's your good arm?'

'Good enough,' grinned the boy.

Benjamin stared at the fresh young face. This time, he wasn't alone. 'You're all right, Sam Fynn,' he smiled. He touched the cat through the thick material. 'If I ever complain about him again, you can stay up here and I'll go down to the orphanage. Thanks Boogie! You're one hell of a cat.'

'Told you he was neat,' declared Sam proudly. 'Hey, the snow's stopped.'

Then man and boy dug furiously for life. A day later, a mountain rescue team banged on the door.

'The woman from Denver never said anything about a kid,' exclaimed the man in charge, retreating from the glowering scarred face and wild, flowing white hair.

'He's my son. Joined me before the snow set in. It's for his development. I'm here on a sabbatical. Sorry to have caused you trouble, but we'll be all right as long as that pilot keeps his feet on the ground.'

'You're crazy, you know that!' the man shaking his head while his team looked on disinterestedly. If the fella wanted to kill himself up here, then why should we stop him. But the kid! Sure takes all kinds.

Benjamin wrote a hurried note to Sally. 'Will you see that she gets it?'

'Sure, but let me leave you with one of our two-way radios.

You say your's is US?'

'Yes. Thanks.'

'Anything else?'

'No. It's all in the letter.'

The team began to move off.

'Watch out for Dickens.'

'Who the hell's he?' the leader scowling.

'You'll know if you meet him.' Ben slammed the door. He was grateful in an ungrateful way. They had meant well, but he resented their intrusion.

'One crazy mother, that,' moaned one of the rescue team.

'Yeah! You believe that about the kid bein' his?'

'None of our business if he is or isn't. I was on a promise, too.'

The other man laughed.

★ ★ ★ ★ ★

Paddy Martin was off the critical list. Tubes fed into his body like roads on a street – seemingly going nowhere in particular, yet arriving at some predetermined destination. His skull had been fractured and his left leg was broken, but his ribs had survived the contact with the Chevvy, thanks to Mona. He had been in a coma for six days, but his enormous constitution and will to live had pulled him through. But he was still weak – and on the danger list.

Sally Brown had brought Benjamin and Sam from the trading post to the hospital. Standing at his friend's bedside, the Englishman wept inside with a cold fury. Nothing had changed below the mountain. It was still the same old Institutionalised Man indulging in his favourite disgusting pastime: greed at any cost and life was the cheapest commodity on sale. Seeing Mona under the bed, he picked up the shillelagh and left the private ward.

Ignoring a doctor's protests for taking the shillelagh, he strode off down the corridor to where Sally had said she would wait with Sam. In his absence, a priest had taken the boy away. Oblivious of the visitors' stares he barged his way along a series of corridors until he saw her straw gold hair outlined against the lilac paintwork.

Sally rose as he elbowed his way between two devious-looking characters with skull-cropped hair, painted with tattoos and emblazoned with earrings and bracelets.

'*Benjamin!*' she exclaimed. 'Whatever's the matter with you? You're really not yourself. Why don't you let a doctor take a look at you?'

'Let's go. Where's the boy?' looking around.

'I'll tell you out at the car.'

'Gone off exploring, has he? If he lets that cat loose, there'll be hell to pay with the doctors.' His face clouded like a river fog. 'You saw him, Sally. Who did this? Were there any witnesses? He'd only just left you, hadn't he? It was attempted murder, you know that! What are the police doing about it? Oh, what a bloody mess. How long has Sam been gone? Where has he . . .'

'One thing at a time, Ben. *Don't rush.* The police are treating it as a hit and run – not homicide. But they said that you might have some idea as to who did it – seeing as you and Paddy were close.'

Benjamin moved towards the door. 'We'll wait for Sam at the car.' He didn't see Sally's downcast expression. 'Yes, I think I know who would do a thing like this that. At any rate, they had the motive.'

'Who? Those hunters you had the fight with?'

He nodded gravely. His eyes burned like coals in his head as he slammed a fist into the palm of his hand. 'I'll find them,' he hissed. 'If it's the last thing . . .'

'*You'll do no such thing, Ben Thompson,*' Sally pushing him into the passenger seat. 'Now listen to me for a change while I tell you a few home truths. You can't go round like a bear with a . . . I'm sorry, I didn't mean it to come out that way, but you know what I mean. You left England leaving some nasty memories behind, and I'm glad you came over here to sort yourself out. But not this way, Ben. You've gone wild. Look at you! You're enough to put the fear up the Good Lord himself. I agree, it's good for a man to try and find himself, but he usually finds out that he already has himself at the end of his search. You may be different . . . But the mountain isn't the answer. It's driving you insane, Ben. You've become an introvert and are running away instead of looking for yourself. The answer isn't up there among all that snow and ice and loneliness; it's down here with us goofballs –

133

Harry told me you used that expression. Well it's a good one, but you're also one. We all are, and you're one of us whether you like it or not.' She looked down at her fingers twiddling with a coat button.

'I wasn't going to say all that out here. In the carpark. It just came out. I wanted to say it at home by the fire where we'd be the only people in the world. But I've spoilt it now.'

Only now, Benjamin saw that her face was strained; the eyes seemed incapable of holding their subject for more than a few seconds. She had been greatly moved by Paddy's misfortune. She was speaking to him, but the words failed to register, like the end of a dream when the sleeper is about to awake.

'. . . It's not Paddy I'm worried about,' she was saying. 'It's you. He'll come out of it, but will you? You know you've got anoxia, don't you. Too much of that fine air up there. Ben, you're a walking time-bomb!'

'Withdrawal symptoms, maybe,' he said morosely as she slipped into drive. 'And I don't like seeing my friends in oxygen tents. What are you doing? *Why aren't you waiting for Sam?*'

'I'll tell you back at the house.'

'Tell me now,' his voice harsh. His hand gripped the steering wheel, forcing her to pull over.

'Ben, that's dangerous. You could have . . .'

'The boy,' he demanded. *'Where's Sam?'*

'Promise me you'll take a tranquilliser when we get back'

'The boy!'

She turned in her seat to face him. 'Somebody wants to adopt him.'

Benjamin went cold and he slumped as the the anger and bitterness dissipated like rain on snow. 'When?' was all he said.

'He's gone to meet them now. The priest came for him while you were with Paddy. There's more, but not here. Are you strong enough?'

She drove off as his head fell onto his chest. Making coffee – she had heard somewhere that alcohol was bad for people in shock – she told him about the prostitute, of why her son was one of her cases and of her meeting with Paddy in the Leprechaun; that the woman had admitted talking to two men calling themselves hunters shortly before the hit and run. She did say that one of the men had a beard and the other was completely bald.'

He sat unflinching and she moved close to him and gently stroked his hair; touched the scar. 'I was over the moon when they told me you and Sam were alive. Oh, it's not fair,' she sobbed. 'All this has thrown things out of control. My emotions are all over the place.'

He put an arm around her shoulders and kissed her forehead. 'I'm sorry. You're doing the worry for all of us. I feel like an alien; like someone who has just walked away from death and is suddenly presented with everyday life. He walks from the operating table out into the street and a passing neighbour says: "Hey Fred, long time no see. Where've you been? Be at the ball game tonight, will we?" It's a crazy all mixed up world away from the mountain. You say that she beat up on her small child?' unable to control his thought pattern.

'Yes. I took him away from her a week ago. She said that one of the men spoke in a queer way. The one with the beard.'

'His jaw was broken in the fight on the timberline. Anything else? but he hardly heard as he slipped back to the boy and his cat. He had been hard on the little blighter, but it was for the lad's own good. And anyway, he had made it clear from the start that he was not welcome. Then there was the Irishman. *Poor Paddy!* What a mess to get himself into. He was a violent man, and, no doubt, had led a violent life, but nonetheless he felt a certain affection for the man. Christ, he saved your bacon more than once, Ben.

'. . . the cops think she's in over her head with the child to be tied in with hit abnd run . . .'

His face had set cruelly with remembrance. The scar whitened where the hair had not regrown. They called this civilisation where a man's stature was judged by his ranking among the monoliths of concrete and steel and of how many secretaries he bedded between meeetings; of starched and shining pink scrubbed doctors with condescending tongues for the sick to shell out their life's savings for sicker hospital wards populated by hit and run victims and people old before their time.

'. . . Paddy had no ID so I vouched for him . . .'

Christ, I'm about to return to this gigantic web of deceit, he thought. And I belong to the biggest hypocrites of them all. Journalists are no heroes in the real world. They haven't learnt about life outside the homogeneous columns of clinical copy which they condescendingly feed to stupid Joe Public to protect Joe public from himself. *Bollocks!* Joe Public is better suited for this world than any hack and always will be; his true heroism far outstrips any to be found among the dipthongs and predicates of slanted headlines: a tramp in the bins holds more feeling and tenderness, honour and valour than any stylised prose from lofty leader writers. Yet I am Institutionalised Man at his worst because I've been to hell and back on Devil Mountain and so I should know better. I wear him like the smell of death on my sleeve. *I'll never be rid of him.* To be truly free of him, I would have to kill him; obliterate him: yes, like my character who chucks himself off the Post Office Tower, I'd have to commit suicide. Is this was I've really come to?

'. . . They said they'd want to interview you when you feel up to it..'

'Humph!'

Ben! You haven't heard a word I've said. Are you feeling alright? Oh. I forgot the tranquilliser. No, don't fuss. I'll not hear of it. It'll calm you down. Your mind is running off with the universe by the second.'

He watched her move across the room to her handbag. She was a marvel! So too were Paddy and the boy. And his cat. But outside of them the mountain had no rival. Thank God he still had them! There he went again: you don't believe in any god, Ben. Not even figuratively speaking! You may have them now, but God has nothing at all to do with it. Like man and love, religion and the so-called true deity escaped him in a sea of pragmatism and theological dialectics. Who needed faith, damn it, assuming you were fighting for your spiritual and temporal life? *And love!* If you needed it you took a woman to bed. You can't love an idea, a myth. Really love it! No woman appreciates being shoved on a pedestal. She needs to be taken, to smell it and be exhausted by the whole physical and mental experience. Compared to that, religion in general and Christianity in particular, seemed like a dried up crab in an oil slick. No, love came with old age and they called it tolerance. But of what, he wasn't sure. Coexistence, now there was something to believe in; fight for.

'You're drifting again,' she said. 'Take this. No, don't worry, it's only a mild sedative really. That's it. You'll feel drowsy soon. I'll be here when you wake up. Relax and you'll sleep well and deep, my darling.'

His head dropped onto her breast. He didn't know why, but he said: 'I love you, Sally.'

She touched his face and smiled. 'I love you, too, Ben. But I hate your mountain.'

Benjamin dropped into a small, shining orchard where he could see just one man picking apples. Everything was gold; gold trees, gold apples, gold sky, even the man was a golden figure. He went over to introduce himself, and when the man turned round, he saw that he was looking at himself.

CHAPTER 10

A sliver of late afternoon sunlight reflected off the ice crusted creek, shooting a momentary silver beam across Dickens' face. He was on his legs clapping in human style as his mate cantered majestically over the scrub. Life was good again, now that the Odd One had taken his mate and the cub away from the mountain.

A shadow rippled over the undulating snow and he looked up as the female eagle floated lazily on a thermal towards the red box canyon. Making a fist, he shook it angrily for he did not like the bird: she was forever out of his grasp.

She arrived hot and wet and steamy and he clubbed her playfully as the eagle changed direction to circle overhead. The two bears fought and rolled happily in the snow; Dickens urging her to mate on the spot knowing she preferred a certain place by the tree-ringed dam.

Frustrated, he began racing in wide circles, calling out loud as the snow cascaded from his giant paws. Content for the moment, she watched his antics with glee, even clapping encouragement as he smashed the ice over the creek and bounded along the snaking bank towards the beaver dam. She knew that soon he would cover her and the playfulness would end. Oh, she wanted him again, but by the dam. She wasn't too pleased about loving on his ice plateau: it was a place of death.

As Dickens sprinted shorter and shorter bursts along the bank, the female knew that it would not be long now: his erection would come and he would mount her immediately. Grunting softly, she led the way over the scrub towards the dam. Dickens charged eagerly after her, galloping noisily around her all the way to the sacred spot.

Raising a wing tip, the female eagle planed across the valley towards the mesa on the higher slopes opposite Devil Mountain. She knew of the he-bear's intentions; wondered about her own man. He seemed to have forgotten 'her' whom she had killed, and whom the man had taken away on his back the day the he-bear had nearly destroyed the man from the timberline. True, they still flapped wings, but he *thought* more of her in the ways that had lapsed while 'she' had been around.

Dropping onto a boulder at the edge of the mesa, she surveyed the valley below. She mustn't stop too long; the children were growing and needed more food than ever. It was amazing the amount that they ate! If they didn't grow faster, the creek would be empty of fish before the spring.

Shaking her great body, she took off and immediately lost altitude as the creek glistened below. Swooping like quicksilver, she caught a large trout and turned for the nest. Crossing the timberline, she saw the frozen footprints belonging to the man and his child. But she knew that they had left for the lowlands. Maybe they were afraid of the great snow falls that always occurred after the steel bird flew over the mountain.

A brief snow squall blew off the rock face and she was lost in the gloom and silence of the high country.

★　★　★　★　★

The bar of the Buffalo Creek Motel had had to be renovated after Paddy Martin's set-to with the hunters. Today, it was crowded with weekend drinkers. Tucked away in a smoky corner of the hubbub, The Beard and Eb sat thoughtfully. The Beard's jaw had knitted perfectly. It had been a week since the hit and run in Denver and tempers were frayed; nerves on edge.

'Looking back, it was stupid, The Beard said under cover of the din. 'I shouldn't have listened to you.'

'Hold it right there, pal!' Eb leaning across the table. 'We're in this together. You didn't see anything wrong with the idea before, so don't now.'

'The whore might talk. She could make a deal with the cops, that's how her kind survives. *They use anybody.*'

'She wasn't the only one on the street,' Eb scratching his shiny dome. 'Why should she be picked up? You're panicking.'

'Because she is what she is, idiot!' The Beard losing his temper. 'Her kind are the eyes and ears of the streets.'

Eb laughed until the rolls of fat in his neck rippled. But his mirth was short-lived as The Beard glared across the table.

'Listen egghead, if she was picked up for routine questioning, OK, she mightn't blab. But that welfare woman and the Mick was visiting had dealings with her, and she might if the cops put two and two together. We hit him outside the welfare woman's place. It all ties in.'

'The welfare woman has no reason to make any connection,' Eb lighting up.

'She might have if the Limey came on the scene! Can't figure out the angle, though. Maybe it's the kid. Maybe the Limey came to town with the Mick – he might even know the welfare woman. If someone gives a description, he'll know it's us.'

Eb's face straightened. 'The Mick's off the critical list – I had someone call. Do you think he saw us?'

'Nah. It was dark and the neons were flashing like Christmas trees. All he saw were headlights. Eradicate the whore and our problems are over.'

140

'It's getting messy,' Eb knifing his dirty fingernails. 'Too many people involved. Up in the mountains it would be simple . . .'

'But we're not up there, are we!' hissed The Beard dangerously. 'Who's losing his nerve now? Remember, you drove the Chevvy, so you're past your neck. Listen,' patting his friend on the arm. 'People go missing all the time in the city. One more'll make no difference.'

'You don't seem too worried about the Limey or the Mick?'

The Beard smiled thoughtfully. 'The Mick will know, but he's half dead. From what I hear, he likes a low profile. And he's still wanted for busting up this place and the job you boys did on the hearse. No, he won't talk. The Limey's a meathead, so there's no problem there. Anyway, we've got alibis in Jake and Wilma. Speaking of the devil, here comes my honourable brother-in-law. Go get the round in and stop worrying.'

'Hi fellas,' greeted Jake. 'There's a woman asking for you in the pool hall. Hooker by the look of her. From Denver, I'd say. Changing your line of business,' he grinned.

Eb caught the steely glint in The Beard's eye. Maybe it was going to be easier than they thought. He whistled all the way to the bar.

★　★　★　★　★

Paddy Martin groaned softly, but otherwise showed no outward sign of life.

The young nurse made several notes on a clipboard and quietly left the room.

Paddy knew he was hurt. Badly. But he didn't feel a thing. The morphine killed everything. Life was one long dream after another. He couldn't control them. It was as though they had taken over his subconscious and delivered him to a land of nerverending technicolour videos – with him in the leading role every time.

Like right now, for instance. He was falling through the clouds – for the umpteenth time since whatever happened to him happened – towards a country he knew vaguely far below surrounded by water. Off to his left he saw Benjamin chopping

141

firewood, while the boy tried to hide behind a cloud from a man he'd never seen before with the cat playing football at his feet. He waved, but none seemed aware of his presence as he continued to fall earthwards.

Corkscrewing past an eagle carrying a fish, he narrowly missed the grizzly he-bear chasing a female across the skies. But downwards, forever downwards, and still failing to recognise the land below, he thought: I should know this place. Hell, it's so familiar . . . That river is like a long winding snake. He closed his eyes as the ground rushed up to meet him.

Blacking for a while, he came to crouching behind a large packing case in a huge, dark shed. He could taste fog in his mouth, and although he couldn't feel it, he sensed that it was intensely cold near the river. He knew there was water nearby because he could hear ships' horns blaring through the mist.

Not long now, he mused. *Not long for what?* He knew – and he didn't. That is, his subconscious knew, but it wasn't telling him. Nevertheless, it was a hell of a place to do what it was he was about to do. Take it easy, Paddy, all will be revealed in time. Just go with things while you're here.

Something triggered in his mind and instantly he knew everything: he was on an operation. The High Command of the IRA had sent him to London – of course, that winding river was the Thames – to eliminate an informer. The man, a Derry man, had been giving information to the British Army about Provo safe houses in Armagh near the border with the Republic. By a stroke of luck, he had been tipped off and the British had spirited him across to the English capital. It had taken time, but the informer had been found living in a bedsit in Camden Town with a gossipy shop girl. He worked as a fork-lift driver on the docks. And that was where he was now – in one of the hundreds of warehouses that lined the London waterfront.

Rubbing his cramped legs – again, he felt nothing, but sensed that they were sore – Paddy changed position only to freeze as the sound of voices came on the river breeze.

Two men moved into the shed from the jetty fifty yards in front of the Irishman. Well done, Delaney, he thought. The perfect set-up. Carefully, he took out the Walther PPK and slipped off the safety. Three to the head for you, boyo. Bring him home, Delaney, as the men moved closer, bring the bastard home.

Only when the unsuspecting victim was several yards away did Paddy make his move. Apart from a mouthful of abuse for Delaney, the man's nerve dropped to stark fear as his executioner moved from his position behind the packing case.

Paddy recited the standard IRA death sentence and raised the Walther; the man pleaded and fell to his knees. The Irishman spun on his heels as a voice rang out ordering him to put up his weapon. Even as Delaney began to run, Paddy shot him through the spine, quickly repeating the process through the informer's head before diving back behind the packing case.

So, the informer had been a patsy all the time: Delaney was the real traitor out to catch Paddy himself. The Special Branch had once more broken Army security, damn them to hell.

His ears whistled as a hail of lead smashed into the wall and floor all round. Then silence before the megaphone voice called out once more. Paddy replied by sending two rounds in the general direction.

Studying a hole in the shed, he estimated that he could just squeeze through onto the jetty. Squirming on his belly, he pulled himself through the gap into the foul tasting London fog. His heart hammered in his breast at the sight confronting him: a dozen motor-boats bristled with rifles, while above on the shed roof, police marksmen held him in their sights.

'Your number's up, Paddy,' he breathed. 'But you'll go down fighting.' He managed to hit two policemen before he was knocked violently backwards, his body riddled with bullets. Lying still and lifeless on the damp jetty, he stared unseeing up at the storm clouds overhead.

He awoke to unconsciousness because his injuries from the car attack refused admittance to consciousness. He was now in a mist-filled box from where he could see Benjamin far above still cutting his wood and Sam still running from the world. Although Dickens had disappeared along with his mate, the eagle still hovered over his life like some winged Damocles Sword and it made him scream. And then everything went black.

The doctor smiled at the young nurse and placed the syringe

back into a tray. 'His heart's excited,' he said, pointing at the screen on the support machine.

'He must be having a dream,' she said.

'Then let's hope he's enjoying it,' replied the doctor. 'With any luck, he should be out of the coma in the next day or so.'

★ ★ ★ ★ ★

It was Benjamin's second week away from the mountain and Sally had cut his hair and trimmed his beard. Dickens' claw marks, however, served as a gruesome reminder of Devil Mountain. Nothing was said about his finger. Carefully, she nursed his mind back to normal. But now there was the hit and run and the boy had been taken from him . . .

Harry Miller had flown up from Cascade shortly after Paddy's hospitalisation and had sat dumbstruck as Benjamin recounted his three months on the timberline. Ben needs treatment, he thought, and from what I can see, Sally Brown is the best person to administer it. 'Do you realise what you look like – *what you've become!* I'm glad I didn't see the hair,' forcing a smile.

Sometimes Benjamin would leave his tale and ramble incoherently or mutter something about a rat and an eagle. He had broken into a sweat talking about living beneath the snow to keep warm. During an ugly outburst, he had rolled over and over on the floor tearing at his clothes, shouting: 'I don't want to drown . . . No Dickens. No . . .'

Harry had shaken his head. 'I was wrong not to have stopped him, Sally,' he had said. 'I could have, but I didn't try hard enough. Anoxia has given him a terrible time. It's crucified that brain of his, but he's far stronger than I gave him credit. Thank God you came along when you did! How involved was he with the boy?'

'Initially, he wasn't,' pouring tea. 'He resented Sam's intrusion in his private world. But eventually, he grew fond of him and maybe that was my fault because I told him that Sam was his responsibility while he was up there. The boy told me he saved him from a mountain lion in a cave after he had fallen down a water-filled pothole. Not a peep from Ben. Lord knows how many things he's keeping to himself! Then the boy's cat saved them both from an avalanche, and I shudder to think of how many escapades he's had with that grizzly. Maybe Paddy knows something, poor man. However, I think Sam and his cat are more responsible for his retaining sanity than he realises. In his mind, the boy is part of the timberline. Symbolical. Ben actually resents being back in civilisation.'

Harry closed his eyes for a moment. 'His resentment can turn to something else, you know. I warned him about mountain living, but he was determined to see it through. I blame myself! We go back years to Fleet Street. So he hasn't found himself! No suicidal tendencies?'

Her face paled. *'No, thank God.* But he's over Rosemary. Finally. She isn't his social conscience any longer. He knows now where they went wrong. It's what happened in his childhood, that bothers me. Apparently it all came back on the mountain. Did he ever mention his younger days?'

'He hinted at some of it. But journalists' bars aren't really the ideal backcloth for matters reminiscence. You mustn't let him go back up there – if he does, he may well never return. I'm sorry to have to say this, but I've seen many cases like Ben's – and he's got more brains than they had which only deepens the problem. Really, you must stop him.'

'I can't, Harry, anymore than you could in the first place. His worlds have switched: he's immune – or thinks he is up there – but he's lost down here. You should have seen him the first time he went to see Paddy! I honestly thought he would get thrown into a padded cell – and I wouldn't have fancied their chances. He can't handle people, that's why the mountain in the first place. It could have been a desert or the bottom of the ocean, they're all the same: no people. He needs time to heal all the hurts, and if it has to be Devil Mountain, then I'll be waiting for him at the bottom when he's ready to rejoin us *'goofballs'.'*

Harry smiled. 'I told him that. He told you?'

'Yes. It's an apt description.'

Harry got up and went to the window. 'I was thinking of him the other day, up there alone in all that goddamned space with nothing but a grizzly for a neighbour: He calmly writing his memoirs or whatever while the bear beats down the door. It gave me the creeps.'

Returning to his chair: 'I don't want to frighten you, but after what happened to Paddy, I think you should go away for a while. And away from any mountains. The plains aren't bad, had some great times there with the wife and kids.'

Sally was nodding her head slowly and blowing into a handkerchief. 'It's all too much for Ben at the moment. It's a novel, not memoirs. I think Sam became a part of the writing by being there. The story is a double tragedy, but now, losing the boy in reality, it has become threefold in his mind. George, my brother-in-law, has a place in Montana. We could go there.'

If the mountain wasn't enough, thought Harry, he has to take on a book and substitute fantasy for reality. Well, he nearly lost it – reality. 'And Sam? he said softly.

'He's gone to good people in Blackhawk. Out of our area, but we felt after all the news coverage a change of environment was imperative for the settling in period. It's a trial situation only. I even . . . It's silly really, a woman's stupid dreams, but I even thought that Ben and I could . . .'

Harry smiled and touched her hand. 'That is truly beautiful.'

Wiping her nose, she added: 'Like Ben, I have also let my characters get too close. I suppose all of us sometime in our lives are guilty of a similar crime.'

Harry stared into his empty tea cup. He remembered Benjamin quoting Rosemary: she had said the same thing. Sally was also a triple tragedy: she stood to lose a half demented man she loved, her one true shot at happiness and possibly the only chance to set up a home for the three of them. Oh boy!

'Leave the hunters to me. I have some pull with the a good precinct guy. He can start with the hooker. Then . . .'

'*She's disappeared.* I know because I took her son away.'

Harry groaned mentally. 'Is the Irishman able to talk yet?'

'The doctors say next week.'

★　★　★　★　★

146

Sam Fynn walked along the garden path. The snow was hard, icy-grey underfoot and uninviting. It wasn't timberline snow. Boogaloo scampered with his pine cone as the boy looked westward past a highrise apartment block across the street and visualised Benjamin working on his pipeline, hunting in the valley or writing his book. It was easiest imagining him working on the pipeline. His symbolical pipeline. Suddenly everything, Virginia and all that revolved around the cabin seemed so far away as to never have existed at all. Picking up the pine cone: *'Didn't it really!'* He was sorry about Paddy.

'*Samuel*,' a woman called. '*Oh Saam-uu-el . . . Boogaalooo.* Time for lunch.'

He forced a smile for Nora Corncliff and her husband, Bill, standing in the doorway. 'They're what I've always wanted, Boogie, but now I want Ben.'

'It's your favourite again, Samuel,' said Bill Corncliff. 'Where did you ever develop such a liking for Irish stew. Was your mother . . .'

'She was from Idaho, sir,' eyeing Kaiser, the alsatian.

'Don't you think Boogaloo gets on with Kaiser, Samuel,' the man trying to cover his gaffe.

'You can call us Mom and Pop,' said Nora Corncliff, giving him a hug. 'Now run along and wash your hands, Samuel.'

You could call me Sam, he thought, taking the stairs two at a time. He stopped as the alsatian let out a loud yelp in the kitchen. *'Yeah, Boogie sure loves Kaiser.'*

CHAPTER 11

Benjamin was impossible: impossible to live with, impossible
with himself, impossible with anyone Sally – she had taken all
her overdue leave – allowed near on medical grounds. But as
winter deepened around the Montana smallholding, he at last
showed signs of improvement.

The property had been in her brother-in-law's family since the
'30s and Sonia had taken George there to forget the horrors of
Vietnam. Run down, almost to the point of delapidation, the two
bedroomed farmhouse with its twenty acres of grassland was
heaven to Benjamin and Sally.

Unless he volunteered, they never spoke of the mountain or the
hunters. The question of Sam and his cat was taboo. Instead, they
talked about their respective countries and the things that mature
lovers talk of with no need to hide like youth behind the bitter-
sweet perfumed pillars of treachery. They witheld no secrets and
the learning was a pleasant voyage across the years where danger
and betrayal were cushioned by experience and simple, straight-
forward honesty.

Physical love came simplest of all: shining, with no youthful delusions of mystique to compensate experience. Yet it rose to a grateful, soul-engulfing climax of two people verging on the autumn of their lives. Passion was rekindled with complete acceptance. Living, loving, talking, they explored hearts and minds and bodies with insatiable longing. The wedding date was set for May.

In early November, Paddy Martin banged on the door with a crutch. The Millers, who drifted in and out of the farmhouse like weekend relations, brought Sam on several occasions; more often, the boy would arrive unnanounced with his cat just as he had always done. Out of earshot, Harry told Paddy that the prostitute had disappeared. The Irishman seemed unconcerned.

Planned to coincide with Sally's birthday, the engagement party was a riotous affair. After a meal in Hardin on the Bighorn River, everybody returned to the farmhouse to further toast the happy couple. The arrival of Indian John and his son brought tears of joy to Sally; Benjamin hugged his old friends. Along with the Millers and Sonia's family – three children and George and Custer the dog who endured a running battle with Boogaloo – Paddy and Sam made up the numbers.

At a quiet moment in the proceedings, Harry took Benjamin outside as a stiffening wind swept off the plains from the Bighorn Mountains far to the south. 'What's your next move?' he asked.

'You're thinking about Immigration,' Benjamin, acutely aware of his disfigurement, turned away. 'I don't like what happened to Paddy,' he growled.

'None of us does. Don't get any fancy ideas about becoming Rambo Two. You've become a hard cookie, but you took a few bad knocks up there. You nearly went insane! Why not come to us for a bit; Hank and Annie never stop talking about you. They would've stayed longer, but they've got mid-term exams.'

'I just can't leave Paddy after all he's done.'

'Bring him with! What do you say?'

Benjamin walked towards a tree near the fenceline. 'Does that job offer still stand? With the face?'

'Ever heard of plastic surgery! They'll make you better than you were – that shouldn't be too difficult. Come and see Gabass and he'll start you in the New Year. Christ, the turnround in editorial staff, you wouldn't believe!'

Benjamin saw Paddy's profile through the open doorway; a bitter, lost man. Harry caught the look. 'What line's he in? Maybe I can fix him up, too.'

'Not ours. I don't think he plans to stay here. He misses Ireland and . . . He doesn't talk about it.'

Harry detected the subtle inference: so Paddy had a secret. But there was that glazed look in Benjamin's eyes. 'You're going back, aren't you,' his voice husky. 'Do you want to screw it up for yourself and Sally?' His voice rose: 'What the hell's the matter? How much finding do you have to do?'

'The book will be completed in spring, I can't let it go. It's bigger than me. The mountain was where I started it, and that's where it'll end. There are still other things I have to do up there.' His voice challenged: 'Jesus Harry, it's only once in my life!'

'*Once, my ass!* I agree, it'll end all right – in more ways than one. Sally, the job and Immigration for a few. Me and Helen for another. You're kind of taking it for granted that Gabass and the rest of us will keep hanging on for Ben Thompson. You're a good journalist, but not that good. Spring, you say. By that time you'll be an undesirable alien. You're supposed to be a highly intelligent man! Instead, you're acting like a goddamned teenager.'

Benjamin's face twisted in a cruel grin. 'Whatever happened to all that hands across the sea stuff?'

Harry purpled. 'That damned mountain's gotten you,' he snarled. 'I warned you! You think you can go round pussy-footing on some nature kick and the world can go to hell. Have I got news for you, pal: you're becoming an embarrassment. I've soft-shoed Gabass and Immigration for an asshole who can't grow up. Go on, hit me. I can see it in your eyes.'

Benjamin's fists unclenched at his side. He didn't like what he was hearing. How had things got so out of hand? Hit Harry! *Christ, an embarrassment! How much have I got into Devil Mountain? Or it into me!*

Harry moved in close. 'I told you last summer that your arguements weren't reasonable. Well, now they're bloody ridiculous. You can finish off your damn book anywhere – if you're a writer. You're taking advantage of hospitality, Ben. You're not the man I knew.'

Benjamin walked along the fence, fingering the snow on the

'Yes Ma'am,' replied Sam. He was sitting in a chair opposite the couple, watching Boogaloo through the window teasing the alsatian near the food bowls. He grinned as the dog yelped and bounded round the garden.

'Oh,' exclaimed the woman in exasperation. 'Really Samuel, Boogaloo is a trifle on the rough side.'

'Now, now, Nora. It's only a kitten. He's playing,' interceded the husband.

'You sang a different tune when you got the last vet's bill,' she said glumly.

Somewhere, a clock struck five and the room fell silent as if the chimes had proclaimed some terrible and odious announcement.

'I'm sorry, Ma'am,' said Sam eventually. 'I'll whistle him inside. He's not a kitten, Sir, he's a runt. Boogie's just on the small side, that's all.'

Bill Cornclift smiled nervously. The tension was mounting. And the lad would persist in calling them 'Sir' and 'Ma'am'. He didn't want to lose the boy: Sam had the makings and Nora had set her heart on him. If it hadn't been for that accident during the factory inspection '. . . *you'll be sterilised, Bill,*' they had said. '*But you'll get well compensated . . .*' How do you get compensated for a thing like that? he had asked himself over the years. Covering his growing fears over keeping the lad: 'Why do you whistle him, Sam? He's not a dog.'

'You can't say "here, Puss-Puss", half way up a mountain. Sounds stupid.'

'Yes, I suppose it does,' glancing once more at his wife.

'Do you like Clint Eastwood, Samuel?' she asked.

'Yes, Ma'am.'

'Good, then that's settled. We'll take in the early show. It's that one about the orangoutang. Odd how they give wild animals names, isn't it, Bill?'

Sam thought of Dickens. That wasn't in the least bit odd. I wonder how Ben's getting along? he thought. He longed for the man and his stupid symbolic pipeline. Apart from a single phone call after the engagement party, there'd been no word. Was that it? Finished! Cut off like a useless limb. Ben said civilisation wasn't good for some people: it changed them. Well, whatever happens, I won't stay here.

153

Boogaloo jumped onto his lap, stretched contentedly, straightened his walking stick tail and drifted off. So did Sam.

When they woke him for the movie, he cried out: 'No Dickens! No!' The Cornclifts didn't know what to make of him.

★   ★   ★   ★   ★

Dickens sniffed the wind. Food! His mate had returned to the box canyon where she would hibernate until the rivers and mountains melted with thunder water. The hunting had been good since the odd one had disappeared with his hairy mate and the cub with its rat-like creature. Today, he would take one of the beavers working on their dam in the creek.

Crossing the timberline, he stopped at the cabin. Icicles hung everywhere; drifts covered the window slats. Waddling closer, he pushed away the snow and stared inside. He grunted at the pack lying in a corner. The odd one hadn't eaten much from the headless animal! Then why did he carry it? Banging the wall in a fit of temper, he loped off through the forest and rolled down the lower slopes into the valley where a cold sun threw diamonds off the splintered ice on the creek.

The grizzly's fur ruffled as wind shot through the valley. Moving off-wind, he stood on his hind legs, snout twitching for a scent of the beaver. Using the drifts for cover, he stomped to the southern end of the valley.

Unaware of the approaching danger, the adult beavers chomped on bark; six-month-old pups played near the underwater lodge. The colony consisted of male and female and four young. Handprint front and webbed hind tracks, congested the morning's light snow on the banks of the creek.

Dickens' moment came as a male pup strayed towards his hiding place. He moved fast – but not fast enough. Dislodging snow from a branch, the 'plop' alerted the young beaver. Darting for a hole in the ice, it disappeared beneath the surface. His presence known, Dickens charged blindly after the family, trying to lessen the angle to the lodge entrance in the hope of catching one of the young. Bounding around in circles, his large claws skated along the creek until he collided untidily with the dam. Looking on angrily as the family vanished beneath the ice, he beat the crust in frustration, his discontent echoing through the timber and into the neighbouring box canyon. Like a spoilt child, he bashed his head against a pine; tore branches and jumped up and down.

Still raging, he galloped out into the snow-laden scrub, bashing the drifts and thumping his chest: temper almost cost him a wounded elk, its blood smell strong. Balancing like a ballerina, he pirouetted as his nose sniffed the wind while the frightened animal stood motionless in the trees ringing the dam. Dickens had lost the Odd One there: he would kill today.

In summer he had been a twelve pointed bull elk. Brownish-grey, antlers shed for winter, he stood almost five feet to the shoulder: nine hundred pounds of injured majesty. Losing his cows to a younger male, he had wandered along the Colorado seeking sanctuary; time to lick his wounds. He had cause to be frightened: his blood smell would alert the wolf packs and cougars from their mountain lairs. Possibly he could outrun the wolves, but not the cats. The grizzly would end things quickly.

The scent now hammered in Dickens' nostrils. He knew the elk was heavier, but it was hurt. It wouldn't survive a long chase. Not needing to stay off windline, he, nevertheless, approached with caution. He knew all about the dangers of a wounded victim. Finally, his rolling gait turned to a trot, then a canter, and, as the elk broke from cover in fear, he charged full tilt in pursuit, kicking up snow clouds that sparkled in his wake.

The chase was on.

Streaking towards the creek, the elk stumbled and regained balance in the loosely packed snow. Turning, he clattered over the ice, eyes bulging, neck muscles taught in a desperate, agonising effort to outdistance his thundering adversary.

Galloping along the bank, Dickens drew level with the tiring elk. Clubbing and clawing, he finally powered home a lethal swing that broke the luckless creature's neck sending it sliding across the ice to slam into the beaver dam.

In less than a minute, hunter and hunted had covered nearly a thousand yards. In less than half that time, Dickens disembowelled the elk before dragging the carcass into the forest. He ate long and well. Too heavy to take to his ice plateau, he slept by his prize while the mountain predators glared from the treeline. On wakening, he tore off several chunks of meat and climbed the mountain while the bobcats closed on the remains of the carcass.

Pausing on the timberline, Dickens glared once more at the cabin: the Odd One would return. His kind always did. This time, he would be waiting.

★ ★ ★ ★ ★

Aghast, Harry Miller listened to Lieutenant Mike Robinson's gruesome tale of how the prostitute had been eaten alive by wolves after apparently losing her way in the forest.

The two men sat in a roadhouse staring at the contents of Sally Brown's dossier on the dead woman – Annaline Kapok – spread over the table. Robinson, quickly digesting the woman's history with practiced ease, trumpeted into an already soiled handkerchief. 'You say this Sally Brown reckons the hooker lied about those guys who hit the Irishman – if they hit him.'

'Sally's a good judge of character – or lack of it,' Harry tearing the wrapper from a fresh pack of filters. 'This is a big favour, Mike. I know you trod on toes to find out about the woman. Since when does a city-loving hooker go on nature rambles in the depths of winter! And probably at night, according to the autopsy. She had to be taken there by someone who knew the country. The woman knew too much and somebody got nervous. She could have connected them to . . .' He stopped as the policeman's pouch-like bags pulsed beneath bloodshot eyes.

'You didn't finish, Harry! the man again blowing into his handkerchief. 'Who are you trying to protect?'

Harry stared at the coffee dregs in the greasy cup. 'The Irishman's had a few close encounters with your boys. Trouble and Immigration don't mix.'

Robinson's eyebrows knitted. 'Go on.'

Harry repeated what little Benjamin had told him about Paddy.

The policeman sneezed violently. 'Damn this cold! You say this guy Thompson, the Limey, has been living on Devil Mountain?'

156

'Something he had to do.'

'One born every minute! Balls or lunacy, I'm not sure which. OK, let's see if I've got this right,' numbering the points on his fingers. 'Your pal goes up a mountain to do his thing and along comes this spud-loving, bar-breaking Mick who brings trouble in his pocket and the two of 'em bust a couple of hunters' heads. Friend Thompson chats up the local grizzly and the enemy hightail it. Next, he gets a call from his fiancée-to-be, that the nomadic Irishman came off second best to an unidentified vehicle, and rushes into Denver like something out of Buffalo Bill's circus. The kid, by the way, how the hell . . . ?'

'Forget him. He's been adopted since – or at any rate, someone's taken him on trial.'

'Poor bastards! Sam Fynn has made more headlines and police bulletins than Legs Diamond and Capone put together.'

'It's simple! All you've got to find out is who she talked to. One thing should lead to another. There had to be other people on the street that night.'

Robinson shook his head. 'This ain't Kojak. The scumbags I deal with have read too many thrillers; seen too many Dirty Harrys. They get scientific! You'll have to be patient.'

Harry grinned as Robinson almost blew his nose off.

'Holy shithooks!' cried the policeman. 'I can get a line on those hunters, but I can't charge 'em with anything. The car'll be long gone or turn out to be hired under a false name from another state; the hooker's in the past tense, so she can't help and the Irishman insists he never saw a thing except the headlights. No, you'll have to play the waiting game. A change for you Press types!'

Harry piqued. 'Explain!'

'*The bear lover*. I'll arrange for his fiancée's protection – just in case – but I think it's him they'll come after. He's the one standing between them and the chair by association – if you see what I mean. The fight! Sorry, but I'm falling for something: 'flu probably. Incidentally, was the boy there during the fight on the timberline?'

Harry felt dizzy. 'They tried to shoot his cat,' he replied. This is getting dirtier, he thought. How did all this come about? Answering his own question: a goddamned news show in Liverpool, that's how! Ben and his bloody mountain.

'He should be OK, but I'll put a man on him, too.'

'You had that look about you just then. The waiting game, you said. You've got somethig in mind for Ben, haven't you. He's a great pal of mine, Mike.' He suddenly felt very old. *What am I doing? All this talk about murder and breaking up decent people's lives. He wants to use Ben to bait two murderers. My own friend!* 'Christ, Mike,' he exploded. 'That would mean . . .'

The police lieutenant's face darkened. 'That's right! He's got to go back up his mountain.'

'You can't be serious! I've just talked him down from it. He's just recovered from a bad dose of anoxia and a near fatal mauling from Dick . . . the grizzly. You know the mountains, Mike. It's inhuman!'

'So is murder and the attempted version,' parried the policeman. 'Talk him back up it. Don't worry, I'll look after him, *but talk him back up.*'

Harry lit a fresh smoke. He fingered the veins rippling on his temple. *Blood pressure,* he thought. *That's all I need.* He stood up, but his legs jellied.

Robinson smiled affectionately. 'I'll speak to the Englishman first. You handle his ladyfriend. It'll be all right on the night, as they say.'

'And the Irishman?'

'I won't blow him to Immigration. There's a little Irish in me, and what you've told me, tells me he doesn't like the way things are being run in the Emerald Isle. Just tell him to keep his nose clean. Hell, would you look at that rain out there: it's coming down in sheets!'

Harry bid the man goodbye and walked through the downpour to his car. Robinson hadn't said it, but he knew the hunters wouldn't return to Denver . . . *He's the one standing between them and the chair* . . . *The bastards expect Ben to go back, too – and I've got to make sure he does. Oh how cruel this blasted existence!*

Switching on the wipers, he stared through the running windscreen. Waiting for his nerves to settle before starting up, he said to the exhaust-fogged rear of Robinson's car skidding off the cinder: 'What do I do? I can't just commit my friend to his death. *Holy, sweet Jesus, what do I do?*'

CHAPTER 12

Harry Miller flopped behind his desk; his head dropped into his hands. The conference had gone badly: Gabass was pushing for the interview with Benjamin, Immigration were rattling and his nerves were frayed over the Hill's reaction to Opec's oil increase. And to cap it all, he couldn't tell Helen about Mike Robinson's plan using Benjamin to lure the prostitute's killer into the open.

His open door admitted the clatter of typewriters attacking the Monday morning behind glass partitions. His own office was fogged with cigarette smoke; stale butts stank from improvised ashtrays. The weekly news conference had shredded everyone's nerves, but Gabass had gone overboard on the political intrigues surrounding the Middle East oil hike. He stiffened at the editor's parting words: 'If Ben Thompson doesn't want the job, that's fine! If he doesn't pitch Friday, nine sharp, he can forget it.' By way of a parting salvo: 'Don't forget that piece on UN costings before lunch.'

Having written most of the article over the weekend, he now

concentrated on the final paragraphs. The phone rang and he jumped nervously, spilling cold coffee over the feature. It was Helen. 'I don't care about dirty Arabs or features,' she said hotly. 'Or who your lunch engagement is with. Cancel! Something's wrong! You haven't had nightmares since Watergate. La Riviera: one on the dot or I'll drag you from that newspaper office – Gabass and all.'

Harry rolled his eyes and replaced the receiver. His glance fell on the wall calendar. 'Jeese,' he muttered. 'The bloody thirteenth. Some Monday!'

'Sir?' A young copy typist stood in he doorway holding a tray of coffee cups.

'Just thinking out loud Melanie,' he grumbled. 'We're in the wrong business.'

The girl eyed him speculatively beneath long lashes. Wiping the mess from the desk, she left grinning as Harry salvaged the UN costings.

Somehow, he survived the morning. The wall clock raced until it said 12.30. Donning hat and coat, he snatched the article and hurried to the subs' department. 'Sorry about the rush, Jim. Gabass wants it before hamburger time.'

A pasty complexioned man in his mid-twenties smiled a smile that said he understood the eccentricities of harrassed editors and egotistical feature writers.

Harry took the stairs two at a time. He arrived breathless and sweating at La Riviera.

Helen, cool and composed, sat at a corner table: they never sat at corner tables. She means business, all right, he thought sullenly.

'You look all in, my dear! Shall I order? Your usual?'

'If you like – no, make it an omelette. Cheese. Stomach's a little on the light side. Monday and all that. Expensive here, isn't it!'

'It makes a change,' replied Helen matter-of-factly. 'Now Mr Political Editor, put your circus away and tell me what's happening in the Miller House on the Hill.'

Benjamin thanked the librarian, picked up his books and

strolled out into the drizzle. He used Helen's tickets twice a week. Walking the two blocks to a small restaurant, he waited for Sally. She drove alternate weekends to Cascade; he took a Greyhound to Denver.

Ordering coffee, he stared idly at fish swimming in a tank in a corner of the room. The coffee came with a smile as he traced the weeks since the engagement party. Paddy had progressed like a superman. Admittedly, he had not kept in close touch with Sam, but he was writing a letter, though omitting the seamier side of the recent events; he had replied to Rosemary, wishing her all the best for the future. Things were fine at the Miller place – at least that's the impression everyone gives, he thought, lapsing into a smile as he remembered the halcyon days since leaving the smallholding . . .

. . . They had left Montana in heavy snow, arriving at Cascade under a frigid, miserable sun and freezing, stiff breezes.

'We could have stayed with Harry,' he said one afternoon as he cast a disapproving eye over the hotel decor. Paddy had been fussed over by Hank and Annie.

'It would have been too much for poor Helen! Anyway, they've got their lives to live, Ben,' coming into his arms. 'Paddy's enough! Besides, I want my man to myself. Do you think we should wait until May, darling? The wedding, I mean.'

Benjamin kissed her on the lips. 'Think I'll run away?' nibbling her ear.

'No,' she smiled. 'I've got you by hook, line and mountain, Mr Thompson. May, it is. It will give me time to sort things out while you master your new job on the Sun.'

But try as he may to think of the future, his face tightened around the scar as Lieutenant Robinson's words slammed inside his head like a sledge hammer on an empty oil drum: *A lot of people seem to be revolving around you . . . You owe it to them to go back up there . . . It may be nothing, but you'll handle it . . . I don't want your bloodbath on my streets . . .'*

Blinking away the memory, he said: 'Do you want to stay in Denver after we're married?'

She shook her head. 'It'd drive you crazy. And that trip back and forth! No, it's much quieter here for my writing man. I'll get a transfer, don't worry.'

He kissed her again. 'You don't mind my writing to Rosemary?'

'I'd have insisted on it. You belong to me, now, and I want her to know it. I'm glad for her too, of course, but I want her to know about us, too.'

Benjamin picked her up and walked to the bed. 'She'll make out. He's in the fashion game as well. You might say she married one of her own designs.'

'*Oh Ben!* What a thing to say.' She giggled. 'Just what do you think you're up to?' as he lowered her onto the bed and undid the clasp at the back of her dress. 'We've just got here!'

'We arrived a long time ago, my love,' kissing her neck and tracing his fingertips over the smooth alabaster of her breasts, enjoying the firm, pink nipples.

'At least let me close the drapes and lock the door,' she breathed, holding up her dress.

They undressed one another; stood facing naked and paining for release. Her eyes showed want, needing his strength upon her; his maleness deep inside her. And then he took her gently, bringing them to a plain of physical and mental calm before hunger consumed their passion, exploding them in an entangled, tortuous, releasing cataclysm that drove them beyond sexual fulfilment to a blessed, peaceful unity.

The telephone shrilled as they lay spent, staring at the ceiling. It was Paddy. 'We're just going for a walk. Call you later.'

'What did he want?' asked Sally later as she stopped the car by the park.

'Just to talk. It's not his cup of tea – being surrounded by family,' linking arms as they passed snow-covered trees and derelict flower beds. Sorry-looking benches squatted like vultures without a victim; grey painted people slouched by, red noses leaking.

'Penny for them?'

'Oh, I was just looking at the lonely people. Mostly lonely people go to parks. Loneliness reminds me of Sam and his boys' home. It's all so . . . So damned institutionalised.'

'Aha, so that's your Institutionalised Man!' sensing his need to talk after love. 'I guess I can't blame you. But there was something

162

else, wasn't there: when you were in the home in Liverpool? That's why you became so close to Sam. It was probably why you rejected his friendship initially, because you didn't want to be reminded of what happened all those years ago.'

'I understood his situation, yes. I was a war baby, an embarrassment for some well-to-do papist family and their unmarried daughter. They had conscience money by the potful and little Ben was offloaded onto a harem of prayer-crazy nuns. That was before being passed on to the bloody Jesuits! *Satan damn them!*' He breathed in deeply, his bitterness portraying a momentary madness in his eyes. 'I never bothered to find out who they were – my parents. There didn't seem much point.'

Sally tightened her grip on his arm; grimaced as the scar whitened through his beard.

'As soon as I could talk – and probably before – they rammed religion down my throat: the catholic version. My life was dominated by decades of the rosary and Stations of the Cross; novenas and the Angelus and never eating meat on Fridays; infernal fasting days and hideously revolting statues with their evil innocence and their bleeding hearts to match the contrived chicanery of it all. I spent more time in church than out of it, confessing about more sins than I knew I'd committed and reciting endless reams of catechism for self-elected sainthood seekers. Maybe words from the mouths of pure, young boys helped their case in the eyes of the Almighty. I never found out. Naturally, like Sam, I rebelled. I had a lad's normal healthy appetite for boyish things, but when I was eleven, the evil men of Loyola's brotherhood tried to stamp all that out as they tried to indoctrinate me in their ways of Mother Church.'

Sally brushed a snowflake from his cheek, content to let him talk it all out. Maybe if he spoke enough of his childhood, the maggot of the Jesuits would be driven out altogether.

'They figured I had a brain,' he was saying. 'That they could turn me into a priest.' He grinned cynically. 'Said it was for my own good; that I had been denied a family in order to serve God all the more. They also said a vocation would tame my rebellious spirit. Well, they tried, but only succeeded in strengthening my resolve to be rid of all things church and catholicism and the evil they stood for. That was when I ran. And I never got caught.'

'You mentioned once that they beat you!' she said softly, knowing he would want to talk that away, too.

'Yes. Apart from one priest, they were a sadistic lot. Several forced relationships on the boys, saying that it was for the greater glory of God's Holy work. The kids were too petrified to speak out because they would be beaten all the harder – and to whom would they appeal? We used to cringe in the dormitory every night waiting to hear the cries as some poor soul was taken off for a pederast's pleasure among his crucifixes and incense. Those howls of fear will always live with me. Always! One boy from Manchester hanged himself from the toilet chain rather than continue being a priest's bed partner. He wasn't old enough to be a lover! One tried it on me and I hid behind the altar in the chapel all night. Needless to say, I was beaten black and blue with a birch cane, but I wasn't touched in any other way. After all that, I couldn't accept any god who allowed all this to happen. Of course, I never accepted the catholic myth of the Holy Trinity; nor could I countenance the Virgin Mary's conception without intercourse. As far as I was concerned, Christ was little more than a Saturday night political rabble rouser. I genuinely felt sorry for Pontious Pilate: his hands were tied politically. Barabas was an excellent ploy for the crucifixion.'

Sally held few beliefs of her own, and had witnessed much cruelty by self-confessed Christians, but to call Christ a political rabble rouser . . . 'Did you ever voice these opinions?'

'Frequently! That's partly why I was beaten. I grew up to respect the individual's right, though, to hold political or religious convicions – or lack of them – as personal and not to be foisted onto another being. The catholic church brainwashes to the exclusion of all else. It is steeped in the blood and tears of a million children screaming their bastardy to a deaf cleric in Rome who concerns himself purely with the garnering of finance and acquisition of land. While nobody should argue over or mock a man's belief – for they are sacred to him – it still doesn't alter my views on Christianity in general – or politics in particular. I make my living from the latter – only by presenting an unbiased viewpoint from a given set of specifics and factual data. I don't necessarily believe in them either!'

'But isn't that... 'Sally bit her tongue. 'Isn't that living a lie, Ben?'

He kissed her cold cheek. 'No. Whether I accept or reject politics as an individual is immaterial as long as my reports are free of all bias as I've said. I see them – politics – as the sole redeeming factor for the survival of the masses, and as such, Christianity's natural enemy in the distribution of power. But I only see myself as a one-off and have little concern of what happens to every Tom, Dick or Harry – not our Harry, of course. As an individual, I am entitled to my opinion. I don't, however, accept communism on any platform – Christ was the original along with his disciples – or any diluted form redolent of concentration camp ideology. We, the British, invented the camps, but what I mean is that any political system that subverts the mind and will of its people is evil and should be exterminated ruthlessly.'

Sally thought for a long time as they walked past a frozen pond with several skaters. 'How about the teachings of Christ? His parables were superb. *The Bible doesn't lie!*'

Benjamin thought about her question while he watched an elderly couple in meagre clothes shuffling through the snow. An ageing mongrel plodded gamely behind. Nodding: 'Their church never made the mistake of parting with a cent,' he said. 'Christ's teachings were well scripted, so too, the parables. They were designed to attract and hold the flock, but nothing any ill paid, down-at-heel hack couldn't best. Originally, the stories were politically instrumental in swaying the Jews from Roman rule. They, and the Bible have been conveniently interpreted to suit prevailing requirements down the centuries: like the tailored news broadcasts of a dictatorship or the gagged Press in South Africa to con the world that apartheid doesn't exist and the lies of Third World black leaders that they have the masses' interests at heart when everyone knows they spend their nations' wealth in Harrods and European flesh spots trying to live up to their Western counterparts. Clerics should stick to missionary work and leave writing to the writers. From cover to cover, the Bible is the most violent, hypocritical, erroneous and diabolical string of half-truths and fiction I've ever read. I can't comprehend why it's the backbone of religious tolerance, love and understanding. It's also the all-time bestseller.'

Sally remained silent as they returned to the car. How could people like the Jesuits get away with all those evil things? She had

165

heard that they were a sort of FBI of catholicism; politically motivated. Of course the comparison stopped at pederasty. It had all a lasting effect on Ben, she thought. It was change-the-subject-time. 'Promise me we'll never talk about those horrid things and those horrid people in our marriage.'

He held her at arm's length. 'Dearest Sally,' he said. 'I love you far too much for that. But you must forgive me if I still have the odd nightmare. The boys crying alone at night . . .'

They embraced and walked on.

Spending the rest of the day planning the wedding, they went over their lives again: matters not spoken about at Indian John's at their first real meeting, nor during their stay at the Montana small-holding. 'Ben,' she said during a quiet moment. 'I know we're over forty, but I want your child.'

They loved that night and all the following day . . .

. . . He looked up as Sally, flushed from the chilly air, came through the restaurant door and kissed him. 'Am I late?' She was bubbly happy.

Benjamin felt his pulse race at the sight and smell of her. 'Do you know that you're the most beautiful woman in the world,' he said. holding her hand over the table.

'Good heavens, can't you wait until after the meal!' Her face radiated happiness. 'You'll have to control your ardour, Ben Thompson, because this working gal is starving. What a day I've had! *And it's the thirteenth!*'

'So it is,' he said softly. 'Would it be anything else!' Something nice has happened to her, he thought. She'll tell me in her own good time.

'Ben, don't ever stop saying those wonderful things to me. You don't know what it does to a woman.'

'And, I'll always mean them.' He called the waitress, loving Sally with his gaze.

Hands on face, she purred: 'I adore you, my darling. Why is it that whenever I'm near you, each time is better than before? Oh, today is such a *wonderful* day.'

He smiled awkwardly. Over dessert, he was about to tell her

about The Beard and his meeting with Lieutenant Robinson, when she leant across the table and said: 'I saw Doctor Abrahams this morning. Benjamin, I'm pregnant.'

★ ★ ★ ★ ★

The Rocky Mountain chain is the afterbirth of a great upheaval of the earth's crust. Millions of years old, this colossal ocean of limestone and rock undulates for three thousand miles from the desert heat of New Mexico to the ice-frozen wastes of the Yukon. In places, it is over three hundred and fifty miles wide: an almost unbeleivable million square miles of untameable wilderness squatting in civilisation's backyard. This prehistoric lunacy forms an irregular ridge of high ground called the Continental Divide; a western watershed where the great American and Canadian rivers are born, are swollen by precipitated rain, ice and snow to empty into the Atlantic, Pacific and Arctic Oceans.

The nomadic plains Indians traversed the mountains on their way to the rich hunting grounds long before the all-plundering Spaniards left the high country in the Sixteenth Century for the more lucrative pickings of what is now Santa Fe. Three hundred years later, the explorers Lewis, Clark and Pike travelled the Northern and Southern Rockies; the great American fur trade flourished among trappers and traders while the conestoga wagons bucked and rolled, blazing open the Oregon Trail, the longest overland route west through the mountain chain.

Of the six chief ranges constituting the Rocky Chain, none this day could compare with the Front Range in the Colorado section of the Middle Rockies: specifically the short distance along the valley footing Devil Mountain where the situation was catastrophic. It had nothing to do with the elements – bad as they were – or the natural grandeur: simply, the mountain animals were in an uproar because the grizzly he-bear who lived on the mountain was on a blood purge as the mid-winter clamped its teeth around earth and sky.

The female eagle flew through the gloom, her great wings almost kissing the tree-tops. Diving from the eyrie, she had hovered high above the creek before floating lazily between the turbulence thrown up by the contours of the land. Ever since killing the rival female from the box canyon, her man had been attentive, allowing her more free time to roam the skies around the great mountain. Nowadays, they only flapped wings in the air when they taught the young ones the secret of flight.

She had sensed of late, the tension in the valley below the he-bear's mountain. It had all seemed to start, curiously enough, about the time of his blundering attack on the beaver family at the south end of the creek. At least, she put it down to that. Then, the killing of the bull elk followed by a spate of senseless attacks on the valley inhabitants. Preferring courtship to hunting, he had seldom eaten much of his kills. So, what kind of winter madness was this? Or had man finally turned his head? She had no idea.

Gliding effortlessly, she saw the animals dart from tree to drift in search of food, the more foolhardy and hungrier flaunting danger hunting far into the open scrub. Dropping onto a rock-smashed pine stump, she saw the beaver colony foraging for roots in the hard-packed snow. Silently, they tested the wind for signs of the grizzly. Instinctively, the cubs began to play, but were soon chased back into the lodge below the creek.

Winging across the valley, she rode the updraughts before skate-landing on the glassy ice-topped mesa. Surveying both ends of the valley, her feathers snatched on the wind: there was movement near the box canyon as snow-backed fur eased from behind the drifts. Elk: the cows that once belonged to the dead bull. She picked out the new leader, proudly cresting a hill, testing for danger. His head suddenly whiplashed and the herd disappeared in a bounding snow mist: forty petrified deer springing twenty feet leaps to safety.

The he-bear was close by.

Leaving the mesa, she hovered in search of small prey, the he-bear's venom now making it a fruitless task. This way and that, she flew in vain: even the wind hushed itself as if straining to catch a tell-tale sound heralding a blur of speed that would end in another sudden death.

Tilting her left wing, dropping her head, she scythed downwards: zigzagging, she looked like some avenging angel patrolling its lifeless boundaries. She caught a speck of tawny grace inside the timber circling the dam: white throat and belly; black tipped tail. The lioness was pining for her dead mate. The he-bear had crushed his life away on the ice-crusted mountain lake close to the man's nest two nights ago. It had been a pitiful sight to see, moreso from altitude. She could feel the cat's sorrow, as she walked aimlessly through the rocks to the forest backing the mesa – away from the mountain. The grizzly's domain.

Life was leaving the valley and the eagle was not prepared for that. Was that another man disease?

The growl came on the windless air and she streaked northwards. The he-bear had cornered a half-grown antelope. In its dilemma, the pronghorn had run into a cluster of giant snowdrifts and was now trying to escape from the white maze before its enemy lunged for the kill. Hovering at a hundred feet, the eagle witnessed the inevitable bloody end: the grizzly struck, ate nothing and lolloped to higher ground.

Angered by this wasteful death worthy of the man disease, she shot dangerously round the bear's head, beating her wings as he tried yet again to snatch her from the sky. Sickened, she sped over the valley to collect her thoughts. Rising above the timberline, she looked down at the man's nest and glided onto the roof. He too, and his family, had run from the he-bear's wrath. Ah, but wasn't that the way of things in the mountains! Nothing stayed for long – and lived.

The wind rushed back and the forest became a sea of crazy motion. Her body feathers rippled and she winged back to the eyrie and the heat of her mate. It was too early to tell the children of the terrible goings-on in the valley.

★　★　★　★　★

Sam Fynn couldn't understand why Boogaloo was losing weight: his backbone felt fragile through the fur. The sneezing had started two days before, the weight-loss, overnight. The cat could hardly stand.

Forlorn, he watched as Boogaloo stumbled across the bedroom, turning his head and miaowing in pain. *'What is it, Boogie?'* he cried. He bent down as the animal excreted, too weak to go outside.

Gently, he carried the cat into the bathroom and cleaned the soiled fur before spongeing off the carpet. Lovingly, he touched the small head. The cat's eyes were half closed, inflamed and runny. It suddenly convulsed in a violent sneezing attack that stretched its tiny body like drumskin: Sam was sure Boogaloo would burst. Just like that! Explode into pieces in front of his eyes on the bathroom floor.

Grabbing a towel, he wrapped up the cat and put him on the bed. Boogaloo tried to nuzzle his face. 'Save your strength, little one,' he said softly. 'If only you could talk.'

He sat on the bed and the cat slept peacefully on his lap until the Cornclifts returned from the supermarket. The afternoon light had failed as night crept into the room. Afraid to wake Boogaloo, he sat in the dark staring at the switch. When Bill Cornclift turned on the light, Sam's face was wet.

'He's got cat 'flu, Sam. It's serious. I hope the vet's not closed. We'll have to hurry.'

Benjamin's words blitzed cruelly inside the boy's head: *'You'll have to get him vaccinated ... You wouldn't want to lose him, then, would you ...'* He had forgotten to get the cat jabbed, what with all the coming and going and everything. There was disease in the city, not so in the mountains. 'Will ... Will Boogie be OK? He's all I've got.'

The man didn't answer, instead picked up Boogaloo and left the room. Sam put on his jacket and followed out to the car. Minutes later, the vet unlocked the door for the two worried faces steaming the glass panel.

Sam quickly explained the cat's short history.

The man sighed. How did you explain to a tear-filled kid that his closest friend was dying! 'Not good! Maybe fifty-fifty. I'll give him an antibiotic, that's all I can do. Cat 'flu is like biliary to a dog. We're helpless. The animal will stand more of a chance with love and care than with anything I can do. I'm sorry, but I have to lay it on the line.'

'Thank you doctor,' Bill Cornclift staring at Sam. 'Are you ready, son?'

Sam's heart was breaking: his world was crumbling there in the clinical, hygienic smelling confines of the vet's surgery. All that had gone before – only for this! Weeping, he picked up Boogaloo and walked to the door.

The man said quietly: 'You'll know in ten days, Mr Cornclift. If you bring the animal back, please leave it in the car. The disease is contageous. No sense in breaking more hearts. My advice is to put the animal down. Kinder on all in the long run.'

Sam turned angrily. 'No,' he shouted. 'I'll make Boogie live! I'll take him back to the mountains where he belongs. Where I belong.' And then he walked to the car.

The vet shook his head. 'If kids grew up caring half as much for humans, I'd consider coming back for a second shot at this life. I remember the boy from the newspapers. He's made national television after he left the circus in Loveland! He's been through a lot with that cat. I wish you luck, Mr Cornclift. Are you adopting him?'

Bill Cornclift smiled appreciatively. 'You're very kind,' was all he said.

CHAPTER 13

Benjamin's interview with Gabass went smoothly and he was appointed senior political correspondent due to several resignations and Harry's contact in Immigration. He was to take over his desk in the New Year. Harry had then taken him to a small bar and persuaded him to return to Devil Mountain.

'If there's no sign of them after a couple of weeks,' he said, 'come on down. That's an order. Officially, I'm your senior on the paper. No sense in tempting a prairie load of providence! I think Mike Robinson's out of court on this one, but he has his methods. How he's survived the city cesspit so long, beats me.'

Benjamin kept Sally's pregnancy to himself: it would only upset his friend in view of what he had asked him to do. He convinced himself that it wouldn't affect Sally too much, for he would be back in no time. Thinking of Robinson, the man had explained things as though he were running the risks; doing a favour.

'I don't want you making out like Custer's last stand,' the police-man had said. 'Just keep your cool and assess the situation.

If they stick to hunting below, they're innocent: if they come up to visit, get your English butt the hell out of it. I'll have somebody waiting nearby to haul 'em in.'

However, it had been a different story with Paddy. The Irishman became embittered by Benjamin's decision and his mood spilled into the Miller home. Hospitality wore thin. On the plus side, he was grateful that the headaches had disappeared and the X-rays had confirmed that his skull had healed: unfortunately, the leg would take a little longer.

On the eve of Benjamin's departure, he said: 'I can't stay here much longer: I'm getting everyone down – *I'm getting me down!* Just sitting like a spastic ogling the television. I've a few dollars, I'll find a place until the leg gets better.'

'Harry found a place for Sally and I. We've taken an apartment until she transfers down here. Why not stay there! You'll be on your own weekdays. She'll be there weekends moving in odds and ends. There's food and beer and no television.

'Bum in the butter, eh, Englishman!' he grinned. 'Ah, good luck to you both.' His face then took on the nearest impression he could achieve to pleading. 'Why don't you wait for me? I'll only be a month at the outside. I know who it was in that car.'

Catching the hate in the Irishman's eye: 'Why didn't you tell Robinson that! It may have made a difference. I've no real back-up.'

'I wanted them to myself! I didn't expect that Yank idiot to send you back alone. I'll stop it! Pass me the phone.'

Benjamin shook his head. 'I won't come into contact with them. Maybe I should tell Sally to stay here with you until it's all over . . . She's . . . '

'In the family way!'

Benjamin paled. 'How did you know?'

Paddy winked. 'Sure there's enough Irishmen running around for us all to know the signs, me bucko. I've delivered three myself! One belonged to a rat I shot – I had no quarrel with his woman. He died about an hour before his son was born. I er . . . said that to you in confidence, Ben.'

'I don't want to know about your cause, Paddy. You know my feelings on that subject and violence in general.'

Changing the conversation: 'How did the little lady take it –

you going back up and all?'

'Not particularly well, but better than I thought she would. She said ... She said she didn't want her child to be fatherless ... '

Paddy beckoned to him and held him close. 'Do what you have to, man. If it's in you, it'll come out one way or the other. If not, you're not the man I took you for. Just keep looking over your shoulder: never stop looking. *Never!* Before you leave, I'm going to put you through plenty of dry firing exercises – don't think you're an expert, it soon wears off. Practice is the thing.'

Benjamin crossed the floor to where Mona lay on a table like a sacred symbol. 'When will you leave her in the cupboard where she belongs? You can't go on indefinitely ... '

'You'll wear your tongue thin, Thompson,' growled Paddy. 'Just you concentrate every second of every day on that riff-raff who'll be coming after you – and that bear who gave you the facelift. You have to come back to her. She is everything: worth a hundred of either of us.'

Benjamin smiled slightly. 'I do believe you're in love a little with her yourself.'

The big man frowned and threw a cushion at Benjamin's head. Benjamin laughed, then looked thoughtfully at the Irishman. 'How did Robinson treat you? Read the riot act about breaking up US saloons?'

'Let's just say we came to an agreement over Immigration. Mind you, that doesn't mean that I won't defend myself should anything ... shall we say, come out of the blue.'

'The Provisionals?'

'Maybe – maybe not! None of your damned business. Jaysus, I never knew a man with such a penchant for involving himself in another man's fight! If you'd done like I said on the timberline, you wouldn't be in this mess now.'

'*Nonsense!* They'd have killed you.'

'Bullshit! It was you they nearly topped. And what if they had taken me! That was my business. You bloody writers don't know when to stay loose! I'm not in an argumentative mood, so just do as I say and just maybe you'll live to play football with junior.'

'I won't get involved in any heavy stuff. Robinson referred to me as a beater: you know, like the ... '

'Bloody grouse, I know.'

174

'Yes. I flush them out and he drops his net. At least that's the idea. Paddy, I've come to know these men. I never knew them before, but now I can feel and smell them. Do you know what I mean?'

'Aye,' Paddy replied wearily. 'It's how every executioner feels before he's called upon to do his duty. It's not for you, Ben! You're a writer, for Christ's sake! Don't involve yourself in blood: because once you do, you'll never be able to shake it off. You'll always feel like you need a bath.'

Benjamin stared at the floor. 'I understand the big country – not as well as them, now – but enough to do what's required. I've a lot going for me, I know, so I'll keep looking over my shoulder. And don't forget, I won't have them killing Dickens or his mate. They butchered his first wife and young. I believe in co-existence more strongly than ever now. Sure, I went a little crazy through lack of oxygen, but I'm OK for this. I . . .'

'Ben,' cut in Paddy, 'they play dirty. Don't get cocky because you feel you know the mountain. They've been at it since their mothers chucked 'em off the tit. They're like nothing else! I'll talk to Robinson again: put a little heavy on him. You'll need more than a little back-up before you're through. Beater or no beater, forget playing policeman to the bear colony, if only for her sake.' Boring deep into Benjamin's eyes: 'For both their sakes!'

Benjamin poured two drinks. 'Here's to the future,' he said.

'Here's to hell,' retorted Paddy. ''Cause that's where you're going, Englishman: with the devil on his mountain.'

Benjamin's hands started to shake and his eyes burned with a loathing he had never felt until this moment.

'More than your hands'll shake before you're finished. But it's natural enough, so don't worry. Whatever you do, don't worry: it's amateurish. Amateurs die.' Tilting his glass, he said added sadly: 'Then go well, Mountain Man.'

★　★　★　★　★

The Beard rubbed red knuckles across his runny nose. 'There, that should do it!' blowing smoky breath into the forest clearing.

Staring with satisfaction at the last of the six traps: 'The time wasn't lost in Nam, Eb, old mate!'

The other hunter smiled crookedly. 'Six little babies,' he chuckled. 'One don't get him, another one will. Good idea of yours: he walks into one of these in winter, an' we remove what's left in spring. Just like the whore: no evidence of human hands. Who knows, maybe that bear pal of his'll eat him up out of the trap.' He belched and guffawed into the spindly sunlight. 'We can take the Mick anytime.'

The Beard pulled out a hip flask and drank. 'Swig?'

Eb emptied half the contents. Wiping his mouth: 'Maybe we'll get that grizzly, too. Two for the price of one. *Perfect!*'

The Beard pocketed the flask and moved off grinning. He was happy. They could forget all about the English idiot – just a cautious visit now and then to reset any animal-sprung traps. Eb might have something there: it was possible they could bag the big grizzly. 'Perfect,' he agreed.

Laughing, they left the timberline, avoiding the trading post on their way back. 'Yeah, that grizzly owes us, Eb!' exclaimed The Beard later as they closed on their vehicle.

'I've been thinking.'

'What's that?'

'Why don't we lit up north for a while? Monatana way! Fresh territory. We can always shoot back for Christmas or whenever.'

The Beard smiled. 'Why not! I believe the women in Jefferson are as horny as the Missouri in full flood!'

'No shit!'

'You better believe it! Have to keep a careful eye on the weather, though. One heavy downpour and those traps'll be out in the open.'

'A point! But the Limey'll be history by then. Oooooh Montan-a-a-a!'

★ ★ ★ ★ ★

The parting was quick. Insisting that Sally not drive him to Indian John's, Benjamin took a lift with one of Robinson's men.

'Bengymen, Bengeymen,' welcomed the old Indian. 'Figured you'd come back!' He beckoned towards the living room where flames crackled and flared in the fireplace. 'Put your gear in the corner and brighten an old man's life. Tell me everything that's happened since we left you at the smallholding. How's Sally? The Irishman? What's happened to the runaway?'

Accepting the whisky, Benjamin filled in the time; Indian John was cock-a-hoop over Sally's pregnancy. 'I'll get the wife to make something for the papoose.'

Speaking with the trust associated with men of the big country, Benjamin explained Robinson's strategy for the hunters. The Indian's leathered face etched tram lines in a worried expression: black eyes slit like miniature oil slicks. 'They are bad men, Bengymen. You must be careful. I watch you move: you know some of the signs, but not all. Not like an Indian. You will take my nephew.'

'No. No, thank you, John. I am honored, but I must do this on my own.'

Indian John studied Benjamin's face silhouetted in the firelight and shook his head. 'Very well. But you must learn something of our ways if you are to survive these men. I will show you that my people haven't lost our heritage or the ways of our ancestors, whittling totem poles or hawking our culture like a piece of candy-floss. I will tell you of our wars with the Longknives and you will understand the need for cunning. Your first lesson will be to think like us: that way, you will be the hunter and not the hunted.'

Grimly, Benjamin relived through the old man's voice, the butchery at Sand Creek, the shame of Wounded Knee and the Indian reprisals in Colorado, Kansas and New Mexico before finally surrendering to General Sheridan after the bloody Red River War. He listened to how men like generals Crook, Miles and Custer led their cavalry against Sitting Bull, Black Kettle and Satanta, of Sioux, Cheyenne and Arapaho revolting against the white man's lies and broken treaties before being reduced to the indignity and inhumanity of the reservations.

But the Indian spiced his people's history with epic stories of the hunt: magnificent full-blooded buffalo charges that filled the great plains with brave deeds; of emotional and sacred initiation ceremonies required by custom of a young buck to attain manhood,

177

and of a people who had loved their land long before the pale-faced settlers came from the east with their disease and their guns and their liqour and their greed. Pride and majesty, ignominy and treachery, Indian John told the history of his people in the simple terms of the woodsman and hunter.

Benjamin listened until the old man eventually drifted to his own words as black-grey embers in the hearth died in the growing light of dawn. Like a statue, he watched the lengthening shadows: thinking, planning, humbling himself as he had done before when he had first gone to the mountain, in preparation for the coming ordeal.

For six weeks, Indian John and his nephew made Benjamin's life a misery as he learnt the ways of the Arapaho. The nephew took him deep into the valleys and forests along the Colorado teaching the secrets of tracking and bushcraft; how to look at a man without being seen, surviving only with one's wits and skills with the bow and knife.

'Gun too noisy, Bengymen,' said the nephew. 'Close up, what is better than the bow or knife!'

In the evenings, Indian John would question him about what he had learned with his nephew; would teach about camouflage: 'The Arapaho stalks like a breath of night wind: he is part of the wilderness and invisible to his enemy. Now Bengymen, tell me what you know about the sounds of the forest and of the traps you will make to catch food and of the berries and the bark that will sustain you until your traps are sprung? Will you shoot with the bow or the rifle? Each has its own use, but remember the bow is silent and will play on an enemy's mind: he will not know from which direction the arrow has been fired. Tell me the spoor of the cottontail rabbit and the song of the sky before the storm? Tell me, Bengymen, what you have learnt of these things?'

Physically demanding, the instruction flew by until one day when the wind howled in from the mountains: 'May your god go with you, Bengymen,' Indian John waving from the forest path that led to the box canyon. 'Always hunt with peace in your heart, wisdom in your head and you will be the victor. I will send my nephew if they pass this way – but I don't think they will make that mistake. Possibly they have returned to the mountain in your absence. If they have, be careful, for nothing will be as it was.'

Rifle slung, bow in hand, Benjamin pressed into the wind shuddering in icy blasts off the rock face and moaning incessantly through the big timber. Spindrifts of snow and icicles cut his face; his eyes watered and back and legs ached from the fresh pack of provisions. God it was cold! He was back.

His plan was simple: drop his stores off at the cabin and then look for the signs; the pictures of killers about to kill again. But not you, Ben, he thought, moving in Indian fashion as he sectioned the terrain, defined canyon sounds and probed every drift and river bend for signs of danger. He saw bear and lion spoor . . . *Concern yourself only with the signs of man, Bengymen . . .*

Before, the trip back and forth through the valley to the trading post had been a casual four hour stroll: now, it was a lengthy, tense, gut-stabbing prowl because a man had nearly died in a Denver street. Fear-sweat iced his face and beard; nerves tightened like bowstring.

Resting inside the forest to drink coffee, his heart jumped as a rabbit broke from cover. The coffee made sickly brown stains down his buckskins and in the snow. Holy God, he thought: now we start. Trading the bow for his rifle, he cocked the weapon and moved off warily, fighting to allay his fears and suppress the instinct to over-react. Acre by acre, bend by bend, he searched for the invisible he knew was there that would betray his enemy. But the unseen eluded him and because of it he became scared. He knew that when he stopped being scared, he would die . . . *remove yourself from fear; perform the obvious without seeming to do so . . . they may be watching – even from afar by the use of traps . . . they will become suspicious if you are. Then you will become the hunted once more . . .*

Benjamin found himself mouthing the Indian's words in order to concentrate all the more. Ignoring the dish, he took the arduous route through the forest to the timberline. The dish was obvious. They would know that. Passing over the sporadic snow dustings painting the hunters' tracks, by last light he merged sore and sweating from the noisy timber in front of the cabin.

179

Relief shone on his face. 'I'm back, Virginia!' he shouted pulling off the snowshoes. Patting the wall, he was about to step inside when caution rang out loud. An hour later, miserable and cold, he finished testing the cabin for boobytraps and finally stepped over the threshold.

Too late to prepare a warning system, he made a fire and prepared a scratch meal of beans and sausages. Food and heat eliminated fatigue and worry as he languished in their sensuality, falling asleep on the dirt floor.

Having returned to the place where he once searched for an inner peace and found a woman, he now had to preserve both.

He awoke stale-mouthed and bleary-eyed to a world of ghosts, memories and stiff limbs. Cabin, timberline and broken pipeline reminded him of Sam and his cat. Turning, he saw the boy's face hovering above the fireplace, Boogaloo's small black head materialising on his shoulder. Shaking his head in disbelief, he heard the Irishman's booming voice: big, strong, dependable Paddy with his red mane of hair and wild beard tugging on the wind. Frightened, he saw Dickens in the doorway staring at him as the hunters' eyes spied from the depths of the forest.

'*Stop it!*' he punched the wall. 'Stop imagining, you fool!'

Storming outside, he thrust his bloodied hand in the snow: it was numb within seconds. Making a fast breakfast, he set about making his defences. The first thing: check if anybody was likely to have had the idea first . . . *think what they would do, knowing what you would do . . .*

Cutting a long thin stick, he searched the area like a sapper for tripwire. He had to assume that everywhere had become a minefield: knee-high snow leant it an almost comical yet macabre sensation. Gradually, working in careful sweeps away from the cabin, he moved along the timberline, his skin prickling nervously with each prod of the stick. Smiling, he remembered waking the rattler in the scrub on his first day back in the summer . . . He stopped before the dish: if anywhere, here. Then he laughed a hysterical and fearful, almost feminine laugh. How bloody silly! How bloody pathetically ludicrously silly: a grown man poking a stick into the snow half way up a mountain for something he didn't know what. They mightn't even be after me! Robinson might have it all wrong; everyone could have exaggerated under pressure.

180

If they do want me, all they have to do is walk up the hill and shoot me . . . *they're hunters, Bengymen. They do what they do best; traps as well as guns . . .*

He squatted on his haunches breathing heavily with stress. 'I must be crazy, thinking what I just did! I'll do the dish later – it's a long way down. I'll finish off the timberline, then . . .' He froze: 'You could have been dead then, you fool,' he scolded himself.

Acting on his own words, he had begun walking without probing. Oh Christ, what a dirty game! he thought picking up the stick. Man once more brings his precious advancement to nature.

Palms clammy inside the gloves, he completed the timberline and made strong coffee laced with whisky. He felt like a prisoner: free to pace his own cell, but one wrong foot outside . . . Maybe that was what they wanted: their victim too afraid to move so they could take him at their leisure. Arapaho or Ben Thompson, they had started to wear him down. The tin mug bounced off the wall . . . *you must learn to control your fear of the unknown: that is your strongest weapon . . .*

Washing the mug with snow, he picked up the stick and rifle and moved towards the forest. Working out and away from his tracks of the previous day, he tested enough ground on which to set his own surprises.

He had almost finished when a squirrel scurried through the sentinels of timber. He stood rigid from the hideous clang as the animal was crushed and skewered between the ugly steel teeth of a trap; his stomach lurched as the stark disgusting reality forged white hot in his brain: blood dripping on snow over jaw-tight steel. *They did want him dead!*

Shock set in and he shivered. One trap! How many more? Where? And that wasn't a place I'd normally walk!

Inching closer, his stick found the limp tripwire attached to a bear trap with a difference: a small tension-release mechanism had been welded on to activate far less than a grizzly's eight hundred pounds. With the squirrel's meagre thirty ounces, they were taking no chances.

Tight faced, Benjamin went back to the cabin as clouds darkened the valley and timberline. Bolting himself in, he took a few gulps of whisky and sat down to think. Like an Indian: an Arapaho! He felt something wet and cold on his thigh. Ashamed, he stared stupidly at the dark patch on his jeans: he had urinated himself.

During an anxious night of half-sleep, he returned to one broiling, airless, sticky afternoon on a bench in St James's Park while working on the girlie magazine. He had gone to the park to be free of the tedium and grossness of the cramped office space at the back of Victoria Station.

He was making some notes regarding character build-up for his book when a seemingly endless tour group of German girls passed by his bench. Opposite, the ducks performed on the sparkling water around Duck Island; alongside, ignoring the sightseers, two squirrels were at play.

Just then, a group of punk rockers brought their peculiar brand of nausea into the park; one of their number firing a pellet gun at the squirrels, half killing one and mercifully missing its mate. Benjamin bent down and picked up the poor animal, but the creature died in his hands, its blood pumping over his suit jacket.

Ignoring his harsh words, the yobos had moved off across the lawns; the park policemen also ignored his complaint, preferring the safer and popular ego-trip of answering the questions of the mini-skirted German girls.

He woke up in a lather of sweat wondering what had happened to the dead squirrel's mate: and in the morning cold of the hut, he thought about the luckless animal caught in The Beard's trap. It too, like the slaying in the Westminster park, was odious and senseless. Were all squirrels destined to be slaughtered so foully just like some humans were destined to die in war?

Remaking the fire, he had an early breakfast and planned his day. In his diary he wrote:

> Unfortuitous circumstances have driven me back to Virginia. But that is not strictly correct, for outside the hit-and-run incident, I longed to return to the mountain and mountain ways . . . I witnessed another of man's brutal passions yesterday – the mutilating of helpless animals. But I must keep my wits about if I am to survive for Sally and the baby . . .

Donning the suit of buckskin over his thermal underwear, he set out for the dish. Picking up his battered wide brimmed hat, he slung a quiver of arrows hung from his waist. The bow was shouldered, the rifle held.

He arrived at the top of the dish as a tepid, glowy sun poked apprehensively through low-hung cumulus. The outlook was not good, but for the time being, the wind had vanished like a sea storm.

He found the second trap early on, a few yards from the top of the incline. Like nothing he had ever seen, he had heard of claymore mines back in the sixties from a war correspondent fresh from the attrocities of an African coup. Anchored to a tree, the convex oblong of death was packed with high explosive and hundreds of steel balls. The tripwire pencil-lined the surface of the snow. Camouflaged with branches, once triggered, the mine would send the lethal projectiles hurtling across the dish to cut its victim in half in a milisecond of bloody overkill.

Keeping his distance in case the mine was boobytrapped, Benjamin fired a shot at the claymore from behind a tree. The explosion shattered the mountain quiet: all manner of animals zigzagged off through the forest. The ricochets rolled over the valley like a procession of drums beating a tatoo on some distant battlefield.

Ex-military men, he thought. The psychology was right: far from the bottom, a tired man would lack concentration to look for the mine; for the man going down, it was too close to the top for him to be ready.

Miserably, he persevered with his gruesome task over six thousand feet to the valley floor.

Wobbly legged from the slow descent, he walked along the iced creek and sat on the beaver dam. It's as safe as anywhere, he thought. Again he asked himself: how many traps had they laid? They were unorthodox, so nowhere was safe, and in a perverse way he felt relieved that he could never relax. At least he couldn't fool himself that such and such a place was *unthinkable* or that The Beard would *never* put a trap there. Yet they couldn't have laid too many mines for fear of killing other hunters or lone fishermen. But as far as the noise factor was concerned, any explosions would be put down to distant thunder claps or disregarded for another military manoeuvre and any report would be lost in the conventional string of military denials. When Paddy picked enemies, he picked professionals.

The male beaver popped up to see the visitor, nodded its head and promptly disappeared.

Benjamin grinned at the thought of his fateful first day after Harry had dropped him off by the Colorado. He could still see the beaver dragging his pack into the river while the trout completed the rout. Hell! That was five months ago. Looking at the beaver dam, he breathed in: it was over five hundred feet long.

'You've been busy, little feller,' he said to where the animal had appeared.

Reasoning that the hunters would return periodically to check their traps – he was certain they were after Dickens and his mate also – after rainfall, he watched the female eagle plummet from a rain cloud onto an unsuspecting prey further along the valley. 'Of course! The air! Because the rain would uncover their infernal contraptions, they were bound to put some in a tree or somewhere off the ground. That's not Arapaho, Ben. *That's eagle!* Thanks my friend,' as the female returned to the eyrie.

Moving back up to the timberline, he shot a small deer and carried it to the cabin. Cooking the legs, he hung strips of meat above the fireplace to smoke. As the moon pushed the sun into the west, he made a brief entry in the diary and turned in: cocked and on safe, the rifle, along with the bow and quiver, leant against the bed.

Rising before dawn, he rubbed for warmth. Making coffee, he unpacked the dozen balls of string and several lengths of rope he had bought off Indian John.

If they came at night, a criss-cross of string would set off a motley symphony of tin cans inside the cabin. Facing east, Virginia possessed a door and window overlooking the valley; it backed west onto the mountain and the ends faced the timberline and rocks at the foot of the water pan respectively. The timberline was an attacking weak point, but they would have good cover east and south from forest and rocks and a reasonable, if angled field of fire from the north inside the treeline. West, where he proposed to put the string, should provide little or no problem from the rock face. They couldn't burn him out; the wood was saturated. Theoretically, that was: there was paraffin and petrol to smoke him out.

What have we brought to the mountain? he thought.

Starting with the timber outside Virginia, he began settting his own traps. Bending thick knee-high branches for fifty feet along the timberline, he roped them to preceding trees with a series of slip knots and fashioned a crude, but effective trip string a few feet in front of the tensioned branches. Anybody touching the string would receive a stout crack on the head. Re-use of the bear trap was tempting, but ruled out for obvious reasons. On finishing his work, he found the lion bones he had used on first arriving on the mountain.

During a late breakfast, he grinned harshly at his handiwork: the difference between life and death.

That afternoon, the cans rattled as he entered in his diary. His heartbeat normalised as a squirrel zipped across the timberline still searching for its dead mate. In the evening, he tried to concentrate on the novel, but eye and mind kept switching to the ominous row of cans. Putting away his work, he drank a whisky and turned in, but the wind rose and the cans jangled and danced ghoulishly in the firelight. Two hours before dawn, he dropped off. It was difficult being an Arapaho!

★ ★ ★ ★ ★

Paddy Martin picked up the phone and dialled New York. 'Yes?' said a voice. 'Things are improving ... You're keeping a low profile. Good! The Irish Special Branch believe you're dead: missing at sea ... *No, no, no!* You'll still have to be patient . . . Plastic surgery, I said plastic surgery . . . Maybe not a year, now. Call in March.' The line went dead.

'March be buggered!' he spat. Continuing in thought: As soon as the hunters are out of the way, I'll take a chance and go back. I might as well die on home territory as out here. He recalled the long evenings discussing the 'troubles' with Benjamin on the timberline. I'm not ashamed to say that I'll miss that daft Englishman. His outlook, though he hated to admit it, was not dissimilar to his dear old Ma. What would Thompson be prepared to die for: A woman? Maybe. An ideal? Probably. The grizzly? *Definitely.* He didn't think countries interested the man enough to die for one. He'd probably be more than willing to die a hundred times over for his damnable pipeline! He was indeed an odd man.

Lighting a cheroot, he settled back on the divan. Sensing Sally's touch on everything, it gave him a peculiar thrill. Steady Paddy, she's spoken for! He cursed as his eyes began to mist: Ben has everything and you have nothing, bucko. That's the top and bottom of it, now. Ach, don't be sorry for yourself; you sacrificed . . . all that, when you joined the boyos. You're a soldier and don't forget just because of a sentimental fool on a hill and the homely smells of a woman.

Drawing on the cheroot, the tears dropped down his face: tears for his dead comrades; tears for his victims; tears for the God he couldn't believe in any more; tears for the women he couldn't love, and most of all tears for his dear Ma who always sat in the parlour with her crippled hands clutching the rosary beads like a drowning man holds onto a spar. He blinked and saw the clean, small Kerry church with its spotless white railings and neat rows of daffodils. She was buried here. He couldn't enter as he couldn't all those years ago when the Special Branch denied him attending her funeral. *His own mother for Christ's sake!* That had been twenty years ago: the last time he had cried . . . *Look for the best in people, Patrick, my son. Then you'll see them . . .* Oh Ma!

He didn't feel the cheroot burn his fingers.

★ ★ ★ ★ ★

'This is McAvoy here. I just spoke to Martin. He's in Cascade . . . Yes, he's still in the mountain districts. I think it's time he left us. There's been a change of heart at home. Anyway, I don't trust him. See to it . . . Yes, the money will be paid into the usual account. Call me on the Yonkers number after it's done – no, I'll be in on this one. Set up a meeting with the others.'

CHAPTER 14

The ice plateau glistened like blue glass in the moonlight. Oddly, there was little wind: nothing moved except a snow mound between two rocks, rising and falling and shuddering like an earth tremor. Beneath, Dickens was enduring another nightmare, his great body heaving violently.

The dreams were always the same: man and his destructive noise of death. He was everywhere: in the valleys along the great fish rivers, fighting with his own kind on the snow covered mountains, in the air dropping man-noises that destroyed his home. Man dominated his every move – like the Odd One who had finally joined their ranks as Dickens had known that he would. Man had poisoned everything with his madness. And it was getting worse; had driven him to kill without reason just like man did. Was that it? he was being moulded like his eternal enemy? A man-made rogue animal?

The ground burst as his head and shoulders errupted through the snow crust. Sauntering ill-tempered across the icy waste, he stopped to complain to the moon with a wheezy splutter that only compounded his discomfort. He looked up once more, for something had caught his eye. Yes, again!

The female eagle swept across the moon, scribbling her shadow over the glinting plateau.

Angrily, he chased the bird's likeness until it disappeared into the darkness in the higher bastions of rock. He seemed to see her more these days, watching, goading from the sky – ever since he had killed the pronghorn. Managing a half-throaty growl, he slouched miserably back across the plateau.

Unsettled, he sat on a ridge watching, smelling his beloved mountain: the damp redolence of rock and time burnt his spirit like a spring madness. He puzzled over the strange tooth plant that had shot from the ground killing the squirrel. He had seen one of those plants eight summers before, eating into the belly of a goat. He had devoured the goat, but the plant had no smell and was hard and tasteless and he had broken a molar.

Rubbing his nose, he yawned. Yes, things had gotten out of control – and he with them. Maybe it was time to leave the mountain! There were planty more. But this one belonged to him: he had been born here and so it belonged to him. His new mate would leave the box canyon after the spring water and show him their children. Who would protect them if he left? For unlike other males, he wanted to stay with his family. Like his last family . . . But it would be different this time.

His breast heaved as he fought his sorrow. He had everthing to live for: man had only himself and he couldn't live with that. After man's downfall there would be nothing left – except hope for Dickens' way of things.

A hint of dawn smudged the horizon above the mesa. A breeze stirred in his nostrils as he picked up the day. A change might be the answer – but he would come back. Where? Ah yes, where the sun was salmoning the high timber across the valley. It could work if man stayed away. He would take her with him.

Pleased with his decison Dickens moved sprightly off the plateau, emerging in the valley as daylight washed the world with morning. Quickly moving over the creek and past the dam, he climbed into the opposite forest and stared back at his mountain. As long as he could see it, he felt safe. Sliding onto his side, sleep came blissfully beneath the trunks of uprooted pine. He would collect her later.

★ ★ ★ ★ ★

Sally thanked the Cornclifts and hurried through the rain-sodden chilly air to the car with Sam. Secretly, by being with him, she felt an unashamed exclusivity for Benjamin, and, in a a stupid, feminine way, she even felt a twinge of jealousy over the boy's closeness to her man.

Driving downtown, she stopped at an icecream parlour. 'Sure it isn't too cold for an Inter-Galactic Whirlwhizz?' she asked as their top coats pooled onto the floor from the backs of chairs.

For reply, Sam's eyes shone at the array of multi-coloured goo adverts.

'When we're alone, you can call me Sally,' she said, ordering two lemonades and Sam's frightening kaleidoscopic mess in an oversized stemmed glass.

'Thank you.'

'This takes me back aways,' the woman sipping through a straw; the boy's top lip lathered with whipped white foam. If it wasn't for the dark circles beneath his eyes, she thought, he's just like any other icecream loving kid. 'How are things going?' opening the conversation. 'I'm sorry to hear about Boogaloo.'

Sam stirred, merged the galactic colours with a finger. 'I don't hang around after school like other kids,' he said miserably. 'I have to get back to Boogie. I'm all he's got. I never know if he's going to be there when I arrive. Can't take him to the vet's surgery 'cause of what he's got. He seems to be improving . . . I don't know,' his voice trailing off. 'He wanted to put Boogie down, did you know that?'

Sally dropped her lashes. There was something definitely unnerving about a child's direct form of questioning. 'I . . . heard about it. Ben has a saying: whatever will be, will be. It's Italian in origin. It applies to many things in life – I think he tried to tell you that.'

Sam seemed preoccupied with lemonade bubbles marching up his glass like transparent soldier ants. 'Boogie's different – he's a fighter.'

'Well, we'll have to wait and see. I asked how you were getting along with the Cornclifts. They're the salt of the earth.'

Sam shrugged awkwardly. 'They're OK, I guess. They call me Samuel.' You can't trust grown-ups, he thought, no matter how they act. Only Ben was different. 'It's not as if I'm against them or anything like that . . . It's just . . . well, they just like to sit quietly and look at me as if I was something from outer space. I don't go anywhere! And I get that feeling that they – Mrs Cornclift especially – don't want me out of their sight. What's the word?'

'Possessive,' Sally fingering her brow in thought. 'I'm sure it only appears that way because you're the first child they've had. You have to give them a chance.'

'Why? Kaiser's treated better than most kids I've known!'

'They can't have children, Sam,' she persisted. 'Bill Cornclift had an accident at work. I daresay Boogaloo gets more than his fair share of attention from you – before his illness,' she added quickly.

Sam grinned. 'Got me on that one! What happened to him? Mr Cornclift?'

'He became sterilised. Do you know what that means?'

Sam shook his head, slurping through the straw. He took a shot in the dark. 'Something to do with his not liking milk?'

Sally didn't laugh. 'No,' she replied softly. 'It means that he and his wife can never produce children of their own. That's why they came to me. You . . . You are taking the place of what they can never have. It's a tremendous responsibility for you, Sam.' She looked into his blue eyes: the circles had darkened.

Sam shuffled his feet beneath the table. 'I can't see Ben,' he said. 'I miss Virginia. Nothing's the same! It's no use pretending, Sally, I hate school because all I can think about is Boogie dying without me around and Ben up his mountain.'

'You'll see Ben – in time. You both have different things to do right now: he has to succeed in his new job and you have to try and concentrate on your lessons. It will be just as hard for him as it will be for you.'

'You love him, don't you.'

'Of course. I thought you would know that,' feeling the intensity of his gaze, and also, she glimpsed, a rival for Benjamin's affection. 'When we're settled, you . . . Boogaloo will come and visit. Often. We'll be moving to Cascade.'

Sam pushed the half eaten icecream away. 'Cascade's a long way from Denver. Kaiser can't be left alone, because he pines over the smallest things and they won't let me come on my own.'

Sally had come across strong-minded, obdurate and overpowering children, but Sam Fynn was in another dimension. What was he growing into? Any which way, Bill and Nora Cornclift would be the losers. But they were aware of the chances they took and the pitfalls; knew that Sam was a difficult case and might not accept their love.

She recalled their grief as they told her about Sam's preoccupation with his cat and what amounted to an unhealthy fascination for the mountain . . . The boy had not talked about Benjamin to the Cornclifts. If the cat died, he would run again: if it lived . . . probably the same. She knew that Benjamin cared for the boy, but the bind was that she was in the middle: she was welfare, ogre and saint, and, along with Benjamin, too old to adopt. It was logical Sam coming to them, but she also knew that it couldn't be for a thousand horrid legal reasons. *Institutionalised* . . . Snap out of it, my girl, you've a job to do.'

She had an idea. Sam needed a break as well as the Cornclifts. Why not pack him off to Montana to that new voluntary centre specialising in non-receptive cases. It would break her heart, but the open air and wide open spaces might do the trick. Yet, in her heart of hearts she knew she was kidding nerself. Mind you, Christmas – and it was just round the corner – would be a good psychological springboard for him to adjust. At any rate, it was worth mentioning to the Cornclifts before Sam got wind of it.

The panic broke two minutes after they returned to the house. Boogaloo had suffered a violent attack. 'It was a relapse.' explained Nora Cornclift. 'He couldn't move. Bill's taken it to the vet.'

'Boogie's not an 'it',' cried Sam defiantly. 'He'll put him down!' Throwing open the door, he dashed out into the rain. Bumping into people, he tore round a corner and into the clinic

Bill Cornclift was talking to a nurse in reception.

191

'*Where is he?*' the boy demanded. 'What have you done with Boogie?'

The man was distraught and looked at the nurse for help. It never came. Putting a hand on the boy's shoulder: 'It's for the best. He won't feel a thing, I'm assured. He's not in any pain, and . . . '

'You wouldn't do it to so easily to Kaiser!' hurled Sam, throwing off the man's hand. Opening doors, he began calling his cat's name.

Grave faced, the vet emerged from a room further along the corridor, a syringe in his hand.

Dodging him, Sam saw Boogaloo lying on a big white table. 'You . . . you've! Boogie's dead,' he choked, afraid to touch the animal and confirm his fears.

The vet put the syringe on the table next to the cat. 'What could you do for him, Sam?' he said sympathetically with just a trace of anger. When would they ever learn, he thought, that animals have to die just like us? A professional, he had long ago immunised himself against weepy children.

'You must let nature take its course. No, he's not dead, but he's not far off it. This is humane,' picking up the syringe. 'Please go home with Mr Cornclift: you're only making it harder on yourself and everyone else by being here.'

Sam's eyes opened like dinner plates. 'You mean you haven't done it!' checking the solution in the surgical instrument. '*Boogie's alive!*' Not waiting for an answer, he took off his jacket and wrapped it around the cat. 'It's only the city,' he exclaimed. 'Like me, Boogie hates it here. I'll take him where he belongs.'

'Sam!' Bill Cornclift looked on in amazement as the boy made for the door.

'You were going to kill him while I was gone,' he accused as Sally and Mrs Cornclift came in wet from the street. 'Is this what you mean by what will be, will be? You were in it, too!' anger-fired eyes confronting Sally. 'You think I'll stay with them after what they've tried to do!'

And then he was back in the rain, doing what he had always done . . . running, running for all he was worth. Packing a few things, he quickly left the house, Boogaloo inside his jacket. 'Take my heat, little feller,' he said gently. 'Let me take the badness out of you. We're going home.'

Sally grimaced at the empty bedroom as Nora Cornclift sobbed to her husband: 'Oh Bill, he's not right for us.'

The man held his wife's hand, trying to absorb her anguish. 'We tried, my dear.'

Kaiser whimpered against his master's leg in confusion.

Lieutenant Robinson's man swore at the rain then dropped his umpteenth soggy cigarette into a puddle as Sally left the Cornclift house. Enveloped in his own miserable condition, he had missed Sam's dash into the street. 'Of all the bloody assignments,' he groaned. 'Kids and cats and bloody rain!'

★ ★ ★ ★ ★

Lieutenant Mike Robinson frowned at his IN tray, over-brimming with routine files, dog-eared and brown with age. Sneezing a hole in a Kleenex, he opened the bottom drawer of a faded bottle green filing cabinet marked: CASES PENDING. Splashing three fingers of bourbon into a plastic coffee cup, he replaced the rye and read the latest report on the two hunters.

'Montana!' he nasalled. The telephone lamented beneath a mass of crime statistics. 'Yeah! No. Come on in, Jim. I'll send someone else to look after the kid. Go home – to dry off! Listen pal, if I can die in the office, I'll do it in company. Get your ass back here. The state provides perfectly good radiators for cold and rainsoaked detectives.' The statistics flew onto the floor as he banged the receiver. *'Home indeed!'*

A black sergeant knocked on the open door. 'Come in, Sol,' said Robinson reaching for another tissue. 'You know what Jim just said to me?'

The man smiled. 'Half the department heard, Lootenant. Jesus H, you havin' one of those days?' eyeing Robinson's coffee cup.

'Where the hell you been? I called half an hour ago.'

The sergeant perched on six inches of clear desk. 'Checkin' with our Irish cousins in Cascade. Right uppity crowd! Seems

193

Martin's flown the coop. They lost him somewhere between the Limey's apartment and the bus station.'

'What the hell's that supposed to mean! Did he go to the station or not?' his eyes screwing for another sneeze.

Waiting for the inevitable explosion to dissipate, the policeman replied: 'That's where our cousins fouled up. This Irishman ain't dumb like the jokes. He took a Greyhound east to Hutchinson.'

'East! If anywhere, he'd go north,' Robinson throwing another tissue into the paper basket.

The sergeant scratched his chin. 'Could be. You see, when the bus unloaded at Kansas, he wasn't on it. That's why I couldn't come right away. A guy answering his description got off at Dodge. He took a bus headin' . . . '

'I know,' Robinson spoke through his teeth. 'North, north-west.'

'You seem sure of that.'

'That's where I've sent his pal.'

'The mother up the mountain!'

'That mother up the mountain is one cute kiddy. Do me a favour, Sol. Remember that Mick you came across when you worked Washington? The one who threatened the heavy on you through the Kennedy tribe?'

The other man palmed his temple in thought. 'McAvoy! This ain't his scene: the IRA don't operate in the Rockies – do they?'

'I hope to Christ not! McAvoy's a sort of emerald guardian angel for the big feller, Martin. Heard through the grapevine he got him off the hook in Cripple Creek. Martin owes him one, or McAvoy's got something on him. If he has, I want to know what that something is.'

'I got the same feelin' when we spoke to Martin at the hospital – like I didn't know his type.'

Robinson almost succeeded in blowing his brains over the desk. 'That's the second pack of Kleenex today! Get back to me on that pronto!'

An hour later, the sergeant reported back. 'Difficult cuss to find,' he said. 'Wouldn't say much. But he was sure Martin wouldn't mess around here. I'd say he's got something on him. Said Martin was going back to Ireland. Soon. Sounded ominous. Sure sounded all fired up at my questions.'

Robinson stared at his sergeant. 'Carrying on the war from Dublin's one thing, Sol, but revenge with murderous intent on my patch is quite another. Get out an APB. Haul Martin in for a chat.'

Alone, Robinson wrestled with himself. Do I have the right to use Thompson as bait? I told him to come down if they showed. Now they're in Montana! I've got Cripple Creek on the Irishman, so he might let something slip. But can I trust him to protect the Limey instead of blowing off those hunters' heads? Still, Immigration's a fine lever.

★ ★ ★ ★ ★

A Boulder patrol car screeched to a halt outside a downtown drugstore. The two policemen levelled their revolvers through the rain at a man leaving the building. Stretching him against the wall, they frisked the suspect, handcuffed and pushed him towards the car.

'OK big boy! Get in,' barked the driver.

'What's all this about?' growled Paddy Martin. 'Where are you taking me?'

'You'll find out,' grinned the other patrolman. 'We're doing the Fed's work for 'em.'

Paddy spat on the sidewalk. FBI, he thought, the equivalent of Britain's Special Branch. Bloody Immigration! Playing silly arses, more like. This sounded like a Robinson tactic.

The car leapt from the curb, lights flashing into the dismal night.

★ ★ ★ ★ ★

Benjamin listened to the golfball hail crashing onto the roof in a deafening crescendo. The ice bullets had ravaged the timberline and valley for over an hour. Surely, it couldn't last much longer.

He had been thinking about the climb to the devil horns eight thousand feet above when the hail erupted.

195

Glancing at some crumpled pieces of paper on the bed, he turned to the poem he had written for the book. It was meant to summarise the ill-fated love between the two agents tormented over conflicting ideals for respective countries. The story had reached a crucial stage where the English SIS man had begun to suspect his Russian counterpart of being a double agent. Their affair had to end; their brief glimpse of happiness blown to oblivion.

Picking up his pen, Benjamin altered the stanzas; changed the metre to flow the passion that was driving his heart like the hail drumming on the cabin roof. Like the title of his book, the poem was called Intelligence Man. Moving closer to the oil lamp, he read the final draft:

> *I aim, you'll die;*
> *I shoot, you missed,*
> *That's how we play the game*
> *. . . God help us!*
>
> *We view the world through intelligence eyes*
> *Loaned by the Service,*
> *And always it is us who die*
> *Or lose to ourselves: the living dead of espionage.*
>
> *We cannot think – conditioned yes,*
> *To save our country from itself*
> *And from an unseen enemy*
> *That hunts us for its own survival.*
>
> *At least hate is not our watchword,*
> *More a deadly game of chess -*
> *A game that nobody wins*
> *And nobody becomes Grand Master.*
>
> *From the bloodied snow of Moscow*
> *To Washington's legal alleys,*
> *Silently, we kill with quieter conscience:*
> *Pawns closer to an unmarked grave.*

I aimed, you're dead;
I hit, you're a statistic,
That's how we play the game
. . . Maybe God won't understand.

Was that how it had been for the man who had given him the idea for the book? Before throwing himself from the London Post Office Tower? He held his head. What kind of men were they really? He too for re-creating the double tragedy. Mind games! Everything was a lurid trick of the brain: it lied like a camera. Or was it blackmail? A sordid exposure of man's soul – if he possessed one – by a sadistic and conniving mind? If so: whose mind? What great intelligence? The government's or the Foreign Service operative's?

He stared at the tin cans, now muted by the cacaphenous hailstones. They too, were a game: foisted on him by the evil of men . . . *Afraid of the unseen enemy that hunts us for its own survival . . .* Bloody true! But not Arapahoe.

You're fantasising again, Ben, he thought, crossing to the window as the hail diminished. Maybe the Arapaho has learnt to separate fact from mental gymnastics. I don't know. 'Whatever?' changing to speech: 'I'm still a novice.'

Moving to the fire, he imagined Sally knitting baby things in the apartment: Paddy nodding off on the divan. He smiled. Me, a father! the thought erasing the dialectics. Looking at the diary resting on a log, he read the day's entry:

Eleven days! Still they haven't come. I miss Sally with every windrush. The book is in its latter stages – thank heaven: it was depressing me. I am stuck for plot – amazing, at the bloody end! So I will re-write the poem – again. The thought excites me . . .

Later, he added:

I have rewritten the poem. It is still bad, but it frightens me. Sometimes insight is a dangerous commodity: alien. I think we will never truly know ourselves. It is this which scares . . . I was reading an old magazine this morning containing the Colorado state song. It was written by one AJ Fynn . . . It brought Sam to mind . . .

Opening the door, he smelt the fresh crushed smell of the forest. Only a storm can do that, he thought: change everything without changing itself. Simple laws of nature! If I could transpose them into human terms, my characters wouldn't have to butcher one another because they couldn't change. Coexistence! Nature's is a better way: absolute; final; free of malice and hate.

Suffering a mood change, he decided against the original plot of lover killing lover: a suicide pact had much more realism and tragedy than a cold blooded killing with a pistol. Somehow it was morally palatable; even passionate in a curiously macabre way. He would have to alter the poem accordingly – no, on second thoughts, maybe not.

Looking through the mist, the eagle delighted his eye. Now there's a shrewd bitch if I ever I saw one! as the giant bird dropped between the foggy layers above the forest. I can't really blame her for that rat. Not really! She's probably got a hungry family to feed somewhere. He pulled a face at the derelict pipeline: at least it worked after a fashion when I needed it, laughing as he remembered himself sitting on the bed like a castaway on a drowning desert island after the broken members had, on one occasion, channelled the rain inside Virginia.

The mountain, invincible as ever, dwarfed the timberline, its peaks beckoning somewhere in the eddying mists just as they had done in the Paradise Pub in Liverpool on that Christmas Eve.

'It'll pass the time away,' Benjamin muttered to the invisible summit. He had been assessing a likely access route from the southern end of the plateau. 'That's if Dickens isn't building his cemetery of bones.'

He grinned, his white hair billowing over the scar. How could a woman love such a face? Thank God Sally does! During the interview, he had promised Gabass that he would present a new face at the Sun offices. 'No sense in petrifying the staff,' the editor had concurred.

The cry, weak and distant like a lonely seagull, trickled through the mire like the night voices along a deserted beach said to be the lost souls of mariners.

He stopped as it came again. Stealthily, keeping to the dish and away from the traps in the trees, he homed in on the sound. Who? Now lifting, the mist wrapped around the voice and changed the timbre: concealed, disguised the owner.

He caught a blur of movement near the forest edge. Something – no, it was human, was close to the sprung ballbearing mine! Who? Breaking from the treeline, he pulled the bow on aim as Sam came into focus.

'You could have died coming here,' he bellowed angrily. 'How did you know I was here?'

'I didn't,' puffed the boy after his climb. 'It's Boogie! You were right: the city's bad for him. I brought him back to get better.'

Benjamin rolled his eyes in defeat. 'You're freezing! Where is he – in your jacket?'

'Yes. You don't mind us coming back? The Cornclifts were nice people . . . but they tried to put Boogie down. I thought that . . '

'You thought what?'

He hung his head. 'Aw shucks, I know different now, but I reckoned hot-headed at the time that Sally had something to do with it. I'm sorry! Nothing was the same and I was confused and miserable. Everything happened so fast: Boogie got ill and you were getting married and going to live in Cascade, so I had to come back up here until spring to save the little feller's life. I'd lost you – I did't want to lose him, too.'

There: it was said. A child's simple, devastating admission of love. Benjamin was in a quandary. No matter how much he wanted the boy with him, his life would be in danger. 'Follow me,' he said acidly, walking back up the dish. 'Give me your pack?'

'Why don't we take the short cut instead of *around* the timberline?'

'Because things have changed. I'll explain later.' What would he explain: that murderers were trying to blow him to bits? 'Hurry, it's coming on to rain.' Suddenly, he stopped. 'Where were you in that hailstorm?'

Sam grinned. 'Crawled between two rocks. Boy, did it come down!'

Benjamin smiled, recalling the time they had walked together away from the unseen pilot and his silent bombs. Somehow, it seemed right that they should be together again on the mountain. Yes, despite the danger, he was truly glad Sam had returned. Damn it, he shouldn't be – *but he was.* Despite welfare! Despite Immigration! *All because of a cat.*

CHAPTER 15

Benjamin did not tell Sam the complete truth about the traps; merely implied that the hunters might cause trouble after the fight on the timberline. As a result, he hunted alone; the boy was content to stay in the cabin with Boogaloo who now showed signs of improvement. In the event of an attack, Benjamin would hold the hunters' fire while Sam made his gettaway either through the rocks down to the southern end of the valley or via the cavern.

Benjamin hoped the two-way radio didn't go on the blink.

'How long will we stay, Ben?' Sam asked reluctantly one late morning. He had been giving Boogaloo sugared water from a syringe to prevent dehydration.

'A week maybe! Remember when we first met? You asked me if I planned climbing the mountain? Well, I think I'll do it while I've got the chance. You'll have to go to Indian John's while I do it. How long has the crisis run?' indicating the kitten.

'The vet said ten days, but it's been much longer. He won't give in. He survived the trip here! I didn't think he would.'

'Hmnn, seems he's got a reasonable chance,' stripping the rifle for cleaning. 'Yesterday, when you went for that walk: where there any tracks?'

'Human? No. Saw bear tracks going down the dish, though! Probably Dickens.'

Benjamin sighed thoughtfully. 'I've a feeling we'll see a lot more of him before we leave.' He shot around as the cans jangled eerily across the room. 'As we planned, Sam. Move it!'

Quickly assembling the weapon, he moved to the doorway, but grinned with relief as a man became entangled in the string at the far end of the timberline.

'Paddy!' he shouted. 'Wait there: don't move! Sam, it's OK.'

Cursing, the big man's face blackened like thunder clouds. 'What the hell is this, Englishman? And me still with my leg dicky. What's with the buckskins?' staring at Benjamin's dress.

'The alarm works. You were dead a minute ago, my friend – the buckskins go with the job, courtesy of Indian John.' Pointing to the leg: 'How did it stand up to the climb?'

'No sense, no feeling,' winked Paddy. 'Wha . . .' as Sam emerged from the rocks.

Benjamin patted the boy's back. 'He'll tell you over coffee.'

'Be damned! It's a decent drink I'm wanting,' allowing Benjamin to pick up his pack. 'Don't break the Bushmills! Best Irish there is.' Glancing at the tin cans: 'Is there anywhere safe? Or are the entire Rockies a bloody no-go area? The place is a bloody mini Belfast!'

'Later.'

Paddy drank deeply inside the cabin. 'I'd back us against the best, wouldn't you, Sam?'

The boy grinned and left the men to talk.

Paddy wiped his lips: 'I'm not here to fight, but protect you – as if you needed it! When they show, we go back down. We only engage them if our lives are endangered. At least that's the theory.'

'What deal have you made with Robinson?' asked Benjamin sus-piciously. 'It isn't like you not to fight!'

'You've heard of the SWAT teams – Special Weapons And Tactics! Robinson's homicide have got a similar outfit of their own; some mish-mash of a task force.' The Irishman chuckled. 'Covers a multitude of sins. He persuaded me to lend a hand. We're to flush 'em out, that's all.'

Benjamin winced. 'To keep your fame from Immigration, more like it! Forget it. Just go back to Ireland – and whatever. Let them do their own dirty work. They can't even keep an eye on Sam. No, go home, Paddy. Go back to your own war.'

Silently the Irishman took Mona from his pack. Holding up the broken pieces, he said with feeling: 'Understand?'

Benjamin shook his head. Celts, he thought.

'I can't go back. There are . . . reasons.'

'Best left unsaid.'

Anyway, I've decided to stay in America – that's the real reason why I let Robinson talk me into it.' His voice went throaty. 'Had a long, hard think in your apartment. Maybe I'm best out of it – the cause. They don't need the likes of me anymore; they've got a new breed coming through. A mean lot, I can tell you. Something you said that first night after we met: 'It's best where it belongs – in the history books.' His head bowed and he fiddled nervously with his fingers.

Astonished, Benjamin handed back the bottle. So Paddy Martin no longer ran! Had faced himself and come to whatever shocking terms had been forced upon him by his own conscience. Touching the man's shoulder, he joined Sam cutting firewood on the timberline.

Paddy leaned on a boulder shaking his large head decisively in the rain as Benjamin clung like a prostrate spider to a jutting pyramid of rock way above the plateau. His body was bruised and his clothes were torn from repetitive sliding down the wet rock face.

'If you want to be another Hillary,' said the Irishman, 'at least start the easy way. It's one obsession after another with you. That route to the fault leading to the main climb is forty feet – almost vertical! You can bypass it in a few minutes by walking round the back of the pyramid. Three blessed days you've been at it! Stupid sod!'

Fingers clamped in crevices, toes cramped and balanced on tiny nibs of rock, Benjamin pressed his face hard against the wet pyramid. Breathing heavy, every fibre in his body ached from the strain. And there it was again! Oh God, he could feel it. He was slipping. His left gave – then the right. Shit!

Paddy grimaced as Benjamin X'd down the rock. 'Oh Christ,' he muttered, as his friend toppled backwards and banged his shoulder. 'Our hunter pals don't have to worry about you – you're doing an admirable self demolition job. Look at you – all rags and blood! *Intellectual, eh!*'

Benjamin rose stiffly, holding his shoulder. 'I'll give it a break for a bit,' he wheezed.

Paddy blew cheroot smoke up the mountain. 'Forty lousy feet! Is it worth it? What the hell are you trying to prove now, Mountain Man?'

'I'm getting there,' Benjmain ignoring the jibe. 'I recognised the crevices.'

Paddy sniggered. 'I should think so: you've been screwing them half the week! Let's go down; this place has ice cubed my love factory.'

'I have to get to that fault. I'll stay on a bit. Where's Sam?'

'Wise! Couldn't take the punishment. He's wandering around somewhere with his moggie . . . Here he is.'

The boy had been exploring the bony plateau. He frowned at Benjamin. 'Haven't you had enough yet! Can't you talk him out of it, Paddy? It's plumb loco.'

'Far be it from me to distract the inner workings of the great English author,' pulling up his collar as the rain grew heavy.

Benjamin swore silently. 'I'll give it one more try, then I'll join you both.'

'I'd make a fortune out of you in the circus,' beamed Paddy. 'OK, Mountain Man, one more shot for mankind.'

Sam rolled his eyes and stood next to Paddy. Periodically, Boogaloo poked his head from the boy's jacket to watch Benjamin's rock climbing antics. 'He won't give in, you know. He's as stubborn as an old mule.'

'I know, son.' There was pride in the Irishman's voice. 'He's that kind of person. Tell him I said that and I'll skin you alive.'

Reaching his previous position, driving rain blurred Benjamin's vision. Twelve inches above his left hand, a slight indent ran diagonally upwards and across the rock: his goal ever since the first fall. After that, it would be plain sailing. All or nothing, he braced himself and edged sideways. Almost there . . . No, don't look down, Ben. Christ, don't do that. Concentrate. But in doing that, he lost balance and reached frantically upwards, his bleeding fingers just hooking into the wet indent. Smiling, he crabbed his way over the top of the pyramid. To the sound of clapping, he came down the easy route, in pain – cold, wet and very relieved.

Sam saw the grizzly first as Dickens appeared from behind an ice cluster fifty yards away, dragging his latest victim.

'Ben,' shouted Paddy. 'Yogi just showed up.'

'Frighten him off! Nothing else. It's his home, not ours!'

'So you found out – eventually,' Paddy cocking his weapon and firing into the air.

Dickens dropped the carcass and growled, but thought better of the man-noise and roared his defiance all the way down to the timberline.

'Jaysus,' snarled the Irishman. 'Why do you have to do these insane things – climb mountains, build pipelines and the like?' Pointing after Dickens: 'After what he did, why don't you kill the bastard – or get off his mountain.'

'Coexistence – remember? It has to work for him, too.'

'You mean the bear's supposed to play this silly game as well! He'll never accept you as long as you've got a hole in your . . . Ah, what's the use!' Mumbling Gaelic obscenities into his beard, he led the way off the plateau.

Like a tattered black shroud held up to the daylight, a myriad pinpricks of light emerged as stars as night threw on its ragged universe.

'Breathtaking, isn't it!' Benjamin re-tensioning the bowstring.

Paddy, bottle in hand, drew on his cheroot and said nothing.

'A heck of a long way,' the boy craning his neck. Boogaloo slept inside his jacket.

'Nearest one's about twenty-five million miles,' Benjamin shouldering the bow.

'Must be big to see them from that distance! I can't imagine so far.'

'It will give you an idea if you think of the sun's diameter –

well over three quarters of a million miles. Some stars are a thousand times that! They say there's over two hundred billion stars glittering blue to white, yellow, orange to red. The colours depend on the star's surface temperature: the sun, for example, is ten thousand degrees Fahrenheit.'

'Sounds like celestial traffic lights for drunken astronauts,' chipped in Paddy, blowing smoke across the universe. 'The North Star, that's all you need to know, out here, Sam.'

'That's the navigation star, isn't it?' the boy rubbing his stiffening neck.

Benjamin nodded. 'On the button, Sam! Polaris is the Latin name. But it's not the brightest by a long shot. Sirius is, in the constellation of Canis Major. Some stars change brightness according to the light they give off. They're called cepheids after the mythological King of Ethiopia, Cepheus. A lot of stars are named after Greek mythological characters.'

'Ceph . . . Who!'

Benjamin laughed. 'Never mind. The king had a daughter called Andromeda – also a constellation – who was chained to a cliff to be eaten by a monster. Fortunately for her, the cavalry arrived in the form of Perseus, the son of Zeus.'

'I've heard of him!' Sam feeling Boogaloo shifting position. 'Saw him at Disneyland three years ago on a Christmas outing.'

Benjamin grinned. 'Did you know he's also called Jupiter? Jupiter's the largest planet in the solar system. Five hundred years before Christ was born, a statue was built in his honour made out of gold and ivory and acclaimed as one of the Seven Wonders of the World. It was forty feet high, but sadly, it went missing somewhere along the line.'

'Probably one of my ancestors pinched it!' Paddy banging his sides with laughter.

'What's so funny?'

'I was just thinking about your forty feet – slithering down that pyramid. You almost disappeared too! In theory, I can't question your motives: in practice, you're a raving lunatic.'

Throwing a quick look at Paddy: 'Any more questions, Sam? Before we go inside and leave the stars to the navigators.'

'Yeah! How do they do that? Navigate?'

'Simple! Say you're on a ship – anywhere. But you have to

have a sextant – don't ask me, I've never used one. It measures the angle each star makes with the horizon. Sailors have an almanac, a book which tells them the earth's position with each star at any given time and they measure the angle. They take three fixes . . . With it so far?'

Sam glanced uncertainly at Paddy before nodding.

'Then they calculate – again, don't ask me – the distance of their ship from each of the three positions. By drawing a line on a map or sea chart, their vessel is where the distance lines meet. In daytime, they 'shoot' the sun at noon in much the same way.'

Tired, Sam followed the two men inside the cabin. Ceph . . . or whoever he was, Greek gods and shooting at the sun: was learning really worth it? His eyes dropped as Benjamin and Paddy talked quietly in the shadows. He wasn't aware of Benjamin tucking him in bed without waking Boogaloo.

Softly, Paddy whistled the Croppy Boy.

Benjamin recalled the night when the Irishman had sung the song around the camp fire. 'Take you back?' he said softly.

The man lit another cheroot. 'Yes,' he replied. 'Funny how music is associated with memories. In a way, I suppose, it's a form of diarising history and the mood of the world through the communal tongue of sound. We make music when we're happy – or sad, use it to stir our hearts in battle or to ease the daily load. Its true magic is its resilience: immortality. Its beauty is the memory that went before.'

Benjamin placed a few logs on the fire: this was what he had missed – the Irishman in reflective moments and the boy never far away. A mental picture of Sally knitting baby clothes completed the idyll. It wasn't wrong wanting them all – was it? Irrespective, could he have them all?

Paddy caught the look. 'Like everything else, music is all part of arriving, growing up. We don't stop until we die – some of us, that is,' grinning. 'Marriage is the first preparation for death. Someone once told me that the joy of dying is accepting eternity with your earthly loved one.'

'They have a valid reason there. I wasn't ready for my first wife. Then, I interpreted love as growing up, but never knowing if, or when, it would stop. I agree, death and love are relative. I see the importance of that now – the difference, yet similarity.'

'Like your characters! Sally said you have a problem with the real and the imaginary?'

'Yes. I live with them. You can't get inside them if you don't understand their individualities – much less your own. You become them: main characters are like brothers, the rest, distant relations – but nevertheless, vital in the overall canvas. Nowadays, I think I can handle Dr Jekyll and Mr Hyde with reasonable parity. Unlike the dubious doctor, I leave the suffering in the surgery. My characters now know I have my life to live, too. But you seem more relaxed with the days!'

Paddy pulled out the Bushmills. 'I think I understand your writer's loneliness – that's what you're talking about, the private hell. Mine's . . . a different brand.' He was picking his words, as if he was still not sure about opening his mind to another man. Even Benjamin. But it's not like that, he thought. Not like kneeling at your first confession! More like being thankful for lifting the burden of the violent years: absolution by recanting to a tried and trusted friend. He'd never gotten that far with a priest hidden behind a black cloth and a crucifix blasting light beneath a solitary globe when the man had always known his voice.

'Loneliness started for me when they shot my father. The English! They dragged him from the boozer for questioning after one of their bigwigs was gunned down on Lodge Day. The IRA caught the real culprit six months later, unable to live with his conscience. But that was too late for my Da. Cooney – the bastard's name – was a Protestant, needless to say, who had a longlasting grudge over something I never found out with my Da. He swore he'd never meant it to go that far – but that's what they all say.'

Benjamin saw the sweat glisten on Paddy's brow: the slow wringing of the hands as his steely eyes glazed with remembrance. He handed back the bottle.

'They executed Cooney in front of me in a waterlogged field; left him with a warning note to any would-be collaborators. Ma – God rest her soul – never got over Da. It was a cover-up, Cooney being an English lackey and all. Da was shot like a dog in an alleyway trying to escape – *so they said.* All very convenient.'

'How old were you at the time?' Benjamin moved by the big man's words.

'An old man of ten! You grew up fast in Ireland, then. I suppose

208

they still do. I had brothers and sisters, but I was the closest to Da. I idolised him. He was never violent or belonged to the Provos, but he believed as fervently in a free and united homeland. Anyway,' he sighed, 'I was considered ripe for the organisation and I joined gladly. There was no glory of a defeated England in my head as was drummed into all of us in the Dublin cellars – just the bitterness of my father's face blown away in that alley. Revenge was my faith and my mistress. One thing led to another and I was sent on operations to Liverpool, Manchester, Birmingham and eventually, London, graduating from messenger to other things. I'll leave that to your imagination. I have much to answer for without dramatising the shame – but remember, you English from your bloody Parliament downwards, segregated and burst my country like a puss-exploded carbuncle. I was a soldier – still am, I suppose – not a murderer or an intruder in someone else's country – fighting for Irish soil. No matter how right he considers his acts, a soldier always feels shame afterwards. Not one's own shame, someone else's: but he feels it because he's the one who has to pull the trigger. The lowly conduit for society in all its hypocricy and ignorance to slake its thirst of hatred. Yes, even stout hearted Republicans without the stomach for fighting have turned against us of late. Every country without exception has had them before, during and after – particularly after – any war.'

He flicked the cheroot into the flames, roaring and sucking up the chimney. 'I got back in the seventies. They had nothing on me, but because of my connections I was thrown in the Maze: H-block. After the usual grilling, they put a hood over my head and made me stand on tip-toe, feet apart and fingertipped to the the wall. Night and day – I never knew which was which – consisted of beatings, debasement and being rolled about naked at night in winter in freezing water with that damnable hood over my face and their damnable white noise – loud radio mush – until I nearly went insane. I was totally disorientated. Then they stopped that infernal noise – a week the Army interrogators said. That may have been true, but I'll never know for sure. It seemed like an eternity. I thought my mind would explode in the blackness of that hood, smelling of my own vomit and stink and the destructive whiteness of that hideous noise interspersed with the screams and sobs and pleas of other men I never saw. I can't describe it even now, but it's something like an invisible dentist driving an invisible wedge into your brain. White! Invisible! *The real hell!* The bloody English revelled in slavery, invented the concentration camp and introduced white noise to an Irishman. Do you understand a little more of the things I do, Ben Thompson?'

Benjamin screwed his eyes, picturing Paddy's naked beaten body while his mind lay a prisoner inside the odious confines of a hood, persecuted with frequency torture sufficient to bring a man to insanity, but not enough to topple him over the edge. What would the Press make of that? And they talk about the Lubyanka! He'd read papers on the horrid subject, confirmed by the man who had leapt off the London Post Office Tower. Torture had indeed become a highly refined art. How far had poor Paddy been?

'They wouldn't let me attend my own mother's funeral, the bastards.' His huge frame shook and Benjamin turned away. 'I was out then – on the run. I escaped. My commanding officer tried to arrange a one day truce, but the gentlemen English denied even that. My own Ma . . . '

Benjamin studied the fire; anything not to look at the big man crying his bitterness in a lonely mountain cabin. He checked the boy was still asleep: the lad could learn nothing from this; it would serve no purpose.

Pulling himself together, Paddy drank and held out the bottle. 'You must have a few loose up top with all that writing and the grizzly. I read your first chapters. You left them open once, a few days after we walloped Davy Crockett and his All Stars.'

'We did, didn't we! Or rather, you did,' Benjamin smiling softly. 'I thought you'd killed that bald headed ape. Yes, I suppose writers have to be scrambled eggs to explain the readers to themselves – and I'm not even a good one! But the reader pays and that's the bottom line: money. A fight against insanity for the fluctuating values of a government's piece of paper. Fool's gold!'

Paddy relaxed, unashamed of weeping in front of this man. 'Once you've made it' though,' he said, 'international bestseller-dom, fame and 'fool's' gold. Not to be scoffed at!'

Benjamin sneered. 'Thirty pieces of silver, not gold! A Judas ransom for prostituting your mind.' He thought for a monent. 'Maybe that's harsh. Writers are nothing special – insecure as sin. But the publishers are the pariahs, the carnivores of creativity;

debase literature to the bestial format of the bank balance. They're nothing but glorified moneylenders with little or no regard for writers: devious little bully men raping creativity for their own profit. I've heard it said that they make writers authors and great authors masters. Bullshit! It's all a great public relation job to con the public into paying increased prices for their titles. Great reapers, publishers! Unless you're lucky, money is like rocking-horse shit to a writer; biased contracts, dubious agents all out to screw the unwary and publishers forever after a free buck. It's a question of working towards a peak. You're no good to anyone until you reach it, and dead afterwards. You have to suffer, bleed your way to the top of the pile. A lot of writers hit their peak when most people are considering retirement! And, of course, the bastards make money after you're dead by re-releasing your old books.'

Paddy laughed quietly so as not to disturb the boy. 'Rocking-horse shit! I've never heard it put that way before. And fame?' tugging his beard.

'Fame is an abstract insincerity. It's a meaningless torture – the price for acceptance. Thankfully, it's a disease writers don't usually suffer from – unless they're politicians on an ego trip. Most people enjoy a good book, but that doesn't necessarily mean that they idolise the author – God forbid! We don't need kudos to survive as do pop or movie stars, but nevertheless, we tend to get used as window dressing by literary snobs rather like the prestigious hotelier who uses the free view of harbour yachts for his privileged clientele, but refuses to serve the salt-stained sweats who crew them. He can't handle plain-speaking sailors anymore than the average person could endure living with a writer: the two don't mix. Thank Christ! Fame is the wrong word, Paddy, in this profession. Achievement is everything – and that can go astray in the lifelong search for lost ideas, the fanatical quest for perfection, booze, gambling, women or other assorted goodies. Pasternak once wrote: Fame's not a pretty sight. Well, that's how I see it. Fame, I never want.'

Paddy spat into the fire, watched the saliva bubble on the glowing logs. 'Well, if nothing else, you have a gift.'

'Gift! Horseshit! It's a curse – a love-hate relationship. You seldom know where one leaves off and the other begins. You're helpless to a degree because it's an extension of yourself. It's like a hungry mongrel – it never leaves you. You play Christmas music in the summer and the neighbours think you've flipped: but it's for mood for a scene in a book. Who waits until Christmas to write a Christmas scene? Then you weep like a fool for your dead characters and hate the damned book in the closing stages and are tempted to rush the final chapters to be rid of the heartache. If you're lucky enough for some bloodsucker of a publisher to annihilate and rebuild on the ashes, you have to relive the hell all over again by re-writing it to his formula. You strive for the perfection you know is beyond you; know you'll never read the thing again in your lifetime – or if you do, you'll be too old to feel the hurt of the younger years of struggle.'

He drank, his eyes uncontrollably ablaze with emotion. He didn't want to talk this way, but now that he'd started, the words kept flooding like a giant tidal wave. 'Hate-love! Hate of the continual search for perfection, of the never-ending sausage machine; love – most of us don't understand it – and the sense of fulfilment, completeness through creativity. No: fame, fortune or gift, they count for nought: it's the pain and joy of sharing your thoughts with another human being and the possessing of the skill to communicate, that really counts. It is responsible work undertaken by people who are mostly walking contradictions. I could go on about writers attacking governments and being a barometer for the national mood, but it's all been said before by drunken writers in the debauched columns of the Sunday nationals.'

'Jaysus! You do have a mind of your own, alright! I thought it was simple: you were a writer, got published and laughed all the way to the Caribbean with a dozen different currencies. And I suppose you're always watching out for plagiarism as well?'

But Benjamin had finished talking. His breast heaved as he pulled hard and long on the Bushmills.

Paddy picked up a piece of burning bark and lit another cheroot. 'Tell me truthfully: would you have it any other way?'

'No.'

'That's what I thought – despite your love-hate tug-of-war.'

'And you?'

'No,' Paddy reaching for the bottle.

'That's what I thought – despite your conscience.'

212

The fire died and they turned in. It had been a long night.

★ ★ ★ ★ ★

The Beard sipped his beer, chalked the cue and broke. 'Spot!' he said as the pool balls clicked on the green cloth. He and Eb were playing two diesel mechanics for drinks and the jukebox.

'Great party, last night!' Eb making a lewd gesture with his hips. 'Montana's the place for me! Heck, those broads did it any way. You were ticking smoothly.'

'Your shot,' The Beard watching rain clouds through a break in the curtains.

Eb made a hash of his shot and grabbed his beer. 'Sorry! Got that redhead again tonight. Hey, you don't look too happy!'

'Have to be moving on again, soon.'

'What!' frowning at The Beard's poker face.

'Rain's about due. We've unfinished business. Remember?'

'Sure . . . but! Aw heck, I was havin' a ball,' now following his partner's gaze up at the clouds. 'But we'll come back, won't we?' like a child whose holiday has been cut short. 'We've found good meat, a market . . . And oh, those dames!'

'Yeah, we'll come back.' But for once, confidence had vanished from The Beard's voice and he didn't believe his own words.

'Hey, you don't sound too sure, old buddy! The Limey ain't no problem.'

'Finish the game,' the hunter replied sourly. Last night he'd had that Vietnam dream again: the one where he and Eb came back soaked with rain and blood only to die in the mountains. But the end always blurred and then he would be alone, sitting on top of a bleeding Statue of Liberty in a rain storm – in football gear for Chrissake! – and then he would awake in a malarial sweat. He'd had it perhaps a dozen times over the last four years. He'd always supported the New York Giants, yet last night he had worn the colours of the Chicago Bears. The bloodstained Statue of Liberty had worn devil horns. He didn't like it, but he'd be darned if it would get him down. He'd been through too much in Asia.

213

He scowled as Eb missed another shot. Awaiting his turn, he sank the eight ball.

'Attaboy!' Eb banging his friend on the back.

Ignoring Eb's delight, he stared up at the sky. Soon, he thought. Rain! It would all finish with the rain.

★ ★ ★ ★ ★

Benjamin made the call from Indian John's. 'Sam's here, Sally,' he said. 'And Paddy! Don't worry, we'll be down in a week or so – probably less. There's been no trouble. Tell Harry that, will you: he'll be concerned.'

He purposely didn't mention the coming rain or the traps. Nor did he talk of climbing Devil Mountain the following day.

'Ben . . . You mean more than life to me. I know you don't believe in Him, but I'm asking God to protect you – all. Please come back, my darling. Remember, you have a child who is growing by the minute.'

Benjamin goosepimpled. 'I know, my love. We'll all be together for our first Christmas,' winking at the old Indian. 'I've written something and left it with John, here, at the trading post so that you can read it while we're on our way down. Nothing can, will go wrong. I found myself when I found you . . . Love was the answer. I have everything to live for now. I truly love you with all my heart, Sally. Go well, my woman.'

'God speed, my only one.'

Indian John took Benjamin's hand: 'I now see the Arapaho in your eye, Bengymen. Do not abuse the honour. You have the trust of an old warrior.'

'Thank you, my friend. Trust is a small word, yet its meaning is far greater than we can ever attain.'

The Indian smiled admiringly as Benjamin left the trading post. Your time is too late, Bengymen, he thought sadly. A hundred years ago, you would have made a great American. You understand the ways of the Indian: the wonder of coexistence.

CHAPTER 16

Benjamin put the small pack on his back. It was that freezing hour before dawn. Paddy was unhappy with the cloud build-up and said so vigorously, but Benjamin insisted on climbing Devil Mountain – hunters or no hunters; rain or no rain. Today was the day.

In a few days he would return to Institutionalised Man.

Sam didn't like the concern registering on the Irishman's face. Visibility, he knew, would be bad up there: zero in places. But, like Virginia, the pipeline, Dickens and the rock pyramid, Benjamin was unstoppable. Climbing the mountain was another of those things he had to do.

Benjamin stroked the cat's head. 'You know, I think he actually likes me, Sam. I believe he's going to make it.'

'*Boogie always did like you, Ben.* You were just too busy to notice. I told you he'd make it living back up here! He likes the mountains. Just you be careful, Dickens growled all last night. Wherever he went before I returned, he's found himself a sore head.'

'I don't think so, Sam. There was havoc in the valley before he left: it's quieter now. Maybe he's like the three of us – at the crossroads.'

Paddy scowled at the glint in Benjamin's eye. 'He's not a human, Ben,' he said gruffly. 'Dickens isn't a Walt Disney trick of photography. Granted, he's had his share of problems with us disturbing his courtship and those . . . hunters, but you've often said you never know when he'll turn.'

Benjamin touched the scar: the skin was hot. He was nervous and wanted to get started: talk at a time like this was scary; counter-productive. He just wanted to go out and damnwell do it!

'Yes, well . . . If he shows up, I'll get back fast. That goes for the rain, too.'

Paddy bit his lip at the reference to the hunters. 'No need,' he said matter-of-factly for Sam's sake. 'Nobody's going anywhere until you get back.'

Benjamin ruffled the boy's hair. 'Take it easy, my boy. We've a lot of talking to do when I get back.'

Sam beamed. 'Are you and Sally going to . . .'

'When I come down,' said Benjamin sternly.

'Don't philosophise too loud up there,' Paddy blowing the red end of his cheroot. 'We don't want any complaints from the heavenly parliament about an English agnostic.'

Benjamin slung the bow and quiver. Seeing Paddy's angry look: 'It's all I need.'

'Don't be stupid, man! Take a rifle. To coin a phrase: What if Dickens has great expectations of you: you're stymied!'

'Not sure I appreciate that remark,' smiled Benjamin looking up at the mountain. It was almost a mile and a half from the timber-line to the devil horns – most of it fairly simple. Nevertheless, he carried an ice pick and a coil of rope, for the final cloud-covered five hundred yards would present the major difficulties. Indian John had told him that many inexperienced climbers like himself had been to the summit. By taking it steady, he had calculated being back at the cabin sometime the following afternoon – the day after at the latest.

They went with him as far as the plateau, Benjamin concentrating on the climb. A moody day in semi-darkness, an undecided wind whistled and moaned like a nagging woman rising from sleep.

216

A very moody day, thought Benjamin, susceptible to great change.

A broad ridge ran south below the main thrust of the mountain, ending in a sheer drop that swept downwards in white and black to collide with the timberlines of adjacent lower peaks that glared upwards like drowning men in some forgotten sea. From here, a steep climb of four thousand feet led to a massive buttress-like projection some two thousand feet below the gruesome chin of the devil head. This awesome passage was draped with enormous folds of wet, shiny rock, twisting and zig-zagging earthwards as if in fear of the evil semblance squatting overhead. Above the buttress, a demanding, deviating section eventually bent onto the head itself, followed by the lethal final approach to Benjamin's destination: the fifteen hundred feet through the clouds over the left-hand ridge.

Even now, the clouds were racing across an anthracite sky; dropping, obscuring the route to the top. If he didn't go now, he never would. Inclement or not, it had to be.

He recalled clear summer days, standing in awe, gazing up from the timberline. The television rescue he had seen in England taken from the airforce helicopter – now seemingly a lifetime away – had not shown the horns ravaged with cloud and violent turbulence. A more sobering thought.

He grinned ruthlessly: today – or tomorrow – he would stand on the summit: conquer Devil Mountain then leave these high places; these terrifyingly beautiful and hostile acres forever. Just for a day in my life, a millisecond in history, I will become man of the mountain: Mountain Man.

Turning to wave a last time to Paddy and Sam – already diminishing in size – he moved off once more. Soon, he was forced to stop where the ridge spewed onto the neighbouring timberlines before tackling the longest haul up to the buttress. It looked a hell of long way up! Adopting his old ploy of resting ten minutes in the hour, he negotiated a tricky overhang promising little but death as billowing cloud swirled all round.

Eventually, hot and cold, he arrived at the buttress and rested inside an alcove. He drank whiskied coffee as cloud and loose snow whipped up with increasing intensity. A rising wind gusted deafeningly across the concave walls of the mountain. Resuming the climb, he forced his aching legs up the gruelling incline to the devil head. With the gale now a constant, clamorous, screeching frenzy, he was continually forced to alter his route around the treacherous ice glaciers that had been invisible from the plateau. Visibility fast approaching zero in every direction, he relied on memory and instinct to reach the base of the chin leading to the left-hand horn.

As he negotiated a precipitous fault jutting out from the main thrust of the mountain, a gut-dropping roaring, gusting wind dispersed the cloud to reveal the rainsoaked miniature canyons and valleys far below. Feet from his side, a vertical wall of glistening rock plunged sickeningly onto the prairie trapped in shadow far to the north; scarps and re-entrants converged in a macabre union to massacre the land.

From up here, he thought, the land appears to be an afterthought in whatever upheaval originally separated the high from the low ground. Indeed, the place where men dwelt seemed dull and unappetising.

Of all his lonely battles, Benjamin had never had to contend with vertigo. Now, sitting to equalise the giddiness, he stared outwards rather than down. But the mesmeric quality of altitude renewed the lightness and contractions of his stomach. And then his illness was erased by violent, rapid change, that blotted out the lowlands, plunging the mountain into mayhem as a freak storm battered the open spaces.

Forced to rest up for the remainder of the day, he endured the bitter cold, listening fearfully to the raging maelstrom until it finally blew itself out in the dark hours. Great peals of thunder crashed eerily between the peaks and echoed off the mountain wall like the vanquished cries of lost Vikings searching for Valhalla.

Dawn fizzled through watery, brassy cloud, billowing softly like a ship's sail on a calm day.

It worried Benjamin: how long would it last? He looked up as a fresh cloud ocean drowned the mountain. As the wind dissipated, he walked upwards through the cloud.

It's like leaving the world behind, he thought, trudging on, higher into the universe.

Saturated, cramped, cold and weary, his head eventually poked through the gloom as the sun beat down from the vast lagoon of blue emptiness above.

Feeling decidedly odd, buried up to his neck in cloud and

218

surrounded by sky and wave upon wave of snow and ice-capped peaks glistening like cathedral glass, he laughed idiotically. Then, like a man expecting some awful apparition, he turned and stood mesmerised: there, marching away on either side, the devil horns threatened to stab the heavens, their massive, jagged tips dipping like obscene fingers into the porridge of rain cloud below.

Finding it difficult to breathe, he estimated the altitude to be around fourteen thousand feet. Partially recovering his composure, fear soon returned as a fresh wind revealed the lowlands, the clouds giving the impression that the land was moving. Giddy, he groped his way up through the cotton-wool; inched slowly over the icy rock of the nearest horn. As his head once more pierced through the cloud, he saw a Jumbo Jet float lazily by, seemingly at arm's length. Sensing conquest, he pushed himself onwards until he crawled over the ridge of the horn – *and nearly off the mountain.*

Elated, heart hammering like a jackhammer, Benjamin had arrived at the desolate pinnacle of Devil Mountain. Open-mouthed, he stared in muted confusion.

Perched on the colossal cantilever jutting from the mountain high above the Rockies, he felt as if he was sitting on the jib of a gigantic crane.

Totally alone, the pain of joy in his heart, he savoured the fleeting moment of peace – and all he said was: *'God . . . God . . . God . . .'*

★   ★   ★   ★   ★

Dickens had smelt the Odd One as he returned to the plateau after an unsuccessful hunt. Perplexed, he had followed the scent towards the buttress. Losing it where the rock dropped into the valleys below the twin peaks, he chose the right hand peak.

He growled softly. Why had the Odd One returned? Man was so unpredictable! Maybe his red-haired mate had complained, so he had wanted to be alone. Mates were like that. You couldn't hunt like you did before courtship, either. Like most males, he lived alone, but of late he had needed female companionship.

219

And there was this great change that was devouring him like the first surge of spring when life held new meanings. He wondered if the Odd One experienced it, too, for he had changed. The grizzly knew about those things. He had read the signs on the wind, felt the pulse of the mountains, their rivers and forests. After all, the Odd One was an animal and not above change. Anything was possible in the mountains.

But what was he doing so high?

The last time man had climbed so far, one had had to be carried off by a larger, noisier bird, than the female eagle. Its smell was bad and it carried other men with their man-noise inside its belly. At least the Odd One hadn't used the killing noise! And he had lived in peace ever since the fight at the ice dam when his face had nearly been taken from him. Should he be spared? How could one spare a man?

Putting aside his great questions, Dickens daydreamed in the gyrating chrysalis of grey. He had never been this high since . . . *She had been a good mate.* His nostrils flared with rage at the thought. But this was still his mountain: his alone.

Padding along the ridge, his temper rose as he arrived at the tip of the horn. The Odd One had vanished. It irritated him. No, they could never live together – with each other or with other men. The Odd One must die.

Waiting for the cloud to lift, his hackels rose as the Odd One's scream broke his reverie. Suddenly, he felt sorry for the man on the other horn, who, as yet, had not seen him. He was not really a man-noise man. But again, his mood changed, rousing his joy of the hunt and the sense of survival.

★ ★ ★ ★ ★

Staring across the cloud hills, Benjamin felt as if he were on an aircraft. His stomach lurched as the wind parted the morass to reveal a hazy map three miles below through multi-layered blotches of cumulus patrolling the lower skies.

Hell, he thought, I'm a child clinging to a branch about to snap and send me crashing into the earth.

He screamed as a freak power-blast sucked him sideways, rolling him towards the edge of the horn. Clawing the rock, the bowstring began to strangle him as it snagged, biting deep into his flesh. For a horrific second, he stared downwards at the earth before crawling back to safety.

Squatting on his haunches, he swallowed the bile vinegaring his throat and began talking to calm his nerves. Speaking to the god whose existence he had doubted since the beatings from the Jesuits, a deluge of emotion laid bare the soul he did not accept.

'Why am I talking like this?' he said. Answering himself in thought: Maybe it's because a man has to talk to someone when he stands on top of a mountain.

A chain reaction of events exploded inside his head; his life passed before his eyes. Impossible to clutch at any particular experience, he pictured the great mysteries: the existence of God and of Heaven and Hell; the definition of Truth and Love and the code that Man should live by, but seldom did.

'I have not accepted,' he said out loud, 'nor rejected Jeus Christ, but the idea of a soul is beyond me. Nor do I accept the Bible as a definitive work on ecclesiastical, moral and social issues. A clever combination of parable and half truth: yes. A domination of minds by a secular intelligence whose script demands obedience and acceptance of an unexplainable and unfathomable faith: certainly.

'I live by principles, not the blind prostratism demanded by clerics to explain so-called divine mysteries. I do not see You, Christ, as the God of Love: war for one, jealousy, revenge, hatred for others. How could You allow these things if You loved the mankind of Your likeness? But I do understand love as much as any man – that is to say: not much at all. It is simply an emotion. Yet I do think that it is this form of expression that we should live by for the advancement and preservation of mankind.

'But there are many types of love violated for self gain. Surely a *principle* is harder to attain; closer to purity than Your sullied variety! My love for Sally, is no more than an acceptance, an agreement of principles formed through respect. That is *not* love: love is the breeding river for hatred. It *is* hatred. It is abstract and simple and complex, impracticable and unbending and damnably frustrating. Most people can't handle it. Few feel its warmth for long – if ever. The boy and Paddy fall into this category of

221

principle. Sure, we don't always agree, but respect is never lost or broken by ulterior motives.'

The wind rose again and hammered his face as he paced back and forth, talking to the earth and sky.

'Let me tell You about Man's interpretation of love! When I was a child, the Jesuit priest schooling us in literature, suffered a heart attack as a result of so-called Christians butchering in Your name. Calling themselves the Divine Interventionists of Jesus Christ, they held a rally in Paris where the priest's parents lived. Their grief was some obscure purist point of scripture which they related to their country's cold-shouldering by the West. The rally erupted into bloodshed as rival religious groups attacked and my teacher's parents – unable to avoid the trouble – were roasted alive after some caring Christian chucked a petrol bomb at their car engine. The Jesuit – and he was one of the decent ones – never recovered and died shortly afterwards. *My point:* he had many years to expound Your code – and no doubt his parents, too – yet You allowed this catastrophe. *Why?* Worse men live! *Or is it that You are more callous than Man?*

'So who goes to Heaven or Hell – if they all believe they are fighting in Your name? Why we should fight at all, seems contradictory to humanitarianism. And maybe that's the nub: we're humans. Heaven and Hell; God and the Angels; Satan and His Devils! All a magnificent fiction to impose a single will upon the many. I would like to believe, but it is all too much . . . '

As he walked back and forth, a speck flew out of the sun. The female eagle hovered above Benjamin before diving back through the clouds into the clutches of winter.

Benjamin's eyes watered from the driving wind; the skin rippled on his face.

'Maybe You are not a person,' he continued, 'but a state of mind: a seed of the brain. I could come to terms with that: but then, from where did that seed originate? Again, mysteries and blind faith. Man is supposed to be created in Your likeness! That's as maybe, but blind faith is no substitute for political or ecological dialectics. I won't go into the Big Bang Theory about all this,' outstretching his arms, 'but I take the six day building programme very philosophically.'

With his hands again clasped tightly behind his back, the

moment of emotion impregnated with the rarified atmosphere moved him to a state of invincibility. He forgot his vertigo; no longer was concerned about being whisked up like a grain of dust, thrown into the great misty hole above the earth and dashed upon the land far below.

Now speaking about his decision to leave England, he categorised Institutionalised Man as a retrogressive sycophant; a sybaritic bureaucrat obsessed with greed and saving face.

Mentally ticking off his list: 'The mountain hunters are evil. Not completely symbolical of Mankind, they are, however, symbolical of the evil dormant in every heart – Your likeness extends beyond mere features. Yet this basic human instinct, this propensity for being bad, is another contradiction to Your holy word. *How so?* You are the God of Revenge, we are told. But if we, the innocent, waited for Your sword, we would eventually be forced to use our own and become worse than the guilty. And be damned for eternity for today's sin as we always have and always will: for is not today also yesterday's tomorrow?'

The eagle returned, remaining in the distance like a spectator expecting a clash of Goliaths.

'These hunters,' waving an arm at a distant valley, 'are a real threat to the ecology and the animals dependent on it for survival. Waiting for Your word, they would become extinct as have the buffalo that once roamed these vast prairies. The dastardly creatures have already destroyed Dickens' first family. I'm not going to allow the slaughter of a second. One day, though, I know Dickens will fall by some bastard's hand, and I won't be there to help. But I am now : *that is what matters.* Even though he would feel nothing by killing me! Don't you see: he's incapable of hatred! If he'd received kindness at the beginning – who knows? A bit like me, I guess. My point is that Man butchers the animals he depends upon. Why? Because he is Man and can be nothing else.

'The hunters have a Devil disease and must be eradicated: Animal versus Man. And Dickens mustn't lose this time. To defy this imbalance, I will gladly be guilty of taking the law into my own hands. And what is that? It is principled symbolism. Yes, I am prepared to sacrifice myself for coexistence. Greedy, idealistic: of course. But my meaning is well founded. Though never agreeing, Sally would understand; that is one of the many reasons I am attracted to her. She carries my child, yet this thing is too great to let pass in my meagre lifetime. *Enough!* It becomes too heavy.'

Squatting once more, he began questioning his right to challenge the existence of the Christian god. But if, as he believed, God did not exist, did he still have the right to challenge nevertheless? It was all a state of mind, really, and personal to the individual.

Where only minutes before, he had been elated, now with its passing, his writer's depression temporarily paralysed his mind. Suddenly, it was finished: he had braved and climbed Devil Mountain. In a horrid, selfish way, Sally, Paddy and Sam were poor consolation for losing the challenge and the ways of the mountain.

Regaining his faculties, he cursed himself for allowing such heinous thoughts. Of course he would live happily with Sally and his friends: for, in them, lay his true strength; his reason to be at ease with himself. And yes, he must do all in his power to adopt Sam. And coexistence? What was written, was written . . .

Channelling his thoughts into capturing The Beard and his crew, he stared at the other peak; gasped fearfully as Dickens glared back through the mist.

'*It can't be,*' he muttered. 'Not up here! It's a trick. The altitude.'

He grinned cruelly: 'Maybe I've flipped at last: high places!' But he cried out loud as fresh cloud swallowed the grizzly, its ominous growls blown on the wind.

Steeling a last look at the world below, he retraced his steps carefully through the scudding cloud. But as he neared the central thrust of the mountain, his heart missed a beat as Dickens came up to meet him.

Benjamin thought fast: there was no way off the horn without passing the grizzly. His only chance lay at the summit: a further half minute of life in which to pray for an idea.

Dickens came on, growling from deep inside his gut. Although his poor sight had lost the Odd One in the falling sky-smoke, the wind had hurled the man's scent into his nostrils.

The temperature plummeted in the thickening cloud as

Benjamin approached the downwards curve of the horn: the tip; space, a scream, then nothing.

Fitting an arrow, he cursed leaving the rifle behind. His heart jolted as Dickens ghosted through the fog. Sighting along the shaft at the he-bear's chest, he knew there would be only one shot. As the string tounched his nose, he felt the bow strain. Now, he thought, before he charges.

A sudden rush of wind rocketed past his head and an explosion of feathers threw Dickens off-balance; the female eagle ripping an ear with her talons.

Amazed, the grizzly sat down holding his head.

Taking advantage, Benjamin hurried towards the main core. Afraid to look back as the bird taunted Dickens, he stumbled onwards in breathless panic with the he-bear's angry roar spurring him on to greater efforts.

I'll never make it, he thought, groping frantically through the cloud. Never knowing when the animal would strike or he would plunge into an invisible gorge, he arrived at the buttress gulping for air. With a mighty roar, the wind demolished the cloud and he was terrorised again by the frightening drops of precipitous rock diving into the distant land.

Unlike the uphill climb, his hasty retreat downwards sent spasms of muscular agony throughout his body. Blessing the eagle for the hundredth time, he calculated that he was now five thousand feet above the timberline.

As the pain eased inside his lungs, he pondered the chances of reaching the plateau. Although he had no right to gauge survival against such a formidible animal, the mental calculations took his mind off the odious fate awaiting him. With the gradient restricting two paces to the yard and the he-bear's unlimited bounds, he estimated he had to be within four hundred feet of Dickens' graveyard before the grizzly emerged from behind the buttress – *if he bypassed the buttress and came the direct route.*

Lower and lower, he climbed; closer and closer to the plateau. A prey to terror with every spine-stabbing, ankle-jerking step, half way down, the eagle overtook on the wing. That meant one thing: Dickens would now be in full pursuit. Glancing nervously over his shoulder, he saw a growing blob move ominously from the buttress.

Benjamin paid for taking his eye off the ground, falling headlong into a shallow declivity. Badly winded, he battled on as the valley features sharpened and the dam discarded its imitation of a puddle. Valuable seconds lost, the fall galvanised another breath-sucking, lung-jabbing efffort as Dickens bounded effortlessly down the mountain.

Benjamin now felt the same fear he had known in the tree by the dam. 'Eagle, where are you?' he gasped in desperation. But the bird had returned to the eyrie.

Providence intervened, however, as Dickens, in his eagerness, overran himself and nosedived into a crater, providing Benjamin with sufficient time to cover the distance to the ridge cutting across the plateau.

Exhausted, he cursed himself onwards until his legs buckled and he toppled helplessly over the top of the ridge to roll and corkscrew screaming several hundred feet down the rock, before skating perilously across the ice-crusted plateau on his back and pitchpoling into a shallow lake.

Stunned and half dead with fright, he dragged himself onto the plateau. A combination of ice and snow having buffeted his fall, he was, nevertheless, badly bruised and cut: his nose was broken in two places and several ribs burned inside his chest. Miraculously – apart from superficial damage – his head had escaped injury.

As the shock wore off, his body trembled violently. Unable to walk, he crawled on all fours as Dickens' roar filled his ears.

Turning, he struggled to his feet as the grizzly hit the plateau twenty yards to his right. Having lost the bow, he took out the hunting knife and brandished it in a futile gesture of defiance.

'Come on,' he croaked. 'Let's finish it. I said I was prepared . . . .A pity we couldn't . . . ' He fainted as a rifle exploded behind his head.

Paddy raised Benjamin's head and gently sponged his forehead. 'How far is it with you?' he groaned. *'Christ, how far?'*

Benjamin saw the Irishman's fiery beard phase through the edge of consciousness and coughed up blood.

'It's OK,' grinned Paddy. 'You swallowed it from your broken snotter. Your ribs are fine, so your lungs aren't punctured. I take it you've just established a new Olympic record for mountain descents. You're definitely running out of lives and into debt.'

226

'Thanks! Dickens? You didn't . . . '

'Not so fast. You were lucky we figured you might get into trouble. Sam and I've been here half the day. What's it like in heaven? You must have upset parliament.'

Sam looked down at Benjamin. 'Oh Ben!' There were tears in his eyes.

'Sam . . . My boy.'

Boogaloo dribbled a stone at his side.

'He's better, Ben. He just walked away from dying!'

Paddy stole Benjamin's eye. 'And so has he, Sam – so has he.'

'Dickens!' Benjamin persisted. 'Did you? Is he . . . '

'I'm getting worse than you,' sighed the Irishman. 'I just gave him some of your medicine – a mouthful of mountain.'

Benjamin smiled. 'The rain kept off.'

Then he fainted again.

CHAPTER 17

It rained solidly for two days and three nights. The timberline was submerged by a thousand torrents cascading down the rock face and obliterating the snow. Thunder boomed through the canyons; lightning cracked the sky with white jagged forks of electricity.

'Now we'll find those infernal traps,' Paddy shouting above the deluge. 'How's the invalid?'

'Much better,' Benjamin peeling off his clothes, and throwing the door open.

'What's this – bath time!' the Irishman laughing.

'You two don't smell too good,' Benjamin, soap in hand dashing outside.

'He's crazy!' Sam shivering as he was gripped by a blast of icy air.

Paddy shrugged and began pulling off his own clothes. 'Won't do

228

you any harm, young feller. Come on, get 'em off. Throw your dirty stuff on the roof: that washing machine in the sky'll get rid of the gunge.'

The downpour took away their breath; a hot, tingling sensation soon enveloped them as steam rose in the lighted doorway.

Boogaloo gave a peculiar look at the naked figures jumping and yelling in the rain.

Drying in front of the fire, Benjamin made hot drinks. The conversation centred on the traps. Seeing little reason now to keep them from Sam, he discussed the lethal mechanisms openly and their probable locations. After all, they were leaving the mountain the day after tomorrow.

The Irishman opened a pack of cheroots. 'You and I can cover quite an area.'

'What about me?' Sam toying with the cat. 'I've got the best eyes here. Anyway, I owe 'em for shooting at Boogie.'

'That's enough of that,' said Benjamin sternly. 'They'll get tried and sentenced. There's enough revenge on this mountain without you cutting in. We only act if they attack us or go for Dickens – otherwise we just draw them out for Robinson.'

The Irishman studied the boy. 'He's got a point, Ben – about his eyes. He's so skinny, he looks like a tree! No one'll see him in good cover. Send him up to the water pan; he'll get a good view up there – plenty of places to hide if things get out of hand.'

'I could always lit out for the trading post and use John's phone. Aw, c'mon, Ben!'

Closetted in thought, Benjamin said: 'If we dissentangle some of the string on the timberline and attach it to our wrists, we'll have a first-rate alarm system. I'm getting to like alarm systems! Whoever sees first, tugs the others. We can work out a code: say one for Dickens, two for other animals and so forth. But the moment the hunters or any humans arrive, Sam, you lie low. This time, there'll be bullets and things flying around the place.'

'*Things?*' Paddy creasing his brow.

'Oh, my surprises on the treeline should help our cause.'

'If Sam sees them, before us,' Paddy inhaling, 'we'll have plenty of time to take the fight to them. They may be good with traps, but that's about it. Hiding to nothing!' winking at the boy. '*Pulling string, indeed!*'

Benjamin poked the fire and Boogaloo jumped as a spark bounced off his nose.

'Plenty of life there, Sam,' Paddy smiling.

After every conceivable eventuality had been analysed, the boy turned in with Boogaloo.

Paddy glanced at Benjamin as light breathing soon came from the bed. 'What are you going to do with him?'

Benjamin looked into the flames and his chin fell onto his chest as he played with his fingers. 'He's blown it with the Cornclifts. I . . . I just don't know.'

'You look upon him as a son, don't you? There's nothing wrong with that. Well, don't you, Englishman?'

Taken aback, Benjamin spluttered a few unintelligible words and threw a log on the fire.

'Whether you do or not, he's one hell-of-an attached to you! While you were visiting the angels, we talked. All he thought about at the Cornclifts was you and this place. He won't care if they give him up: *I'd say he's counting on it!* He said he used to watch the mountains from the garden. Apparently – so he thinks – the cat had the same symptoms. Mind you, the black bastard's almost human.'

Benjamin avoided the man's searching gaze; continued playing with his fingers.

'I don't know how adoption works, but I do know human beings. That kid loves you. He's even made a bow like yours.'

'I didn't know,' Benjamin starting to his feet.

'That, and a few other things,' Paddy pouring himself a stiff tot. 'He's too embarrassed to show it to you because it's not up to Arapaho standard. He emulates everything you do – just like any son does. Are you blind? It's pathetically beautiful. You and I are insecure because of what we are. We'll never change. But Sam's more afraid than insecure: afraid of losing you when this is all over. The authorities may tell him where to *go,* but Sam knows where he's *at.* And that's one prairie load of difference, as your pal Harry would say.'

Benjamin half-smiled into the fire. Harry: what a pal! Facing the other man: 'Out with it, Irishman! It's a night for sorting things.'

'Don't think I'm intruding, but I've seen the longing in Sally's eyes. Maybe she can pull a few strings. Sam's a one-off, and you're the only one who's come close to handling the little shit. What I'm trying to say is: whatever you do, do it fast, because when we go down this mountain, he's going one way. It's a life sentence to him.'

'Remember, I'm an immigrant – like you.'

'No, I'm something else!' Taking a piece of crumpled paper from his pocket, he dropped it on the table. 'Should interest you. He threw it away. Kid's embarrassment – like the bow. I'm hitting the sack. Sweet dreams, *Mountain Man*.'

Benjamin scowled at this latest jibe. Snatching the paper, he moved for the fire's light. Slowly, he read the scrawled hand:

My first Poettry by sam fynn, Virginia, Devil Mountain

I live on a mountain with ben
and Boogaloo my cat
I'm still an orfen at ten
but I guess i'm lucky at that

paddy he's a good guy
helps ben and me round the place
the three of us gets by
two beerds and my CLEAn face

we bild things and mess around
hunt an fish from sunup
BeN'S pipeline fell to the ground
with hIm i like growin up

I aint no poet as you can see
whoever reads this poem of mine
but I do know I'm HAPPY
with BEN and BOOGIE on the timberline

(note by myself – I did this when i shouldda bene chopping wood.

Benjamin reached for the bottle and wept quietly.

Silence held the liquid dawn as the two men went in search of the traps. Water, snow and melting ice ran underfoot as they moved warily along the timberline.

'There'll be more snow,' exclaimed Benjamin.

'We won't be around to see it.'

'What about Robinson and this task force you're supposed to be in? They might drag you back up.'

'I don't think so. We'll probably sort out our trapping friends if they pitch – if not, we disappear. I've got things to do.'

Benjamin wheezed a cough and held his ribs. 'I won't ask what. Look, the only place – apart from the valley – I haven't checked, is the forest at the back of my surprises.'

They waved to Sam crossing the timberline towards the water pan.

'You made up your mind about him?'

'Private.'

'Of course. Poem clinch it?' Paddy grinning.

Benjamin looked away.

Starting at the dish, they worked back towards Virginia, until Paddy's scream shattered the quiet.

Benjamin raced to the spot where his friend had disappeared. Horrified, he found the Irishman standing on a dead antelope in a deep hole.

'The heathen bloody sods! It could've been me. Would you *look* at this poor bastard.'

Benjamin examined the trap closely. His face hardened at the two rows of needle-sharp stakes protruding from the animal. Luckily, Paddy had landed feet first on the carcass, but a stake had pierced his calf muscle.

Gritting his teeth, Benjamin helped the big man free as a roar echoed across the timberline.

'Oh no,' groaned Paddy. 'Yogi's come a'callin'. Get rid of your pet.'

Benjamin sprinted back to Virginia as Dickens began pulverising the cabin walls. Firing above the grizzly's head, he scowled as the animal bounded into the rocks nearby. Returning for Paddy, they made the cabin just ahead of the boy; Boogaloo shooting between Paddy's legs.

'Well,' said Benjamin, 'that puts paid to that for the time

being.' Crossing to the splintered window slats, he peered outside. 'He's somewhere nearby.'

'Never mind him: help me with this damned leg! Paddy flopping onto the bed.

'Roll up your trouser leg! Sam: hot water, my lad.'

The wound wasn't deep, but Benjamin gave a tetanus shot after cleaning and salting the injury. Applying a tourniquet, he said: 'Loosen it every ten minutes or so. Isn't that the leg you broke?'

'Not its year!' Paddy hiding the pain. 'If it hadn't been for that antelope . . .'

'One of the traps, huh!' Sam playing with the cat.

Benjamin nodded as he opened a bottle of whisky.

'Bit early for you, isn't it?'

'For the wound.'

Paddy profaned in Gaelic and snatched the bottled as the spirit ate into the open wound. 'Jaysus, you're not fit to be a bloody horse doctor.'

'Ben,' shouted Sam. 'Dickens; he's back. Look!'

Just then, the grizzly's head burst through the slats, his fangs drooling as he roared at the three friends.

'Holy Jaysus . . . ' Paddy backing into a corner.

As they retreated from the bear, Boogaloo charged, his claws digging into Dickens' snout.

'Boogie!' cried Sam, as the cat hung from the grizzly's nose. 'Get away from there.'

But before Dickens could crush the life out of his tenacious adversary, Boogaloo dropped safely to the floor. Raving, the bear pulled his head from the shattered window slats and pounded the wall with renewed ferocity.

But Boogaloo, hadn't finished his assault. Leaping up to the window, he spat at Dickens through the hole and made a sound like an air raid siren.

'Such language!' Paddy grinning. 'He's got 'em, I'll give him that.'

'Got what?' asked Sam as the cat dropped to the floor once more and began cleaning itself.

'Never mind,' said Benjamin monitoring Dickens as he slouched off along the timberline, complaining to the sky as cans jumped and bobbed.

'The choir is silenced forever,' Paddy flopping back on the bed. 'The cans are dead. No more! Yogi's got a mean temper.'

'Hell!' exclaimed Benjamin. 'If he smells that antelope, he won't be as lucky as you.' Grabbing his rifle, he ran outside and fired into the air, sending Dickens galloping far down the dish. 'I'll remove those stakes. That's the third trap!'

'Be right there,' said Paddy. 'Just let the blood circulate.'

'Stay where you are,' ordered Benjamin. 'Sam, guard the bugger. I mean it, Paddy. You're not fit. I can handle it!'

Ignoring the protests, he moved onto the timberline.

Grinning at the Irishman's discomfort, the boy watched Benjamin move into the forest.

Benjamin trod carefully against the steep gradient. He found a further two traps, both of which had whiplash mechanisms to swing their luckless victim crashing into a wall of stakes cunningly secured to a tree trunk.

Coming to a break in the timber, he saw Dickens trundling back and forth below in the scrub. Nerves on edge, he jumped at the light footfall behind.

'What the hell!' he snapped. 'I told you to stay with Paddy. I found two more – it isn't safe here.'

Serious faced, the boy said: 'I was careful. I followed your tracks. I wanted to talk, so I gave Paddy the slip.'

Boogaloo rubbed affectionately against Benjamin's leg.

'I see you've brought your back-up!' Benjamin's face dark with anger. 'It could have waited. You've left an injured man alone. It had better be good.'

'I think it is. I'm sorry, but what I have to stay can't be said with Paddy around. It's private.'

'Go on,' Benjamin dropping onto one knee.

'The Cornclifts won't take me and Boogie back, will they?'

'Can you blame them? Anyway, what of it?'

Sam lowered his head and talked to his feet. 'Why can't you and Sally take us on? We don't eat much! I'd learn to spell right and add up . . . And Boogie likes you really.'

Benjamin sighed. 'Oh Sam, my boy – if life were that simple! Even if we could – and I admit we've talked about it – the authorities don't work as fast as your feelings – or Boogie's. There are rules: made to help, not confuse. Sally and I are in our forties:

middle-age and youngsters can be an explosive formula. You'll find that out, one day.'

'I'm nearly eleven! We get along fine. You always said we were partners – *or have you forgotten?*'

'That's uncalled for,' protested Benjamin as the boy's poem shot across his mind. 'You're making it difficult. I'm an immigrant: I have no rights, and certainly no claim on an American child. Your country-men would go ape if . . . if Limey's took their jobs and then started on their offspring.'

Sam stuck out his chin defiantly. 'I ain't got no kin! I'm free to choose, and I choose you and Sally.'

'You've a long way to go before you can make your own decisions. If I were you . . .'

'You made your own decisions,' interrupted Sam. 'You did!'

'My case was different.'

'How?'

'I was older, for a start – and I don't think you're eleven. I had more education at the back of me, and I was stronger in every department. I regret it now. I'd have been a more complete person with a solid family background. I'm sorry, you'll have to abide by the authorities this time.'

'I love you, Ben. I don't want to lose you.'

Benjamin stared at the fresh face, so vulnerable and young. Damn it, what do I say to him? 'I have a saying: What will be, will be.'

The boy nodded sullenly, as if a great sentence had just been passed, committing him to a life of searching for what other kids took for granted.

'At least tell me how you *feel!* Or are you just a good actor? I'm not one of the characters you twist to fit the story. Remember, I was around when you talked to the wind and shouted your craziness at the mountain. And Boogie saved you from the aeroplane! We saw you at your lowest, Ben, and helped by being with you. We didn't *have* to come back here from the circus – we wanted to be *with* you. Just give Boogie and I a sign. No matter where we end up, I want to be able to tell Boogie you cared a bit.'

Benjamin's temper flared, but evaporated instantly. 'You damn well deserve a belt for some of the things you just said. But you're right, I am an actor – but not a good one. Every writer has to be something of the bloody kind. You're not a character, Sam: you're a veritable pain in the rectum. I'm not proud of what happened to me after Dickens' attack. I didn't ask you or your cat to come up this mountain – or Paddy. I came here to – oh, never mind. I inherited you both. I . . . I like having you and Boogie around. The truth is, Sam, I can't hold out any hope. I would be wrong to say otherwise. But I promise you, I'll try. That's all.'

Sam hugged him and Benjamin felt the lad's hot tears. 'Son,' he said lovingly.

Tenderly, the boy held his face and kissed the scar. 'Boogie agrees,' he smiled.'

'Agrees what?'

'That maybe it's us should be looking after you.'

Boogaloo sat grinning his cat's grin.

Dickens crouched behind a boulder sniffing the air. He too, seemed to have reached some weighty decision. Yet he still wasn't sure about the Odd One: the man still hadn't used the man-noise against him despite his numerous attacks.

The hunters kept to the trees at the northern end of the valley. Using cover, they approached the dish. They did not see the grizzly.

'Reckon the Limey's done for?' Eb scowling at his waterlogged boots.

'If he didn't leave,' replied The Beard. 'He's an asshole. No one'll miss a crazy, but we don't take no chances! We'll go up through the timber.'

As it will, the unexpected struck fast: Dickens smelt man and his mate's scent simultaneously. She had left her hibernation den to walk in the valley; a happy, pregnant stroll. Dickens knew she would soon be in the hunters' view. Suffering flashbacks of his dead family, he galloped to warn her.

Startled at his cries, she saw the hunters appear from a dip in the land.

Hearing the echoes, Benjamin and Sam moved for a clearer view. Watching Dickens running in agitated circles around the female, they grimaced as two smaller objects came into the picture.

'Got them! spat Benjamin. 'Sam, you want to help – now's the time. Get Lieutenant Robinson. Indian John's got his number. Hurry, I'll be alright.' As an afterthought: 'Boogie'll make his way back to the cabin.'

'Sure you'll be OK?'

'Sure,' his exasperation showing. *'Now move out!'*

Greed rushed The Beard's decision as Dickens' echoes came on the wind. If the Limey's croaked already, he thought, it'd be loco to throw away all that fur. Word had filtered to the lowlands about Benjamin's near fatal climb. If he isn't, hell, I'll take the bastard at my leisure.

The two men spread out. Now from behind separate rocks, they waited for their victims.

The female was obstinate. Dickens clubbed her reproachfully on the head before pushing her onto the windline. *Why did females forget these things?*

Her fear blazed for man with his deadly noise. The male had saved her and the unborn. *But what about him?* How long could he spring around and thrash his claws while she escaped? Man was so dominant. So evil.

Sadly, she nuzzled his face and returned to the den.

Seeing the hunters go to ground, Benjamin cross-grained over the lower slopes of the adjoining mountain. He knew Dickens was waiting for his mate to leave. Rifle cocked, he held on to the new bow and quiver of arrows – a present from the old Indian – and raced through the pine down to the valley. He couldn't let them take the grizzly now: not after everything they'd been through together.

Heading for a rocky outcrop a hundred yards from the hunters' ambush position, he dropped panting and sweating profusely as Dickens' roar invaded the valley.

Firing two rapid shots across the animal's path, he stopped the grizzly before sending a third at the hunters.

'What the . . .' The Beard diving to the ground.

Eb cursed as he scoured the valley for the attacker. 'See him?' he yelled angrily.

'That shot came from the high ground,' grunted The Beard, suddenly recalling his dream. 'It must be the Limey! Who else?'

'The Mick's been seen around lately,' returned Eb, spitting out a wad of chewing tobacco.

'Maybe, but I don't think so. The Englishman's a fit bastard.'

Eb had known fear only twice in his life: as a child, when he had almost beaten a rival gang member to death, and during the last patrol with The Beard before pulling out of Nam in the rain. Cut off from the main force, they had held out for a week until reinforcements arrived.

Nervous sweat dripped onto his rifle as it had done then. How had the Limey survived the traps? He'd actually stalked them for Chrissakes! Jesus H. Friggin' Christ!

The Beard mentally apppraised the Englishman. He could have taken them alright! But instead, he had frightened off the he-bear and only fired a warning shot. Maybe he had been up here too long! But there was something not right about the whole damn thing – something stank and was scaring the shit out of him: this wasn't the same man they had beaten before the snows. This one had returned because he liked the high country: he was a goddamned freak of nature who thought more of animals than men.

That's what it was: oh mother-fucking Son of God, he walks with death.

He cried out as another shot threw dirt into his face. His dream came into focus. After all this time, why was this happening to him now?

Benjamin ordered the hunters to drop their weapons and walk slowly towards the creek. 'I've been thinking,' he growled at Eb. 'I doubt there were any snakes like you at the Alamo,' his foresight opening the man's face from eyebrow to chin. 'Now we're even! I'll settle for the boy's cat, later.'

The Beard collapsed as his foot found the man's genitals. *'Remember?'* he hissed.

They stared in disbelief at the disfigured man in buckskins, his long white hair plaited Indian style.

'Get up,' Benjamin firing between the two men. 'Now you run the arrow!'

'We're . . . WHAAAT!' Eb's face white with fear.

Putting on a face, The Beard returned: 'Our Limey friend's been readin' too many Wild West stories. He doesn't . . . '

He groaned as the rifle stock smashed into his cheekbone.

Suppressing his loathing, Benjamin shouldered the weapon and fitted an arrow.

Still in shock, the hunters watched the shaft slice into the sky before plummetting into the forest at the foot of Devil Mountain.

'You're outta your skull,' yelled Eb, holding his torn face. 'We'll kill you for this. I'll tear your heart out and feed it to that grizzly you fancy. You haven't got the balls, you . . .'

'If you don't move off, the next one goes through your guts.'

Bewildered, the men looked at one another before shuffling off towards the forest. Throwing worried glances over their shoulders, one unspoken fact was rapidly becoming a horrid reality: *the Englishman had said nothing about the traps.* Did that mean that he knew where they were? Or which ones had gone off?

Sweat streaked down their foreheads as the terrible realisation dawned: *the bastard could be leading them right into their own goddamned traps for Chrissake!*

When they reached the forest, Benjamin put his weapons on a rock by the creek and fell into a relaxed trot. Moving away from the hunters' line of retreat, he started up the steep incline.

Dickens had been confused many times in his life, but never like today. He had seen the Odd One leave the rocks and beat the killers of his family. The man had used his man-noise to give life. Was that what the Odd One had done before – and the red haired mate yesterday on his loving ground. And twice he had nearly ended the man's days; attacked his den and given him no peace.

If all this was confusing, the Odd One had not ended the killers' days, but set them free!

Maybe he had only wished to share the mountain: *but not with these men!*

Following the three men from a distance, he thought it more than strange that the Odd One had left his man-noise and stick-throwing weapon behind. He sensed for the first time that the Odd One had no need of these things. He had named him well.

Unaware of the he-bear's presence, Benjamin moved stealthily through the pine ... *When you find them Bengymen, tread softer than the deer ... hasten slowly like the cougar ...*

His plan was simple: force them up to the timberline and administer his own justice before Sam brought Robinson and the task force. Paddy would approve. If the hunters set off one of their own traps, so much the better. If not, they would tell him where they were before Robinson arrived.

He felt no remorse; no recriminations for his actions. No time to moralise, he thought. Morals are best preserved in the paper-clean columns of the Press. Nobody gets hurt there. This is the real world.

They'll think I'm armed, his thoughts returning to the hunters. They'll split up to even their chances. He stopped at the first track: The Beard! Moving on, he heard laboured breathing and broken twigs; grinned as sunlight reflected on a disturbed wet branch.

He prepared himself.

Within visual distance of each other, the hunters grappled with the steepening incline. Nearing the timberline, they understood the Englishman's silence: four traps had been sprung. Assuming the ballbearing mine had gone off at the dish, too, that still left the one in the . . . He'd even cut the stakes where the antelope had died! Only the bones were left after the wolves – yet he had survived.

They saw the timberline briefly before being caterpulted painfully forward by Benjamin's whip-traps. Stunned, they came round as the Englishman stepped from the forest.

'Ready when you are,' his voice menacing.

Paddy hobbled from the cabin. 'I see you've brought something to play with!'

The hunters ogled at the Irishman as if he were a ghost.

'A bad mistake, you leaving me alive in the street, boys! Now Ben, show me what you've learnt.'

The Beard stood shakily; Eb wobbled on jellied legs. As they recovered, Benjamin sprang. Lightning jabs to The Beard's face and stomach, toppled the man; a sharp kick to Eb's testicles sent him vomitting into the pine.

'An improvement, to be sure,' Paddy applauding. 'Mind you, I think you cheated a bit with that penalty kick.'

He grinned approvingly as Benjamin beat the two men ruthlessly to a pulp.

His mind still screaming at the hunters' nefarious plans with the traps, Benjamin finally went to the cabin for rope to tie up the men. He spun as Dickens galloped from the forest, the beast's fangs sinking deep into Eb's chest.

Horrified, he watched as the he-bear slammed the screaming hunter to the ground, bursting the man's body over the timberline.

The Beard ran for the trees as the heavens opened; the flash storm erasing the timberline in seconds.

Dickens growled out in fury at the sky: like the Odd One, he too, felt cheated as he leapt up the rock face and vanished into the swirling mist.

'You won't find the bearded bastard in this,' Paddy yelled. 'Let's get inside. Where's Sam?'

'Half way to the trading post, I hope,' running to the cabin. Towelling off, he cursed. 'I left my weapons down by the creek.'

'So what!' Paddy reaching for the whisky. 'The cavalry should arrive tomorrow. Just sit back and enjoy the rest of the day. The danger's passed.'

Offering the bottle: 'You know, I'm proud of you – not for what you did – but for what you didn't. Do you think the wolves'll leave enough of that bastard for Robinson? Dead, maybe, but he's evidence.'

'Rain might kill the scent; probably not. You can't kid the animals. Quite frankly, I don't give a damn.'

'You *are* mad! *Upset* mad.'

They drank in silence. Suddenly it was over: so quick; unexpected. Wasn't that life!

CHAPTER 18

The Beard shivered in front of the stove. Both his and Eb's rifle stood propped against the far wall of the hunting lodge bar. He was angry at being interrupted by an Indian refusing to leave the room. Two of the Rangers had eventually thrown the man out while he told his story.

Straightfaced, he continued his amended version of the fight on the timberline. 'Third time in twelve months,' he added for effect, 'that the grizzly attacked old Eb an' I.'

The Head Ranger coughed in thought. Up to now, a blind eye had been turned to the Englishman and his peculiar taste for high places. Reasons had been given on compassionate grounds by some bigwig on the Springs Sun – well, didn't the paper provide good coverage when needed – and latterly, pressure had arrived in the shape of that pushy and arrogant Lieutenant Robinson from the 'Heavy Mob'.

He shook his head wearily. But this unprovoked attack by the Englishman and his Irish pal changed the entire ballgame. The shit was going to hit the fan! *Oh brother, was it!*

'Crazy! Been up there too long,' The Beard measuring his performance in the men's faces. 'It's the Limey's fault. Completely off his trolley. But the Mick's in with him.'

Highlighting Eb's death, he convinced the Head Ranger to go after the grizzly while he slipped off and sorted out the duo on the timberline. Put carefully, his plan negated the presence of the Police Department.

Christ, he thought, not while I'm seeing to the bastards. If things go wrong, Wilma and that idiotic husband of hers will swear I left Denver a few days before the hit and run. The whore's already been written off as misadventure. Best it stays that way! A punch-up on a mountain's no reason to suspect a homicide. A little more acting and I'm home and dry.

But the man was not entirely convinced. 'Crazy, you say,' shot the Ranger. 'Bloody maniacs by the sound of it! Once Robinson arrives, we'll move in. That grizzly hampered the chopper rescue last year, you know. Got worldwide coverage.'

The Beard scowled. 'Nah! Why wait for the city boys! Take 'til Christmas – and they'll grab the headlines.' Saving the traps for his *pièce de résistance,* he grinned: 'I want a dig at them before the law shows.'

'I don't know . . . We should wait...'

'You'd be doin' America a favour – oh did I forget to mention the traps?'

'Whaaaat!'

The atmosphere became hostile as the men gathered closer.

'Before . . . Before we was bushwhacked, we came across some traps. Shit, you should've seem 'em. Evil bastards! I tell you...'

'What kind?' snarled the Ranger.

Embellishing the story, The Beard played on their feelings. When he had finished, the Head Ranger said: 'Think you're up to it? You've taken a hammering.'

'It's personal! You know? Five minutes with each is all I ask.' More like a few seconds through a sniperscope, he thought.

'You're one helluva guy,' smiled the Ranger. 'Right, fellas?'

The men chorussed approval.

'I'll call Robinson after you've had your 'five minutes'. OK! Rain's set in for the night. No one's going up there – or down. We leave first light. Just you rest up now, Mister.'

The Beard let himself be helped to a bedroom. Tomorrow, he thought. Then that's it! Tough on old Eb, but that's the way it goes.

A frown creased his brow as the Indian passed in the narrow corridor. 'Damned buck,' he muttered under his breath. 'Seen him somewhere before.'

★ ★ ★ ★ ★

McAvoy scrutinised the three men in the hotel room. Recruited by his FBI contact, they were the best in the business. Expensive but the best. Following the black sergeant's call concerning Paddy Martin, he had received permission to execute the man.

Finishing his summary, he said: 'He's trouble, gentlemen. Martin was one of our top people in London. Now, he's an embarrassment. And that's dangerous for the organisation. If he were caught by MI5, they'd shoot him full of scopolamine or whatever truth drug they use nowadays. Many covers would be blown in England – not to mention the political repercussions both at home and here.'

The men nodded across the smoky room.

'He's still living with an eccentric Englishman – of all people! - on a mountain. At this stage, I don't want the Englishman hit: he's a journalist with a bit of pull. I doubt Martin would have talked about us, but you never know in our line of business. Pressure's a curious thing. If we find to the contrary, the Englishman's history.'

The men grinned coldly. Another John Bull would make no difference.

'When do we leave?' enquired one man.

'We fly to Stapleton this evening. A car will take us to the location; a few hours drive at most. We'll be briefed by our man on the way as to the best access to the subject. Retain your aliases, but no weapons. They'll be provided. Questions?'

'Just one,' said a bullnecked individual. 'How close are Denver Police monitoring the subject?'

'They're nowhere near the killing ground,' assured McAvoy. 'They wouldn't tell me why they wanted him. He's just in the frame for questioning. Well be in and out so fast...'

Exchanged glances were followed by the donning of raincoats.

'Board separately at JFK and meet up in Denver. Until tonight, gentlemen.'

McAvoy left the room immediately; the three executioners followed at five minute intervals.

★   ★   ★   ★   ★

Harry Miller kissed Helen and hurried through the rain to the garage.

'Be careful,' she called. She was anxious over her husband's decision to join Robinson at Devil Mountain.

Harry rushed back to the porch. 'I know what you're thinking, but I feel responsible for Ben. And Mike Robinson isn't all that bad. I'll stay with Sam and Sally at the trading post. *Promise!* I'll be OK. See you tomorrow with the whole gang. Oh, get Ben's appointment confirmed at the clinic. That scar gives me the habdabs.'

Kissing him again, Helen watched the tail-lights disappear from the driveway. His night vision is awful, she thought. This rain doesn't help.

The pick-up left Cascade and joined the main traffic north to Denver. Staying over at Sally's apartement, he would drive them to Indian John's first thing in the morning.

Thank God the kid kept his head, he thought, and made that call to Sally. Pondering the Irishman's position, he reasoned that he was the right man for Benjamin to have around – injured or not.

He cursed as a wheel hit a discarded tyre. 'Hell, the eyes aren't what they used to be.'

★   ★   ★   ★   ★

At two o'clock in the morning, Lieutenant Mike Robinson was bad-tempered-wide-awake. The weather had disrupted all communications with Ranger Headquarters at Fort Collins, at Clear Creek and Sulphur.

'There's no way I'm letting Sol take in a team without a scout,' he grumbled into an empty coffee cup. 'If this backfires!'

The political ramifications were swept aside as the black sergeant arrived with hamburgers and fresh coffee.

'Breakfast Mike!'

'Thanks Sol. Still no word?'

The man shook his head. 'Can't get over how that orphan gave us the slip! Can't the Indian's nephew take us to this darned mountain? Save time.'

'Not even the Almighty could in this weather!' Robinson rubbing his eyes. 'My pension's really on the line this time. If someone gets hurt, you'll inherit my desk ahead of schedule. If we can't get through by – glancing at his watch – five, we'll roll. Between the Ys and Zs, you'll find jungle juice. Shoot it.'

The sergeant dragged open the filing cabinet drawer. Miller must be some guy to get him into this state, he thought. 'Do yourself a favour and hand this over to the Feds, Lootenant. This Thompson guy and the Mick ain't US citizens. Why bust your lily white ass?'

Robinson blew his nose. 'Wish I could, Sol, but I'm too far up the creek. It got out of hand with the hooker's demise – and a certain Irish congressman wants no adverse publicity connecting the IRA this side of the Big Pond. I owe Miller one. Back in '63 after JFK got it, he held back on a story to give me breathing space on a cert pick-up. It cost him a scoop on CIA activity in Miami. Connected – so he said – with the assassination.'

'No shit! So, what gives now?' downing the bourbon.

'The Feds owe me a couple, too. If the visibility improves, we'll get a chopper over that goddamned timberline. See to it. Hell, the Twentieth Century and Nature's still screwing us all!'

'Why can't they come up with a radio that works in all weathers? Pisses me off! The kid said shots were fired.'

'Yeah, yeah, yeah! Team still awake?'

'Bitching like a fishmonger's wife.'

'Keep the bastards on their toes. Nah, stand them down. But no one goes home for a quickie.'

Just a few hours, Thompson, thought the policeman. Hang in there. He jumped as the phone shrilled beneath a fresh batch of crime statistics. 'Yeah! You sure? Holy shithooks . . . Well, keep on it. It has to be the Micks' heavy brigade . . . You've what? No kidding! I'll send flowers to the hospital. A granddaddy eh! Look, I got to go. Keep in touch. *Soooool.*'

The sergeant came at the run.

'We've got ourselves a problem. Bill Tovey just called – you worked with him I recall.'

'Sure. He just retired.'

'Seems he invested in a gas station just off the 119 outside Boulder. Guess who just filled up?'

'The President,' grinned the sergeant.

'Piss off, Sol. McAvoy. And he had company: three big goons in the back. The driver's a local in fruit. He's also Irish. They were heading for the mountains. This thing is really giving me the screaming shits. Kick ass, I want the show on the road in fifteen minutes. And Sol: no fuck-ups. Everything that has to work had better – *or else!*'

Quickly, he dialled a number and got through to Harry Miller. Without mentioning the Irishmen, he said: 'We're pulling out now. Thompson's OK. It's gotten heavy, pal, so you and the Brown woman stay put. I mean it. Show and I'll book you both for obstruction . . . Oh by the way, there's a letter for the lady. The Indian told me before the lines went down. I'll have it sent on: Special D.'

Palming his bloodshot eyes, he threw on the service overcoat.

When I retire, he thought, *I'll retire.* No gas stations and spy jobs for Michael Stanislow Robinson.

After a hitch tracing the duplicate key for the radio cupboard, he rasped into the sergeant's ear: 'The asshole who went off duty with the original, his fanny belongs to me. The second we get back!'

'Lootenant.'

★ ★ ★ ★ ★

Half an hour behind the police vehicles, Harry drove through the deluge. Just as Robinson had been unsuccessful in stopping him, he had found similar stubborness in Sally Brown.

'Something's happened, I just know it,' she said. 'He isn't sure about all this, is he? Robinson!' And when Harry didn't speak, she said: 'Men! Always sticking together.'

Harry winced and concentrated on the driving. His eyes were killing him.

She wondered what Benjamin had written. It was so like him at a time like this. He'd write a story in No Man's Land. Oh please, dear Lord, keep my man safe! There's so much to live for.

The doctor had told her it would be a Christmas child.

The pick-up was swallowed by the blackness and her anxiety was exacerbated by the vehicle skidding occasionally on the wet surface.

'I'm sorry, Harry. That was selfish of me. I didn't mean to...'

'I know, honey. I know. We both love him.'

Despite taking turns to keep watch, neither man found the solace of sleep. Prisoners of the present, they were also captives of the recent past concerned about the near future.

At six o'clock, Benjamin lit the kerosene lamp and wrote the final entry in his mountain diary:

> . . . *In a few hours, Paddy and I will leave the mountain. Forever. It does not belong to us anymore: with hindsight, it never did. I think Dickens will be happy then. It is not quite dawn and we feel a sense of loss, for, however harsh, Devil Mountain has enriched our lives. We are decidedly better people for the experience, despite the pathological attentions of The Beard and his cronies. Boogaloo sits by my side waiting patiently for his young master: a truly noble animal . . . I felt something at the summit, but am not sure if it was a presence or some trick of the altitude . . .*

Paddy yawned and poked the fire for the last heat. 'Guess we might as well get ready,' he said drowsily.

Benjamin snapped the diary shut and went across to his pack.

Boogaloo jumped onto the bed as the two men moved quietly in the lamplight.

Paddy wrapped Mona's two halves in a blanket.

'That was a shame,' said Benjamin softly.

'Aye. But it shows Ma still cares for her wayward son,' he smiled. 'Finished?'

'Only the writing to cram in somewhere. It's always the last wherever I go.'

'Rain's stopped. Might get a little sun to see us down. Fancy a stroll before we go down?'

'You can tell me about your plans.'

Boogaloo miaowed as they picked up their rifles and left the cabin: then fell asleep on Sam's pack.

The moon bobbed above the forest like a Christmas lantern on a wave of wispy cumulus, lighting the timberline with weeping, silver tears.

'You know, it's sad,' Benjamin sitting on a piece of broken pipeline.

'What is?' Paddy joining him.

'I haven't seen a rainbow here. Of all places!'

'Ah, you'd have to go to Ireland for that,' smiled the Irishman. Poets! he thought.

'We're like that,' reading the man's eyes. 'Well, don't keep me in suspense.'

'Don't laugh, but I might make a bid for that doss house in Denver – the not-so Jolly Leprechaun.'

'Where's the money coming from – if it's for sale?'

'It will be,' Paddy lighting up a cheroot. 'I've a few bob tucked away in Ireland nobody knows about. I'll get rid of the riff-raff and install a good Irish showband. All it needs is a new image. I might even make an exception for you – after you've had a facial.'

Benjamin touched the scar. 'Harry's sorting out a specialist. But how will you convince the present owner his time's up?'

The reply was killed as a bullet thudded into the pipeline between the two men, followed by a fusillade of fire across the timberline.

'Martin,' a voice boomed. 'Come out with your hands up. You haven't a chance.'

'This is where I came in,' said Paddy.

'Who the hell is it?' Benjamin staring through the gloom.

'A shadow from the past. Whatever happens, Ben, please stay out of it. This is Irish business. This one's *my* mountain. Understand?'

'Yes, but . . .'

'No buts – just stay out Englishman.'

Benjamin stared as he walked to the centre of the timberline, breathed in deeply as three men with rifles surrounded the Irishman. Crouching behind the pipeline, he picked up snippets of heated conversation as Paddy argued with a fourth man who was obviously the leader.

'So you see, McAvoy,' growled Paddy, 'I've made up my mind: I want out. I'll no longer be a thorn in your side if I go my own way. But, if you have to have it your way, then I can't stop you! Just leave him alone,' pointing towards Benjamin.

'The mad Englishman!' McAvoy screwing up his eyes to penetrate the gloom. 'We've no quarrel with him – if he knows nothing...'

'I told you, he's ignorant. Let that be an end to it.'

'Let's hurry up,' said one of the men. 'It'll be light soon and the place will be crawling with police.'

'A minute, if you please,' McAvoy walking around Paddy like a prizefighter appraising his opponent. 'You see, I know about Lieutenant Robinson and his amateur theatrical group. Losing your touch, aren't you, Martin! Do you really mean to finish it! Why should I accept your word? You could be up to your old tricks – you were one of the best . . . You know the rules.'

'I'm tired. I can't explain it to a man of your disposition. Walk away or pull the bloody trigger.'

As daylight slowly permeated the timberline, a cry came from one of the men as Eb's mutilated corpse came into view.

'What the . . .' McAvoy taken aback. 'Who . . . What the devil is that?'

'Holy Jaysus, he's been eaten,' said one of the men. 'What Devil's work have you and your English friend been up to Martin?'

'Not us, bollocks! His pal, Yogi – or should I say, Dickens.'

'*Dickens!*' spat McAvoy. 'This is no time to stuff around, Martin. Who the shit is Dickens?'

'An eight hundred pound eight foot grizzly, that's who. Ben swears by him.'

'You,' McAvoy calling to Benjamin. 'Get out here. Is what he

251

said true about the bear?'

'Every word,' Benjamin moving cautiously, the rifle held at his side..

'Drop it,' ordered McAvoy.

'I've calculated that I can take at least two of you before you get me. I don't like intruders. Especially men with guns who attack my friends – that includes the animals.'

'*You what* . . . Cheeky bastard, I'll . . .' one man losing patience.

'Wait,' called McAvoy, trying to defuse the situation. 'Our fight isn't with you.'

'Then tell the IRA to get the hell off my mountain,' Benjamin swinging the rifle on aim. 'I'll take you first, Mister.'

Even as Benjamin spoke, the executioners fired through the gloom. Diving sideways, he fired in mid-air, one bullet finding McAvoy's chest, killing him instantly; another took an attacker in the throat.

While Paddy scrambled to pick up McAvoy's fallen weapon, a heart-stopping, nerve-jangling roar blasted from the pine as Dickens crashed through the forest and burst onto the timberline.

The two remaining executioners fled for the safety of the forest, only to be catapulted backwards after triggering one of Benjamin's whip-traps.

Dickens pounced in a flash, tearing one of the men apart in a blind fury.

Realising his mistake to run for the forest, the other man scrambled after Benjamin and Paddy in a dash for the cabin. Collapsing against the wall, he sobbed for breath, pure terror etched on his face.

After several minutes, his frenzy cooled, Dickens roared a final warning before bounding back up to the plateau.

'I'm going for the walk you and your cronies interrupted,' said Benjamin angrily. 'Give me half an hour, Paddy, then we'll go down.'

Boogaloo followed him onto the timberline.

'You don't have to wait,' snarled the Irishman to the gunman.

Still in shock, he replied: 'Not with whatever that maniac's planted out there,' he gasped. 'I'll go with you. You'll be givin' those two a Christian burial, now won't you!'

'Paddy pushed his face into the other man's: 'What do you think, asshole?'

'You can forget about ever returning home, Martin. You're an evil son-of-a-bitch . . .'

Paddy's fist felled the man with a single blow. 'Hold your venomous tongue where my Ma's concerned. I should kill you for that, but my pal would object – believe it or not! Until we leave, abstain from all speech and you'll live for another Angelus.'

Spitting out blood and broken teeth, the man gurgled: 'You're mad – both of you! What's he doing out there?'

Paddy pulled out the whisky. 'Saying goodbye to some old friends.'

'Friends?'

'The kind I left for Erin long ago; the ones you never had.'

CHAPTER 19

Chaos rocked the trading post. On arrival, Harry and Robinson almost came to blows. Sally too, gave vent to her feelings, accusing the Police Department of flagrant inefficiency.

Finally, Indian John put an arm around her shoulder and said: 'You will lose all through emotion.'

'What the hell's that supposed to mean?' fumed Robinson.

'Never mind,' sweeping the air with his arm. 'My nephew here has learnt some of the bad ways of the whites, but he...'

The lieutenant jabbed an accusing finger: 'Cut the racial crap! You got your own back at the Little Big Horn. Get to the point, Mister.'

'Now listen . . .' began Harry, but the old Indian cut him short.

'They were Sioux: I am Arapaho, White Man. If you'd have let me continue, I was about to say that for once my nephew's drinking habits may prove advantageous.'

The room fell silent as the Indian spoke quietly, but firmly. 'He was in the hunting lodge last night. He saw this man with the beard arrive and heard his pack of lies about Bengymen and the Irisher.' Repeating The Beard's story, he said vehemently: 'I think this snake has cut the telephone wires to the lodge. I called Ranger Headquarters just now, and they say they can't get through to the men there. Headquarters are sending men to the mountain now to cut off this evil man. Call the Rangers, Lieutenent: there will be many men with guns on the mountain today. It is best everyone knows where everyone is.'

'How come I couldn't get through from Denver?' snarled Robinson.

Indian John grinned his solitary tooth. 'We are closer here. These things happen in the mountains. It is getting light and your men have a long walk.'

Robinson went to the phone. 'Where's the kid?'

'Sleeping in the back room,' said Harry.

'I'll look in on him,' Sally grateful to leave the smokefilled room of men.

Harry stopped her in the doorway. 'Everything's going to be a prairie full of laughs after this. You'll see.'

Sally smiled jadedly and entered the small bedroom. Instantly she returned, her face chalk white. 'He's gone! He's gone to Ben and his cat.'

'Shit!' moaned the sergeant. 'He must have been listening at the door. Cunning little . . .'

'OK,' drawled Robinson. 'You figure that's what he's done, Harry?'

Harry nodded. 'Have you a spare rifle, Mike?'

'No way Hosai!'

'Then that's just tough shit, isn't it!'

Indian John smiled his secret smile. 'You love him, too. Bengymen always spoke highly of you. Stay with my nephew. He will bring you back down.'

'Sol, Harry here starts playing John Wayne – you put his lights out. I know Helen thinks I'm pigshit, pal, but I have the job to thank for that. You journalist types ain't *all* roses!'

The task force was assembled and ready to move to Devil Mountain. Robinson was to remain at the trading post and act as a relay between his force and the Ranger Headquarters team.

'They'll RV with you in the box canyon somewhere north east of here. Got the frequency and call signs?'

The sergeant grinned. 'We'll get 'em down, Lootenant. Still nothing from those other guys from the lodge?'

The lieutenant shook his head. 'Left an hour ago according to a runner from Ranger HQ – but you've got less to travel.'

'But they are used to the ways of the mountains,' said Indian John.

'Move off,' growled Robinson, glaring at the Indian in the doorway. 'Remember, there's a kid up there,' he called out. 'Call in every half hour. I'll give you a radio check in a few minutes. Good hunting. Go easy, Harry. *I mean it.*'

Harry waved to the man and smiled at Sally before falling in step alongside the Indian's nephew.

Robinson stopped in front of Sally. 'I know what you think of me, Ma'am. And I don't blame you. But Ben had to go back up – there was no other way. I take no pleasure in all this. It . . . wasn't easy. I just want you to know that.'

Sally slapped his face and stormed into the trading post.

Indian John found her crying in the small bedroom. He held an envelope in his wrinkled hand. 'Don't judge him too harshly,' he said. 'His kind is necessary. He's like that because of us. Robinson will never go home to anyone. Here,' handing over the letter. 'The one I told you about on the phone. I'l bring some tea.'

Sally sat on the bed and opened Benjamin's letter. Somewhere, she heard Robinson curse into his radio through the open door. Closing it, she read:

Dear Sally,

Just a note to keep your spirits up – and mine. In a few days, we will be together: forever. I live for that.

I wrote a bad poem for my book and I just can't get it right: I hope this is an improvement. Don't laugh – it's about our dotage.

Like us, Virginia's weathered
Not unkind years, My Love.

256

The timberline too, where we met
On Devil Mountain a heaven above.

Burning seasons turned to ice
Captured by the eagle's eye,
All now a bygone age
Beneath a rolling, restless sky.
In your dotage, stop awhile
For the madding Colorado,
For all its frenzied landscapes
That joined us long ago.

Virginia was an old friend;
The mountain older still:
But it's you I really sought –
Not that lonely hill.

All my love,
Ben.
PS: look after our child. You are pregnant, aren't you.
I sense it. Maybe Sam will complete the family!
Maybe!!!

Blowing her nose, she turned as Indian John set down a tray and frowned at her tears.

'You know all about the wild, but little of a squaw's happiness.'

He smiled. 'Drink and eat. My wife's cookies are the best in the mountains. I told Bengymen to fatten you: squaws don't breed on empty bellies.'

Sally pulled a face. 'You'll be at the wedding?'

The Indian winked. 'He has more taste with his women than with his tracking.'

'Oh, get along with you. *And it's not women – it's woman.*'

Indian John smiled wisely into her face.

★ ★ ★ ★ ★

257

A brassy sun blurred through the pine as Boogaloo dribbled a cone at Benjamin's feet. The forest, a catacomb off yellow slants, squelched underfoot as he strolled casually towards the dish.

'Weather's picked up, Boogie! First stop for you in Denver is the vet for a jab.'

Stroking the animal, his eyes strayed towards the valley. How I love this place, he thought. He looked at the scar by the water pan and a sadness wrenched his heart for the dismembered pipeline.

'It was necessary, Boogie.'

The cat deftly pushed the cone around small stones at his feet. 'You wouldn't be out of place where I come from.'

Suddenly, he caught a glimpse of Dickens romping above the water pan. I don't think we're really enemies, he thought.

Boogaloo suddenly stopped playing and arched his back; his coat fluffed as he glared into the forest.

'What is it, little feller?'

The cat ran up the slope and hissed into the pine, his walking-stick tail scything with agitation.

Benjamin turned as his name came on the breeze. 'It's OK, Boogie, it's only Sam. Over here,' he called.

The boy came puffing through the trees. 'Ben,' he gulped. 'H... he's on the . . . way. The one with the beard. The Rangers . . . He told them...'

'Calm down; get your breath back.' His face darkened as Sam related The Beard's duplicity and Robinson's dilemma with communications at the trading post.

'Good work, my boy. Pick up your cat. We haven't a moment to lose.'

Paddy frowned as they confronted him outside the cabin.

'I don't need this kind of involvement,' said the hitman.

Paddy rubbed his bad leg and told the man to be quiet. 'This bearded shit will most likely arrange a decoy so as he can get a bead on us, Ben.'

Benjamin agreed and checked his ammunition. 'But what about the Rangers he conned at the lodge?'

'Hmmn, that's the nub! Then there's Robinson's All Stars. There could be over thirty guns on the mountain – all popping off out of the woodwork! And those from the lodge will be all fired up with lies and bullshit. All for one grizzly!

'Well, they'll all be disappointed.'

'*What!* What's that, you say? If you're thinking what I think you're thinking, Ben Thompson, this isn't any time for playing silly buggers.'

'All I need is a little time. He'll be up on his plateau. I'll get him off the mountain and the hell and gone before they arrive. Create a diversion of your own: use this sod if you have to,' indicating the hitman. 'You should be a past master at that.'

'I said forget it, Ben!' Paddy grabbing him by the collar. 'Mother of God, Englishman, you'd be safer in Belfast on Lodge Day.'

'Is he risking his life for a bear – the one that ate the hunter?' asked the hitman.

'Shut up!' boomed Paddy. 'You get out there and bring McAvoy's carcass in here if you want something to do – unless you prefer a stroll down the mountain on your lonesome.'

'Ben, you can't,' put in Sam. '*You can't . . .*'

'I'll be alright. Nobody's here yet. None of this is any of Dickens' fault.'

Determination chiselled Benjamin's face as he explained his reaffirmed comittment to coexistence. 'I refuse to be swayed,' he said finally. 'I'll be back before the fun starts. I have a fondness for that crazy bear . . . I've shared his home.'

Paddy shrugged angrily and opened the whisky bottle. 'Well, I hope it isn't the grave you're going to, Englishman. Don't stand there; get on and tell Yogi to move mountain for the day . . . *shared his home.*'

Benjamin smiled thinly and strode for the door.

'Good luck, Ben. From me and Boogie.'

'Try Pop.'

'*Whaat!*' but Benjamin had already stepped through the door and was running along the timberline.

Paddy swore silently and made the sign of the cross.

Dickens stopped to scratch his back against a rock and urinate. He was still irritated over the killers on the timberline. He would go on destroying all that came to his home, threatening his survival.

He growled as a shadow swept across the plateau. Looking up, he wrung his great claws at the female eagle as she planed overhead before dropping effortlessly onto the cabin roof.

Dismissing her, he recollected the events of the day. When the sun had woken the valley, he sat by the lake where the Odd One drank. He saw the man and the fearless rat-like creature look at him before the cub called from the trees. Apart from that and a couple of lions keeping distance, little had happened to break the simple monotony of his day.

Once more testing the wind, he stiffened: man was near. The hairy-faced killer had returned.

Moving swiftly, he bounded forwards; growled angrily as the man-noise showered rock splinters into his face and shoulder. Moving onto windline, he became maddened by the obnoxious smells of other men moving up through the forest.

They had come for him at last! Helpless, he began running in large circles, hoping to elude the terrible noise of death.

At least she was safe.

Benjamin clambered over the rocks near the cabin, entering the forest. He could hear the Rangers from the hunting lodge battling upwards through the pine. Reaching the scar, he took cover as The Beard's shot echoed across the mountain.

Scrabbling upwards, he stopped to watch Paddy start his diversion using the hitman as unwilling bait. And then he saw The Beard edging round a boulder off to his right.

White hot anger electrified his body and mind as the hunter fired again at Dickens exposed on the vast plateau.

'*Higher!*' he yelled. 'Go higher, you idiot!'

Too late to chase the grizzly off Devil Mountain, Benjamin made up his mind to force the animal as high as possible. If he could elude the Rangers until last light, Dickens would have every chance in the dark hours.

It's a long shot, Ben, he thought. But it's all Dickens has. Coexistence has! God, what a time to think about symbolism. Catching another sight of The Beard, he fired a warning shot over the man's head.

'The next one's for you,' he yelled. 'Leave the grizzly alone. *Haven't you done enough!*'

The Beard cursed as his face was cut from flying rock. 'Bastard,' he yelled. 'It's too late, Limey, for the likes of you and me. Born after our time. I'm gonna kill you both – you and the he-bear. And you know why: because you're both scum. Weak scum. I'm strong! The hunter. That's the way of things. Of course, you might save your lousy hide if you hightail it while I'm nailin' the grizzly.'

Another round from Benjamin told him different. Genuine fear gripped the back of his throat as he heard the Englishman working his way towards him.

His dream returned. 'Not now,' he croaked. 'Not on top of everything else.'

On hearing the first shot, the female eagle had left the cabin roof and circled five hundred feet above the valley. Bad tempered, she looked down at the men crawling over the lower slopes of the mountain. The food would be late. How would she explain this to the children? She sensed the mountain's future was in the balance.

Swooping over the scrub, she saw a group of men being led by a man the shade of the dark rock beneath her nest. She thought all men were the colour of her eggs; the same as the sky sickness that fell in winter.

Skimming the forest roof, she spotted more men, but these were the men who sometimes took her eggs and smaller animals from the valley and brought them back again after many moons. They always wore the same skins; different to other men.

Dropping one wing, she zoomed back over the plateau where the he-bear still ran in defiant circles. She saw the killer of his family behind a rock, and the ugly mate of the man who had returned to live on the mountain.

Everybody was flapping wings. *A truly strange day.*

Then she saw the man himself, crossing the plateau after the he-bear. More madness! Did men ever learn? Had the climb achieved nothing? She could not tell the young of this madness yet – but something told her the time was close at hand.

Gliding over the southern end of the plateau, she banked sharply for a last look at the timberline. The dark man and his followers were arguing among themselves as they joined the egg stealers near the man's nest.

She and her man seldom flapped wings any more. She saw to that. Arrowing into the blue high above the misty devil horns, she turned for home. It was time for the youngsters' first flying lesson. Now that was something to look forward to. Let men sought out men's things.

The Beard had clambered back to the water pan, the salt of exertion heavy and sticky in his mouth. The Limey's plan was obvious: to drive the he-bear higher. A quick glance confirmed the untouched sixth trap nearby. It had been a fair bet that the man would go there sooner or later.

Pity, he thought, wiping the grime from his face. He looked sideways as the sound of raised voices came from the timberline.

He spat against the rock as Paddy came in sight, followed by Robinson's men. Damn it! I cut the lines; doctored the Rangers' radios. And there's that bloody Indian again! Christ! That was where he'd seen him: he was from the trading post. He'd heard everything! That changed things. It wouldn't take long before the truth emerged – *if it hadn't already.*

He had to get off the mountain: fast.

His dream descended like a curse as the police and Rangers gathered round Eb's remains and the new corpse belonging to McAvoy. Suddenly, he was back in Nam: hounded, marked for death and betrayed by a country sacrificing its young men through the blunders of high command and the whims of Washington capitalists and idealists.

Danger sparked madness in his brain and he grinned viciously. Let 'em all come, he mused, as the devil-horned Statue of Liberty materialised in the rock. The hell with it all; this is as good a place as any to die.

His rifle barrel glinted in the sun as he saw the Irishman look up at his position.

'I tell you, I saw a reflection,' argued Paddy. 'He's up there by the water pan. If he's not there, where the hell is he? You brought him!'

Harry grabbed the nearest Ranger. 'The hunter: the one who sold you down the Colorado?'

'He was here a moment ago!'

'Aw heck, it was longer than that.'

'Nah, I saw him just now.'

The police sergeant moved across to Paddy through the press of bodies. 'Where? Exactly?'

Paddy pointed and began limping along the timberline. He turned as Sam arrived at his side. 'Christ, will you never do as you're told! Get back inside – and take that cat. And – thanks. You and Ben . . .'

Leaving the sentence unfinished, he hurried towards the water pan.

Harry took Sam back to the cabin. 'It's about time we met, young man. You've turned my whole family upside down. We've got a whole prairie load of talking to catch up on, Mr Fynn.'

'Hey,' yelled the sergeant. 'Where's the Mick going?'

'Don't let *him* hear you calling him that,' replied Sam. 'He ain't particular.'

'That's his friend – and mine – up there,' said Harry.

'Then what's the Lim . . . the Englishman up to?'

'Taking care of coexistence, if I know him,' replied Harry. 'Just get that bearded monster. That's why you're here.'

'Taking care of . . .' Deciding against argument, the police sergeant gave rapid orders to his men and the Rangers and chased after Paddy, now out of sight in the rocks.

Benjamin stopped as Dickens sprang from behind a rock cluster. Throwing his arms about wildly, he screamed in frustration for the grizzly to go higher. To his amazement, the he-bear suddenly turned and raced up to him before galloping back over the plateau.

The Beard, he thought. Is it possible? He wants the killer of his family.

Dickens gradually worked his way back along the plateau

towards the water pan. His fear, now very real, told him constantly that death was near. But he would protect the Odd One. The killer would not kill again on his mountain. Other men may take him, but this one would not.

Summoning all his strength, he threw everything into a final defiant charge across the plateau, his growl booming once more across the valley. Arriving at the gulley that led down to the pan, he stopped, nostrils flaring, saliva creaming from his open mouth.

The smell above all smells was close. Again, his torment rose.

Sprinting back across the plateau, Benjamin fired above Dickens' head in an effort to get the animal away from where The Beard must surely be hiding.

Closer and closer, his lungs threatened to burst inside his chest. His mind screamed: Get away, Dickens. He'll kill you. Go up to the horns; go higher until darkness. I'll take you up the canyons. *But get away from the water pan . . .*

His mouth went dry as The Beard appeared from behind a huge boulder, rifle on aim. Again, he fired above Dickens' head, yelling for all he was worth. But the words hardly came after his wheezing run across the plateau.

Yet the distance was closing: a hundred yards . . . seventy five . . . fifty . . .

His head swam with fatigue and his body ached, but he could see The Beard plainly now, twenty yards off to his right.

'Dickens: go up your mountain, damn you,' he sobbed, diving sideways as a bullet spat chunks of rock at his feet.

Dickens had come to a halt; heard the man-noise and saw the Odd One hit the ground. Confused, he turned as the hairy mate called out nearby.

'Ben,' shouted Paddy. 'For the love of God, get in cover. Forget the bloody bear! The murdering bastard's somewhere in those rocks to your front. I can't get a bead from here. Get in bloody cover, man, and stay there!'

Sweat poured down The Beard's face and his eyes had glazed. The Mick! This was it. This was his destiny! The dream pressed down upon him like a leaden weight, crushing all reason, all will to survive. Destroy the enemy, it said. Just like Nam: *kill, kill, kill.*

Peering through a V in the boulder, he grinned as Benjamin ran in front of the grizzly. What kind of lunatic is he? he thought, ignoring the Irishman's order to throw down his weapon.

Laughing crazily, he placed his rifle into the V and lined up the sight, alternating between Benjamin and Dickens.

In the ensuing silence, still unsure, Dickens moved off to Benjamin's left. The wind had shifted; the scent gone. In doing so, he moved closer to The Beard's hiding place.

Benjamin saw the rifle protrude through the V and he ran towards Dickens, hoping to increase his own angle of fire.

'*Nooooooooo,*' he yelled.

Again pacing himself between Dickens and The Beard, he saw hostility for the hunter in the grizzly's eyes. For a fleeting moment, they had become united; forged by the flame of tolerance against the evil man with the gun.

Reaching out, Dickens touched Benjamin on the shoulder and groaned helplessly. The grizzly's eyes were wet.

Stroking Dickens' snout, he said: 'It won't happen to you. Not again.' Turning to The Beard: 'You murdered his family! Where does the world go when you've killed them all? Fight me, you . . .'

Paddy cried out as Benjamin was knocked backwards into the he-bear by the high velocity round. But before he could move, the grizzly had streaked up the boulder towards The Beard.

The hunter grinned savagely, his eyes now flashing with madness. He was going to live after all! Just the grizzly. Slowly does it; watch the breathing . . . His stomach dropped as the rifle jammed and his dream drowned him as Dickens clubbed him off the boulder and onto the unsprung trap in the water pan.

Mortified, Paddy ignored The Beard's screams as the large steel teeth skewered the hunter's body, and watched the tragic scene to his front.

Groaning sorrowfully, Dickens stood hind legged over Benjamin's body beating his breast in a pathetic lament.

Hearing the police sergeant and his men in the rocks, Paddy walked out into the open. 'Go on, bear, damn you. He died for you. Don't waste it.'

As if understanding, Dickens beat his head and then bounded up the mountain.

Dropping to his knees, Paddy held Benjamin's bloodsoaked body in his arms. 'Oh, you beautiful, beautiful man,' he wept. 'You walked where I never could.'

When the task force arrived, the Irishman was unconsolable.

★ ★ ★ ★ ★

A sprinkling of snow sugared the timberline as the service ended.

Ashen faced, Sally placed wild flowers on Benjamin's grave. 'The seeds will always bloom for him.'

In turn, they honoured him: Indian John, an eagle's tail feather; Sam crossed the bow and quiver over the neatly placed stones.

When it was over, Sally turned to Helen Miller. 'Don't you think it was a lovely act, Harry getting the Rangers to rebuild his pipeline.'

Helen nodded and looked at Sam still standing at the graveside.

'He'll be the eldest brother,' said Sally, touching her large stomach.

As they walked from the grave, Paddy, Harry and Indian John stood a moment, each with their final thoughts.

Rest well, Bengymen, smiled the Arapaho. Your story is told – may you live longer than the mountains.

The women joined them. 'Thanks for your Mother, Paddy.'

The Irishman put an arm around Sally and looked towards the crucifix at the head of the grave: his beloved Mona. 'He was worthy of her. A man among men.'

'This hill will never be lonely again,' she said.

'Pardon?' said Harry.

Sally shook her head. 'Just something he wrote.'

As they moved off, Sam picked up the pine cone Boogaloo had dribbled to the grave and placed it next to Mona.

'That's from Boogie, Ben.' Then he followed them down the mountain.

★ ★ ★ ★ ★

The cubs scampered behind the female through the valley and past the beaver dam.

From afar, Dickens watched them before climbing through the forest to the clump of wild flowers where the Odd One slept. This had become his favourite place for the past three years.

Stopping briefly at Virginia, he bounded across the timberline to the spot ablaze with colour and smelt its sweetness. Beating his great breast, his echoes cut the valley as they had always done.

Then he growled happily as he climbed towards the clouds.

The female eagle broke flight from her man and the young as the grizzly left the timberline. Gliding onto Mona, she suddenly felt old. Yes, she thought, nothing ever comes to the mountain and lives long.

One beat of her powerful wings and she swept upwards to rejoin her loved ones.

★ ★ The End ★ ★

Future work from Sean Edge
for Anfield Publications:

Poetry/Short Stories

A Man and his Words

THE AUTHOR

Born in 1945 of Irish-American parents, Sean Edge was educated in Liverpool. Travelling extensively throughout North and South America, he lived in the Caribbean before settling in the former colony of Rhodesia.

Published and broadcast in verse whilst writing numerous short stories and the first draft of *Mountain Man*, his literary work was interrupted in the mid '70s when he worked for a special department of the Army, collating information in the bush war against the Communist terrorist forces of Joshua Nkomo and Robert Mugabe.

Moving to South Africa, he studied the geopolitical and military situations for future novels while engaged as a chief sub editor and feature writer.

Returning to England in 1988, he wrote for newspapers and magazines before turning his energies towards novels. He is currently working on a historical saga, a book of poetry and a collection of short stories. His work has been featured on the BBC.

Mr Edge lives in the south of England with his wife and a multitude of animals.